PENGUIN 🐧 CLASSICS

CASTLE RACKRENT *and* ENNUI

MARIA EDGEWORTH was born in 1768, the eldest daughter of Richard Lovell Edgeworth, a wealthy Irish landlord, who went on to marry three more wives after the death of Maria's mother and had twenty-two children in all. Interested in education and in the practical applications of science, he had a considerable influence on his daughter and, together, they wrote *Practical Education* (1798). Maria Edgeworth went to school in England for some years and returned to Ireland at fourteen, spending the rest of her life there with her family. Her first publication was *Letters to Literary Ladies* (1795), a plea for women's education; she went on to establish a high reputation with her writings over the next forty years. *Castle Rackrent* (1800), her first novel, centred on Irish life and pioneered the Anglo-Irish novel, and probably the colonial novel too. A second Irish tale, *Ennui* (1809), established her reputation as a realistic portrayer of Irish life. Her work was greatly admired by Scott, who acknowledged his debt to her Irish novels in the Postscript to *Waverley* in 1814. Her other works based on Irish life are *The Absentee* (1812) and *Ormond* (1817). She also wrote novels depicting contemporary English society, such as *Belinda* (1801), *Leonora* (1806), *Patronage* (1814) and *Helen* (1834), and many popular lessons and stories for and about children, including *The Parent's Assistant* (1796–1800), *Moral Tales* (1801) and *Popular Tales* (1804).

MARILYN BUTLER is a Rector of Exeter College, Oxford. She was educated at Oxford University and has taught both there and at Cambridge, where she was King Edward VII Professor of English Literature from 1986–1993. Her books include *Maria Edgeworth: A Literary Biography* (1972), *Jane Austen and the War of Ideas* (1975), *Peacock Displayed* (1979), *Romantics, Rebels and Reactionaries* (1981) and *The Collected Works of Mary Wollstonecraft* (1989), which she co-edited with Janet Todd.

MARIA EDGEWORTH

CASTLE RACKRENT
and
ENNUI

Edited by MARILYN BUTLER

PENGUIN BOOKS

PENGUIN BOOKS

Published by the Penguin Group
Penguin Books Ltd, 27 Wrights Lane, London w8 5TZ, England
Penguin Putnam Inc., 375 Hudson Street, New York, New York 10014, USA
Penguin Books Australia Ltd, Ringwood, Victoria, Australia
Penguin Books Canada Ltd, 10 Alcorn Avenue, Toronto, Ontario, Canada M4V 3B2
Penguin Books (NZ) Ltd, 182–190 Wairau Road, Auckland 10, New Zealand

Penguin Books Ltd, Registered Offices: Harmondsworth, Middlesex, England

This edition first published 1992
7 9 10 8 6

Printed in England by Clays Ltd, St Ives plc
Set in 10/12 Monophoto Baskerville

CONTENTS

INTRODUCTION

Castle Rackrent and *Ennui*, the first of Maria Edgeworth's four Irish tales, are two ambitious and deeply original novels. *Castle Rackrent* (1800), the shorter, has the bigger name. It features in literary histories as a comic masterpiece, a landmark in the European novel, an importantly innovative fiction. *Ennui* (1809), much less well known, will come to most readers as a genuine surprise. It is a fictional allegory on a sweeping scale, which represents an age of political revolution for Ireland as for France, and uncovers the social and economic revolution in train in Northern and Western Europe. When *Castle Rackrent* and *Ennui* are paired, as two related studies of the same historical process, they read as perhaps the boldest, most innovative and most influential contribution to English-language fiction by a woman writer before Charlotte Brontë and George Eliot. They have the best claim to pioneer the nineteenth-century social novel which, more self-consciously and more precisely than its eighteenth-century predecessor, criticizes and remoulds the reader's perception of modern social life.

Castle Rackrent came out in January 1800 to very little critical notice, largely no doubt because it was anonymous and unconventionally short, but in April of the same year the Edgeworths were told that George III was amused by it; in 1805, that it was a favourite of Pitt, the Prime Minister.[1] The third edition of 1801 carried Maria Edgeworth's name on the title-page: henceforth none of her fiction or book-length non-fiction appeared anonymously, however unfeminine the topic. There were three more London editions before the first *Collected Edition* of 1825, as well as pirated editions in Dublin and America. A complete German translation appeared in 1802, following extracts in French from the Glossary in the influential Genevan journal, the *Bibliothèque Britannique* ('Traits remarquables des mœurs des Irlandais'). After this more Irish works by Maria Edgeworth were always eagerly awaited, and *Ennui* (1809), *The Absentee* (1812) and *Ormond* (1817) all attracted more extensive and more favourable reviews than *Castle Rackrent* had been able to command.

Ennui was in its fourth edition by 1813, and had arrived at classic status, as incidental comments about it by well-placed literary intellectuals show. Germaine de Staël, the leading European woman of letters, 'est charmée d'*Ennui*', Étienne Dumont, a Genevan intellectual and collaborator with Jeremy Bentham, told Edgeworth in 1813.[2] Byron read and approved of it. Francis Jeffrey generally avoided noticing novels in his prestigious *Edinburgh Review*; he not only carried articles on each Edgeworth book as it came out in the first decade of the century, but himself praised *Ennui* as 'perfect' and up to 'the best tales of Voltaire'.[3] Sydney Smith suspected that her dissolute clergyman Buckhurst Falconer in *Patronage* (1814) was a caricature of himself, and he angrily complained in terms that show how high the reputation of *Ennui* then stood – 'Everything else I have read of hers I thought very indifferent, even her tale [*Ennui*].'[4]

But the three later Irish tales have not weathered well, with the partial exception of *The Absentee*, which has benefited from being the usual choice to make up a volume with *Castle Rackrent*. The Everyman edition of these two tales, which first appeared with an Introduction by Brander Matthews in 1910, re-emerged at intervals later in the century. The two most scholarly and well-annotated editions of any Edgeworth novel are George Watson's *Castle Rackrent* (Oxford: O.U.P., 1964, reissued in the World's Classics series from 1971), and W. J. McCormack's and Kim Walker's *The Absentee* (Oxford: O.U.P., World's Classics, 1988). There has been at least one modern edition of *Ormond* (Irish University Press, 1971). It is *Ennui* that seems to have fallen into almost total neglect. Apart from late nineteenth-century collected editions of Edgeworth's fiction, it was last published (together with *Castle Rackrent*, *Irish Bulls* and two short tales) by Routledge in 1884.

With *Castle Rackrent*, 'Tales and Sketches' of the life of a particular locality became an important nineteenth-century form. Edgeworth had Irish contemporaries and successors in Sydney Owenson (later better known by her married name of Lady Morgan), the Banim brothers, Charles Lever, Samuel Lover and William Carleton; Scots successors in Scott, John Galt, James Hogg and J. G. Lockhart, and Continental successors from Balzac and George Sand in France to Turgenev, Gogol and Chekhov in Russia. The scale of these fictions of small provincial living has varied so much that we now have difficulty in thinking of a single tradition; too much of the best modern fiction is always provincial fiction, located anywhere from Bengal to Montana. Early nineteenth-century opinion responded to novels of national identity and nation-building of the size and range of Scott's. Twentieth-century taste has preferred something more anecdotal, such as the delicately occasional short stories of Chekhov.

Nineteenth-century critics proved more willing over time to accept women writers as miniaturists than as national novelists. At first Scott, writing a Postscript to *Waverley* in 1814, warmly acknowledged Edgeworth's Irish tales as the model for his own portrayal of Scotland on the big historical stage: 'she may be truly said to have done more towards completing the Union [of Ireland with Britain, 1800] than perhaps all the legislative enactments by which it has been followed up'.[5] But near the end of his life he distances himself from his women contemporaries Austen and Edgeworth by suggesting that he works on a bigger scale. 'I can do the big bow-wow strain better than anyone going,' he says, which sounds amiably self-mocking until it is related to his last compliments to his women rivals for their beautifully-done small work:

> He spoke with praise of ... Miss Austen ... 'There's a finishing-off in some of her scenes that is really quite above everybody else. And there's that Irish lady, too ... – Ay, Miss Edgeworth – she's *very* clever, and best in the little touches too. I'm sure in that children's story ['Simple Susan'] – where the little girl parts with her lamb, and the little boy brings it back again, there's nothing for it but just to put down the book and cry.'[6]

Out of Edgeworth's substantial *œuvre* of three-decker novels, tales and prolific educational writings he picks one of the children's stories as what is most memorable – because, as it happens, he is no longer remembering much. The irony is that Scott's 'big' topics – social change, national identity, English hegemony – feature first in Edgeworth's *Castle Rackrent* and *Ennui*. Indeed for modern readers Edgeworth's handling of these themes often has the advantage because it is fresh, odd, complex and sceptical. Ireland was more a colony than Scotland, and Edgeworth wrestles with the practical, political and ethical consequences of her country's colonial status. The contribution her nineteenth-century readers acknowledged, to the literature of class, for post-colonial readers takes on new shape as a contribution to the literature of class, race and gender: a remarkably intuitive, perceptive and far-reaching portrait of an unequal society.

Edgeworth herself writes so self-effacingly of *Castle Rackrent* that she gives the impression it is merely mimicry. She even implies that John Langan, the Irish steward of her father's estate, took the lead and 'dictated' the tale:

> The only character drawn from the life in *Castle Rackrent* is Thady himself, the teller of the story ... I heard him when first I came to Ireland, and his dialect struck me, and his character, and I became so acquainted with it that I could speak it without effort: so that when, for mere amusement, without any ideas of publishing, I began to write a family history as Thady would tell it, he seemed to stand beside me and dictate and I wrote as fast as my pen could go, the characters all imaginary.[7]

This account, written in 1834, must not be taken at face value, even if its modesty has run like a contagion through the critical literature on *Castle Rackrent*.[8] The reliable aspects of this letter presumably include its declaration that the tale had a very early provenance, and originated in speech rather than in writing. The first point matters because the date of publication of *Castle Rackrent*, 1800, has resounding implications in Irish history as the year of Ireland's constitutional Union with England. Though Edgeworth had lived in Ireland for two years as a child, she must mean by 'when first I came' her return from an English school in 1782, at the age of fourteen, to live permanently on her father's estate in County Longford. About a decade appears to have passed before she 'began to write a family history as Thady would tell it'. In 1819, a relative by marriage reported that *Castle Rackrent* was written eight years before publication.[9] Rather stronger family sources merely say the tale began as an attempt to amuse her favourite aunt and confidante, her father's sister Mrs Margaret Ruxton, who lived within reach of Edgeworthstown in County Meath. In fact Maria Edgeworth was living in Bristol with her family in 1792 and for most of 1793. After her return home she spent part of the winter of 1793–4 renewing her friendship with Mrs Ruxton, who was convalescing from an illness, and the correspondence between the two households confirms that Edgeworth was telling Langan stories at this time. If the book was partly written well before publication, this winter would seem the earliest likely date.

As for the latest date of writing, *Castle Rackrent* must have been sent to the family's London publisher (the celebrated Joseph Johnson, leading literary publisher of the 1790s) quite early in the autumn of 1799, since it was on sale by early January 1800. It was only while the text was being printed that the Edgeworths decided that an explanatory Glossary was necessary. The printer added it after the Preface, since the preliminaries were as usual the last part of the book to go to press.

But though the writing of the Glossary can be pinpointed in the autumn of 1799, there is almost no contemporary evidence about when Edgeworth worked on the narrative, Thady's supposed contribution. Her letter to Mrs Stark in 1834 says that the annals of the last of the Rackrents, Sir Condy, which are longer than those of Sir Patrick, Sir Murtagh and Sir Kit put together, were added two years after the rest. In October 1798 Edgeworth wrote to D. A. Beaufort, an Irish statistician and geographer and the father of her new stepmother Frances Beaufort Edgeworth, to inquire if he had anything 'to add alter or correct in the Rack Rent families'. Beaufort must have had a manuscript to read, and to be of a publishable length it would have had to include the sequel. Taking all the clues together, it seems likely that the annals of the first three Rackrents belong substantially or completely to a time that was relatively tranquil locally, 1794-5. The Condy part and the complete written version were composed in the years 1796-8, when Ireland's endemic local unrest became politicized, and far more threatening to an England at war with revolutionary France. Their neighbourhood was drawn eventually into a state of armed rebellion in which the Edgeworths found themselves undesignedly caught up.

Few novelists of either sex were as well qualified to make the running with social realism as Edgeworth, put by her intellectual father through a training in what we would call economics and sociology, the new 'sciences of man' of the French and Scottish Enlightenment. In his youth R. L. Edgeworth had been to France and had even met Rousseau. Since then he had married, and lost, a strongminded second wife, Honora Sneyd, who had persuaded him of the unsoundness of the views Rousseau propounded in *Émile* (1762) on the education of women – which were, in short, that girls should be reared to be passive, submissive and attractive, the playthings and helpers of men. As a first project for his daughter in 1782, R. L. Edgeworth set her to translate for publication a moderately revisionist educational book of the Rousseauistic school, Mme de Genlis's *Adèle et Théodore*. Though the book was withdrawn at the last moment when a rival translation appeared, it was now established that the fourteen-year-old Edgeworth was to be an author, and in the French Enlightenment mode. Much of the reading matter of this Irish household emanated from France, and it is an important, neglected fact about her apprenticeship as an artist that the French books that seemed to impress her most before 1800 showed how low-life topics could be handled with wit and style, as art rather than ideology.

Throughout her career Edgeworth drew on English novels she thought of as classics, by Richardson and Fielding, Burney and Inchbald. But she also knew the French encyclopedists, and from the outset her narrative art plainly relates to the theories as well as to the practice of French masters of the philosophic tale, Voltaire and J.-F. Marmontel. More charming, delicate and observant than Voltaire, Marmontel (1723–99) also supplied a celebrated series of articles on literature to Diderot's *Encyclopédie* in the 1760s. His *Contes moraux* (Amsterdam, 2 vols., 1763), a collection of tales introduced by one of the author's graceful essays, were quickly available in England in French and English. It was probably through this volume that Marmontel became Edgeworth's literary mentor and model.

Marmontel's most sustained account of the tale nevertheless occurs in his literary essays in the *Encyclopédie*, afterwards collected in a volume called *Éléments de Littérature* (1789). Here he places the form in a European tradition originating in the Renaissance with Ariosto and Boccaccio, but most completely mastered in modern times by the Frenchman La Fontaine; Prior in verse and Swift in prose are, some way behind, the best of the English.[10] The form's prerequisites are that it handles comic materials, and should be short; even La Fontaine can err by going on too long. The writer 'must present to the mind's eye the scene, the dumb-show, the action, but in choosing these details he must have regard only for what counts as truth to nature or to behaviour'. What he adds, by way of sophisticated commentary for his reader, offsets the scene by being 'witty, subtle and arch'. Then:

> The most striking parts of the tale are the scenes of dialogue. It is there that manners can be vividly caught, subtly indicated, delicately shaded; a skilful painter can with slight touches, brilliantly true to life, produce animated groups and living pictures. The better these groupings are composed, the more life and exquisite truth they will give to the dialogue. It is in situation that character is brought into play; it is in the play of character, and in their particularity, that the interest of the scene lies.[11]

The very essence of the tale, and certainly for Marmontel the source of its wit, resides in the social dialogue it conducts, a duplication and echo of the dialogues that make up much of the narration: a further play of voices, between the subjects on the one hand, the teller and the collusive reader on the other. The author must always seem aware of the distance between the polished world he or she inhabits together with the reader, and the rustic world they peep into. A tale's effects necessarily include a sense of exclusion from a happy scene, nostalgia for a lost innocence; for Voltaire and Marmontel the social fissure becomes itself a prime matter for comment. A tale has then a point, often enforced by a sharp twist or 'grain of salt' at the end. A story which is not self-consciously intellectual and thematic, which instead aims to lose itself in a world of its own imagining, should be called by a different name – 'a narrative which was nothing but a string of happenings without a common aim to join them together would be a novel and not a tale'.[12]

Edgeworth published one collection of fiction simply called *Moral Tales*. In the same year, 1801, she asked her readers to think of the three-volume *Belinda*, which certainly looks like a novel, as another moral tale. Her preference for the term has become an obstacle to many modern readers, and has given rise to all sorts of misunderstandings, exemplified by one modern critic's odd belief that Edgeworth in her day was received as essentially the writer of conduct books.[13] But the problem for us really lies in the word 'moral', which we associate with heavy didacticism; the French-style tale, quite another form, aims at lightness, contrast, subversiveness, surprise.

Edgeworth's main surprise for her English reader is to frame scenes of Irish peasant life – the 'vulgarest' stratum of British society – within this supremely elegant format. Her subversion is to bring Irish humour and French wit into conjunction.

However humble and 'natural' some of its origins, then, *Castle Rackrent* evolves as a sophisticated experiment directed at an existing slot in world literature. Like Marmontel's stories, it comes supplied with a Preface which defends and in modern terminology 'theorizes' the domesticity of the materials: the public taste for anecdote is 'philosophical', the 'fine fancy of the professed historian' may be either artificial or mendacious, it is from 'careless conversations' and half-finished sentences that we can get at 'real characters'. It is for his truth-telling capabilities that we prefer an informant like the illiterate Thady, who 'pour[s] forth anecdote[s], and retail[s] conversations, with all the minute prolixity of a gossip in a country town' (p. 62).

The notion that this fictional character tells 'true history', or anything resembling 'a plain unvarnished tale', is of course itself mendacious. In the Preface Edgeworth (or, to judge by the style, her father) is appropriating a vein of populist sentiment fashionable in revolutionary times, and usable not only by radicals but by conservatives, to imply that ordinary folk have a homely wisdom not found in their liberal, utopian betters. In practice, *Castle Rackrent* does not rely on Thady's wisdom, but on our ability to see through his folly. The 'true' theme, the ruin of the estate, is apparent to us, the 'philosophical' interpreters whom the Preface addresses, but not to the characters, their memorialist Thady included. Wholly displaced in its intellectual concerns from the naive world-view of the small-town gossip, the story becomes a microcosmic version of Gibbon's *Decline and Fall*, an inventive and bizarre study of a localized system in terminal decay.

Like Swift and Voltaire before her, Edgeworth with her ironic philosophic tale succeeds from the outset in making a fool of unwary commentators. Almost all earlier critics and some recent ones agree in finding Thady plain, simple and above all loyal. Recently, however, the consensus has begun to swing the other way. More and more critics are claiming that 'the heart of the matter' lies in his character and more particularly in his motivation, which is no longer found transparent. Is he loyal at all to the masters he professes to serve? Could he be a thieving rogue, the accomplice of his son Jason, who ends up in possession of his master's estate? Whom does he represent? – for modern readers are quicker to see that Thady represents people other than himself. To Tom Dunne, he stands for the disaffected rural Catholic masses of the 1790s, the 'peasant jacquerie' which in real life accompanied an invading French army virtually to the gates of the town of Longford in 1798.[14] To P. F. Sheeran 'poor Thady', 'old Thady', 'honest Thady' is most memorable as a man without a proper name or stable identity, an unpersoning that arises from his people's defeat: he is 'a superb portrayal of colonised man'.[15] Dunne cordially picks up this reading, and uses it to make Thady seem unusually malignant, a direct threat to his colonial masters' security: 'Thady is a Caliban in the guise of a quaint stage-Irish Ariel, his devious and false servility a direct product of the colonial system, and destined, through his crucial aid for his son, to be its nemesis.'[16]

An unusually meticulous documenter, Edgeworth puts certain constraints on our freedom to interpret her work. *Castle Rackrent* narrates the annals of a landlord family which is not only of native Irish descent (and presumably Protestant in a very recent generation) but which continues to mix with other families of the same stock. It never avowedly locks on to a contemporary public event: instead, its 'facts and manners' are declared on the title-page to derive from the period before 1782. The Ireland drawn here by Edgeworth is visibly the product of a long history as an English colony; but by placing her fiction 'in history', Edgeworth asks us not to limit it to a commentary on Ireland in 1800. The book is complex, even kaleidoscopic, and however seductive the appearances we have to test further its typing as a colonial novel.

With their astonishing introduction of Thady's voice, the opening pages of *Castle Rackrent* subvert the common expectations of their day. The Shandean irrelevance of the opening words, 'Monday morning', sends the first signal that classical order and formal convention have been suspended. As an act of mimicry the voice of Thady works on a number of levels, an idiolect influenced not only by linguistic factors such as the rhythms of Gaelic, but by 'cringing and flattery', as Edgeworth calls it in *Ormond*, or the 'equivocating, exculpatory or supplicatory' language of the lifelong inferior.[17] Symbolically it is important that Thady does not play the part of a peasant or tenant (as most of Edgeworth's sympathetic 'lower Irish' characters do), but that of a family servant, a universally recognizable figure for social inferiority. The strongest historical objection to interpreting Thady as archetypal colonial man is the fact that his literal role, that of serving man, is more generally familiar and has stronger ideological connotations in the eighteenth century.

Thady himself has an understanding of his own *métier*. Loyal servants get away with putting their fingers into the till, provided they exercise reasonable restraint. 'Cuteness' or 'acuteness' is a trait Thady acknowledges – in fact is proud of – in himself. During young Sir Kit's absence abroad he connives with his son Jason and with the agent in buying up bits of the estate below the market price – 'I spoke a good word for my son, and gave out in the country that nobody need bid against us' (p. 74). Sometimes he admires a Rack-rent for being ''cute' in his own interest – like Condy when he orders a clod of earth to be transplanted to his neighbour's estate, so that a Rackrent tenant can swear the land he stands on is Condy's. While in theory Thady is naive, what he says and what he doesn't say may plainly be determined by partisanship or cunning. When Sir Condy signs away a jointure of £500 to his wife Isabella, to be paid from the encumbered estate before any debts, Thady neither comments nor tells Jason about it, clearly to the surprise of Condy as well as Jason.

It takes a determined sentimentalist to find Thady consistently lovable. He lacks feeling for anyone except a born Rackrent and a born M'Quirk, and even towards the small group he is attached to his services are patchy. Whatever we may think of his coolness towards Jason, his willingness on two different occasions to act as Condy's pandar with his own great-niece Judy M'Quirk is not wholly amiable. He is consistently out of sympathy with the Rack-rent wives, and a *de facto* accomplice in Sir Kit's seven-year incarceration of his young Jewish bride because she will not give up her jewels to him. His summing-up of Sir Kit's career is remarkable for its economy with the truth – 'he was never cured of his gaming tricks; but that was the only fault he had, God bless him' (p. 81).

Even Thady's love for the last Rackrent is first contaminated with self-interest: like his fellow-servant the huntsman, he sucks up to the boy Condy because he is the heir. Iain Topliss, in general a shrewd and observant reader of the Irish tales, finds Thady's tears moving in the scene where Condy is driven by Jason to sign the estate away – 'Jason said, which I was glad of, that I was no fit witness, being so old and doting.'[18] Read primarily for these tears the sequence would seem sentimental; it manages to avoid being so largely through our prior knowledge that Thady has an unacknowledged role in Condy's disaster. It was he who taught his 'white-headed boy' to gamble, and to consider the drunkard Sir Patrick Rackrent the model of a popular Irish gentleman. Condy will die in the act of imitating Sir Patrick's feat of tossing off a full horn of claret, an echo of the scene with which Thady's memoir opens, when Patrick kills himself by the same method.

While boasting of Sir Patrick's feats in the drinking line, Thady seems on the point of acknowledging their futility:

He is said also to be the inventor of raspberry whiskey, which is very likely, as nobody has ever appeared to dispute it with him, and as there still exists a broken punch-bowl at Castle Rackrent, in the garret, with an inscription to that effect – a great curiosity. (p. 67.)

That quick slur on Sir Patrick's achievements is for the knowing reader only. Thady cannot detach himself from the Rackrents, for reasons that become clear only with Condy's ruin. If the last Rackrent funeral has an intensity foreign to all the previous ones, it is because it ends Thady's feudal employment and so severs his relations with the land. Without Condy he ceases to be the equivocal figure, the landlord's servant, who is actually part of the system, and begins to utter complaints that come a great deal nearer to speaking for the landless mass of the population. Marianne Elliott, in her valuable study of the 1798 Rebellion, argues that 'big' politics still had only a small part to play before the mid 1790s in the lawlessness endemic in so much of rural Ireland. Gangs of local terrorists such as the Whiteboys of the Irish Midland counties committed murders, killed or maimed cattle, and burned houses and crops, not directly on behalf of their religion, still less of their nationhood, but in resentment of landlords installed by English law as sole possessors of the land. Under the earlier Brehon law, the clan occupied the land, and those who were now tenants, cotters, labourers and beggars naturally interpreted this 'remembrance' in their own favour.[19] A mythology of land and loss of land provides the topos of popular Irish culture, especially Gaelic song, ballad, folk-history and memory, in the eighteenth century.

Thady's language has much more variety than most descriptions of it suggest. Edgeworth does not convey regional speech through the Victorian convention of misspelling, a device which signals the speaker's ignorance and linguistic incompetence. Instead she adjusts her rhythm and syntax so that it seems possible for the reader to 'hear' an Irish inflection. This general technique allows for considerable shifts in vocabulary as Thady moves from the annals of one master to the next. The brilliantly condensed narrative of the regime of Sir Murtagh and his lady is given in a language thickened by Anglo-French legal terminology, the linguistically archaic remnant of a decayed feudal system. As Condy nears his sodden end Thady, a parodic bard, provides the native Irish caoinan or funeral song in praise of the dead chief – at once a gesture of traditional loyalty and a last act of courtly flattery.

Thady's speech and also his character change as his world changes. Though his fictional lifespan binds the four Rackrents together over about half a century, their 'manners' suggest a considerably longer history, and Thady's language hints at a longer one still. Sir Patrick's lifestyle looks back to a tribal world; Sir Murtagh's Anglo-French legal language reminds us that both Irish and English shared the experience of colonization by the Normans. By incorporating so much historical freight into this local version of English, Edgeworth gives Irish peasants a past roughly coexistent with Burke's version of England's past in his *Reflections on the Revolution in France* – a span of roughly six centuries back to the Conquest. Absorbing Sir Murtagh's archaic terminology, Thady reminds us that English carries the evidence of not one but two Norman conquests a century apart, successful French invasions of the English as well as the Irish. The archaeological layering of Thady's idiom provides a cultural history of his people, the hybrid stock of late eighteenth-century Ireland. Whatever the topic, the language also says that native and settler, *colon* and *colonisé*, have experienced centuries of coexistence.

For Edgeworth, unlike Burke, history is not a usable model. Thady's nostalgia is what misleads him, and us; it is at the heart of his unreliability. He is one of the classic instances of that device so brilliantly handled in eighteenth-century narrative, the unreliable first-person narrator, a line with (again) the Swift of *Gulliver's Travels* and *A Modest Proposal* at its head. Much nearer to Edgeworth in time, Godwin in *Caleb Williams* (1794) also provides a narrator who is a servant, and on that account an unreliable, morally corrupted exponent of his master's character and actions. The themes of *Caleb Williams* and of *Castle Rackrent* are closely bound up with one another, since each is a hostile study of the class system and of its impact on the morals and attitudes of both the master and the servant class. But resemblances between Edgeworth's work and Godwin's may stem from their shared part in the discourse of class, which was fast becoming the master-discourse in representations of the public sphere. Edgeworth's debts to Swift are more formal. His narrative writing gives her a variety of models not committed to the continuous plot and to naturalism: allegory or parable, as we shall see, and also the old comic tradition of the satirical critique or 'anatomy' of contemporary intellectual obsessions. Edgeworth could be seen as Swift's end-of-century counterpart: where he as a Tory satirizes modern intellectual innovations, secularization, scientism and self-sufficiency, she as a Whig satirizes nostalgia, sectarianism, parochialism and blind loyalty.

While not binding on the reader, an author's intentions and responses to her text are often deeply suggestive. Edgeworth did leave a clue that showed she had in mind the Swiftian mode of political allegory, even if the project was never completely implemented. 'As I have lived so will I die, true and loyal to the family' is Thady's governing maxim, and in Edgeworth's mind it appears to be associated with an Irish political figure. She indicates her interest in these sentiments in a list of pencilled manuscript corrigenda, most never executed, which appear in her handwriting on the first flyleaf of an Edgeworth family copy of the first edition of *Castle Rackrent*.[20] The first entry reads 'page fifth True & loyal to the family write a note on Loyal High Constable'. The real-life 'Loyal High Constable' is James Butler, 2nd Duke of Ormond (1666–1745), who in 1688 left the service of James II for that of William and Mary, served these monarchs and after them Queen Anne, but was attainted in 1715 by the new Whig ministry of George I. He fled to France, made contact with the Jacobite court in exile, and commanded a Spanish fleet taking supplies to the British Jacobite insurgents in 1718. A hero to some, a traitor to others, Ormond remained a focus of Irish Jacobite sentiment throughout the earlier eighteenth century.

How should we read the fact that Thady's proudly proclaimed loyalty to an old family fallen on evil times reminded Edgeworth of Ormond's loyalty to the Stuarts; additionally, or alternatively, of the loyalty of at least one of her Edgeworth ancestors to the exiled Ormond?[21] Even if the Duke's services to four successive Stuarts do offer tantalizing parallels to Thady's services to the Rackrents, *Castle Rackrent* in its published form hardly reads like a fully sustained political allegory. This is too particularized a provincial estate easily to stand in for the politics of the nation. (Galt's *Annals of the Parish* (1821), in so many ways a Scottish version of *Rackrent*, resembles it in 'shadowing' the sixty-year reign of George III, while stubbornly retaining its sense of locality.) Yet it is significant that some of the best recent commentators have seen Anglo-Irish fiction in general as characterized by 'a tendency towards allegory'.[22] *Ennui* confirms that in Edgeworth's Irish tales allegory is indeed an important technique for introducing wider issues of Irishness. It reappears in most characters who represent traditional Celtic and Catholic Ireland, such as Thady, Ellinor the nurse in *Ennui*, Grace Nugent and Count O'Halloran in *The Absentee*, Corny in *Ormond*. Thady cannot be read adequately until he is read on two levels, the second of which elevates him socially to the level of the very different Irish servant still identifiable in the phrase 'true and loyal to the family'.

Even without our knowing that many forms of intellectual conservatism, including Jacobitism, merged to make the portrait of his 'loyalty', Thady would prompt comparison with the narrator-heroes of a modern allegorist, Kazuo Ishiguro. In two remarkable studies of precarious twentieth-century empires, the Japanese (*An Artist of the Floating World*) and the British (*The Remains of the Day*), Ishiguro appoints a loyal servant of each system to narrate the process of its downfall. Like Ishiguro's Mr Stevens, the English butler who tells the story of an English country house and its neo-Fascist owner in *The Remains of the Day*, Thady lacks a general social ethic. He believes that his responsibilities end at the boundaries of the estate, and within the boundaries he does as his master tells him. The reader becomes all the more aware of a world which is not the estate, of a politics the butler shuts out, of an entire ethical dimension which the system he serves works to deny. Provoked into compensating for the narrator's complacency, we call up the tottering empire for ourselves. That is an appropriate reader's response to *Castle Rackrent*. Edgeworth may be at her most persuasive as an unabashed critic of the dying feudal Ireland, rather than as the writer the Union made her, the utopian prophet of a new nineteenth-century commercial empire.

Thady's Irish voice dominates the book for most readers, but never without competition. It first comes in the tones of the so-called editor, to whom Thady, being illiterate, is obliged to dictate his memoirs. The Preface establishes the editor as a scholar, presumably male, who frames the narrative within the general discourse (unknown to Thady) of private and public history. Next (in the first edition) the reader encounters the Glossary, in which the editor sets out in a thoroughgoing style to interpret Thady to us, and so ironizes and subverts his version of his masters and their world.

With the Glossary, Edgeworth takes to an extreme Marmontel's goal of a cross-cultural dialogue. Entries range from the scholarly note on a linguistic usage to the short occasional essay on a social ritual, such as the Irish funeral. The editor is introduced not like Thady as someone with distinctive, vulnerable personal traits, but as the unassailable representative of more advanced culture. 'He' (again) is highly educated, knowledgeable, superior, worldly-wise and interested in everything, in strong general contrast with Thady's ignorance of anyone's affairs but his own. This emphatic disjunction between the narrative and editorial sections of the book makes *Castle Rackrent* quite unlike Beckford's oriental tale *Vathek* (1787), a rare earlier example of an annotated prose fiction, where the voice of the narrator of the tale is as ironic and knowing as that of the editor of the notes. If in its weight of scholarly impedimenta *Castle Rackrent* resembles any near-contemporaneous narrative form, it is the long, annotated Romantic poem, commonly set in the feudal past or in the East. A distinction between the emotional, primitive, feminine, Eastern narrative poem and the rational, analytic, masculine and Western notes is made, for example, in Southey's *Thalaba the Destroyer* (1801) and *The Curse of Kehama* (1810), in Byron's *Childe Harold* I and II (1812) and *The Giaour* (1813), in Shelley's *Queen Mab* (1813) and Moore's *Lalla Rookh* (1817).

Just as the portrayal of Thady is illuminated by the comparativist insights of post-colonialist criticism, so is the overall structure of *Castle Rackrent* and the part played by its second voice – which can be seen as speaking through the Glossary, Preface and footnotes in the name of metropolitan knowledge and linguistic correctness, both forms of mental authority. We may see in the schizophrenic quality of the narration – one half warmly and humorously Irish, the other half coolly and rationally English – the split cultural personality of the colonizer.[23]

Castle Rackrent could from the outset have been classed as a tale about Ireland, a tale about the 'lower orders', a tale rather surprisingly written by a woman almost entirely about men: the feature common to all these topics is an unequal social relationship. Forms of modern criticism that draw on anthropology and particularly on structuralism, whether they are primarily concerned with class, race or gender, all potentially have something to contribute to the topic of *Castle Rackrent*. In the decade of the French Revolution, as the work of Paine and Godwin illustrates, class was easily the most visible and the most controversial of the inequalities, and its vocabulary was commonly borrowed in discussions of what we would call gender, religion and race. 'Can man be free, if woman is a slave?' demanded P. B. Shelley, following Wollstonecraft; and Henry Grattan, leading parliamentarian of Anglo-Ireland: 'The Irish Protestant can never be free until the Irish Catholic has ceased to be a slave.'[24] Approaching *Castle Rackrent* in the light of its own cultural politics means taking heed of the current language of class.

In 1800, when almost all fiction in English was first published in London, and all of it was written in standard English, what must have struck readers as most remarkable about *Castle Rackrent* was that the tale itself was written in a 'provincial' variant of the English language. Even its claims to a special authenticity as history and experience rest on the fact that it provides a space in which native Irish voices can appear to speak uncensored, uninterrupted – 'out of the face', in the Irish expression (see the Glossary, p. 133), which means, precisely, not edited by anyone else. By 1800 non-standard speech appeared, if anywhere, in dialogue given to minor characters: no dialect 'speaker' had enjoyed the fictional status, and licence, allowed to Thady. Rather than imposing herself (through the Glossary) on Thady's world, Edgeworth in 1800 would surely read as a writer retiring to the margins of her own picture. Challenging and topical questions were raised by a text claiming to make a more philosophical history out of gossip, a new fictional world out of traditions, laws, feelings and ideas peculiar to Ireland and realizable only through an Irish form of language.

The Glossary admittedly opens as if its function is to ridicule Thady and the Irishness he stands for. It seems an act of aggression that his oratorical act of commencement – 'Monday morning' – is at once undercut by an editorial note which tells a landlord's anecdote about lower-class Irish laziness. Again, it is easy to find the first footnote obnoxious, incorporating a dehumanizing description by Spenser of the people whose land he was taking by force. But, significantly, Spenser too wrote his tract on Ireland in the form of a dialogue. The very different views taken of the Irish cloak by Eudoxus and Irenius, Spenser's two speakers, express deeply divided and old English responses to the Irish – sometimes an ancient, romantic, learned people, with an infinitely seductive history; at other times beggars and outcasts, thieves and murderers. That dichotomy surfaces once more in the first long Glossary entry, on the Ullaloo, or Irish funeral wail. Edgeworth quotes at length from a sympathetic article in *Transactions of the Royal Irish Academy* on ancient Irish funeral rites, and goes on to deflate it with an amused piece of rapportage on the customs of the present day. The penultimate Glossary note, on wakes, repeats the dialoguic pattern. In fact, all the substantial notes – other relevant ones deal with fairy-mounts, docking the entail, and the raking pot of tea – act out incompatible points of view. As though to demonstrate the hermeneutic function of the gloss, one interpretation follows another, without engaging in argument or moving towards a resolution.

Even more than Thady's diversified idiolect, the Glossary is inconsistent and paradoxical. It intrudes on Ireland, often ungraciously, by professing to interpret it; logically it weakens its own position by its many internal contradictions. First cousin to the encyclopaedia and the general journal, the glossary is a form typical of the Enlightenment which more easily appears to destabilize a text than to impose coherent monolithic meaning. Certainly the Glossary to *Castle Rackrent* avoids those orthodox judgements, moralistic or polite, which women writers especially were under some pressure to adopt. A decade later Edgeworth compiled another Irish glossary – to the book of Mary Leadbeater, an Irish Quaker, *Cottage Dialogues among the Irish Poor* (1811). Edgeworth's Preface on that occasion makes another strong declaration in favour of homely, informal knowledge, as opposed to classical knowledge, and in favour of the accurate reporting of what peasants really say, not what lady moralists want them to say. But in Edgeworth's Glossary to the Leadbeater volume the improving tone is noticeably more insistent than in the Glossary to her own tale. One note in *Castle Rackrent* that keeps its power to surprise us is the Glossary entry on the raking pot of tea (pp. 135–6), which overturns a series of icons, including modern academic ones, about what a proper lady of 1800 should write and what she should not.

It is after midnight, and the end of an Irish party. The men are still drinking downstairs, or they have fallen asleep. Upstairs the women dash from room to room, gathering their correspondence (love-letters?), unlocking a torrent of gossip, laughter and complaint, admitting perhaps the occasional audacious male, and not forgetting a favourite woman servant: 'The merit of the original idea of a raking pot of tea evidently belongs to the washerwoman and the laundry-maid.' As in the annual late-medieval Feast of Fools, when the populace clowned in church, the women overturn orders they are expected to observe at other times. This is not conventional footnote material. Nor is its masculine complement, the note R. L. Edgeworth contributed on wakes (pp. 137–8), which gives an uncensorious account of the amorous finale of a lower-class Irish funeral. Nor is the touchingly rough translation of the Estonian poem of peasant protest (pp. 128–9), which seems to invade the Glossary on behalf of sub-cultures generally.

If parts of the Glossary celebrate a non-literate world, they side in this with Thady's narrative – which is described in the Preface, as we have seen, as 'domestic anecdote' and 'gossip'. The Preface goes on to hint that the 'real-life' materials out of which Thady's story is made are themselves anecdotes, reminiscences, belonging to the Edgeworth family and their neighbours. It looks as if there can be no strict polarization between the 'feminine' gossip of an elderly Irish male narrator, and the 'masculine' commentary of an equally fictional English male editor. One view of the presence of an element such as gossip in polished fiction is that its charm and seductiveness is temporarily allowed, only to be contained after all by the writing around it.[25] But *Castle Rackrent* includes material significantly close to the author's heart which falls on the subversive side: not merely much of her own family history and not merely the women's late-night party, but that other women's party in which the tale originated, the conversational session on her aunt's sofa which began the process of turning spoken anecdote into written narrative.

Some notes now neutralized by time must have struck early readers as risky. The Glossary's second entry, on the Irish idiom 'let alone', cites as an authority the linguistic scholar and notorious democrat John Horne Tooke, one of the three defendants in the treason trials of 1794. It is no accident that a theorist of language was also a leading radical intellectual in the period of the American and French revolutions.[26] Dictionary-makers and grammarians, Samuel Johnson on the high-cultural side and Tooke and Francis Grose on the popular, took issue over the authority of polite, literary language or the 'naturalness' (and thus for some the legitimacy) of the vulgar spoken language, including dialect and slang. A novel published in dialect in 1800 enters this debate, inevitably on the popular side. Popular rhetorical positions already familiar to contemporaries include a taste for a vulgar domestic history – of the kind declared by the Preface from its opening sentence, and borne out in the Glossary, again virtually at the outset, when the second note declares its unabashed reliance on Tooke as an authority.

By the late twentieth century the best-known contribution to the debate about the historical relations of the masses with language and culture is William Wordsworth's Preface of 1800 and 1802 to his *Lyrical Ballads* (1798). Wordsworth does not introduce the contentious name of Tooke, though Coleridge at this time was recommending Tooke's theories to his friend. Nor does he allude to the prior existence of claims that the *speech* of the common people, in all its local variety, had its own history, its own expressiveness, its own value as a field of knowledge. As though hoping to steer clear of existing controversies, Wordsworth evades the problem that in real life bred inequality – the difference between provincial speech and slang on the one hand, and on the other educated speech and the formal written language. By claiming to believe in an essential simple language, that of people close to nature who speak from the heart, he denies this difference, and glosses over the real-life class hostilities and hierarchies associated with the claim of the upper orders alone to have the requisite competence to write and speak correctly. By distancing himself from the actual speech of the poor people whose *visual* features he and Dorothy Wordsworth render so graphically, by not letting their voices speak distinctly in his poetry, Wordsworth sidesteps the most stubborn obstacles to cross-class dialogue: the fact that educated speakers hear lower-class or provincial speakers as coarse or ignorant, while the uneducated hear the educated as domineering and contemptuous.

Though the Preface to *Lyrical Ballads* makes a case for demotic language, neither it, nor Wordsworth's poems and letters, advance the claims of dialect;[27] but dialect was precisely what was at issue and in use by most partisans of the simple side of the linguistic class divide. Edgeworth's publications on dialect in essentially the same years as Wordsworth's, *Castle Rackrent* (1800) and *Irish Bulls* (1802), give a much more precise representation of demotic or localized speech than Wordsworth, and do identify the issue as one of class and hierarchy expressed through language. They seek to persuade the educated reader to accept a plurality of (English) languages, varying both by region and by class.

In a letter to a schoolfriend written shortly after her return to Ireland in 1782, Edgeworth declares that English is the language used for transactions between tenants and landlords in County Longford but (revealingly) that Irish is the language preferred when the lower orders quarrel among themselves.[28] The virtual absence of reference to the Irish language in the Irish tales is her equivalent of Wordsworth's decision to steer clear of dialect. By 1800 some Celticists were developing a nationalist case for the historical Irish language as the authentic sign of 'native Irish' ethnic identity. In advancing her own claims for the expressiveness and dignity of the English used by the Irish lower classes, Edgeworth always implicitly opposes the notion that the Irish language has unique significance. On occasion she is franker, and openly declares that to encourage Irish would be retrograde and divisive.[29]

No part of *Castle Rackrent* goes far into the question of the language the book is written in. This issue, along with that of aristocratic cultural hegemony and metropolitan centrism, was opened by the Edgeworths for the first time in 1802 in their jointly authored *Essay on Irish Bulls*. Though half as long again as *Castle Rackrent*, *Irish Bulls* serves it much as Wordsworth's Preface serves the *Lyrical Ballads*, as a theoretical commentary composed very much after the creative event. R. L. and Maria Edgeworth again attempt a Swiftian vein of irony for the essayistic opening and close of the new book, but by general consent handle Swift's manner very awkwardly. The best that can be said of *Irish Bulls* is that it ought to be a much better book than it is, for its views on linguistic variation are admirably liberal, and it shows the potential of a form much in vogue at the political close of the eighteenth century, the learned and humorous anthology of vulgar materials. Later chapters are again cast as a dialogue – an Englishman, a Scotsman and an Irishman find themselves shut up together on a long coach journey, and they pass the time debating national identity, national difference, and language. As a whole the book examines the English preconception that the Irish frequently make blunders or 'bulls' when speaking English, and so betray their national or ethnic stupidity. It concludes that a nasty vein of cultural superiority accounts for English jokes about Irish–English speech – which deserves a new, imaginative style of analysis.

The so-called bull is found universally; some of the classic Irish ones also occur in other languages; the English lower-class idiom, which is less metaphorical and witty than the Irish, could more reasonably be considered stupid. The Edgeworths support their case by introducing along the way a dozen or so speeches by lower-class Irish men and women which were taken down, they say, shortly after they were heard. Most of these were given as testimony before a magistrate or judge – an educated auditor, then, and plainly often R. L. Edgeworth himself. The degree of plausibility in these oral materials varies a lot. Most sound too composed for accuracy and, because the book's argument focuses not on linguistic particularity but on eloquence, relatively few dialect expressions are recorded. The result is surprisingly formal and correct from the author of *Castle Rackrent* and of the low-life scenes in *Ennui*. There is, however, a striking exception, a speech in an unusually particularized idiom which R. L. Edgeworth heard as it was publicly delivered. The speaker appeared

> in a court of justice, upon his trial for life or death. A quarrel happened between two shoeblacks, who were playing at what in England is called pitch-farthing, or heads and tails, and in Ireland, head or harp. One of the combatants threw a small

paving stone at his opponent, who drew out the knife with which he used to scrape shoes, and plunged it up to the hilt in his companion's breast. It is necessary for our story to say, that near the hilt of this knife was stamped the name of Lamprey, an eminent cutler in Dublin. The shoeblack was brought to trial. With a number of significant gestures, which on his audience had all the powers that Demosthenes ascribes to action, he, in a language not purely attic, gave the following account of the affair to his judge:

'Why, my lord, as I was going past the Royal Exchange I meets Billy – "Billy," says I, "will you sky a copper?" – "Done," says he – "Done," says I; and done and done's enough between two jantlemen. – With that I ranged them fair and even with my hook-em-snivey – up they go. – "Music!" says he – "Skulls!" says I; and down they come three brown mazards. "By the holy! you flesh'd 'em," says he. – "You lie," says I. – With that he ups with a lump of a two-year-old, and lets drive at me. I outs with my bread-earner, and gives it him up to Lamprey in the bread-basket.'[30]

The passage is straightway submitted to several pages of linguistic commentary, an analysis which aims simultaneously at wit and at seriously demonstrating how figurative the language of the Irish common people is. Almost all the shoeblack's terms are correctly shown to be metaphors which are evidently accepted popular language. 'Heads' on a coin become for example 'skulls' and 'mazards', and (since the Irish halfpenny showed a harp) 'tails' could be 'harp' or 'music'. The facetiousness apart, the analysis is sharp and effective, but it is the feat of hearing, remembering and labouring to record such language that really tells. As a guarantee of fidelity, some terms are still current in parts at least of Britain: verbs like 'sky', 'ups', 'outs', 'flesh'd' and the pithy 'bread-basket' for stomach. Moreover the racing term 'two-year-old' for a medium-sized rock seems to be a substitution typical of urban humour, and not at all typical of the country idiom in which Edgeworth's Irish tales generally deal, a distinction which seems to confirm the accuracy of R. L. Edgeworth's ear.

The Edgeworths clearly have skills necessary to scholars dealing with oral materials before the age of the tape recorder – powers of observation, of memory and of mimicry, all in relation to speech. To develop and exercise such powers one must respect variation in speech and believe in the value of accumulating knowledge of social behaviour. So-called 'popular antiquarians', the incipient anthropologists of the day, had become interested in fieldwork within the populace of the British Isles; novelists thus far had not. It is difficult for metropolitan writers, when putting words in the mouths of provincial or colonized people, not to introduce naive characteristics, the half-covert equivalent of the 'bull'. The witnesses in *Irish Bulls* may flatter the Anglo-Irish magistrate or election candidate with whom they converse, but in the context of this argument they are not shown doing it in the wheedling, servile tones of the colonized. And like many of the eloquent talkers briefly encountered in the Irish tales, they benefit from the discontinuities of tone Edgeworth habitually uses, her practice of isolating a speech or an anecdote as a single event, unique to its place and time, which asks us to consider it just as it is. Avoiding absorption into the Edgeworths' standard written English, the shoeblack and his kind never become 'characters' – as they might well do in a novel written by anyone but Edgeworth herself. They are more like passers-by snapped by a photographer, autonomous, resilient, and somewhat mysterious.

In 1802, the year *Irish Bulls* appeared, Maria Edgeworth spent some months with her father and stepmother in Paris, where she had her first experience of intellectual high society; they came home via Edinburgh and Glasgow, where she had her second. From her travels Edgeworth acquired her first intellectual correspondents, and a new notion of her ideal reader.[31] The fiction Edgeworth writes from 1804 imagines for itself a cosmopolitan circle located in the metropolitan centres of Paris, London, Edinburgh, Glasgow, Geneva, Dublin. Even when set partly in Ireland, no later tale of hers restricts itself to a single Irish estate, or indeed to a single country. Her notion of society becomes expressly generalized, the modern cultural condition as defined by economics, sociology and social psychology. Meanwhile more London-oriented novelists, who soon included Austen and even Scott, concentrated for their main medium on the long narrative and its specialized techniques, such as the fluid rendering of time, and mood-management through the use of place. Because of the long ascendancy of the nineteenth-century novel, any previous experiments less blatantly signalled than those of Sterne have tended to look like naivety. Modern readers do indeed have to accept that Edgeworth's tales will not rank *as novels* beside those of her successors and leading contemporary rivals. Instead they have to be read as texts with their own purposes, achievements, and projected clever readers.

The intellectual first fruit of Edgeworth's tour of 1802–3 was the tale *Ennui*, drafted in 1804–5, though 'two-thirds rewritten' before publication in 1809.[32] Her adoption of a theme as sophisticated as 'ennui', a significantly French word, indicates that she is putting much of her earlier work behind her. Where before she specialized mainly in 'simple' materials – tales about children or the lower orders – she now for some years wrote mainly about the wealthy. Her working notes for *Ennui* survive, five closely-written pages in a notebook which, to judge by its other contents, was probably compiled at the revision stage, 1805–7. Here she briefly lists anecdotes supplied from a cosmopolitan range of reading, her own and her friends', to illustrate the upper-order pastimes of eating, drinking, gaming, spending, and boredom. The courts of the despots Louis XIV and Frederick the Great of Prussia figure more than other sources in both the notebook and the tale, partly because entertaining recent memoirs of old-regime societies were currently fashionable in post-revolutionary Paris. The first five chapters of *Ennui*, professedly Lord Glenthorn's memoirs of his own first twenty-five years, are really a general essay on the uses and abuses of great wealth under late eighteenth-century aristocratic governments. They are given in the form of the 'confessions' of a wealthy man, a parodic equivalent of Rousseau's *Confessions* of a provincial.

Following the five chapters set in English high life come twelve set in a world almost wholly unfamiliar, at least in literature before 1800: the mixed but generally very poor society that surrounds the hero's vast estate in the west of Ireland. By reading *Ennui* in a single volume with *Castle Rackrent* we foreground these chapters and extract what is Irish in the tale. The first edition bound and sold it with quite different companion-works, and readers consequently read it somewhat differently. *Ennui* was published in 1809 as the first volume of the three-volume *Tales of Fashionable Life*, a collection of five stories of varying length. Three years later the second series of *Tales of Fashionable Life* appeared: five more tales, of which the longest was again Irish (*The Absentee*), and again had pride of place – in the sixth and last volume, which rounded off the series. Thus the two tales, which ambitiously represent Ireland as a complex society in the process of becoming modern, embrace eight more stories treating English life at its wealthiest and most incipiently decadent. One London-based story in each series – *Madame de Fleury* (1809) and *Émilie de Coulanges* (1812) – has a titled French emigrée as a heroine. Within each series, Edgeworth maintains a balance between the lives and vocations of women and of men. The goal is a stylish portrait of oligarchy or plutocracy not special to one country, but pointedly located within a Britain conceived as uncentred, many-layered, equally a home to Irish peasants and to Parisian aristocrats fleeing from revolution.

R. L. Edgeworth supplied a stiffly written General Preface to the first series, in which he claimed that the Fashionable Tales illustrated a project on which Maria Edgeworth had worked at his request – *Professional Education* (1808), a treatise on vocational education for sons of the gentry. R. L. Edgeworth seems to succumb here to the well-known temptation of valuing that aspect of someone else's work that most resembles one's own. It is true that as early as February 1805 he persuaded his daughter to embark on a course of 'solid reading' for *Professional Education*,[33] and that reading for the chapters in the treatise on (for example) the education of princes and of lawyers fed details into the tale as well. But the thinking that has gone into *The Tales of Fashionable Life*, and especially *Ennui*, is much more capacious than the ideas needed for *Professional Education*, and it clearly should not be credited to the novelist's father. Because it was not really relevant to family partnerships and projects, Edgeworth still wrote privately of her work as mere entertainment. But the text itself, complex and diverse, has left us with the evidence we need to understand the curious and exciting experiment in innovative social fiction and sociology that she now embarked on.

These subtle, devious purposes were signalled by the Italian epigraph which first appeared on the title-page of the second edition (December 1809), probably supplied by a friend and reader (such as Lady Moira, knowledgeable in Italian) who spotted its appropriateness:

Everyone listened smilingly to the pretty little tales, in

which they all saw the faults of other people rather than their own; or if they suspected their own, they believed that no one else would do so.

It is then at once 'a pretty little tale' and a narrative with hidden significance. In outward appearance a story of other people, it covers a story about oneself. Though formally a fictional travelogue, it is more profoundly – as an epigraph to one chapter hints – about happiness and self-realization at home. A novelty because of the way it represents one people, the Irish, it is also a parable of Western society in an age when its old regimes, dominated by property-owning magnates, are severely under challenge.

Among recent commentators on allegorical narrative, it is another Anglo-Irish writer, the poet Louis MacNeice, who seems to have launched a suggestive discussion of the *Irish* dimension of such 'double-level' writing. To this mode, for which he prefers the term 'parable', MacNeice recruits Spenser (*The Faerie Queene*) and Swift (*The Tale of a Tub*); a critic on whom he draws is a fellow-Ulsterman, C. S. Lewis, author of the study of medieval and Renaissance romance, *The Allegory of Love*.[34] In the 1930s the most sceptical and matter-of-fact of leading English poets, MacNeice after the war worked in radio, and for his experimental radio dramas found himself increasingly drawn to devices which could give prose the same allusiveness and tension as poetry. Edgeworth did not share that motive with MacNeice, yet she may have shared others. Their Anglo-Irishness arguably throws up problems of personal and national identity, for which double meaning becomes an appropriate means of expression. And certainly she too is richly indebted to both Spenser and Swift. While her adoption of an unexpectedly complex narrative vehicle may be coincidence, she seems to use it far more elaborately in her Irish tales than in her English. It is through the allegorical plot of a tale such as *Ennui* that she is able to explore a subject hitherto unfamiliar in fiction, the schismatic nature of modern Irishness, and the problem this represents for individual men and women in the age of dawning nationalism.

One productive way of reading *Ennui* is as a re-writing of *Castle Rackrent* on terms intelligible to a liberal sophisticated cosmopolitan readership. The reading is all the more persuasive because it is clear that each of Edgeworth's later Irish tales is in some sense explicitly a sequel to or re-working of *Castle Rackrent*.[35] The Glossary to *Castle Rackrent* could stand in front of both tales, so thoroughly do its entries (and those of the footnotes) seem to pick out the inconsequential bricolage that in Edgeworth's writing evokes Irish estate life. A footnote to *Castle Rackrent* comments on the fondness of the lower-class Irish for their by now old-fashioned wigs. In *Castle Rackrent* this fixes our attention on Thady's characteristic gesture when puzzled, to remove his wig and scratch his head. But the same action occurs at a very significant point in the plot of *Ennui*, when the hero's foster-brother the blacksmith has to be induced to remove his wig so that his bare pate can be examined for its tell-tale scars.

Again, *Castle Rackrent* has a satirical footnote about the banshee, 'a species of aristocratic fairy' which appears in the shape of 'a little hideous old woman' to warn the family in some great house that one of them is soon to die: old Ellinor's sudden appearance before Glenthorn at his gate is the most striking manifestation of the banshee in either novel. Funerals play a commanding part in the Glossary, and also in both tales. There is even a repeat in *Ennui* of the scene in *Castle Rackrent* in which a leading character shams death in order to overhear what his dependants and supposed friends think of him. In *Castle Rackrent* there is no scene that really illustrates that most intriguing of Glossary entries, 'the raking pot of tea', but in *Ennui* the hoydenish behaviour of the ladies at Ormsby Villa, and especially their prank of locking up Geraldine with Glenthorn in a temple dedicated to a woman deity, Minerva, fits the Glossary's description of an unlicensed, indecorous interlude snatched by women, 'low life above stairs'.

Containing all this detail and more suggestive of a controlling allegory, *Ennui* repeats *Rackrent*'s framing plot – the annals of the last four members of a falling Irish dynasty, the arrival of a new regime. In each case a strongly characterized male narrator is used, who incidentally 'confesses', knowingly or unknowingly, a great deal about himself; readers become more or less aware of distortions of vision and unreliable interpretations, belying the tale's pervasive matter-of-factness. Glenthorn, a less obvious 'original' than Thady, nevertheless matches Thady as his pair: in the first tale, the cheating servant looks up at his incompetent masters, in the second the incompetent master looks down on his cheating servants. Finally, the wild scenes in the latter days of Glenthorn castle, before its destruction by

27

fire, seem to belong more naturally in *Castle Rackrent* than in *Ennui*, and to signal the end of an old world evoked by both tales together. On the level of allegory, this falling system signifies something obviously greater than a single estate, but it is *Ennui*, within *Tales of Fashionable Life*, which intimates that we should not think of the débâcle as peculiar to Ireland. The portrait fits 'us', not 'them'. It represents the challenge to the old political order which had been felt in every Western European polity since 1790.

Though Edgeworth has passing affinities with the Godwin who wrote *Political Justice* and *Caleb Williams*, those hostile portrayals of 'things as they are', it would be altogether misleading to think of Godwin and the still more partisan Tom Paine as sources for Edgeworth's circumspect, generalized study of revolutionary Ireland in *Ennui*. By far the most suggestive text for a political reading of the Irish tales is Adam Smith's *The Wealth of Nations* (1776), the first major book R. L. Edgeworth gave her to read when he took her from her English boarding-school in 1782. Smith's contemporaries were more aware than are many of his modern admirers of facets of his work that reappear in Edgeworth: his severe, satirical eye for non-productive people and practices in all walks of society, from the highest downwards, and an evolutionary model of history. The passages from *The Wealth of Nations* most relevant to Edgeworth are easy to find, since they tend to occur in the celebrated opening chapters which unfold his labour theory of value. Here Smith sets out in non-technical language why it is not gold, silver or paper money that constitute wealth: 'labour ... is the only universal as well as the only accurate measure of value'.[36] In Book II he pursues some of the radical implications of this principle, especially in a provocatively written chapter which distinguishes between productive and unproductive labour. The labour of a 'manufacturer' (that is, a worker or factory hand) generally adds to the value of the material he works on, and so is productive. On the other hand the labour of the menial servant 'does not realize itself ... in any vendible commodity'; such services 'perish in the very instant of their performance'. In this respect the menial servant has points in common with 'some of the most respectable orders' in society, who are similarly unproductive: 'the sovereign', suggests Smith imperturbably, 'with all the officers of justice and war who serve under him'.[37]

Tom Paine developed the argument about the unproductivity of the monarch and the central bureaucracy to such notorious effect in his *Rights of Man*, Part II (1792) that Edgeworth probably had qualms about bringing the case home to the nation's leaders. But she has taken hints from the list of unproductive occupations Smith gives, after royalty:

> In the same class must be ranked, some both of the gravest and most important, and some of the most frivolous professions: churchmen, lawyers, physicians, men of letters of all kinds; players, buffoons, musicians, opera-singers, opera-dancers, &c.[38]

While Thady in *Castle Rackrent* and Joe Kelly in *Ennui* are both unproductive servants, it is Kelly who has Smith's hallmark on him. He is a 'buffoon,' a kind of 'player', and idleness personified – as well as a cause of idleness in Glenthorn. Even Joe's acknowledged qualities, without his covert hatred and treachery, come near to bringing down Glenthorn's house, estate and order.

Before Hegel made the topic of the master–servant relationship his own, the French revolution generation knew it in Smith's sharply politicized form as typically a backstairs alliance, by insinuation an unnatural liaison, which cuts right across the old hierarchical pride of rank, and also frustrates the concern of the new bourgeois order with production. Smith's tone becomes polemical when he introduces the matter of the domestic favourite:

> The rent of lands and the profits of stock are everywhere . . . the principal sources from which unproductive hands derive their subsistence . . . [Owners of land and stock] might both maintain indifferently either productive or unproductive hands. They seem, however, to have some predilection for the latter. The expence of a great lord feeds generally more idle than industrious people.[39]

Smith's analysis of the curious reciprocity, the mutual support and mutual destructiveness prevailing between the 'high' and 'low' parties to a bad alliance, anticipates what the Tunisian Albert Memmi has to say of the interdependence of the *colon* and the *colonisé* within the colonial relationship. Smith, and after him the generation of Paine and Godwin, analyse 'aristocracy' the system much as

Fanon, Memmi, Said and others analyse colonialism: as a relationship enslaving not only the dependants but the privileged, who are similarly reduced to passivity and weakness. Thus, disappointed of his hopes of marrying Geraldine, an Irishwoman and his social equal, the magnate Glenthorn demeaningly seeks the friendship of the entertaining, manipulative Kelly, who lures him away from his proper concerns on his estate, and for a while makes him the dupe of rebels who would take his life as well as his property.

When Adam Smith develops his discussion of the landed proprietors he associates himself with the work of the French 'œconomists', or physiocrats, headed by Quesnai. Drawing on the analysis of the French school, he puts land foremost as a source of national wealth. He also adopts the French division of agricultural producers into two groups – proprietors (landlords who draw rents and do not farm) and cultivators of land (farmer-owners, tenant-farmers and agricultural labourers). Again he mixes the classes, but this time in order to produce a large heterogeneous productive grouping which fills society's middle ground, in the place normally occupied by the quite differently conceived middle class or 'middling sort'. Smith in fact uses a utopian tone rare with him to describe the cheerful cooperation between the comfortably-off and the poor within productive rural communities.[40] On the other hand he becomes more laconic than usual when he considers the contribution of his first group of landowners, the large proprietors. Their productive input is what they spend on maintenance and improvement. Since this expenditure earns the cultivator profits, Smith finds it reasonable that it earns the proprietor rent. But his tone becomes warmer and more pointed when he turns to examine all the necessary expenses of the cultivator or tenant-farmer – what *he* has to lay out on maintenance costs, improvements and labour, plus the costs of a large household:

> ... unless [these expenses] are regularly restored to him, together with a reasonable profit, he cannot carry on his employment upon a level with other employments; but, from a regard to his own interests, must desert it as soon as possible, and seek some other. That part of the produce of the land which is thus necessary for enabling the farmer to continue his business, ought to be considered as a fund sacred to cultivation, which if the landlord violates, he necessarily reduces the produce of his

own land, and in a few years not only disables the farmer from paying this racked rent, but from paying the reasonable rent which he might otherwise have got for his land. The rent which properly belongs to the landlord, is no more than the neat produce which remains after paying ... expences ... laid out in order to raise the gross ... produce. It is because the labour of the cultivators affords a neat produce ... that this class of people are ... distinguished by the honourable appellation of the productive class.[41]

This passage supplies a general gloss to Edgeworth's writing about the estate in all her Irish tales. From the beginning she singles out unproductive proprietors (not merely absentees) as the main targets of her satire. Judging that Ireland has what Smith would deem an unreconstructed aristocracy, she creates a memorable race of idle landlords, beginning with the Rackrents, whose extortions or 'rack-renting' deplete not only the farmer's and labourer's subsistence, but their own wealth and the wealth of the nation. Plainly she is not merely mining Smith for convenient material, but documenting and amplifying his case from Irish sources, much as Arthur Young does in his Smithian *Tour in Ireland* (1780), another book Edgeworth much admired.[42]

The strong French associations of Smith's 'physiocrat' passages – which are among the most identifiable of those Edgeworth uses – were controversial in the decade or so after French revolutionaries had put some of the proposals into practice.[43] Edgeworth's Irish tales have not been much linked with controversy. Quite the contrary indeed: read in the narrow context of Irish *realpolitik*, her emphasis on the camaraderie between a farmer-landlord or a reforming agent and friendly tenants looks bland and emollient, an example of the Anglo-Irish liberal's wishful thinking. Alternatively, her supposed identification with landowners is seen as an uncritical partiality for her own family interest. When her format is rejoined with Franco-Scottish political economy her Irish fiction takes on a wholly new energy. Its discernibly French brand of liberalism is both universal and contentiously topical, giving these tales of Irish estate life an impressive range of reference.

Though there have been a number of efforts to read *Castle Rackrent* as an allegory of, say, the fall of 'the Protestant Nation',[44] *Ennui* and the two subsequent Irish tales are normally taken for rather simpler chronicle-plots loosely based on travel writing. How then can we feel confident that sufficient signs of a 'dark conceit' exist for a reasonably quick reader to pick up? The first need is to identify the plot, with its immediate allusions to *Castle Rackrent*, and its remoter Gothic reverberations, as the symbolic rather than the particularized fall of a house and order. The second is to notice the precise dating of the central, melodramatic events of the plot – in 1798, a year of terrible slaughter and of the disintegration of Ascendancy Ireland. The third is to notice that the hero's make-up and behaviour are not the particularized traits of an individual but the previously known diagnosis of a species.

Glenthorn is a sick man who suffers two near breakdowns in the course of the action, one at the time of his twenty-fifth birthday in England, when he is riding out with pistols in his pocket, intending to kill himself; the other in Ireland when, turned down by Geraldine, his lassitude returns. He is suffering from hypochondria, a nervous condition well documented in eighteenth-century medicine and long recognized as the masculine equivalent of the woman's ailment, hysteria. John Mullan has given a valuable account of early to mid-century discussions of hypochondria, and their relevance to the am-bivalent fashionable character-trait, sensibility, which is both a sign of refinement and personal distinction, and a symptom of social over-cultivation, degeneracy and madness. What Mullan does not go on to say is that one of the later authorities on hypochondria, who is in fact Edgeworth's acknowledged main source, the Scottish doctor William Cullen, sees the nervous complaint as specifically the occupational disease of the idle rich.[45] Most of what Glenthorn actually does in the book – his aristocratic English 'dissipations' of spending, gambling, gourmandizing, prize-fighting and democratic politics – are Cullen's proposed remedies for the wealthy classes' chronic want of occupation: and travel, particularly travel with a purpose, is the activity Cullen specially recommends. Thus far Glen-thorn personifies the aristocrat; when he resigns his earldom and becomes plain Christy O'Donoghoe, he takes on the characteristics of the professional who must rely on his own energies and talents. In this phase he tests some of the propositions about personal and social ethics Adam Smith advances in the *Theory of Moral Sentiments* (1759).

He has become one of the poor men whose drive to attain fortune keeps in 'continual motion the industry of mankind', and commands general admiration.[46] He represents successively two different class styles, which are also two different (Smith would say successive) social philosophies and systems.

The two great Irish public events embraced by the action are the Rebellion and its direct political consequence, Ireland's constitutional Union with England. Glenthorn acts for the Anglo-Irish ruling order, by abdicating his old role of feudal ruler after the Rebellion, and by re-training as (eventually) a professional administrator. Of the two public events, the Rebellion is represented, if thinly; the Union is not directly introduced. Nevertheless, it is surely no accident that the novel's events span the decade 1795 to 1805, for the Union, here rendered only symbolically, signifies the shift from one form of state system to another, and is actually the tale's unspecified axis.

Unless the symbolic implications of the plot are allowed for, interpretations of the Irish tales can become tediously level and prosaic. Of the good twentieth-century writing on Edgeworth's Irish fiction, most probably comes from Irish historians, concerned to place Edgeworth on the Irish public scene at the time of writing. Edgeworthian commentary has frequently belonged to a style of work identified with R. B. McDowell, who has done more than any other modern historian to establish the range and complexity of Irish political attitudes in the Union period.[47] The historians Michael Hurst, Oliver MacDonagh and Tom Dunne, along with historical literary critics such as Thomas Flanagan and W. J. McCormack, have tended to identify Edgeworth with the positions of her politically active father, and to categorize them both within the appropriate political subsection of the Irish gentry. The Edgeworths usually figure in a grouping which before 1800 included many of the larger and more anglicized landowners: families willing in principle to accept Catholic emancipation, and to vote with various degrees of commitment for 'progress', or a gradual amelioration of poverty, backwardness and sectarian hatred by way of education and agrarian reform.

In this way Thomas Flanagan, W. J. McCormack, Tom Dunne and Iain Topliss, who between them have written most of the best recent Edgeworth criticism, have all at different times concluded, with different kinds of emphasis, that she positions herself behind the windows of the Big House. Michael Hurst, writing not on the novels but on family papers of the second quarter of the nineteenth century, emphasizes how representative of their class the Edgeworths became, as first the removal of the legislature to Westminster, and in 1829 the passing of Catholic Emancipation, reduced the influence and prestige of the larger Whiggish landowner. Hurst's topic is confined to the more conservative half of her long life; but even those working on the tales written in her thirties and forties do not these days often hear the sceptical, 'philosophical' tones and the wit which Edgeworth picks up from Smith. At the worst her reformist agenda can be made to read like enlightened self-interest, and the none-too-subtle pursuit of social control by a member of what is, for practical purposes, London's fifth-column in Ireland.

Edgeworth's reception has been much affected by twentieth-century Irish cultural politics. In the somewhat philistine nationalist ambience of the generation after the founding of the Irish Republic in 1922, her work was unsympathetically noticed by critics such as Stephen Gwynn.[48] 'Big House' attitudes do not seem her only problem; the taint of Unionism, a cleaving to the English connection, is a failing harder to live down. Again, Edgeworth's Unionism has been less often read from her own work than glossed externally, through the politics of her family and especially her father.

As member of the Irish parliament for the pocket borough of St John's Town, R. L. Edgeworth played his practical part in history in July 1800 by casting his vote (against Union) in the division which put an end to the life of the Dublin legislature. This was the odd outcome of his study of the issue, largely from books headed by Arthur Young's *Tour in Ireland*, but also from conversations with Irish neighbours and letters exchanged with friends among the intellectuals and entrepreneurs of the English Midlands. The matter of Ireland's incorporation with greater or mainland Britain had for the last century been presented as an economic debate within the discourse of classical Machiavellian republicanism. Irishmen such as William Molyneux, author of *The Case for Ireland* (1698), and the politician and writer Robert Molesworth, argued that under a mixed constitution a nation's trade was part of its polity, a proper concern of the state, and perhaps the most crucial aspect of policy for the state's subjects.[49] For many mainstream writers after the 1688–9 Revolution, the 'real' (i.e. economic) issue becomes whether Ireland should remain the first of Britain's colonies (and thus *de facto* a trading competitor), or incorporate with the heart of what was already termed the Empire, in the expectation of gaining favoured terms of trade. As R. L. Edgeworth put it in a letter to Darwin of 31 March 1800 and afterwards repeated in *Irish Bulls*, 'such a Union as would identify [i.e. make identical or merge] the nations, so that Ireland should be as Yorkshire to Great Britain, would be an excellent thing'.[50]

Edgeworth was indeed persuaded by his intellectual friends in the English Midlands, and by his own reason, that he should vote for Union on economic grounds. But what counted in the end were the emotions and loyalties of his Irish Protestant friends and parliamentary colleagues, the most ardent 'patriot' opponents of the bill at this time. Like so many Anglo-Irishmen on so many occasions, he chose to follow his heart down the Irish road, and voted against – while pretending that he was guided by something loftier and more English: disgust at the bribery that was needed to get the act through. No wonder R. L. Edgeworth yearned for a single legislative act, equally desired by both sides, which would have healed over the Anglo/Irish schism in his own make-up.

In his Field Day pamphlet, 'Heroic Styles: the tradition of an idea', Seamus Deane has diagnosed even the giant of modern Irish poetry, W. B. Yeats, as suffering from 'the pathology of literary Unionism'.[51] Deane also implicates Edgeworth, for whom the term is more literally applicable. It is in fact crucial to any modern understanding of her writing that we identify the central symbolic role of the Union in *Ennui* and afterwards in *The Absentee*. But the cruder implications of her Unionism for us need tempering by three considerations, two historical and one artistic. She was writing in the immediate context of the traumatic events of 1798, when she and her family witnessed atrocities, and were themselves threatened, as a Rebellion of Protestants as well as Catholics was bloodily put down. 'A share in the empire' had long represented, in Scottish as well as Irish discourse, a way of containing English greed and exclusivity, rather than of putting down the aspirations of the other peoples of the British Isles. But beyond all this, the first literary treatment of Union to which she put solely her own name – *Ennui* – brings the issue pointedly and originally down to the personal level. At the point in the plot where chronology would lead us to expect a reference to the passing of the Union as a public event, she substitutes a symbolic equivalent: the exchange of rank, income and ethnic identities by two English–Irish Earls of Glenthorn; the chequered, shifting identity and many re-namings of 'Christy O'Donoghoe'. Fantastically, we see in the doubling and merging of 'Christy' the meltdown of the polarized class and national identities that have divided key characters until now. Edgeworth tackles the problem of the Union in a highly individual style. She makes it the pivot of a theoretical, visionary history, distanced from deeply divided Irish politics.

As she worked on her own tale, Edgeworth also helped her father to write a more public statement about the post-Union public sphere, which has an intricate and illuminating relationship with *Ennui*. This is through their anonymous review (*Edinburgh Review* 10 (1807)) of John Carr's superficial travel-book, *The Stranger in Ireland* (1806). (See Appendix, pp. 324–42.) The article duplicates some scenes from the tale, such as the boisterous duping of Lord Craiglethorpe by Irish practical jokers, and Glenthorn's own inattentive visit to Killarney. The burlesque parts of the review prove more suggestive than their limp equivalents in the tale, since they draw the reader into the witty and bookish Dublin subculture that remains hidden from Carr. Then the Edgeworths conclude the article more conventionally, with the direct policy-debating, along liberal, gradualist, Whiggish lines, that is left out of the work of fiction. Comparing Edgeworth's two treatments of Carr shows how she is drawn to eclectic materials derived from a very wide cultural and social range – and at the same time how strongly she remains aware of genre, or perhaps rather of audience. It is because politics are there in semi-hidden form that *Ennui* is so interesting. But the absence from *Ennui* of overt politics, such as the article's, is of interest too.

A work of fiction may be at once minutely localized in what it represents and very large in its sense of an audience: as that greatest of Irish books, Joyce's *Ulysses*, manifestly is. A crude explanation for the internationalism of much of Ireland's literature in English is the materialist one: a nation of four million or so provides a small market to sustain such a steady flow of ambitious literature as that of modern Ireland. But Edgeworth's strange approach to the identity and integrity of her characters (to be examined next), and her elaborate procedures to invent a multinational readership, suggest that far more complex needs and motives are also in play. Because the pattern repeats itself, we may reasonably suspect it occurs naturally in a culture threatened over the centuries by a large and greedy neighbour. In the late twentieth century the dramatist Samuel Beckett, the novelist Brian Moore and the poet Paul Muldoon have followed the example of Shaw, Wilde and Joyce and positioned themselves offshore, at a tangent to Ireland's own history. The international theme in *Ennui* and more particularly in *Ormond*, the polished distancing of social conflict in both, have proved with time one of the more Irish features of Edgeworth's Irish tales.

At the time of their appearance, *Ennui* and *The Absentee* looked intellectually ambitious, and earned a style of criticism that prided itself on being philosophical. The reception of the completed *Tales of Fashionable Life* in 1812 was warmer even than that of the group which included *Ennui* in 1809. Prestigious journals not normally in accord – the Whig *Edinburgh Review*, the Tory *Quarterly Review* and the Dissenter *Eclectic Review* – praised the ethical seriousness of the whole enterprise, but especially the vivacity and accuracy of the two Irish tales. Though Henry Stephen and William Gifford, writing in 1809 in the Tory and Anglican *Quarterly Review*, had renewed an old complaint against the Edgeworths' pointedly secular views on education, its reviewer in 1812 delivered what was probably the most thoughtful and influential notice of her career as a novelist. Its author was the essayist and politician John Wilson Croker, who had briefly been Chief Secretary for Ireland and was now in what must in wartime have been a busy office, that of Secretary to the Admiralty. The telling point of Crocker's review is his careful distinction between documentary realism and a form of realism still rarer in fiction, the intelligent analysis of the social scene. On both points he thinks Edgeworth compares well with any contemporary:

> In this department [of *manners*] . . . we do not know that she has, in the whole circle of literature, a rival except the inimitable authors of *Gil Blas* and *Don Quixote*; and the discrimination with which the *individuality* of her persons is preserved through all the varieties of rank, sex and nation, gives to her story a combined charm of truth and novelty [and] creates an interest more acute than fiction (if fiction it can be called) ever excited.

The difference between Edgeworth and almost all predecessors is in effect that she portrays 'character' as both a question of individual personality and a question of social class. Fully to exercise her abilities here she seems to need her Irish scene, what is for the English reader another place, since this enables her to sketch a national community in its complex stratifications. Previous writers had tried to catch 'Irishness', Croker says, and in doing so achieved caricature. Her breakthrough lies

> in the accurate discrimination of the various classes of Irish society . . . Other writers have caught nothing but the general feature, and in their description, everything that is Irish is pretty much alike . . . To Miss Edgeworth . . . it was reserved to separate the genus into its species and individuals, and to exhibit the most accurate and yet the most diversified views that have ever been drawn of a national character.[52]

Over the review as a whole, Croker insists on the importance of Edgeworth's power to analyse or break down, and her power to synthesize or combine. He frankly declares that her intellectual excellence rises above her *métier* as a writer of fiction, and his language is unmistakably that of the natural sciences – 'to separate the genus into its species and individuals'. He sees her modern-seeming commitment to detailed, verifiable knowledge playing a considerable part in the development of a strongly utilitarian and distinctively nineteenth-century aesthetic.

Once more the polymath Adam Smith illuminatingly generalizes the issue. Smith left among his papers an essay concerned incidentally with aesthetics and more centrally with the psychology of the reception and construction of knowledge in the social or natural sciences. When two friends, the chemist Joseph Black and the geologist James Hutton, published the posthumous collection of Smith's ungathered papers, *Essays on Philosophical Subjects* (1795), they opened the volume with the impressive general essay, 'The Principles which lead and direct Philosophical Enquiries: illustrated by the History of Astronomy'. In exploring the psychology of knowledge, primarily in the natural sciences, Smith adopts a vocabulary he could have found in Hogarth or in Burke's *Enquiry on the Sublime and Beautiful* (1757). His key terms, surprise and wonder, are associated with aesthetics and particularly with the pleasure we experience from form and order:

With what curious attention does a naturalist examine a singular plant, or a singular fossil, that is presented to him? He is at no loss to refer it to the general genus of plants or fossils; but this does not satisfy him ... It stands alone in his imagination, and as it were detached from all the other species ... [R]ather than that it should stand quite by itself, he will enlarge the precincts, if I may say so, of some species, in order to make room for it; or he will create a new species on purpose to receive it, and call it a Play of Nature ... But to some class or other of known objects he must refer it, and betwixt it and them he must find out some resemblance or other, before he can get rid of that Wonder, that uncertainty and anxious curiosity excited by its singular appearance, and by its dissimilitude with all the objects he had hitherto observed.[53]

Such a passage applies to much of Edgeworth's fictional and essayistic writing on Ireland, to *Irish Bulls* as much as to *Ennui* and *The Absentee*, because all present to the reader 'knowledge' of Ireland in a carefully prepared way. In the two tales a fictional hero, involved with Ireland yet ignorant about it, confronts something like the ladder of knowledge proposed by Smith. First comes the datum, spectacle or particular curiosity which surprises us. The peculiarity of Edgeworth's Irish realist scenes, and also of her educational writing, is that such curiosities are handled so that they excite the surprise and wonder of the *reader*, though not necessarily of the relevant fictional character. Moments we receive as odd and unaccountable, demanding our further thought, occur in *Ennui* after the supposedly English hero arrives in Ireland. The first of note comes in Chapter VI, when Glenthorn encounters Paddy, the witty and enterprising Irish coach driver; the next, when he arrives after midnight at his castle; a third, when he steps out the following morning to find his dismayingly numerous tenants, who bow, and bow, and return day after day in the hope of having a word with him.

In fact the wonder he immediately experiences does not drive Glenthorn to the philosophic irritation engagingly described by Smith. While he has that name, Glenthorn is never a philosopher, and he does not ask himself why the Irish poor seem as unique and inexplicable as they do. Nor does he learn from his surrogate the English tourist Lord Craiglethorpe, nor from other non-Irish interpreters of the current scene, good and bad, such as the agents M'Leod and Hardcastle, nor from the friendly peasants who try to 'read' the Rebellion for him. The reader, on the other hand, *is* to pursue the explanations Glenthorn keeps evading. As Croker notices, Edgeworth's social realism is not so much an aesthetic effect as a psychological strategy, designed to engage the reader throughout the book by first stimulating and then satisfying his or her curiosity about Ireland. He gives a medical or psychological rather than an aesthetic explanation for a style of realism that isolates an individual occurrence and also seeks to relate it to formal classifications (genus, class). His effort and Edgeworth's, to express realism in the terminology of science, parallel Smith's to write of astronomy in the language of the arts.

Edgeworth's favourable reception must owe a lot to the absence of another active major novelist immediately before Austen and Scott came on the scene. But she also reaped the reward of her Scottish intellectual ambience, which, as the basis of economic and utilitarian thinking in the period, provided a middle-class middle ground. Reviewers understood her because they too were general intellectuals, not specialists as poets seemed, and because they worked like her. In its eclectic contents, its kaleidoscopic diversity and its informativeness, the *Review* and the individual review-article had points in common with an Edgeworth tale. By plainly allowing her tales to seem influenced by *Reviews* (or encyclopaedias) as the medium of knowledge, Edgeworth secured reviewers as allies. She gave Croker lively, memorable, seemingly authentic passages to quote, and large issues, both of artistry and of public policy, to comment on. The Irish tales might have been tailored to enter discourse via the secondary route of the serious review-article.

Croker did most of what she could have asked of him. But she appealed to him specifically on the basis of her truth-telling claims, and for this Edgeworth the writer of polished fables also had to pay. His laudatory article begins with a stern itemizing of her failings, and heading the list come the devices that are too self-consciously fictional for his tastes – especially her use of coincidence, or of traditional, non-naturalistic turns in the plot, which we might be willing to call fantasy but which Croker terms 'violent and unnecessary vicissitudes of fortune and feeling'. Among the most offensive examples is the discovery made by the hero of *Ennui* that he was

changed as a baby with his foster-brother. Noting that such incidents
are not marginal but key to Edgeworth's plots, Croker tantalizingly
shows he guesses why she uses them. But 'we cannot reconcile ourselves to extreme improbabilities, and events barely within the verge
of nature, which excite wonder instead of interest, and disgust rather
than surprise'.[54] This is that taboo against the use of invented materials in proximity with fact, which has limited the modern historian's
freedom to experiment, and incidentally constrained realist fiction
too. Here it means that Croker will not read those elements in the
Irish tales that, as we shall see, encode some of their subtlest and
most suggestive meanings.

Croker's bluff approach set an unfortunate precedent when it came
to spotting the crucial undercurrents of an Edgeworth text. It was for
instance a tricky assignment, but a brave one, for a woman author in
this period to 'cross-dress' as a sexually experienced and moderately
dissolute young male narrator. Some of the texts from which she
quotes to construct her portrait of aristocratic dissipation in the
opening chapters are notably scandalous.[55] Even if Glenthorn's vices
are sanctioned by a medical textbook, and moderate enough at that,
Edgeworth risks provoking middle-class distaste for a lifestyle based
on hedonism and the experimental sampling of pleasures. Unfortunately Glenthorn's occupational malaise of indolence also works to
distance the reader from the vivid Irish world he is supposed to
mediate for us. Some of the psychological insights offer real compensations, but few reviewers or critics, early or late, have dwelt on these.
Cocooned in his neurosis, Glenthorn for most of the action can hear
but only faintly respond to voices unlike his own, belonging to
strangers who speak monologues rather than entering into dialogue.
In the opening sequence in England, injured and shamming death, he
for once hears his servants' honest opinion of him – and, as so often in
his life, he is unable to respond. Later, recovering from his head injury,
he drifts in and out of sleep while Ellinor tells him stories, as though he
is still her sick child. In the uncensorious scene in which he finds his
adulterous wife packing to leave him, this poor little rich girl proves as
emotionally blocked as he is: they cannot talk over what has happened,
or decide together what to do. Lady Glenthorn, who is never given a
Christian name, anticipates other repressed wives in Edgeworth's
fiction, such as the impressively realized Lady Sarah in *Vivian* (1812).

Once in Ireland, Glenthorn (like Goethe's Wilhelm Meister, who precedes him, and Scott's Waverley, who follows) remains half immobilized, as though participating in his own dream. He meets a procession of Irish figures whose energetic speeches elicit from him only short, faint replies: Paddy the driver, his loquacious tenants, his Scottish agent M'Leod, his neighbour's agent Mr Hardcastle, Lady Geraldine, Joe Kelly, Christy – and Ellinor, who rounds off these narratives with the world-turning story of his real parentage. In all Glenthorn's encounters with these people, it is they, not he, who are the animate figures and the real agents of the plot. These effects are of course part of the scheme of the book, and Glenthorn, suffering from an ailment identifiable at once as the male neurosis and the aristocratic neurosis, makes a fascinating object of study for a sharpeyed woman writer. But readers of fiction tend to empathize with central characters unless clearly directed to do otherwise. There are other distinguished cases in this period of good novels with 'unreliable' or distanced narrators, such as *Caleb Williams* and *Frankenstein*, both of which remained in low critical repute until relatively recently because the alienation effect being used remained under-defined – by the authors concerned as well as by their critics. And so the presentation of Glenthorn is in all probability the key factor in the book's relative unpopularity.

Though the contending agents M'Leod and Hardcastle have good moments, the tale's strongest voices belong to dialect-speakers or to women. Whatever the rank, Irish voices are distinctive. Lady Geraldine is described as having a style and intonation that is unmistakably Irish, though nearer French than English. Simply as a talker, humorous and outspoken, she gives Irish upper-class conversation a plausible timbre of difference – even if some of her conversation now sounds not so much brilliant as over-assertive. Her status as an Irish patriot and spokesperson is established clumsily and schematically, by her speeches against the slavish copying of English visitors merely because they are English; and her teasing of Craiglethorpe has none of the wit of the Irish literary warfare of the 1770s on which it is remotely based (see Appendix). On the other hand, the scene where Geraldine, as Irish woman, receives the proposal of Glenthorn, as English man, and to his astonishment refuses him is one of those satisfying upsets of the favourite's form, by which novelists of the period – Frances Burney, Robert Bage, Austen and Edgeworth – lightly queried society's structures of power.

It is more special to Edgeworth that Glenthorn meets Geraldine between 1796 and 1798, when Anglo-Ireland is toppling and Irish nationhood is asserting itself. Her name links her to the Fitzgeralds or Geraldines, for centuries the dominant aristocratic family in the Irish Midlands, where the Edgeworths lived. This is a bold move, since it also has to be a reminder of the highest-ranking United Irishman, Lord Edward Fitzgerald, who died in prison after his capture in the 1798 Rebellion; Geraldine's strong personality may suggest that of Fitzgerald's Irish–French wife, Pamela.[56] The Fitzgerald associations are complex ones in post-Union Ireland: a family long since Protestant, whose most recent representative was pro-Catholic and pro-French to the point of 'jacobinism'; but also the line of the assertive earls of Kildare, whose first prominent representative reached Ireland with the Anglo-Norman Earl Strongbow in 1170.

Geraldine dominates the book's central chapters. By refusing to marry Glenthorn, she anticipates his own later rejection of his estate, name and title. At this point Edgeworth's mannered, artificial plotting, her use of repetition and duplication as well as coincidence, sweeps most of the leading characters on to a roundabout, where they stay for the rest of the action. Geraldine's new husband Cecil Devereux seems very like the professional man Glenthorn becomes after he has lost his fortune. A further oddity is that Cecil comes close to sharing a name with Glenthorn's second wife, Cecilia Delamere. Glenthorn does just this when he changes his surname (for a third time) to Cecilia's. Meanwhile Geraldine and Cecilia also 'sound alike', in a different sense. Each defies her mother in order to marry the man of her choice, proceeds to find her husband a professional career, and plainly means to share his work. The high degree of artifice in the second half of *Ennui* turns it from a fictionalized travel narrative into what must be read as an allegory involving all the Irish characters together.

But why at the very centre of the book should Geraldine, this key character, depart for *India*? In *Belinda*, her most ambitious work of fiction before *Tales of Fashionable Life*, Edgeworth proposes marrying her heroine to a West Indian – Mr Vincent, a man of English descent whose family has made a fortune from its Caribbean plantations. Edgeworth felt sympathy, a fellow-feeling, with West Indians: the qualities she gives to Vincent, warmth and impulsiveness, were ones normally attributed in her family circle to herself. Several times she connects, significantly, the *speech* of the Irish and the West Indian, two colonized peoples.[57]

But *Ennui* hardly establishes the connectedness of Lady Geraldine with the Indian masses. Prevented by her gender, her relative poverty and the masculine/colonial system from doing anything worthwhile at home, Geraldine escapes to India to play her 'natural' role, which is frankly one of governing. Geraldine–Cecil set off not, clearly, to embark on the essentially commercial career of the typical Company employee a generation earlier, who was liable to return home a rich 'nabob'; nor were they imitating the careers of the Edgeworths' neighbours and acquaintance the Irish Wellesley brothers, who had been engaged between 1800 and 1805 in a spectacular but also contentious campaign of imperial conquest and annexation.[58] About 1800, British India was, like Ireland, in a state of transition. What before 1795 had been three scattered territories administered by a mercantile company for the purposes of trade were fast enlarging into an empire even larger than that of the Moghuls, which had to become the responsibility of the British state. In the first three decades of the nineteenth century India became the focus of much idealistic thinking by middle-class intellectuals – evangelicals and utilitarians or 'philosophical radicals' – who saw it as a terrain for great social experiments in the spiritual and material betterment of an entire population.[59] If Edgeworth had belonged to a less secular family and had been born a generation later, she might have sent out her second hero (as Charlotte Brontë sends St John Rivers in *Jane Eyre*) to convert the Hindu heathen. If she had been born a generation earlier, she might have had high-minded republican anxieties about the corrupting influence of eastern trade, luxury and despotism on an over-extended empire.

When she despatches her Geraldine–Cecil partnership to India, Edgeworth emphasizes their civilian role. Their appointment, achieved with Glenthorn's help and through political influence in Dublin, seems the natural consequence of Ireland's incorporation in the heart of the empire. The Irish must henceforth claim their full share, with the English and Scots, in Britain's mission to bring prosperity, stability and some version of Protestant individualism to populations caught until then in systems breeding only poverty, superstition and inertia. Cecil Devereux, blocked like Geraldine from leading the Irish out of much the same plight, sees the door of opportunity opening for him in India. By developing her plot this way, Edgeworth implies that she is not much interested in debating the right to rule other peoples; she views government, especially the government of the empire, as a benign force – the means of disseminating education and enlightenment from the centre, and the employer of a new progressive civil service.

Nineteenth-century novelists quite frequently use Africa and India as a kind of moral trampoline, a place where characters go for healthy moral exercise, and to get the kudos of turning a bad old world into a brave new one. We have naturally grown sceptical of idealism in this form, especially of its links with profits and more often careers; but then the form may always quite obviously have had more to say on conditions at home than on the nominal topic, 'abroad'. In the period of rapid development of the professions, around 1800, no profession was as open to talent, or as independent of wealthy patronage, as writing. Most writers of the age emerged from the provinces or from families involved in non-affluent 'learned trades' (the humbler ranks of the clergy and of lawyers, or booksellers, printers, and so on). Their paymasters the publishers represented a similar 'interest'. The most persuasive accounts of the sociology of Western European culture about this time, such as Robert Darnton's for France, show authors and readers forming a network of uninfluential, unfranchised and uncapitalized groupings within the middle and lower middle class.[60] This could explain why novel plots so typically encode dreams of social advance and empowerment, the instinctive compensations of individuals who in real life know frustration. Heroes and heroines rise in the world, however nobly indifferent for much of the plot to the lure of wealth and rank. Since such sudden promotions tend to seem implausible, especially in the realistic domestic novel, 'the colonies' become one imaginary terrain for their realization, and the feudal past another. The fantasy of an escape for Geraldine and Devereux to 'somewhere else' is an optimistic alternative glimpsed at the centre of *Ennui*, at a point when the rich Glenthorn is most hopelessly sunk in passivity and inertia. While modern interpreters could see this fantasy serving a collective project of Western dominance, contemporaries might think it exposed what was desirable but unavailable in an inert colonial society such as Ireland.

As one of the novel's leading women, Geraldine is flanked by others – Glenthorn's first wife; his nurse, Ellinor; his second wife, Cecilia. Of these, Ellinor the nurse is much the most interesting and original creation, helped by a role that is maternal rather than sexual. As his mother in babyhood, Ellinor is Mother Ireland, Cathleen ni Houlihan, stubborn and earthy, the most emotive and influential figure in the hero's life. The figuring of Irish identity as an old, poor woman emerged in the course of the eighteenth century, it is now commonly argued, because Ireland was indeed emasculated and generally disempowered at this time. But Edgeworth, a woman writer, makes more of the stereotype. The presence in *Ennui* of *three* symbolic women figuring Ireland complicates matters; so does the contrast in character between Geraldine (strong, witty, optimistic) and Ellinor (disappointed and regressive).

Supposedly his foster-mother but in fact his natural mother, Ellinor proves the real mistress of Glenthorn's destiny. She appears during his twenty-fifth birthday celebrations, just when he is riding out to kill himself. She both 'kills' him in his English existence by causing a near-fatal accident, and brings him to life as an Irishman by inducing him to return to Ireland. One of the means she employs is story-telling of the Irish past – always, significantly, stories of Irish rebelliousness against English rule, a fact which gives an added dimension, that of plausibility, to the subsequent association of her sons with the 1798 Rebellion. Much later in the plot, she brings the hero's reign as an earl to an end, killing him once more, by revealing the true history of his birth or rather infancy. Though the baby motif has some comic associations, its tragic potential is realized for Ellinor. The cultural differences between mother and son prevent them from understanding each other's wants. Each gives the other unwise material gifts that, as in a fairy-tale, prove burdensome and alienating. Her distress when her son gives up her gift of the earldom kills Ellinor, and she dies without being reconciled to him.

Cecilia, associated more prosily with the Glenthorn estate to which she is heir, lacks the symbolic resonances of Ellinor and Geraldine. But her appearance in the plot just after Ellinor dies has a touch of the uncanny about it: both of them are after all autochthonous creatures, who represent that part of the land of Ireland to which the hero's fate is tied. Since Cecilia enters only in the schematic closing chapters, neither her personality nor her world ever takes on the density of specification of the earlier chapters on the estate. The third and last of the hero's changes of identity, from O'Donoghoe to his wife's name of Delamere, seems especially arbitrary. Edgeworth in fact seems to want to amuse experienced novel-readers with an elaborate play on the celebrated ending of one of the best-regarded English novels, Frances Burney's *Cecilia*. There, the middle-class heroine, Cecilia Beverley, lost her fortune because her aristocratic fiancé Mortimer Delvile would not change his name to hers, since to do so offended his pride of caste and of gender. Burney's heroine is persuaded to give up her name and social identity, and to become Cecilia Delvile. Rearranging the counters, reversing the outcome, Edgeworth has the shadowy Cecilia Delamere emerge at the finale as the triumphant meritocrat who absorbs the dual personality representing feudalism, Glenthorn-O'Donoghoe. This is the last of the hero's transformations, and the Irish humiliations already visited on him by Geraldine now appear complete.

Even by Edgeworth's non-naturalistic standards, the last six chapters of *Ennui* represent an extreme case. It becomes a series of bizarre games, of which the most flamboyant, the change at nurse, is also the most consciously and wittily narrated. Normally when this folk-motif is used, some sign remains on the baby or the baby-clothes which allows him or her to be identified. *Ennui* jokes cheerfully at this usual way of handling the business. The child who should have become the earl was not born with a birthmark, but was handed over (of course) to a drunken servant, who dropped him on the fender at three days old. When Christy is persuaded to uncover his bald pate, it displays all sorts of signs – not merely the aristocratic (though non-hereditary) cicatrice on which the traditional plot depends, but the plebeian dents and lumps of a youth spent 'at fairs, fighting with the boys of Shrawd-na-scroob'. As educationalists, the Edgeworths followed Locke in their almost devout belief in the formative influence of acquired over innate characteristics. The contrasting characters of the true and false earls side in *Ennui* with the environment lobby, by proving that earls are made and not born. Christy's skull, as densely written over as a phrenologist's model head, itself cancels the sign of his aristocratic beginnings. Meanwhile Edgeworth slyly bestows on a doctor who is none other than the real-life Sylvester O'Halloran, expert reader of Ireland's origins, the task of deciphering Glenthorn's skull – on which, of course, there is nothing either ancient or infantile to be found.[61]

Ennui is a far more selfconsciously literary book than *Castle Rackrent*, and it is always referring to other books. Why not, then, to the fairy-tales that Ellinor tells? The central character is no common land-owner, after all, but a hero who falls under a spell once an old woman in a red cloak enters his life. After she lures him to Ireland, she eventually waves her wand again, and he awakens from his trance to find himself plain Christy O'Donoghoe who, penniless and obscure, has to set out alone into the world to make his living. From this point the former Glenthorn doubles with the serio-comic figure of the blacksmith-earl – who also undergoes a traditional temptation and trial as master of the enchanted castle, finds the wonderland a nightmare, and wakens with relief to resume his old work at the forge. The presence of so folkloric a plot underlines the essential fictionality of a tale which can offer only a resemblance of truth. But the role-playing and role-swopping of the two foster-brothers *is* eventually the truth of the tale, for it symbolizes their interdepend-ence and equality. It becomes impossible to say which brother is more Irish, which more English, or which earns more credit for generosity and brotherliness. If they can both be seen to lose the Glenthorn estate, they can also both be said to earn it. Each abdi-cates as an owner of Glenthorn, a role which made him unhappy, and each returns there to do a job of work he is professionally trained to do. While this may contain a lesson about knowing your lot in life, it also contains one about the true value that inheres in labour.

However 'real' the scenes at Glenthorn may seem as a near-documentary record of Irish life, *Ennui*'s containing fable of shapeshifting and magical transformations warns us to keep our distance from the characters and what befalls them. Yet in this second Irish tale, as in the first, we can recognize the clear outlines of a great deal of documented family and neighbourhood history.[62] If in *Castle Rackrent* Edgeworth draws on family records and local gossip dating in the main from times past, in *Ennui* she renders the years 1795–8 as a recognizable version of the scenes her letters were recording month by month. This too is gossip, and identifiably so of course to many of her Irish readers, if not to the wider cosmopolitan readership. In 1795 R. L. Edgeworth fell out with his more zealous Protestant neighbours and fellow-magistrates. In February 1796 he stood as a candidate in a local by-election, and was defeated. In 1798 he and his family were forced to flee their home because the countryside around Edgeworthstown (nowadays known by its Irish name, Mastrim) was in the hands of Catholic rebels. When he took his family to the nearby Protestant town of Longford for refuge, R. L. Edgeworth was nearly lynched by a Protestant mob which suspected him of trying to signal with his new invention, a telegraph, to the French army camped dangerously close at hand.[63] As these episodes figure in Chapters XII–XV of *Ennui* they appear scrambled, as though in code, and the most interesting feature of the disguise is their apportionment between three characters, the 'brothers' Glenthorn, Christy the blacksmith and Ody. All three are suspected of sympathy with the rebellion, and each experiences violence or the threat of violence from one or other group of extremists. In the act of representing her father's ostracism and time of danger (which, as a most partisan daughter, Edgeworth herself found traumatic in real life), she separates him into a trio who straddle, fantastically, the Irish/Anglo-Irish divide.

In her creative re-presentation of these very emotive events, Edgeworth performs similar imaginative self-divisions. The violent years that repeat themselves somewhat schematically in *Ennui* are probably the years in which the Condy sequence in *Castle Rackrent* was written. In letters written to her aunt and cousin at this time, she is reporting the family's social isolation anxiously, and writing emotionally about her home as a place of refuge. Though Thady is at times a distanced and satirized character, in this part of the tale at least he appears to speak her own strong emotional attachment to the enclosed world of the family and the estate. In sentiment, Ellinor can equally sound like the character in *Ennui* closest to the tone and value-system of her creator. In short, Edgeworth's real-life allegiances are not being simply reproduced in the tales – where, on the contrary, her self-positioning is as complex and unstable as her representation of the Anglo-Irish landlord hero.

The imaginative terrain Edgeworth shapes in fiction after *Castle Rackrent* is generally a world of productive change and of social reconciliation; for individuals, of re-making or empowerment. Her children's stories were often contrasted with fairy-tales (unfavourably, by Lamb, Coleridge and eventually Scott) because of their realistic settings. Actually they share with many fairy-tales the child's fantasy of becoming a free agent, temporarily escaping the grip of powerful adults. Her novels and tales for adults, so practical, well documented, well informed and worldly-wise, do not strike the reader at first sight as fantasies, yet *Ennui* for one repeats insistently that we must adopt that way of reading. The revolution the Irish have just failed to achieve is offered them in fantasy, in Edgeworth's drastically restyled version of social transformation. They are imagined getting their seat at the international dining-table; health, wealth and the pursuit of happiness lie immediately before them. The real world of the immediate past has turned turtle in this very special country, which appears to be in the grip of a trio of larger-than-life, faintly supernatural women, capable of making anything happen.

Edgeworth is everywhere a strong resister of stereotyping, and all her tales use individualized women who are often unusually energetic and articulate. The Edgeworth heroine has always been thought of as notably well-educated and rational, that is less feminine than other writers' heroines. Just as characteristically, her older women are dominant, even domineering: Lady Delacour in *Belinda* (1801), Lady Davenant in *Helen* (1834) and Mrs Beaumont in *Manoeuvring* (*Tales of Fashionable Life*, 1st series, 1809). On the face of it the women characters in her Irish tales, especially *Castle Rackrent*, are simply less salient, even if Lady Geraldine, Lady Oranmore in *The Absentee* and Mrs Annaly in *Ormond* have at least an honorific place among Edgeworth's women of power. But her Irishwomen really deserve special attention as a group, because they have a part in a narrative itself more significantly political than the tales set in England, and because their symbolic roles (again, a feature unique to her writing on Ireland) have to do directly or implicitly with national consciousness. Women characters could seldom be given such resonant roles in the domestic novel. In fact it is probably no accident that women writers such as Edgeworth, Hamilton, Owenson, Porter and Ferrier authored the first handful of 'national tales' in the early 1800s. The imagined community and the empowered woman tend to appear in a symbiotic relation, each needing the other as a condition of existence.

In both *The Absentee* and *Ormond*, some leading women characters
are more solidly drawn, that is more naturalistic, both psychologi-
cally and in their social circumstances, than the women of the first
two Irish tales. *The Absentee* scores at once with its alienated Irish
social climber, Lady Clonbrony, the clever, plain and equally alienated English heiress Miss Broadhurst, and a gallery of comic types
from Lady Clonbrony's thankless guests to the hapless Irish hostess
Mrs Raffarty. Yet in its heroine Grace Nugent *The Absentee* repeats
the essentially allegorical notion of characterization used in *Ennui*.
Grace's name is the title of an Irish popular air. In real life the
Nugents were leading Catholic gentry of the Irish Midlands, known
for their principled attachment to their religion and for their service
in European Catholic armies. The name of Grace's mother, Miss St
Omer, evokes the French Catholic seminary in which Irish boys
were commonly trained for the priesthood before the establishment
of Maynooth in 1795. The answer to who she is must be, a representative of the well-born dispossessed Catholic gentry of Ireland.

What happens to Grace Nugent is somewhat odder, and it is
again an echo of the plotting of *Ennui*. She has a shadowy namesake
and double, a peasant girl, also Grace, who seems to exist in order
to make the heroine a type rather than an individual. As a character
she seems to have no traits of her own except a desire to return to
Clonbrony, and to take the absentee family of that name back to
Ireland with her. But the closing stages of the plot are held up for an
examination not so much of Grace's own moral character as that of
her mother, long considered not to have been legally married to her
father, an English officer in a foreign army. The decoding of this
mystery again requires the services of a character based on the real-
life Irish Catholic historian, Sylvester O'Halloran. By proving the
purity of Grace and Grace's female line, the Count O'Halloran of
the tale again repeats the scholarly achievement of the Dr O'Halloran of real life: he proves the legitimacy and innate nobility of
Catholic Ireland, and prepares the way for their reconciliation with
the Anglo-Irish Protestant gentry.[64]

Edgeworth's allegorical Irishwomen are a particularly strange variant of an insufficiently discussed type – the figure of a woman as a
symbolical national leader, as she features in the writing of some
women novelists from the late eighteenth century. By virtue of her
articulacy, her involvement in politics and her influence on events,

this embodiment of women's social frustrations is a quite different figure from the peasant girl Marianne, used as an emblem of revolution by French male artists in the 1790s, and more saliently in 1830. Edgeworth began *Ennui* before the appearance of two novels which resemble it by writers she considered rivals – Lady Morgan's *The Wild Irish Girl* (1806), which has an Irish-speaking patriot heroine, and Germaine de Staël's *Corinne* (1808), whose heroine is in effect an Italian nationalist agitator. *Ennui* and *The Absentee* virtually coincided with two more nationalist novels from Lady Morgan – a woman-centred political fantasy, *Ida of Athens* (1809), and a striking novel featuring a Hindu priestess and set in India, *The Missionary* (1811). In both Morgan's oriental novels, a Western male travellor seduces and also contends with a woman who is by birth a social leader, and (somewhat strangely) a recognized focus of national consciousness. Mary Shelley's *Frankenstein* (1818) has only an incidental place in this sequence, but her historical novel of ideas, *Valperga* (1823) is important to it. Of its two leading women, one, Beatrice, represents late-medieval religious faith, and the other, the Countess of Valperga, the same period's emerging secular idealism and its political expression, republicanism: the book is named, then, after a city-state, but the name does double duty as the title of a woman. George Eliot's heroine Romola, who has much in common with the Countess of Valperga, is now the best known of this line of empowered but tragic figures.

The late eighteenth-century trope of the nation as a woman does not enjoy a good press in modern times. Assumed to be typically a feature of men's writing, it is thought to reflect the low esteem in which both women and lesser (that is, defeated) nations are held. Even if persuaded that women authors were attracted to the device, modern feminists might well opine that they had no real right to bolster the dignity of an imagined heroine at the expense of her imagined subjects. In practice the woman novelist who imagines such a heroine generally sees to it that her authority is as short-lived and problematic as Glenthorn's reign as earl. The power of an Ida, Corinne or Romola remains notional, even slippery: it is not shown being actively maintained through money, political intrigue, or the shedding of soldiers' blood. Where a male head of state would have inherited power or wealth unopposed, the woman often finds herself robbed of greatness by the men she trusts, most painfully by an unscrupulous lover (Shelley's Castrucci, Eliot's Tito). Far from simply allowing a woman protagonist to act out clichés from the early nineteenth-century masculine historical or colonialist yarn, the woman's version identifies the politicking and the wars as particularly male pursuits, and holds them up to scrutiny. Both the political concept, might is right, and the ideal of masculinity emerge undercut from this series of fictions. And here *Ennui*, a naturalized representative of the genre, seems quite typical of it, since the tripartite figure of Mother Ireland, Ellinor-Geraldine-Cecilia, lacks power in herself, and yet morally 'masters' the unmanly leading man, Glenthorn-O'Donoghoe.

In current feminist work on autobiography it is often observed that women writers generally seem to have experienced difficulty in using the first person. Edgeworth's fondness for male narrators, and her tendency to divide herself among diverse characters, male and female, illustrates this penchant for invisibility; nowhere more than in *Castle Rackrent*, that best sustained of masquerades. Little has been written about *Castle Rackrent*'s feminist implications, and not much about its women – with the limited exception of Sir Kit's incarcerated bride, the first of the nineteenth-century novel's Madwomen in the Attic.[65] The victimized Jewish Lady Rackrent is a female Babylonian captive within a monstrously masculine society, in which no one, least of all 'her' Irish servants, show her any mercy. But in her enforced passivity and silence 'the Jewish' is untypical of Rackrent women. Sir Murtagh's lady is a better litigant than Sir Murtagh, and a better extortioner from the tenants. When she survives her husband, the first of the Rackrent line of wives to do so, she drives away with most of the capital realizable from their joint regime. In due course Thady sees off both Sir Kit's wife and Sir Condy's, each in a depleted condition, each clutching what she has been able to salvage of her husband's money and her own. None of these consorts shares Thady's uncritical admiration for her husband and for his estate. The last of them, Sir Condy's cast-off mistress Judy M'Quirk, speaks for all the Rackrent women, that alternative dynasty which until now has lacked a spokesperson:

> And when Judy came up that evening, and brought the childer to see his honour . . . he gives 'em all round guineas

a-piece. 'Hold up your head,' says my shister to Judy . . . 'for who knows but we may live to see you yet at the head of the Castle Rackrent estate?' 'May be so,' says she, 'but not the way you are thinking of.' . . . 'Sure you wouldn't refuse to be my lady Rackrent, Judy, if you had the offer?' says I. – 'But if I could do better!' says she . . . 'Why, what signifies it to be my lady Rackrent, and no castle? sure what good is the car, and no horse to draw it?'

Shrewd and tough, Judy means to take the best option that offers for herself and her children. She adjusts to the future, and the future is delivering Thady's anglicized and upwardly mobile son, Jason Quirk. The three-way dialogue between Thady, his elderly sister and her granddaughter Judy is one of the longest reported conversations in the book, and the only one in which Thady encounters a direct refutation, a counter-view that he is puzzled how to answer. 'I was never so put to it in my life: between these womens . . . So I said not a word more.' Edgeworth's heart may incline in this conversation, as so often, to Thady, but her head equally surely goes with Judy, the peasant woman with a past whose only miscalculation now is to overrate her chances with her cousin Jason. Judy gets the general point right, that the nineteenth century is coming in, with or without her. For its toughness, its unobviousness, its feeling for the community, its recognition that people in communities contend, that open-ended last conversation is the best answer to the question: why read Edgeworth's Irish tales?

Marilyn Butler
King's College
Cambridge

NOTE ON THE TEXT

The texts of *Castle Rackrent* and *Ennui* are reprinted from the collected *Tales and Novels by Maria Edgeworth*, 18 vols. (London: Baldwin & Cradock, 1832). A fourteen-volume collected edition, *Tales and Miscellaneous Pieces*, appeared in 1825, in which misprints only were corrected and not all of these. Maria Edgeworth was invited to correct the 1832 edition, and she did so, with the result that some tenacious errors were weeded out, and some alterations made, all of them minor. The other difference between 1832 and any earlier edition of Edgeworth's fiction is that it makes a switch to more modern punctuation conventions, above all to quotation marks rather than dashes for dialogue. By the late eighteenth century, the punctuation of novels, relatively a mass medium, had become essentially standardized, leaving little if anything to the discretion of the individual writer. It seems fair in the circumstances to offer modern readers not the now archaic-looking format of a generation earlier, but a text that still looks familiar and natural.

As texts for editing, *Castle Rackrent* and *Ennui* represent a marked contrast. Both books took some years to evolve, but Edgeworth reported that she wrote down the final version of *Castle Rackrent* quickly and easily. 'There was literally not a correction, not an alteration, made in the first writing, no copy, and as I recollect, no interlineation; it went to the press just as it was written.'[1] One result seems to have been that by Edgeworth's later standards *Castle Rackrent*, published in January 1800 by Joseph Johnson, contained more than its share of inconsistencies and rough passages, which afterwards needed tidying up.[2] A very early afterthought, the Glossary, was done in time to appear in the first edition. A further list of pencilled corrections seems to have been made early in an Edgeworthstown copy, but most of these were not implemented.[3] A plan by R. L. Edgeworth to add another generation to the family for the fifth edition of 1810 met with successful resistance from his daughter: material which could have been used for this purpose in fact became *The Absentee*.[4]

Ennui, which appeared in 1809 as the first of the *Tales of Fashionable Life*, first series, was substantially worked on and perhaps drafted as early as 1804, but further revised and added to in 1806–7. A notebook containing anecdotes and plot-motifs for *Ennui* seems to have been in use at the later of those dates. By then Edgeworth, a successful author, seems to have been particularly anxious to maintain her reputation for polish and elegance. The text has been carefully worked over and on the whole it has few misprints, though some appear in its many quotations from French and Italian. Its most interesting variant is the footnote, added in the fourth edition of 1813, which gives readers' anecdotes about travelling in Ireland.[5] Here, as in all Edgeworth's glossaries and appendices, there is some blurring of the normal boundaries between fact and fiction, or what conventionally is the author's and what the reader's.

BIBLIOGRAPHY

1. *Biography and Letters*

Marilyn Butler, *Maria Edgeworth: A Literary Biography* (Oxford: Clarendon Press, 1972).

Christina Colvin, *Maria Edgeworth: Letters from England 1813–1844* (Oxford: Clarendon Press, 1971).

Maria Edgeworth in France and Switzerland (Oxford: Clarendon Press, 1979).

Mrs Frances Edgeworth (ed.), *Memoir of Maria Edgeworth with a Selection from her Letters*, 3 vols (privately printed, 1867).

A. J. C. Hare (ed.), *Life and Letters of Maria Edgeworth*, 2 vols (London: Arnold, 1894).

See also:

H. E. and H. J. Butler (eds), *The Black Book of Edgeworthstown and Other Edgeworth Memories, 1585–1817* (London: Faber & Gwyer, 1927).

2. *Modern Criticism and History*

Marilyn Butler, *Jane Austen and the War of Ideas* (Oxford, 1975). (*See also* Biographies, *above.*)

John Cronin, *The Anglo-Irish Novel, I: The Nineteenth Century* (Belfast: Appletree, 1980).

Donald Davie, *The Heyday of Sir Walter Scott* (London: Routledge, 1961).

Denis Donoghue, 'Being Irish Together', *Sewanee Review* 84 (Winter 1976).

Tom Dunne, *Maria Edgeworth and the Colonial Mind* (Dublin: National University of Ireland, 1985).

'Haunted by History: Irish Romantic Writing, 1800–1850', in Roy Porter and M. Teich (eds), *Romanticism in a National Context*

(Cambridge: C.U.P., 1988), pp. 68–91.

Marianne Elliott, *Partners in Revolution: the United Irishmen and France* (New Haven: Yale U.P., 1982).

Thomas Flanagan, *The Irish Novelists, 1800–1850* (New York: Columbia U.P., 1959).

Michael Hurst, *Maria Edgeworth and the Public Scene* (London: Macmillan, 1969).

Donald MacCartney, 'The Writing of History in Ireland, 1800–1830', *Irish Historical Studies* 10 (September 1957), 347–62.

W. J. McCormack, *Ascendancy and Tradition in Irish Literary History, 1793–1939* (Oxford: Clarendon Press, 1985).

(ed., with K. Walker), *The Absentee* (Oxford: World's Classics, 1988).

Oliver MacDonagh, *The Nineteenth-century Novel and Irish Social History* (Dublin: National University of Ireland, 1970).

Ireland: The Union and its Aftermath (London: Allen & Unwin, 1977).

States of Mind: A Study of Anglo-Irish Conflict (London: Allen & Unwin, 1983).

R. B. McDowell, *Irish Public Opinion: 1750–1800* (London: Faber, 1944).

Ireland in the Age of Imperialism and Revolution (Oxford: Oxford University Press, 1982).

Roger McHugh and Maurice Harmon, *A Short History of Anglo-Irish Literature* (Dublin: Wolfhound Press, 1982).

Albert Memmi, *The Coloniser and the Colonised* (in French, *Portrait du colonisé*, Paris, 1957; English translation by Howard Greenfield, London: Souvenir Press (Condor Books), 1974).

James Newcomer, *Maria Edgeworth* (Lewisberg: Bucknell U.P., 1973).

P. F. Sheeran, 'Some Aspects of Anglo-Irish Literature from Swift to Joyce', *Yearbook of English Studies* 13 (1983), 97–115.

Iain Topliss, 'The Novels of Maria Edgeworth: Enlightenment and Tutelage', Ph.D. thesis for Cambridge University, 1985.

Alan Warner, *A Guide to Anglo-Irish Literature* (New York: St Martin's Press; Dublin: Gill & Macmillan, 1981).

CASTLE RACKRENT

*An Hibernian Tale taken from facts
and from the manners of the Irish squires before the year 1782*

The prevailing taste of the public for anecdote has been censured and ridiculed by critics who aspire to the character of superior wisdom: but if we consider it in a proper point of view, this taste is an incontestible proof of the good sense and profoundly philosophic temper of the present times. Of the numbers who study, or at least who read history, how few derive any advantage from their labours! The heroes of history are so decked out by the fine fancy of the professed historian; they talk in such measured prose, and act from such sublime or such diabolical motives, that few have sufficient taste, wickedness, or heroism, to sympathize in their fate. Besides, there is much uncertainty even in the best authenticated ancient or modern histories; and that love of truth, which in some minds is innate and immutable, necessarily leads to a love of secret memoirs, and private anecdotes. We cannot judge either of the feelings or of the characters of men with perfect accuracy, from their actions or their appearance in public; it is from their careless conversations, their half-finished sentences, that we may hope with the greatest probability of success to discover their real characters. The life of a great or of a little man written by himself, the familiar letters, the diary of any individual published by his friends or by his enemies, after his decease, are esteemed important literary curiosities. We are surely justified, in this eager desire, to collect the most minute facts relative to the domestic lives, not only of the great and good, but even of the worthless and insignificant, since it is only by a comparison of their actual happiness or misery in the privacy of domestic life that we can form a just estimate of the real reward of virtue, or the real punishment of vice. That the great are not as happy as they seem, that the external circumstances of fortune and rank do not constitute felicity, is asserted by every moralist: the historian can seldom, consistently with his dignity, pause to illustrate this truth: it is therefore to the biographer we must have recourse. After we have beheld splendid characters playing their parts on the great theatre of the world, with all the advantages of stage effect and decoration, we anxiously beg to be admitted behind the scenes, that we may take a nearer view of the actors and actresses.

Some may perhaps imagine, that the value of biography depends upon the judgement and taste of the biographer: but on the contrary it may be maintained, that the merits of a biographer are inversely as the extent of his intellectual powers and of his literary talents. A plain unvarnished tale is preferable to the most highly ornamented narrative. Where we see that a man has the power, we may naturally suspect that he has the will to deceive us; and those who are used to literary manufacture know how much is often sacrificed to the rounding of a period, or the pointing of an antithesis.

That the ignorant may have their prejudices as well as the learned cannot be disputed; but we see and despise vulgar errors: we never bow to the authority of him who has no great name to sanction his absurdities. The partiality which blinds a biographer to the defects of his hero, in proportion as it is gross, ceases to be dangerous; but if it be concealed by the appearance of candour, which men of great abilities best know how to assume, it endangers our judgement sometimes, and sometimes our morals. If her grace the Duchess of Newcastle, instead of penning her lord's elaborate eulogium, had undertaken to write the life of Savage, we should not have been in any danger of mistaking an idle, ungrateful libertine for a man of genius and virtue.[2] The talents of a biographer are often fatal to his reader. For these reasons the public often judiciously countenance those, who, without sagacity to discriminate character, without elegance of style to relieve the tediousness of narrative, without enlargement of mind to draw any conclusions from the facts they relate, simply pour forth anecdotes, and retail conversations, with all the minute prolixity of a gossip in a country town.

The author of the following Memoirs has upon these grounds fair claims to the public favour and attention; he was an illiterate old steward, whose partiality to *the family*, in which he was bred and born, must be obvious to the reader. He tells the history of the Rackrent family in his vernacular idiom, and in the full confidence that Sir Patrick, Sir Murtagh, Sir Kit, and Sir Condy Rackrent's affairs will be as interesting to all the world as they were to himself. Those who were acquainted with the manners of a certain class of the gentry of Ireland some years ago will want no evidence of the

truth of honest Thady's narrative: to those who are totally unacquainted with Ireland, the following Memoirs will perhaps be
scarcely intelligible, or probably they may appear perfectly incredible. For the information of the *ignorant* English reader, a few notes
have been subjoined by the editor, and he had it once in contemplation to translate the language of Thady into plain English; but
Thady's idiom is incapable of translation, and, besides, the authenticity of his story would have been more exposed to doubt if it were
not told in his own characteristic manner. Several years ago he
related to the editor the history of the Rackrent family, and it was
with some difficulty that he was persuaded to have it committed to
writing; however, his feelings for '*the honour of the family*', as he
expressed himself, prevailed over his habitual laziness, and he at
length completed the narrative which is now laid before the public.

The editor hopes his readers will observe that these are 'tales of
other times': that the manners depicted in the following pages are
not those of the present age: the race of the Rackrents has long since
been extinct in Ireland; and the drunken Sir Patrick, the litigious
Sir Murtagh, the fighting Sir Kit, and the slovenly Sir Condy, are
characters which could no more be met with at present in Ireland,
than Squire Western or Parson Trulliber[3] in England. There is a
time, when individuals can bear to be rallied for their past follies
and absurdities, after they have acquired new habits, and a new
consciousness. Nations as well as individuals gradually lose attachment to their identity, and the present generation is amused rather
than offended by the ridicule that is thrown upon its ancestors.

Probably we shall soon have it in our power, in a hundred instances, to verify the truth of these observations.

When Ireland loses her identity by an union with Great Britain,[4]
she will look back with a smile of good-humoured complacency on
the Sir Kits and Sir Condys of her former existence.

1800.

CASTLE RACKRENT

Monday morning.^G

Having, out of friendship for the family, upon whose estate, praised be
Heaven! I and mine have lived rent-free, time out of mind, voluntarily
undertaken to publish the MEMOIRS of the RACKRENT FAMILY, I
think it my duty to say a few words, in the first place, concerning
myself. My real name is Thady Quirk, though in the family I have
always been known by no other than '*honest Thady*', – afterwards, in
the time of Sir Murtagh, deceased, I remember to hear them calling
me '*old Thady*', and now I'm come to 'poor Thady'; for I wear a long
great coat* winter and summer, which is very handy, as I never put
my arms into the sleeves; they are as good as new, though come
Holantide⁵ next I've had it these seven years; it holds on by a single

---

* The cloak, or mantle, as described by Thady, is of high antiquity. Spencer, in his
'View of the State of Ireland', proves that it is not, as some have imagined, peculiarly
derived from the Scythians, but that 'most nations of the world anciently used the
mantle; for the Jews used it, as you may read of Elias's mantle, &c.; the Chaldees also
used it, as you may read in Diodorus; the Egyptians likewise used it, as you may read
in Herodotus, and may be gathered by the description of Berenice, in the Greek
Commentary upon Callimachus; the Greeks also used it anciently, as appeared by
Venus's mantle lined with stars, though afterwards they changed the form thereof
into their cloaks, called Pallai, as some of the Irish also use: and the ancient Latins
and Romans used it, as you may read in Virgil, who was a very great antiquary, that
Evander, when Æneas came to him at his feast, did entertain and feast him sitting on
the ground, and lying on mantles: insomuch that he useth the very word mantile for
a mantle,

' – Humi mantilia sternunt':

so that it seemeth that the mantle was a general habit to most nations, and not
proper to the Scythians only.'
Spencer knew the convenience of the said mantle, as housing, bedding, and cloth-
ing.
'*Iren.* Because the commodity doth not countervail the discommodity; for the
inconveniences which thereby do arise are much more many; for it is a fit house for
an outlaw, a meet bed for a rebel, and an apt cloak for a thief. First, the outlaw being
for his many crimes and villanies, banished from the towns and houses of honest men,
and wandering in wastes places, far from danger of law, maketh his mantle his house,

button round my neck, cloak fashion. To look at me, you would hardly think 'poor Thady' was the father of attorney Quirk; he is a high gentleman, and never minds what poor Thady says, and having better than fifteen hundred a year, landed estate, looks down upon honest Thady; but I wash my hands of his doings, and as I have lived so will I die, true and loyal to the family.[7] The family of the Rackrents is, I am proud to say, one of the most ancient in the kingdom. Every body knows this is not the old family name, which was O'Shaughlin, related to the kings of Ireland – but that was before my time. My grandfather was driver to the great Sir Patrick O'Shaughlin, and I heard him, when I was a boy, telling how the Castle Rackrent estate came to Sir Patrick; Sir Tallyhoo Rackrent was cousin-german to him, and had a fine estate of his own, only never a gate upon it, it being his maxim that a car was the best gate. Poor gentleman! he lost a fine hunter and his life, at last, by it, all in one day's hunt. But I ought to bless that day, for the estate came straight into *the* family, upon one condition, which Sir Patrick O'Shaughlin at the time took sadly to heart, they say, but thought better of it afterwards, seeing how large a stake depended upon it, that he should by act of parliament, take and bear the surname and arms of Rackrent.[8]

Now it was that the world was to see what was *in* Sir Patrick. On coming into the estate, he gave the finest entertainment ever was heard of in the country: not a man could stand after supper but Sir Patrick himself, who could sit out the best man in Ireland, let alone the three kingdoms itself.[G] He had his house, from one year's end to another, as full of company as ever it could hold, and fuller; for rather than be left out of the parties at Castle Rackrent, many gentlemen, and those men of the first consequence and landed estates in the country, such as the O'Neils of Ballynagrotty, and the Money-gawls[9] of Mount Juliet's Town, and O'Shannons of New Town Tullyhog, made it their choice, often and often, when there was no room to be had for love nor money, in long winter nights, to sleep in

and under it covereth himself from the wrath of Heaven, from the offence of the earth, and from the sight of men. When it raineth, it is his pent-house; when it bloweth, it is his tent; when it freezeth it is his tabernacle. In summer he can wear it loose; in winter he can wrap it close; at all times he can use it; never heavy, never cumbersome. Likewise for a rebel it is as serviceable; for in this war that he maketh (if at least it deserves the name of war), when he still flieth from his foe, and lurketh in the *thick woods* (*this should be black bogs*) and straight passages waiting for advantages, it is his bed, yea, and almost his household stuff.'[6]

the chicken-house, which Sir Patrick had fitted up for the purpose of accommodating his friends and the public in general, who honoured him with their company unexpectedly at Castle Rackrent; and this went on, I can't tell you how long – the whole country rang with his praises! – Long life to him! I'm sure I love to look upon his picture, now opposite to me; though I never saw him, he must have been a portly gentleman – his neck something short, and remarkable for the largest pimple on his nose, which, by his particular desire, is still extant in his picture, said to be a striking likeness, though taken when young. He is said also to be the inventor of raspberry whiskey, which is very likely, as nobody has ever appeared to dispute it with him, and as there still exists a broken punch-bowl at Castle Rackrent,[10] in the garret, with an inscription to that effect – a great curiosity. A few days before his death he was very merry; it being his honour's birth-day, he called my grandfather in, God bless him! to drink the company's health, and filled a bumper himself, but could not carry it to his head, on account of the great shake in his hand; on this he cast his joke, saying 'What would my poor father say to me if he was to pop out of the grave, and see me now? I remember when I was a little boy, the first bumper of claret he gave me after dinner, how he praised me for carrying it so steady to my mouth. Here's my thanks to him – a bumper toast.' Then he fell to singing the favourite song he learned from his father – for the last time, poor gentleman – he sung it that night as loud and as hearty as ever with a chorus:

'He that goes to bed, and goes to bed sober,
Falls as the leaves do, falls as the leaves do, and dies in October;
But he that goes to bed, and goes to bed mellow,
Lives as he ought to do, lives as he ought to do, and dies an
   honest fellow.'[11]

Sir Patrick died that night: just as the company rose to drink his health with three cheers, he fell down in a sort of fit, and was carried off; they sat it out, and were surprised, on inquiry, in the morning, to find that it was all over with poor Sir Patrick. Never did any gentleman live and die more beloved in the country by rich and poor. His funeral was such a one as was never known before or since in the county! All the gentlemen in the three counties were at it; far and near, how they flocked: my great grandfather said, that to see all the women even in their red cloaks, you would have taken

them for the army drawn out. Then such a fine whillaluh!^G you
might have heard it to the farthest end of the county, and happy
the man who could get but a sight of the hearse! But who'd have
thought it? just as all was going on right, through his own town they
were passing, when the body was seized for debt – a rescue was
apprehended from the mob; but the heir who attended the funeral
was against that, for fear of consequences, seeing that those villains
who came to serve acted under the disguise of the law: so, to be sure,
the law must take its course, and little gain had the creditors for
their pains. First and foremost, they had the curses of the country:
and Sir Murtagh Rackrent, the new heir, in the next place, on
account of this affront to the body, refused to pay a shilling of
the debts, in which he was countenanced by all the best gentlemen
of property, and others of his acquaintance; Sir Murtagh alleging
in all companies, that he all along meant to pay his father's debts
of honour, but the moment the law was taken of him, there was
an end of honour to be sure. It was whispered (but none but
the enemies of the family believe it), that this was all a sham seizure
to get quit of the debts, which he had bound himself to pay in
honour.

It's a long time ago, there's no saying how it was, but this for
certain, the new man did not take at all after the old gentleman; the
cellars were never filled after his death, and no open house, or any
thing as it used to be; the tenants even were sent away without their
whiskey.^G I was ashamed myself, and knew not what to say for the
honour of the family; but I made the best of a bad case, and laid it
all at my lady's door, for I did not like her any how, nor any body
else; she was of the family of the Skinflints, and a widow; it was a
strange match for Sir Murtagh; the people in the country thought
he demeaned himself greatly,^G but I said nothing: I knew how it
was; Sir Murtagh was a great lawyer, and looked to the great
Skinflint estate; there, however, he overshot himself; for though one
of the co-heiresses, he was never the better for her, for she outlived
him many's the long day – he could not see that to be sure when he
married her. I must say for her, she made him the best of wives,
being a very notable stirring woman, and looking close to every
thing. But I always suspected she had Scotch blood in her veins; any
thing else I could have looked over in her from a regard to the
family. She was a strict observer for self and servants of Lent, and all

fast days, but not holidays. One of the maids having fainted three times the last day of Lent, to keep soul and body together, we put a morsel of roast beef into her mouth, which came from Sir Murtagh's dinner, who never fasted, not he; but somehow or other it unfortunately reached my lady's ears, and the priest of the parish had a complaint made of it the next day, and the poor girl was forced as soon as she could walk to do penance for it, before she could get any peace or absolution, in the house or out of it. However, my lady was very charitable in her own way. She had a charity school for poor children, where they were taught to read and write gratis, and where they were kept well to spinning gratis for my lady in return; for she had always heaps of duty yarn from the tenants, and got all her household linen out of the estate from first to last; for after the spinning, the weavers on the estate took it in hand for nothing, because of the looms my lady's interest could get from the Linen Board to distribute gratis.[12] Then there was a bleach-yard near us, and the tenant dare refuse my lady nothing, for fear of a lawsuit Sir Murtagh kept hanging over him about the water-course. With these ways of managing, 'tis surprising how cheap my lady got things done, and how proud she was of it. Her table the same way, kept for next to nothing; duty fowls, and duty turkies, and duty geese,[G] came as fast as we could eat 'em, for my lady kept a sharp look-out, and knew to a tub of butter every thing the tenants had, all round. They knew her way, and what with fear of driving for rent and Sir Murtagh's lawsuits, they were kept in such good order, they never thought of coming near Castle Rackrent without a present of something or other – nothing too much or too little for my lady – eggs, honey, butter, meal, fish, game, grouse, and herrings, fresh or salt, all went for something. As for their young pigs, we had them, and the best bacon and hams they could make up, with all young chickens in spring; but they were a set of poor wretches, and we had nothing but misfortunes with them, always breaking and running away. This, Sir Murtagh and my lady said, was all their former landlord Sir Patrick's fault, who let 'em get the half year's rent into arrear; there was something in that to be sure. But Sir Murtagh was as much the contrary way; for let alone making English tenants[G] of them, every soul, he was always driving and driving, and pounding and pounding, and canting and canting,[G] and replevying and replevying,[13] and he made a good living of trespassing cattle; there was always some tenant's pig, or horse, or cow, or calf, or goose, trespassing, which was so great a gain to Sir Murtagh, that he did not like to hear me talk of repairing fences. Then his heriots[14] and duty work[G] brought him in something, his turf was cut, his potatoes set and dug, his hay brought home, and, in short, all the work about his house done for nothing; for in all our leases there were strict clauses heavy with penalties, which Sir Murtagh knew well how to enforce; so many days' duty work of man and horse, from every tenant, he was to have, and had, every year; and when a man vexed him, why the finest day he could pitch on, when the cratur was getting in his own harvest, or thatching his cabin, Sir Murtagh made it a principle to call upon him and his horse; so he taught 'em all, as he said, to know the law of landlord and tenant. As for law, I believe no man, dead or alive, ever loved it so well as Sir Murtagh. He had once sixteen suits pending at a time, and I never saw him so much himself; roads, lanes, bogs, wells, ponds, eel-wires, orchards, trees, tithes, vagrants, gravelpits, sandpits, dunghills, and nuisances, every thing upon the face of the earth furnished him good matter for a suit. He used to boast that he had a lawsuit for every letter in the alphabet. How I used to wonder to see Sir Murtagh in the midst of the papers in his office! Why he could hardly turn about for them. I made bold to shrug my shoulders once in his presence, and thanked my stars I was not born a gentleman to so much toil and trouble; but Sir Murtagh took me up short with his old proverb, 'learning is better than house or land'.[15] Out of forty-nine suits which he had, he never lost one but seventeen;[G] the rest he gained with costs, double costs, treble costs sometimes; but even that did not pay. He was a very learned man in the law, and had the character of it; but how it was I can't tell, these suits that he carried cost him a power of money; in the end he sold some hundreds a year of the family estate; but he was a very learned man in the law, and I know nothing of the matter, except having a great regard for the family; and I could not help grieving when he sent me to post up notices of the sale of the fee-simple of the lands and appurtenances[16] of Timoleague. 'I know, honest Thady,' says he, to comfort me, 'what I'm about better than you do; I'm only selling to get the ready money wanting to carry on my suit with spirit with the Nugents of Carrickashaughlin.'

He was very sanguine about that suit with the Nugents of Carrick-

ashaughlin. He could have gained it, they say, for certain, had it
pleased Heaven to have spared him to us, and it would have been at
the least a plump two thousand a year in his way; but things were
ordered otherwise, for the best to be sure. He dug up a fairy-mount* ^G
against my advice, and had no luck afterwards. Though a learned
man in the law, he was a little too incredulous in other matters. I
warned him that I heard the very Banshee† that my grandfather
heard under Sir Patrick's window a few days before his death. But
Sir Murtagh thought nothing of the Banshee, nor of his cough with
a spitting of blood, brought on, I understand, by catching cold in
attending the courts, and overstraining his chest with making himself
heard in one of his favourite causes. He was a great speaker with a
powerful voice; but his last speech was not in the courts at all. He
and my lady, though both of the same way of thinking in some
things, and though she was as good a wife and great economist as
you could see, and he the best of husbands, as to looking into his
affairs, and making money for his family; yet I don't know how it
was, they had a great deal of sparring and jarring between them.
My lady had her privy purse – and she had her weed ashes,^G and
her sealing money^G upon the signing of all the leases, with something
to buy gloves besides; and besides again often took money from the
tenants, if offered properly, to speak for them to Sir Murtagh about
abatements[18] and renewals. Now the weed ashes and the glove
money he allowed her clear perquisites; though once when he saw
her in a new gown saved out of the weed ashes, he told her to my
face (for he could say a sharp thing), that she should not put on her
weeds before her husband's death. But in a dispute about an abatement, my lady would have the last word, and Sir Murtagh grew
mad;^G I was within hearing of the door, and now I wish I had made

* These fairy-mounts are called ant-hills in England. They are held in high reverence
by the common people in Ireland. A gentlemen, who in laying out his lawn had
occasion to level one of these hillocks, could not prevail upon any of his labourers to
begin the ominous work. He was obliged to take a *loy*[17] from one of their reluctant
hands, and began the attack himself. The labourers agreed, that the vengeance of the
fairies would fall upon the head of the presumptuous mortal, who first disturbed them
in their retreat.
† The Banshee is a species of aristocratic fairy, who, in the shape of a little hideous old
woman, has been known to appear, and heard to sing in a mournful supernatural
voice under the windows of great houses, to warn the family that some of them are
soon to die. In the last century every great family in Ireland had a Banshee, who
attended regularly; but latterly their visits and songs have been discontinued.

bold to step in. He spoke so loud, the whole kitchen was out on the stairs.[G] All of a sudden he stopped and my lady too. Something has surely happened, thought I – and so it was, for Sir Murtagh in his passion broke a blood-vessel, and all the law in the land could do nothing in that case. My lady sent for five physicians, but Sir Murtagh died, and was buried. She had a fine jointure settled upon her, and took herself away to the great joy of the tenantry. I never said any thing one way or the other, whilst she was part of the family, but got up to see her go at three o'clock in the morning. 'It's a fine morning, honest Thady,' said she; 'good bye to ye,' and into the carriage she stept, without a word more, good or bad, or even half a crown; but I made my bow, and stood to see her safe out of sight for the sake of the family.

Then we were all bustle in the house, which made me keep out of the way, for I walk slow and hate a bustle; but the house was all hurry-skurry, preparing for my new master. Sir Murtagh, I forgot to notice, had no childer;* so the Rackrent estate went to his younger brother, a young dashing officer, who came amongst us before I knew for the life of me whereabouts I was, in a gig or some of them things, with another spark along with him, and led horses, and servants, and dogs, and scarce a place to put any Christian of them into; for my late lady had sent all the feather-beds off before her, and blankets and household linen, down to the very knife cloths, on the cars to Dublin, which were all her own, lawfully paid for out of her own money. So the house was quite bare, and my young master, the moment ever he set foot in it out of his gig, thought all those things must come of themselves, I believe, for he never looked after any thing at all, but harum-scarum called for every thing as if we were conjurers, or in a public-house. For my part, I could not bestir myself any how; I had been so much used to my late master and mistress, all was upside down with me, and the new servants in the servants' hall were quite out of my way; I had nobody to talk to and if it had not been for my pipe and tobacco, should, I verily believe, have broke my heart for poor Sir Murtagh.

But one morning my new master caught a glimpse of me as I was

---

* *Childer:* this is the manner in which many of Thady's rank, and others in Ireland, *formerly* pronounced the word *children.*

looking at his horse's heels, in hopes of a word from him. 'And is that old Thady?' says he, as he got into his gig: I loved him from that day to this, his voice was so like the family; and he threw me a guinea out of his waistcoat pocket, as he drew up the reins with the other hand, his horse rearing too; I thought I never set my eyes on a finer figure of a man, quite another sort from Sir Murtagh, though withal, *to me*, a family likeness. A fine life we should have led, had he staid amongst us, God bless him! He valued a guinea as little as any man: money to him was no more than dirt, and his gentleman and groom, and all belonging to him, the same; but the sporting season over, he grew tired of the place, and having got down a great architect for the house, and an improver for the grounds, and seen their plans and elevations, he fixed a day for settling with the tenants, but went off in a whirlwind to town, just as some of them came into the yard in the morning. A circular letter came next post from the new agent, with news that the master was sailed for England, and he must remit £500[19] to Bath for his use before a fortnight was at an end; bad news still for the poor tenants, no change still for the better with them. Sir Kit Rackrent,[20] my young master, left all to the agent; and though he had the spirit of a prince, and lived away to the honour of his country abroad, which I was proud to hear of, what were we the better for that at home? The agent was one of your middle men,* who grind the face of the poor, and can never bear a man with a hat upon his head: he ferretted the tenants out of their lives; not a week without a call for money, drafts upon

---

* *Middle men.* – There was a class of men termed middle men in Ireland, who took large farms on long leases from gentlemen of landed property, and set the land again in small portions to the poor, as under-tenants, at exorbitant rents. The *head landlord*, as he *was* called, seldom saw his *under-tenants*; but if he could not get the *middle man* to pay him his rent punctually, he *went to his land, and drove the land for his rent*, that is to say, he sent his steward or bailiff, or driver, to the land to seize the cattle, hay, corn, flax, oats, or potatoes, belonging to the under-tenants, and proceeded to sell these for his rents: it sometimes happened that these unfortunate tenants paid their rent twice over, once to the *middle man*, and once to the *head landlord*.

The characteristics of a middle man *were*, servility to his superiors, and tyranny towards his inferiors: the poor detested this race of beings. In speaking to them, however, they always used the most abject language, and the most humble tone and posture. – '*Please your honour*; *and please your honour's honour*,' they knew must be repeated as a charm at the beginning and end of every equivocating, exculpatory, or supplicatory sentence; and they were much more alert in doffing their caps to these new men, than to those of what they call *good old families*. A witty carpenter once termed these middle men *journeymen gentlemen*.

drafts from Sir Kit; but I laid it all to the fault of the agent; for, says I, what can Sir Kit do with so much cash, and he a single man? but still it went. Rents must be all paid up to the day, and afore; no allowance for improving tenants, no consideration for those who had built upon their farms: no sooner was a lease out, but the land was advertised to the highest bidder, all the old tenants turned out, when they spent their substance in the hope and trust of a renewal from the landlord. All was now set at the highest penny to a parcel of poor wretches, who meant to run away, and did so, after taking two crops out of the ground. Then fining down the year's rent[G] came into fashion; any thing for the ready penny; and with all this, and presents to the agent and the driver,[G] there was no such thing as standing it. I said nothing, for I had a regard for the family; but I walked about thinking if his honour Sir Kit knew all this, it would go hard with him, but he'd see us righted; not that I had any thing for my own share to complain of, for the agent was always very civil to me, when he came down into the country, and took a great deal of notice of my son Jason. Jason Quirk, though he be my son, I must say, was a good scholar from his birth, and a very 'cute lad: I thought to make him a priest,[G] but he did better for himself: seeing how he was as good a clerk as any in the county, the agent gave him his rent accounts to copy, which he did first of all for the pleasure of obliging the gentleman, and would take nothing at all for his trouble, but was always proud to serve the family. By-and-bye a good farm bounding us to the east fell into his honour's hands, and my son put in a proposal for it: why shouldn't he, as well as another? The proposals all went over to the master at the Bath, who knowing no more of the land than the child unborn, only having once been out a grousing on it before he went to England; and the value of lands, as the agent informed him, falling every year in Ireland, his honour wrote over in all haste a bit of a letter, saying he left it all to the agent, and that he must set it as well as he could to the best bidder, to be sure, and send him over £200 by return of post: with this the agent gave me a hint, and I spoke a good word for my son, and gave out in the country that nobody need bid against us. So his proposal was just the thing, and he a good tenant; and he got a promise of an abatement in the rent, after the first year, for advancing the half year's rent at signing the lease, which was wanting to complete the agent's £200, by the return of the post, with all which my master wrote back he was well satisfied. About this time we learned from the agent as a great secret, how the money went so fast, and the reason of the thick coming of the master's drafts: he was a little too fond of play; and Bath, they say, was no place for a young man of his fortune, where there were so many of his own countrymen too hunting him up and down, day and night, who had nothing to lose. At last, at Christmas, the agent wrote over to stop the drafts, for he could raise no more money on bond or mortgage, or from the tenants, or any how, nor had he any more to lend himself, and desired at the same time to decline the agency for the future, wishing Sir Kit his health and happiness, and the compliments of the season, for I saw the letter before ever it was sealed, when my son copied it. When the answer came, there was a new turn in affairs, and the agent was turned out; and my son Jason, who had corresponded privately with his honour occasionally on business, was forthwith desired by his honour to take the accounts into his own hands, and look them over till further orders. It was a very spirited letter to be sure: Sir Kit sent his service, and the compliments of the season, in return to the agent, and he would fight him with pleasure to-morrow, or any day, for sending him such a letter, if he was born a gentleman, which he was sorry (for both their sakes) to find (too late) he was not. Then, in a private postscript, he condescended to tell us, that all would be speedily settled to his satisfaction, and we should turn over a new leaf, for he was going to be married in a fortnight to the grandest heiress in England and had only immediate occasion at present for £200, as he would not choose to touch his lady's fortune for travelling expences home to Castle Rackrent, where he intended to be, wind and weather permitting, early in the next month; and desired fires, and the house to be painted, and the new building to go on as fast as possible, for the reception of him and his lady before that time; with several words besides in the letter, which we could not make out, because, God bless him! he wrote in such a flurry. My heart warmed to my new lady when I read this; I was almost afraid it was too good news to be true; but the girls fell to scouring, and it was well they did, for we soon saw his marriage in the paper to a lady with I don't know how many tens of thousand pounds to her fortune: then I watched the post-office for his landing; and the news came to my son of his and the bride being in Dublin, and on the way home to Castle

Rackrent. We had bonfires all over the country, expecting him down the next day, and we had his coming of age still to celebrate, which he had not time to do properly before he left the country; therefore a great ball was expected, and great doings upon his coming, as it were, fresh to take possession of his ancestors' estate. I never shall forget the day he came home: we had waited and waited all day long till eleven o'clock at night, and I was thinking of sending the boy to lock the gates, and giving them up for that night, when there came the carriages thundering up to the great hall door. I got the first sight of the bride; for when the carriage door opened, just as she had her foot on the steps, I held the flam^G full in her face to light her, at which she shut her eyes, but I had a full view of the rest of her, and greatly shocked I was, for by that light she was little better than a blackamoor, and seemed crippled, but that was only sitting so long in the chariot. 'You're kindly welcome to Castle Rackrent, my lady,' says I (recollecting who she was); 'did your honour hear of the bonfires?' His honour spoke never a word, nor so much as handed her up the steps – he looked to me no more like himself than nothing at all; I know I took him for the skeleton of his honour: I was not sure what to say next to one or t'other, but seeing she was a stranger in a foreign country, I thought it was right to speak cheerful to her, so I went back again to the bonfires. 'My lady,' says I, as she crossed the hall, 'there would have been fifty times as many, but for fear of the horses and frightening your ladyship: Jason and I forbid them, please your honour.' With that she looked at me a little bewildered. 'Will I have a fire lighted in the state room to-night?' was the next question I put to her, but never a word she answered, so I concluded she could not speak a word of English, and was from foreign parts. The short and the long of it was I couldn't tell what to make of her; so I left her to herself, and went straight down to the servants' hall to learn something for certain about her. Sir Kit's own man was tired, but the groom set him a talking at last, and we had it all out before ever I closed my eyes that night. The bride might well be a great fortune – she was a *Jewish* by all accounts, who are famous for their great riches. I had never seen any of that tribe or nation before, and could only gather, that she spoke a strange kind of English of her own, that she could not abide pork or sausages, and went neither to church or mass. Mercy upon his honour's poor soul, thought I; what will become of him and his, and all of us, with his heretic blackamoor at the head of the Castle Rackrent estate! I never slept a wink all night for thinking of it; but before the servants I put my pipe in my mouth, and kept my mind to myself; for I had a great regard for the family; and after this, when strange gentlemen's servants came to the house, and would begin to talk about the bride, I took care to put the best foot foremost, and passed her for a nabob²¹ in the kitchen, which accounted for her dark complexion and every thing.

The very morning after they came home, however, I saw how things were plain enough between Sir Kit and my lady, though they were walking together arm in arm after breakfast, looking at the new building and the improvements. 'Old Thady,' said my master, just as he used to do, 'how do you do?' 'Very well, I thank your honour's honour,' said I; but I saw he was not well pleased, and my heart was in my mouth as I walked along after him. 'Is the large room damp, Thady?' said his honour. 'Oh, damp, your honour! how should it but be as dry as a bone,' says I, 'after all the fires we have kept in it day and night? it's the barrack-room^G your honour's talking on.' 'And what is a barrack-room, pray, my dear?' were the first words I ever heard out of my lady's lips. 'No matter, my dear!' said he, and went on talking to me, ashamed like I should witness her ignorance. To be sure, to hear her talk one might have taken her for an innocent,^G for it was, 'what's this, Sir Kit? and what's that, Sir Kit?' all the way we went. To be sure, Sir Kit had enough to do to answer her. 'And what do you call that, Sir Kit?' said she, 'that, that looks like a pile of black bricks, pray, Sir Kit?' 'My turf stack, my dear,' said my master, and bit his lip. Where have you lived, my lady, all your life, not to know a turf stack when you see it, thought I, but I said nothing. Then, by-and-bye, she takes out her glass, and begins spying over the country. 'And what's all that black swamp out yonder, Sir Kit?' says she. 'My bog, my dear,' says he, and went on whistling. 'It's a very ugly prospect, my dear,' says she. 'You don't see it, my dear,' says he, 'for we've planted it out, when the trees grow up in summer time,' says he. 'Where are the trees,' said she, 'my dear?' still looking through her glass. 'You are blind, my dear,' says he; 'what are those under your eyes?' 'These shrubs,' said she. 'Trees,' said he. 'May be they are what you call trees in Ireland, my dear,' said she; 'but they are not a yard high, are they?' 'They were planted out but last year, my lady,' says I, to soften matters between them, for I saw she was going the way to make his honour mad with her – 'they are very well grown for their age, and you'll not see the bog of Allyballycarricko'shaughlin at-all-at-all through the screen, when once the leaves come out. But, my lady, you must not quarrel with any part or parcel of Allyballycar-ricko'shaughlin, for you don't know how many hundred years that same bit of bog has been in the family; we would not part with the bog of Allyballycarricko'shaughlin upon no account at all; it cost the late Sir Murtagh two hundred good pounds to defend his title to it and boundaries against the O'Leary's who cut a road through it.' Now one would have thought this would have been hint enough for my lady, but she fell to laughing like one out of their right mind, and made me say the name of the bog over for her to get it by heart, a dozen times – then she must ask me how to spell it, and what was the meaning of it in English – Sir Kit standing by whistling all the while; I verily believed she laid the corner stone of all her future misfortunes at that very instant; but I said no more, only looked at Sir Kit.

There was no balls, no dinners, no doings; the country was all disappointed – Sir Kit's gentleman said in a whisper to me, it was all my lady's own fault, because she was so obstinate about the cross. 'What cross?' says I; 'is it about her being a heretic?' 'Oh, no such matter,' says he; 'my master does not mind her heresies, but her diamond cross, it's worth I can't tell you how much; and she has thousands of English pounds concealed in diamonds about her, which she as good as promised to give up to my master before he married, but now she won't part with any of them, and she must take the consequences.'

Her honey-moon, at least her Irish honey-moon, was scarcely well over, when his honour one morning said to me, 'Thady, buy me a pig!' and then the sausages were ordered, and here was the first open breaking-out of my lady's troubles. My lady came down herself into the kitchen, to speak to the cook about the sausages, and desired never to see them more at her table. Now my master had ordered them, and my lady knew that. The cook took my lady's part, because she never came down into the kitchen, and was young and innocent in housekeeping, which raised her pity; besides, said she, at her own table, surely, my lady should order and disorder what she pleases; but the cook soon changed her note, for my master made it a principle to have the sausages, and swore at her for a Jew herself, till he drove her fairly out of the kitchen; then, for fear of her place, and because he threatened that my lady should give her no discharge without the sausages, she gave up, and from that day forward always sausages, or bacon, or pig meat in some shape or other, went up to table; upon which my lady shut herself up in her own room, and my master said she might stay there, with an oath: and to make sure of her, he turned the key in the door, and kept it ever after in his pocket. We none of us ever saw or heard her speak for seven years after that:* he carried her dinner himself. Then his honour had a great deal of company to dine with him, and balls in the house, and was as gay and gallant, and as much himself as before he was married; and at dinner he always drank my lady

* This part of the history of the Rackrent family can scarcely be thought credible; but in justice to honest Thady, it is hoped the reader will recollect the history of the celebrated Lady Cathcart's conjugal imprisonment. – The Editor was acquainted with Colonel M'Guire, Lady Cathcart's husband; he has lately seen and questioned the maid-servant who lived with Colonel M'Guire during the time of Lady Cathcart's imprisonment.[22] Her ladyship was locked up in her own house for many years; during which period her husband was visited by the neighbouring gentry, and it was his regular custom at dinner to send his compliments to Lady Cathcart, informing her that the company had the honour to drink her ladyship's health, and begging to know whether there was any thing at table that she would like to eat? the answer was always, 'Lady Cathcart's compliments, and she has every thing she wants.' An instance of honesty in a poor Irish woman deserves to be recorded: – Lady Cathcart had some remarkably fine diamonds, which she had concealed from her husband, and which she was anxious to get out of the house, lest he should discover them. She had neither servant nor friend to whom she could entrust them; but she had observed a poor beggar woman, who used to come to the house; she spoke to her from the window of the room in which she was confined; the woman promised to do what she desired, and Lady Cathcart threw a parcel, containing the jewels, to her. The poor woman carried them to the person to whom they were directed; and several years afterwards, when Lady Cathcart recovered her liberty, she received her diamonds safely.

At Colonel M'Guire's death her ladyship was released. The editor, within this year, saw the gentleman who accompanied her to England after her husband's death. When she first was told of his death, she imagined that the news was not true, and that it was told only with an intention of deceiving her. At his death she had scarcely clothes sufficient to cover her; she wore a red wig, looked scared, and her understanding seemed stupefied; she said that she scarcely knew one human creature from another; her imprisonment lasted above twenty years. These circumstances may appear strange to an English reader; but there is no danger in the present times, that any individual should exercise such tyranny as Colonel M'Guire's with impunity, the power being now all in the hands of government, and there being no possibility of obtaining from parliament an act of indemnity for any cruelties.

Rackrent's good health, and so did the company, and he sent out always a servant, with his compliments to my lady Rackrent, and the company was drinking her ladyship's health, and begged to know if there was any thing at table he might send her; and the man came back, after the sham errand, with my lady Rackrent's compliments, and she was very much obliged to Sir Kit – she did not wish for any thing, but drank the company's health. The country, to be sure, talked and wondered at my lady's being shut up, but nobody chose to interfere or ask any impertinent questions, for they knew my master was a man very apt to give a short answer himself, and likely to call a man out for it afterwards; he was a famous shot; had killed his man before he came of age, and nobody scarce dared look at him whilst at Bath. Sir Kit's character was so well known in the country, that he lived in peace and quietness ever after, and was a great favourite with the ladies, especially when in process of time, in the fifth year of her confinement, my lady Rackrent[23] fell ill, and took entirely to her bed, and he gave out that she was now skin and bone, and could not last through the winter. In this he had two physicians' opinions to back him (for now he called in two physicians for her), and tried all his arts to get the diamond cross from her on her death-bed, and to get her to make a will in his favour of her separate possessions; but there she was too tough for him. He used to swear at her behind her back, after kneeling to her to her face, and call her in the presence of his gentleman his stiff-necked Israelite, though before he married her, that same gentleman told me he used to call her (how he could bring it out, I don't know) 'my pretty Jessica!'[24] To be sure it must have been hard for her to guess what sort of a husband he reckoned to make her. When she was lying, to all expectation, on her death-bed of a broken heart, I could not but pity her, though she was a Jewish; and considering too it was no fault of hers to be taken with my master so young as she was at the Bath, and so fine a gentleman as Sir Kit was when he courted her; and considering too, after all they had heard and seen of him as a husband, there were now no less than three ladies in our county talked of for his second wife, all at daggers drawn with each other, as his gentleman swore, at the balls, for Sir Kit for their partner, – I could not but think them bewitched; but they all reasoned with themselves, that Sir Kit would make a good husband to any Christian but a Jewish, I suppose, and especially as he was now a reformed rake; and it was not known how my lady's fortune was settled in her will, nor how the Castle Rackrent estate was all mortgaged, and bonds out against him, for he was never cured of his gaming tricks; but that was the only fault he had, God bless him.

My lady had a sort of fit, and it was given out she was dead, by mistake: this brought things to a sad crisis for my poor master, – one of the three ladies showed his letters to her brother, and claimed his promises, whilst another did the same. I don't mention names. Sir Kit, in his defence, said he would meet any man who dared to question his conduct, and as to the ladies, they must settle it amongst them who was to be his second, and his third, and his fourth, whilst his first was still alive, to his mortification and theirs. Upon this, as upon all former occasions, he had the voice of the country with him, on account of the great spirit and propriety he acted with. He met and shot the first lady's brother; the next day he called out the second, who had a wooden leg; and their place of meeting by appointment being in a new ploughed field, the wooden-leg man stuck fast in it. Sir Kit, seeing his situation, with great candour fired his pistol over his head; upon which the seconds interposed, and convinced the parties there had been a slight misunderstanding between them; thereupon they shook hands cordially, and went home to dinner together. This gentleman, to show the world how they stood together, and by the advice of the friends of both parties, to re-establish his sister's injured reputation, went out with Sir Kit as his second, and carried his message next day to the last of his adversaries: I never saw him in such fine spirits as that day he went out – sure enough he was within ames-ace[25] of getting quit hand-somely of all his enemies; but unluckily, after hitting the tooth pick out of his adversary's finger and thumb, he received a ball in a vital part, and was brought home, in little better than an hour after the affair, speechless on a hand-barrow, to my lady. We got the key out of his pocket the first thing we did, and my son Jason ran to unlock the barrack-room, where my lady had been shut up for seven years, to acquaint her with the fatal accident. The surprise bereaved her of her senses at first, nor would she believe but we were putting some new trick upon her, to entrap her out of her jewels, for a great while, till Jason bethought himself of taking her to the window, and showed her the men bringing Sir Kit up the avenue upon the hand-barrow, which had immediately the desired effect; for directly she burst into tears, and pulling her cross from her bosom, she kissed it with as great devotion as ever I witnessed; and lifting up her eyes to heaven, uttered some ejaculation, which none present heard; but I take the sense of it to be, she returned thanks for this unexpected interposition in her favour when she had least reason to expect it. My master was greatly lamented: there was no life in him when we lifted him off the barrow, so he was laid out immediately, and *waked* the same night. The country was all in an uproar about him, and not a soul but cried shame upon his murderer; who would have been hanged surely, if he could have been brought to his trial, whilst the gentlemen in the country were up about it; but he very prudently withdrew himself to the continent before the affair was made public. As for the young lady, who was the immediate cause of the fatal accident, however innocently, she could never show her head after at the balls in the county or any place; and by the advice of her friends and physicians, she was ordered soon after to Bath, where it was expected, if any where on this side of the grave, she would meet with the recovery of her health and lost peace of mind. As a proof of his great popularity, I need only add, that there was a song made upon my master's untimely death in the newspapers, which was in every body's mouth, singing up and down through the country, even down to the mountains, only three days after his unhappy exit. He was also greatly bemoaned at the Curragh,[G] where his cattle were well known; and all who had taken up his bets formerly were particularly inconsolable for his loss to society. His stud sold at the cant[G] at the greatest price ever known in the county; his favourite horses were chiefly disposed of amongst his particular friends, who would give any price for them for his sake; but no ready money was required by the new heir, who wished not to displease any of the gentlemen of the neighbourhood just upon his coming to settle amongst them; so a long credit was given where requisite, and the cash has never been gathered in from that day to this.

But to return to my lady: – She got surprisingly well after my master's decease. No sooner was it known for certain that he was dead, than all the gentlemen within twenty miles of us came in a body, as it were, to set my lady at liberty, and to protest against her confinement, which they now for the first time understood was against her own consent. The ladies too were as attentive as possible, striving who should be foremost with their morning visits; and they that saw the diamonds spoke very handsomely of them, but thought it a pity they were not bestowed, if it had so pleased God, upon a lady who would have become them better. All these civilities wrought little with my lady, for she had taken an unaccountable prejudice against the country, and every thing belonging to it, and was so partial to her native land, that after parting with the cook, which she did immediately upon my master's decease, I never knew her easy one instant, night or day, but when she was packing up to leave us. Had she meant to make any stay in Ireland, I stood a great chance of being a great favourite with her; for when she found I understood the weathercock, she was always finding some pretence to be talking to me, and asking me which way the wind blew, and was it likely, did I think, to continue fair for England. But when I saw she had made up her mind to spend the rest of her days upon her own income and jewels in England, I considered her quite as a foreigner, and not at all any longer as part of the family. She gave no vails[26] to the servants at Castle Rackrent at parting, notwithstanding the old proverb of '*as rich as a Jew*', which, she being a Jewish, they built upon with reason. But from first to last she brought nothing but misfortunes amongst us; and if it had not been all along with her, his honour, Sir Kit, would have been now alive in all appearance. Her diamond cross was, they say, at the bottom of it all; and it was a shame for her, being his wife, not to show more duty, and to have given it up when he condescended to ask so often for such a bit of a trifle in his distresses, especially when he all along made it no secret he married for money. But we will not bestow another thought upon her. This much I thought it lay upon my conscience to say, in justice to my poor master's memory.

'Tis an ill wind that blows nobody no good – the same wind that took the Jew Lady Rackrent over to England brought over the new heir to Castle Rackrent.

Here let me pause for breath in my story, for though I had a great regard for every member of the family, yet without compare Sir Conolly, commonly called, for short, amongst his friends, Sir Condy Rackrent, was ever my great favourite, and, indeed, the most universally beloved man I had ever seen or heard of, not excepting his great ancestor Sir Patrick, to whose memory he, amongst other instances of generosity, erected a handsome marble stone in the church of Castle Rackrent, setting forth in large letters his age, birth, parentage, and many other virtues, concluding with the compliment so justly due, that 'Sir Patrick Rackrent lived and died a monument of old Irish hospitality.'

CONTINUATION OF THE MEMOIRS OF THE RACKRENT FAMILY[27]

History of Sir Conolly Rackrent

Sir Condy Rackrent, by the grace of God heir at law to the Castle Rackrent estate, was a remote branch of the family: born to little or no fortune of his own, he was bred to the bar; at which, having many friends to push him, and no mean natural abilities of his own, he doubtless would, in process of time, if he could have borne the drudgery of that study, have been rapidly made king's counsel, at the least; but things were disposed of otherwise, and he never went the circuit but twice, and then made no figure for want of a fee, and being unable to speak in public. He received his education chiefly in the college of Dublin;[28] but before he came to years of discretion lived in the country, in a small but slated house, within view of the end of the avenue. I remember him bare footed and headed, running through the street of O'Shaughlin's town, and playing at pitch and toss, ball, marbles, and what not, with the boys of the town, amongst whom my son Jason was a great favourite with him. As for me, he was ever my white-headed boy:[29] often's the time when I would call in at his father's, where I was always made welcome; he would slip down to me in the kitchen, and love to sit on my knee, whilst I told him stories of the family, and the blood from which he was sprung, and how he might look forward, if the *then* present man should die without childer, to being at the head of the Castle Rackrent estate. This was then spoke quite and clear at random to please the child, but it pleased Heaven to accomplish my prophecy afterwards, which gave him a great opinion of my judgement in business. He went to a little grammar-school with many others, and my son amongst the rest, who was in his class, and not a little useful to him in his book learning, which he acknowledged with gratitude ever after. These rudiments of his education thus completed, he got a-horseback, to which exercise he was ever addicted, and used to gallop over the country while yet but a slip of a boy, under the care of Sir Kit's huntsman, who was very fond of him, and often lent him his gun, and took him out a-shooting under his own eye. By these means he became well acquainted and popular amongst the poor in the neighbourhood early; for there was not a cabin at which he had not stopped some morning or other, along with the huntsman, to drink a glass of burnt whiskey out of an eggshell, to do him good and warm his heart, and drive the cold out of his stomach. The old people always told him he was a great likeness of Sir Patrick; which made him first have an ambition to take after him, as far as his fortune should allow. He left us when of an age to enter the college, and there completed his education and nineteenth year; for as he was not born to an estate, his friends[30] thought it incumbent on them to give him the best education which could be had for love or money; and a great deal of money consequently was spent upon him at college and Temple. He was a very little altered for the worse by what he saw there of the great world; for when he came down into the country, to pay us a visit, we thought him just the same man as ever, hand and glove with every one, and as far from high, though not without his own proper share of family pride, as any man ever you see. Latterly, seeing how Sir Kit and the Jewish lived together, and that there was no one between him and the Castle Rackrent estate, he neglected to apply to the law as much as was expected of him; and secretly many of the tenants, and others, advanced him cash upon his note of hand value received, promising bargains of leases and lawful interest, should he ever come into the estate. All this was kept a great secret, for fear the present man, hearing of it, should take it into his head to take it ill of poor Condy, and so should cut him off for ever, by levying a fine, and suffering a recovery to dock the entail.[G] Sir Murtagh would have been the man for that; but Sir Kit was too much taken up philandering to consider the law in this case, or any other. These practices I have mentioned, to account for the state of his affairs, I mean Sir Condy's, upon his coming into the Castle Rackrent estate. He could not command a penny of his first year's income; which, and keeping no accounts, and the great sight of company he did, with many other causes too numerous to mention, was the origin of his distresses. My son Jason, who was now established agent, and knew every thing, explained matters out of the face to Sir Conolly, and made him sensible of his embarrassed situation. With a great nominal rent-roll, it was almost all paid away in interest; which being for convenience suffered to run on, soon doubled the principal, and Sir Condy was obliged to pass new bonds for the interest, now grown principal, and so on. Whilst this was going on, my son requiring to be paid for his trouble, and many years' service in the family gratis, and Sir Condy not willing to take his affairs into his own hands, or to look them even in the face, he gave my son a bargain of some acres, which fell out of lease, at a reasonable rent. Jason set the land, as soon as his lease was sealed, to under-tenants, to make the rent, and got two hundred a-year profit rent; which was little enough considering his long agency. He brought the land at twelve years' purchase two years afterwards, when Sir Condy was pushed for money on an execution, and was at the same time allowed for his improvements thereon. There was a sort of hunting-lodge upon the estate, convenient to my son Jason's land, which he had his eye upon about this time; and he was a little jealous of Sir Condy, who talked of setting it to a stranger, who was just come into the country – Captain Moneygawl was the man. He was son and heir to the Moneygawls of Mount Juliet's town, who had a great estate in the next county to ours; and my master was loth to disoblige the young gentleman, whose heart was set upon the lodge; so he wrote him back, that the lodge was at his service, and if he would honour him with his company at Castle Rackrent, they could ride over together some morning, and look at it, before signing the lease. Accordingly the captain came over to us, and he and Sir Condy grew the greatest friends ever you see, and were for ever out a-shooting or hunting together, and were very merry in the evenings; and Sir Condy was invited of course to Mount Juliet's town; and the family intimacy that had been in Sir Patrick's time was now recollected, and nothing would serve Sir Condy but he must be three times a-week at the least with his new friends, which grieved me, who knew, by the captain's groom and gentleman, how they talked of him at Mount Juliet's town, making him quite, as one may say, a laughingstock and a butt for the whole company; but they were soon cured of *that* by an accident that surprised 'em not a little, as it did me. There was a bit of a scrawl found upon the waiting-maid of old Mr Moneygawl's youngest daughter, Miss Isabella, that laid open the whole; and her father, they say, was like one out of his right mind, and swore it was the last thing he ever should have thought of, when he invited my master to his house, that his daughter should think of such a match. But their talk signified not a straw, for, as Miss Isabella's maid reported, her young mistress was fallen over head and ears in love with Sir Condy, from the first time that ever her brother brought him into the house to dinner: the servant who waited that day behind my master's chair was the first who knew it, as he says; though it's hard to believe him, for he did not tell till a great while afterwards; but, however, it's likely enough, as the thing turned out, that he was not far out of the way; for towards the middle of dinner, as he says, they were talking of stage-plays, having a playhouse, and being great play-actors at Mount Juliet's town; and Miss Isabella turns short to my master, and says, 'Have you seen the play-bill, Sir Condy?' 'No, I have not,' said he. 'Then more shame for you,' said the captain her brother, 'not to know that my sister is to play Juliet to-night, who plays it better than any woman on or off the stage in all Ireland.' 'I am very happy to hear it,' said Sir Condy; and there the matter dropped for the present. But Sir Condy all this time, and a great while afterwards, was at a terrible nonplus; for he had no liking, not he, to stage-plays, nor to Miss Isabella either; to his mind, as it came out over a bowl of whiskey punch at home, his little Judy M'Quirk, who was daughter to a sister's son of mine, was worth twenty of Miss Isabella. He had seen her often when he stopped at her father's cabin to drink whiskey out of the eggshell, out hunting, before he came to the estate, and, as she gave out, was under something like a promise of marriage to her. Any how, I could not but pity my poor master, who was so bothered between them, and he an easy-hearted man, that could not disoblige nobody, God bless him! To be sure, it was not his place to behave ungenerous to Miss Isabella, who had disobliged all her relations for his sake, as he remarked; and then she was locked up in her chamber, and forbid to think of him any more, which raised his spirit, because his family was, as he observed, as good as theirs at any rate, and the Rackrents a suitable match for the Moneygawls any day in the year: all which was true enough; but it grieved me to see, that upon the strength of all this, Sir Condy was growing more in the mind to carry off Miss Isabella to Scotland, in spite of her relations, as she desired.

'It's all over with our poor Judy!' said I, with a heavy sigh, making bold to speak to him one night when he was a little cheerful, and standing in the servants' hall all alone with me, as was often his custom. 'Not at all,' said he; 'I never was fonder of Judy than at this present speaking; and to prove it to you,' said he, and he took from my hand a halfpenny, change that I had just got along with my tobacco, 'and to prove it to you, Thady,' says he, 'it's a toss up with me which I should marry this minute, her or Mr Moneygawl of Mount Juliet's town's daughter – so it is.' 'Oh, boo! boo!'* says I, making light of it, to see what he would go on to next; 'your honour's joking, to be sure; there's no compare between our poor Judy and Miss Isabella, who has a great fortune, they say.' 'I'm not a man to mind a fortune, nor never was,' said Sir Condy, proudly, 'whatever her friends may say; and to make short of it,' says he, 'I'm come to a determination upon the spot;' with that he swore such a terrible oath, as made me cross myself; 'and by this book,' said he, snatching up my ballad book, mistaking it for my prayer book, which lay in the window; 'and by this book,' says he, 'and by all the books that ever were shut and opened, it's come to a toss-up with me, and I'll stand or fall by the toss; and so, Thady, hand me over that *pin*† out of the ink-horn,' and he makes a cross on the smooth side of the halfpenny; 'Judy M'Quirk,' says he, 'her mark.'‡ God bless him! his hand was a little unsteadied by all the whiskey punch he had taken, but it was plain to see his heart was for poor Judy. My heart was all as one as in my mouth when I saw the halfpenny up in the air, but I said nothing at all; and when it came down, I was glad I had kept myself to myself, for to be sure now it was all over with poor Judy. 'Judy's out a luck,' said I, striving to laugh. 'I'm out a luck,' said he; and I never saw a man look so cast down: he took up the halfpenny off the flag, and walked away quite sober-like by the shock. Now, though as easy a man, you would think, as any in the wide world, there was no such thing

---

* Boo! boo! an exclamation equivalent to *pshaw* or *nonsense*.

† *Pin* read *pen*. It formerly was vulgarly pronounced *pin* in Ireland.

‡ *Her mark*. It *was* the custom in Ireland for those who could not write to make a cross to stand for their signature, as was formerly the practice of our English monarchs. The Editor inserts the fac-simile of an Irish *mark*, which may hereafter be valuable to a judicious antiquary –

Her

Judy × M'Quirk,

Mark.

In bonds or notes, signed in this manner, a witness is requisite, as the name is frequently written by him or her.

as making him unsay one of these sort of vows* which he had learned to reverence when young, as I well remember teaching him to toss up for bog-berries on my knee. So I saw the affair was as good as settled between him and Miss Isabella, and I had no more to say but to wish her joy, which I did the week afterwards, upon her return from Scotland with my poor master.

My new lady was young, as might be supposed of a lady that had been carried off, by her own consent, to Scotland;³¹ but I could only see her at first through her veil, which, from bashfulness or fashion, she kept over her face. 'And am I to walk through all this crowd of people, my dearest love?' said she to Sir Condy, meaning us servants and tenants, who had gathered at the back gate. 'My dear,' said Sir Condy, 'there's nothing for it but to walk, or to let me carry you as far as the house, for you see that back road is too narrow for a carriage, and the great piers have tumbled down across the front approach; so there's no driving the right way, by reason of the ruins.' 'Plato, thou reasonest well!' said she, or words to that effect, which I could no ways understand; and again, when her foot stumbled against a broken bit of a car-wheel, she cried out, 'Angels and ministers of grace defend us!' Well, thought I, to be sure if she's no Jewish, like the last, she is a mad woman for certain, which is as bad: it would have been as well for my poor master to have taken up with poor Judy, who is in her right mind, any how.

She was dressed like a mad woman, moreover, more than like any one I ever saw afore or since, and I could not take my eyes off her, but still followed behind her, and her feathers on the top of her hat were broke going in at the low back door, and she pulled out her little bottle out of her pocket to smell to when she found herself in the kitchen, and said, 'I shall faint with the heat of this odious, odious place.' 'My dear, it's only three steps across the kitchen, and

---

* *Vows* – It has been maliciously and unjustly hinted, that the lower classes of the people in Ireland pay but little regard to oaths; yet it is certain that some oaths have great power over their minds. Sometimes they swear they will be revenged on some of their neighbours; this is an oath that they are never known to break. But, what is infinitely more extraordinary and unaccountable, they sometimes make and keep a vow against whiskey; those vows are usually limited to a short time. A woman who has a drunken husband is most fortunate if she can prevail upon him to go to the priest, and make a vow against whiskey for a year, or a month, or a week, or a day.

there's a fine air if your veil was up,' said Sir Condy, and with that
threw back her veil, so that I had then a full sight of her face; she
had not at all the colour of one going to faint, but a fine complexion
of her own, as I then took it to be, though her maid told me after it
was all put on; but even complexion and all taken in, she was no
way, in point of good looks, to compare to poor Judy; and with all
she had a quality toss with her; but may be it was my over-partiality
to Judy, into whose place I may say she stept, that made me notice
all this. To do her justice, however, she was, when we came to know
her better, very liberal in her housekeeping, nothing at all of the
skin-flint in her; she left every thing to the housekeeper; and her
own maid, Mrs Jane, who went with her to Scotland, gave her the
best of characters for generosity. She seldom or ever wore a thing
twice the same way, Mrs Jane told us, and was always pulling her
things to pieces, and giving them away, never being used, in her
father's house, to think of expence in any thing; and she reckoned,
to be sure, to go on the same way at Castle Rackrent; but, when I
came to inquire, I learned that her father was so mad with her for
running off, after his locking her up, and forbidding her to think any
more of Sir Condy, that he would not give her a farthing; and it was
lucky for her she had a few thousands of her own, which had been
left to her by a good grandmother, and these were very convenient
to begin with. My master and my lady set out in great style; they
had the finest coach and chariot, and horses and liveries, and cut
the greatest dash in the county, returning their wedding visits; and
it was immediately reported, that her father had undertaken to pay
all my master's debts, and of course all his tradesmen gave him a
new credit, and every thing went on smack smooth, and I could not
but admire my lady's spirit, and was proud to see Castle Rackrent
again in all its glory. My lady had a fine taste for building, and
furniture, and playhouses, and she turned every thing topsy-turvy,
and made the barrack-room into a theatre, as she called it, and she
went on as if she had a mint of money at her elbow; and, to be sure.
I thought she knew best, especially as Sir Condy said nothing to it
one way or the other. All he asked, God bless him! was to live in
peace and quietness, and have his bottle or his whiskey punch at
night to himself. Now this was little enough, to be sure, for any
gentleman; but my lady couldn't abide the smell of the whiskey
punch. 'My dear,' says he, 'you liked it well enough before we were

married, and why not now?' 'My dear,' said she, 'I never smelt it, or I assure you I should never have prevailed upon myself to marry you.' 'My dear, I am sorry you did not smell it, but we can't help that now,' returned my master, without putting himself in a passion, or going out of his way, but just fair and easy helped himself to another glass, and drank it off to her good health. All this the butler told me, who was going backwards and forwards unnoticed with the jug, and hot water, and sugar, and all he thought wanting. Upon my master's swallowing the last glass of whiskey punch my lady burst into tears, calling him an ungrateful, base, barbarous wretch! and went off into a fit of hysterics, as I think Mrs Jane called it, and my poor master was greatly frightened, this being the first thing of the kind he had seen; and he fell straight on his knees before her, and, like a good-hearted cratur as he was, ordered the whiskey punch out of the room, and bid 'em throw open all the windows, and cursed himself: and then my lady came to herself again, and when she saw him kneeling there bid him get up, and not forswear himself any more, for that she was sure he did not love her, nor never had; this we learnt from Mrs Jane, who was the only person left present at all this. 'My dear,' returns my master, thinking, to be sure, of Judy, as well he might, 'whoever told you so is an incendiary, and I'll have 'em turned out of the house this minute, if you'll only let me know which of them it was.' 'Told me what?' said my lady, starting upright in her chair. 'Nothing at all, nothing at all,' said my master, seeing he had overshot himself, and that my lady spoke at random; 'but what you said just now, that I did not love you, Bella; who told you that?' 'My own sense,' she said, and she put her handkerchief to her face and leant back upon Mrs Jane, and fell to sobbing as if her heart would break. 'Why now, Bella, this is very strange of you,' said my poor master; 'if nobody has told you nothing, what is it you are taking on for at this rate, and exposing yourself and me for this way?' 'Oh, say no more, say no more; every word you say kills me,' cried my lady; and she ran on like one, as Mrs Jane says, raving, 'Oh, Sir Condy, Sir Condy! I that had hoped to find in you –' 'Why now, faith, this is a little too much; do Bella, try to recollect yourself, my dear; am not I your husband, and of your own choosing; and is not that enough?' 'Oh, too much! too much!' cried my lady, wringing her hands. 'Why, my dear, come to your right senses, for the love of heaven. See, is not the whiskey punch, jug and bowl, and all, gone out of the room long ago? What is it, in the wide world, you have to complain of?' But still my lady sobbed and sobbed, and called herself the most wretched of women; and among other out-of-the-way provoking things, asked my master, was he fit for company for her, and he drinking all night? This nettling him, which it was hard to do, he replied, that as to drinking all night, he was then as sober as she was herself, and that it was no matter how much a man drank, provided it did no ways affect or stagger him: that as to being fit company for her, he thought himself of a family to be fit company for any lord or lady in the land; but that he never prevented her from seeing and keeping what company she pleased, and that he had done his best to make Castle Rackrent pleasing to her since her marriage, having always had the house full of visitors, and if her own relations were not amongst them, he said that was their own fault, and their pride's fault, of which he was sorry to find her ladyship had so unbecoming a share. So concluding, he took his candle and walked off to his room, and my lady was in her tantarums for three days after; and would have been so much longer, no doubt, but some of her friends, young ladies, and cousins, and second cousins, came to Castle Rackrent, by my poor master's express invitation, to see her, and she was in a hurry to get up, as Mrs Jane called it, a play for them, and so got well, and was as finely dressed, and as happy to look at, as ever; and all the young ladies, who used to be in her room dressing of her, said, in Mrs Jane's hearing, that my lady was the happiest bride ever they had seen, and that to be sure a love-match was the only thing for happiness, where the parties could any way afford it.

As to affording it, God knows it was little they knew of the matter; my lady's few thousands could not last for ever, especially the way she went on with them, and letters from tradesfolk came every post thick and threefold with bills as long as my arm, of years' and years' standing; my son Jason had 'em all handed over to him, and the pressing letters were all unread by Sir Condy, who hated trouble, and could never be brought to hear talk of business, but still put it off and put it off, saying, settle it any how, or bid 'em call again to-morrow, or speak to me about it some other time. Now it was hard to find the right time to speak, for in the mornings he was a-bed, and in the evenings over his bottle, where no gentleman chooses to be disturbed. Things in a twelvemonth or so came to such a pass there was no making a shift to go on any longer, though we were all of us well enough used to live from hand to mouth at Castle Rackrent. One day, I remember, when there was a power of company, all sitting after dinner in the dusk, not to say dark, in the drawingroom, my lady having rung five times for candles, and none to go up, the housekeeper sent up the footman, who went to my mistress, and whispered behind her chair how it was. 'My lady,' says he, 'there are no candles in the house.' 'Bless me,' says she, 'then take a horse and gallop off as fast as you can to Carrick O'Fungus, and get some.' 'And in the mean time tell them to step into the playhouse, and try if there are not some bits left,' added Sir Condy, who happened to be within hearing. The man was sent up again to my lady, to let her know there was no horse to go, but one that wanted a shoe. 'Go to Sir Condy, then; I know nothing at all about the horses,' said my lady; 'why do you plague me with these things?' How it was settled I really forget, but to the best of my remembrance, the boy was sent down to my son Jason's to borrow candles for the night. Another time in the winter, and on a desperate cold day, there was no turf in for the parlour and above stairs, and scarce enough for the cook in the kitchen; the little *gossoon** was sent off to the neighbours, to see and beg or borrow some, but none could he bring back with him for love or money; so as needs must, we were forced to trouble Sir Condy – 'Well, and if there's no turf to be had in the town or country, why what signifies talking any more about it; can't ye go and cut down a tree?' 'Which tree, please your honour?' I made bold to say. 'Any tree at all that's good to burn,' said Sir Condy; 'send off smart and get one down, and the fires lighted, before my lady gets up to breakfast, or the house will be too hot to hold us.' He was always very considerate in all things about my lady, and she wanted for nothing whilst he had it to give. Well, when things were tight with them about this time, my son Jason put in a word again about the lodge, and made a genteel offer to lay

---

* *Gossoon*, a little boy – from the French word *garçon*. In most Irish families there *used* to be a barefooted gossoon, who was slave to the cook and the butler, and who in fact, without wages, did all the hard work of the house. Gossoons were always employed as messengers. The Editor has known a gossoon to go on foot, without shoes or stockings, fifty-one English miles between sunrise and sunset.

down the purchase-money, to relieve Sir Condy's distresses. Now Sir Condy had it from the best authority, that there were two writs come down to the sheriff against his person, and the sheriff, as ill luck would have it, was no friend of his, and talked how he must do his duty, and how he would do it, if it was against the first man in the country, or even his own brother; let alone one who had voted against him at the last election, as Sir Condy had done. So Sir Condy was fain to take the purchase-money of the lodge from my son Jason to settle matters; and sure enough it was a good bargain for both parties, for my son bought the fee-simple of a good house for him and his heirs for ever, for little or nothing, and by selling of it for that same, my master saved himself from a gaol. Every way it turned out fortunate for Sir Condy; for before the money was all gone there came a general election, and he being so well beloved in the county, and one of the oldest families, no one had a better right to stand candidate for the vacancy, and he was called upon by all his friends, and the whole county I may say, to declare himself against the old member, who had little thought of a contest.[32] My master did not relish the thought of a troublesome canvass, and all the ill-will he might bring upon himself by disturbing the peace of the county, besides the expence, which was no trifle; but all his friends called upon one another to subscribe, and they formed themselves into a committee, and wrote all his circular letters for him, and engaged all his agents, and did all the business unknown to him; and he was well pleased that it should be so at last, and my lady herself was very sanguine about the election; and there was open house kept night and day at Castle Rackrent, and I thought I never saw my lady look so well in her life as she did at that time; there were grand dinners, and all the gentlemen drinking success to Sir Condy till they were carried off; and then dances and balls, and the ladies all finishing with a raking pot of tea[G] in the morning. Indeed it was well the company made it their choice to sit up all nights, for there were not half beds enough for the sights of people that were in it, though there were shakedowns in the drawing-room always made up before sunrise for those that liked it. For my part, when I saw the doings that were going on, and the loads of claret that went down the throats of them that had no right to be asking for it, and the sights of meat that went up to table and never came down, besides what was carried off to one or t'other below stairs, I couldn't but pity my poor master, who was to pay for all; but I said nothing, for fear of gaining myself ill-will. The day of election will come some time or other, says I to myself, and all will be over; and so it did, and a glorious day it was as any I ever had the happiness to see. 'Huzza! huzza! Sir Condy Rackrent for ever!' was the first thing I hears in the morning, and the same and nothing else all day, and not a soul sober only just when polling, enough to give their votes as became 'em, and to stand the browbeating of the lawyers, who came tight enough upon us; and many of our freeholders were knocked off, having never a freehold that they could safely swear to, and Sir Condy was not willing to have any man perjure himself for his sake, as was done on the other side, God knows, but no matter for that. Some of our friends were dumb-founded, by the lawyers asking them: Had they ever been upon the ground where their freeholds lay? Now Sir Condy being tender of the consciences of them that had not been on the ground, and so could not swear to a freehold when cross-examined by them lawyers, sent out for a couple of cleaves-full of the sods of his farm of Gulteeshinnagh:* and as soon as the sods came into town he set each man upon his sod, and so then, ever after, you know, they could fairly swear they had been upon the ground.† We gained the day by this piece of honesty.G I thought I should have died in the streets for joy when I seed my poor master chaired, and he bareheaded, and it raining as hard as it could pour; but all the crowds following him up and down, and he bowing and shaking hands with the whole town. 'Is that Sir Condy Rackrent in the chair?' says a stranger man in the crowd. 'The same,' says I; 'who else should it be? God bless him!' 'And I take it, then, you belong to him?' says he. 'Not at all,' says I: 'but I live under him, and have done so these two hundred years and upwards, me and mine.' 'It's lucky for you, then,' rejoins he, 'that he is where

---

33 * At St Patrick's meeting, London, March, 1806, the Duke of Sussex said he had the honour of bearing an Irish title, and, with the permission of the company, he should tell them an anecdote of what he had experienced on his travels. When he was at Rome, he went to visit an Irish seminary, and when they heard who he was, and that he had an Irish title, some of them asked him, 'Please your Royal Highness, since you are an Irish peer, will you tell us if you ever trod upon Irish ground?' When he told them he had not, 'O then,' said one of the order, 'you shall soon do so.' Then they spread some earth, which had been brought from Ireland, on a marble slab, and made him stand upon it.
† This was actually done at an election in Ireland.

he is; for was he any where else but in the chair, this minute he'd be in a worse place; for I was sent down on purpose to put him up,* and here's my order for so doing in my pocket.' It was a writ that villain the wine merchant had marked against my poor master for some hundreds of an old debt, which it was a shame to be talking of at such a time as this. 'Put it in your pocket again, and think no more of it any ways for seven years to come, my honest friend,' says I; 'he's a member of parliament now, praised be God, and such as you can't touch him: and if you'll take a fool's advice, I'd have you keep out of the way this day, or you'll run a good chance of getting your deserts amongst my master's friends, unless you choose to drink his health like every body else.' 'I've no objection to that in life,' said he; so we went into one of the public houses kept open for my master; and we had a great deal of talk about this thing and that. 'And how is it,' says he, 'your master keeps on so well upon his legs? I heard say he was off Holantide twelvemonth past.' 'Never was better or heartier in his life,' said I. 'It's not that I'm after speaking of,' said he; 'but there was a great report of his being ruined.' 'No matter,' says I, 'the sheriffs two years running were his particular friends, and the sub-sheriffs were both of them gentlemen, and were properly spoken to; and so the writs lay snug with them, and they, as I understand by my son Jason the custom in them cases is, returned the writs as they came to them to those that sent 'em; much good may it do them! with a word in Latin, that no such person as Sir Condy Rackrent, bart., was to be found in those parts.' 'Oh, I understand all those ways better, no offence, than you,' says he, laughing, and at the same time filling his glass to my master's good health, which convinced me he was a warm friend in his heart after all, though appearances were a little suspicious or so at first. 'To be sure,' says he, still cutting his joke, 'when a man's over head and shoulders in debt, he may live the faster for it, and the better, if he goes the right way about it; or else how is it so many live on so well, as we see every day, after they are ruined?' 'How is it,' says I, being a little merry at the time; 'how is it but just as you see the ducks in the chicken-yard, just after their heads are cut off by the cook, running round and round faster than when alive?' At which conceit he fell a laughing, and remarked he had never had

* *To put him up* – to put him in gaol.

the happiness yet to see the chicken-yard at Castle Rackrent. 'It won't be long so, I hope,' says I; 'you'll be kindly welcome there, as every body is made by my master; there is not a freer spoken gentleman, or a better beloved, high or low, in all Ireland.' And of what passed after this I'm not sensible, for we drank Sir Condy's good health and the downfall of his enemies till we could stand no longer ourselves. And little did I think at the time, or till long after, how I was harbouring my poor master's greatest of enemies myself. This fellow had the impudence, after coming to see the chicken-yard, to get me to introduce him to my son Jason; little more than the man that never was born did I guess at his meaning by this visit: he gets him a correct list fairly drawn out from my son Jason of all my master's debts, and goes straight round to the creditors and buys them all up, which he did easy enough, seeing the half of them never expected to see their money out of Sir Condy's hands. Then, when this base-minded limb of the law, as I afterward detected him in being, grew to be sole creditor over all, he takes him out a custodiam[34] on all the denominations and sub-denominations, and every carton and half carton[G] upon the estate; and not content with that, must have an execution against the master's goods, and down to the furniture, though little worth, of Castle Rackrent itself. But this is a part of my story I'm not come to yet, and it's bad to be forestalling: ill news flies fast enough all the world over.

To go back to the day of the election, which I never think of but with pleasure and tears of gratitude for those good times; after the election was quite and clean over, there comes shoals of people from all parts, claiming to have obliged my master with their votes, and putting him in mind of promises which he could never remember himself to have made; one was to have a freehold for each of his four sons; another was to have a renewal of a lease; another an abatement; one came to be paid ten guineas for a pair of silver buckles sold my master on the hustings, which turned out to be no better than copper gilt; another had a long bill for oats, the half of which never went into the granary to my certain knowledge, and the other half were not fit for the cattle to touch; but the bargain was made the week before the election, and the coach and saddle horses were got into order for the day, besides a vote fairly got by them oats; so no more reasoning on that head; but then there was no end to them that were telling Sir Condy he had engaged to make their sons excisemen, or high constables, or the like; and as for them that had bills to give in for liquor, and beds, and straw, and ribands, and horses, and postchaises for the gentlemen freeholders that came from all parts and other counties to vote for my master, and were not, to be sure, to be at any charges, there was no standing against all these; and, worse than all, the gentlemen of my master's committee, who managed all for him, and talked how they'd bring him in without costing him a penny, and subscribed by hundreds very genteelly, forgot to pay their subscriptions, and had laid out in agents' and lawyers' fees and secret service money the Lord knows how much; and my master could never ask one of them for their subscription, you are sensible, nor for the price of a fine horse he had sold one of them; so it all was left at his door. He could never, God bless him again! I say, bring himself to ask a gentleman for money, despising such sort of conversation himself; but others, who were not gentlemen born, behaved very uncivil in pressing him at this very time, and all he could do to content 'em all was to take himself out of the way as fast as possible to Dublin, where my lady had taken a house fitting for him as a member of parliament, to attend his duty in there all the winter. I was very lonely when the whole family was gone, and all the things they had ordered to go, and forgot, sent after them by the car. There was then a great silence in Castle Rackrent, and I went moping from room to room, hearing the doors clap for want of right locks, and the wind through the broken windows, that the glazier never would come to mend, and the rain coming through the roof and best ceilings all over the house for want of the slater, whose bill was not paid, besides our having no slates or shingles for that part of the old building which was shingled and burnt when the chimney took fire, and had been open to the weather ever since. I took myself to the servants' hall in the evening to smoke my pipe as usual, but missed the bit of talk we used to have there sadly, and ever after was content to stay in the kitchen and boil my little potatoes,* and put up my bed there; and every post-day I looked in the newspaper, but no news of my master in the house; he never

---

* *My little potatoes* – Thady does not mean, by this expression, that his potatoes were less than other people's, or less than the usual size – *little* is here used only as an Italian diminutive, expressive of fondness.

spoke good or bad; but as the butler wrote down word to my son Jason, was very ill used by the government about a place that was promised him and never given, after his supporting them against his conscience very honourably, and being greatly abused for it, which hurt him greatly, he having the name of a great patriot in the country before. The house and living in Dublin too were not to be had for nothing, and my son Jason said, 'Sir Condy must soon be looking out for a new agent, for I've done my part, and can do no more: – if my lady had the bank of Ireland to spend, it would go all in one winter, and Sir Condy would never gainsay her, though he does not care the rind of a lemon for her all the while.'

Now I could not bear to hear Jason giving out after this manner against the family, and twenty people standing by in the street. Ever since he had lived at the lodge of his own, he looked down, howsomever, upon poor old Thady, and was grown quite a great gentleman, and had none of his relations near him; no wonder he was no kinder to poor Sir Condy than to his own kith or kin.* In the spring it was the villain that got the list of the debts from him brought down the custodiam, Sir Condy still attending his duty in parliament, and I could scarcely believe my own old eyes, or the spectacles with which I read it, when I was shown my son Jason's name joined in the custodiam; but he told me it was only for form's sake, and to make things easier than if all the land was under the power of a total stranger. Well, I did not know what to think; it was hard to be talking ill of my own, and I could not but grieve for my poor master's fine estate, all torn by these vultures of the law; so I said nothing, but just looked on to see how it would all end.

It was not till the month of June that he and my lady came down to the country. My master was pleased to take me aside with him to the brewhouse that same evening, to complain to me of my son and other matters, in which he said he was confident I had neither art nor part; he said a great deal more to me, to whom he had been fond to talk ever since he was my white-headed boy, before he came to the estate; and all that he said about poor Judy I can never forget, but scorn to repeat. He did not say an unkind word of my lady, but wondered, as well he might, her relations would do nothing

* *Kith* and *kin* – family or relations. *Kin* from *kind; kith* from we know not what.

for him or her, and they in all this great distress. He did not take any thing long to heart, let it be as it would, and had no more malice, or thought of the like in him, than a child that can't speak; this night it was all out of his head before he went to his bed. He took his jug of whiskey punch – my lady was grown quite easy about the whiskey punch by this time, and so I did suppose all was going on right betwixt them, till I learnt the truth through Mrs Jane, who talked over their affairs to the housekeeper, and I within hearing. The night my master came home thinking of nothing at all but just making merry, he drank his bumper toast 'to the deserts of that old curmudgeon my father-in-law, and all enemies at Mount Juliet's town'. Now my lady was no longer in the mind she formerly was, and did no ways relish hearing her own friends abused in her presence, she said. 'Then why don't they show themselves your friends,' said my master, 'and oblige me with the loan of the money I condescended, by your advice, my dear, to ask? It's now three posts since I sent off my letter, desiring in the postscript a speedy answer by the return of the post, and no account at all from them yet.' 'I expect they'll write to *me* next post,' says my lady, and that was all that passed then; but it was easy from this to guess there was a coolness betwixt them, and with good cause.

The next morning, being post-day, I sent off the gossoon early to the post-office, to see was there any letter likely to set matters to rights, and he brought back one with the proper post-mark upon it, sure enough, and I had no time to examine, or make any conjecture more about it, for into the servants' hall pops Mrs Jane with a blue bandbox in her hand, quite entirely mad. 'Dear ma'am, and what's the matter?' says I. 'Matter enough,' says she; 'don't you see my bandbox is wet through, and my best bonnet here spoiled, besides my lady's, and all by the rain coming in through that gallery window, that you might have got mended, if you'd had any sense, Thady, all the time we were in town in the winter.' 'Sure I could not get the glazier, ma'am,' says I. 'You might have stopped it up any how,' says she. 'So I did, ma'am, to the best of my ability; one of the panes with the old pillow-case, and the other with a piece of the old stage green curtain; sure I was as careful as possible all the time you were away, and not a drop of rain came in at that window of all the windows in the house, all winter, ma'am, when under my care; and now the family's come home, and it's summer time, I never thought no more about it, to be sure; but dear, it's a pity to think of your bonnet, ma'am; but here's what will please you, ma'am, a letter from Mount Juliet's town for my lady.' With that she snatches it from me without a word more, and runs up the back stairs to my mistress; I follows with a slate to make up the window. This window was in the long passage, or gallery, as my lady gave out orders to have it called, in the gallery leading to my master's bedchamber and hers. And when I went up with the slate, the door having no lock, and the bolt spoilt, was a-jar after Mrs Jane, and as I was busy with the window, I heard all that was saying within.

'Well, what's in your letter, Bella, my dear?' says he: 'you're a long time spelling it over.' 'Won't you shave this morning, Sir Condy?' says she, and put the letter into her pocket. 'I shaved the day before yesterday,' says he, 'my dear, and that's not what I'm thinking of now; but any thing to oblige you, and to have peace and quietness, my dear' – and presently I had the glimpse of him at the cracked glass over the chimney-piece, standing up shaving himself to please my lady. But she took no notice, but went on reading her book and Mrs Jane doing her hair behind. 'What is it you're reading there, my dear? – phoo, I've cut myself with this razor; the man's a cheat that sold it me, but I have not paid him for it yet: what is it you're reading there? did you hear me asking you, my dear?' 'The Sorrows of Werter,' [35] replies my lady, as well as I could hear. 'I think more of the sorrows of Sir Condy,' says my master, joking like. 'What news from Mount Juliet's town?' 'No news,' says she, 'but the old story over again, my friends all reproaching me still for what I can't help now.' 'Is it for marrying me?' said my master, still shaving: 'what signifies, as you say, talking of that, when it can't be help'd now?'

With that she heaved a great sigh, that I heard plain enough in the passage. 'And did not you use me basely, Sir Condy,' says she, 'not to tell me you were ruined before I married you?' 'Tell you, my dear,' said he; 'did you ever ask me one word about it? and had not you friends enough of your own, that were telling you nothing else from morning to night, if you'd have listened to them slanders?' 'No slanders, nor are my friends slanderers; and I can't bear to hear them treated with disrespect as I do,' says my lady, and took out her pocket handkerchief; 'they are the best of friends; and if I had taken their advice – But my father was wrong to lock me up, I own; that was the only unkind thing I can charge him with; for if he had not locked me up, I should never have had a serious thought of running away as I did.' 'Well, my dear,' said my master, 'don't cry and make yourself uneasy about it now, when it's all over, and you have the man of your own choice, in spite of 'em all.' 'I was too young, I know, to make a choice at the time you ran away with me, I'm sure,' says my lady, and another sigh, which made my master, half shaved as he was, turn round upon her in surprise. 'Why, Bell,' says he, 'you can't deny what you know as well as I do, that it was at your own particular desire, and that twice under your own hand and seal expressed, that I should carry you off as I did to Scotland, and marry you there.' 'Well, say no more about it, Sir Condy,' said my lady, pettish like – 'I was a child then, you know.' 'And as far as I know, you're little better now, my dear Bella, to be talking in this manner to your husband's *face*; but I won't take it ill of you, for I know it's something in that letter you put into your pocket just now, that has set you against me all on a sudden, and imposed upon your understanding.' 'It is not so very easy as you think it, Sir Condy, to impose upon *my* understanding,' said my lady. 'My dear,' says he, 'I have, and with reason, the best opinion of your understanding of any man now breathing; and you know I have never set my own in competition with it till now, my dear Bella,' says he, taking her hand from her book as kind as could be – 'till now, when I have the great advantage of being quite cool, and you not; so don't believe one word your friends say against your own Sir Condy, and lend me the letter out of your pocket, till I see what it is they can have to say.' 'Take it then,' says she, 'and as you are quite cool, I hope it is a proper time to request you'll allow me to comply with the wishes of all my own friends, and return to live with my father and family, during the remainder of my wretched existence, at Mount Juliet's town.'

At this my poor master fell back a few paces, like one that had been shot. 'You're not serious, Bella,' says he; 'and could you find it in your heart to leave me this way in the very middle of my distresses, all alone?' But recollecting himself after his first surprise, and a moment's time for reflection, he said, with a great deal of consideration for my lady, 'Well, Bella, my dear, I believe you are right; for what could you do at Castle Rackrent, and an execution against the goods coming down, and the furniture to be canted, and an auction in the house all next week? so you have my full consent to go, since that is your desire, only you must not think of my accompanying you, which I could not in honour do upon the terms I always have been, since our marriage, with your friends; besides, I have business to transact at home; so in the mean time, if we are to have any breakfast this morning, let us go down and have it for the last time in peace and comfort, Bella.'

Then as I heard my master coming to the passage door, I finished fastening up my slate against the broken pane; and when he came out, I wiped down the window seat with my wig,* and bade him a good morrow as kindly as I could, seeing he was in trouble, though he strove and thought to hide it from me. 'This window is all racked and tattered,' says I, 'and it's what I'm striving to mend.' 'It *is* all racked and tattered, plain enough,' says he, 'and never mind mending it, honest old Thady,' says he; 'it will do well enough for you and I, and that's all the company we shall have left in the house by-and-bye.' 'I'm sorry to see your honour so low this morning,' says I; 'but you'll be better after taking your breakfast.' 'Step down to the servants' hall,' says he, 'and bring me up the pen and ink into the parlour, and get a sheet of paper from Mrs Jane, for I have business that can't brook to be delayed; and come into the parlour with the pen and ink yourself, Thady, for I must have you to witness my signing a paper I have to execute in a hurry.' Well, while I was getting of the pen and ink-horn, and the sheet of paper, I ransacked my brains to think what could be the papers my poor master could have to execute in such a hurry, he that never thought of such a thing as doing business afore breakfast, in the whole course of his life, for any man living; but this was for my lady, as I afterwards found, and the more genteel of him after all her treatment.

I was just witnessing the paper that he had scrawled over, and was shaking the ink out of my pen upon the carpet, when my lady

---

* Wigs were formerly used instead of brooms in Ireland, for sweeping or dusting tables, stairs, &c. The Editor doubted the fact, till he saw a labourer of the old school sweep down a flight of stairs with his wig; he afterwards put it on his head again with the utmost composure, and said, 'Oh, please your honour, it's never a bit the worse.'

It must be acknowledged, that these men are not in any danger of catching cold by taking off their wigs occasionally, because they usually have fine crops of hair growing under their wigs. The wigs are often yellow, and the hair which appears from beneath them black; the wigs are usually too small, and are raised up by the hair beneath, or by the ears of the wearers.

came into breakfast, and she started as if it had been a ghost! as well she might, when she saw Sir Condy writing at this unseasonable hour. 'That will do very well, Thady,' says he to me, and took the paper I had signed to, without knowing what upon the earth it might be, out of my hands, and walked, folding it up, to my lady.

'You are concerned in this, my lady Rackrent,' says he, putting it into her hands; 'and I beg you'll keep this memorandum safe, and show it to your friends the first thing you do when you get home; but put it in your pocket now, my dear, and let us eat our breakfast, in God's name.' 'What is all this?' said my lady, opening the paper in great curiosity. 'It's only a bit of a memorandum of what I think becomes me to do whenever I am able,' says my master; 'you know my situation, tied hand and foot at the present time being, but that can't last always, and when I'm dead and gone, the land will be to the good, Thady, you know; and take notice, it's my intention your lady should have a clear five hundred a year jointure off the estate afore any of my debts are paid.' 'Oh, please your honour,' says I, 'I can't expect to live to see that time, being now upwards of fourscore years of age, and you a young man, and likely to continue so, by the help of God.' I was vexed to see my lady so insensible too, for all she said was, 'This is very genteel of you, Sir Condy. You need not wait any longer, Thady;' so I just picked up the pen and ink that had tumbled on the floor, and heard my master finish with saying, 'You behaved very genteel to me, my dear, when you threw all the little you had in your own power along with yourself, into my hands; and as I don't deny but what you may have had some things to complain of,' – to be sure he was thinking then of Judy, or of the whiskey punch, one or t'other, or both, – 'and as I don't deny but you may have had something to complain of, my dear, it is but fair you should have something in the form of compensation to look forward to agreeably in future; besides, it's an act of justice to myself, that none of your friends, my dear, may ever have it to say against me, I married for money, and not for love.' 'That is the last thing I should ever have thought of saying of you, Sir Condy,' said my lady, looking very gracious. 'Then, my dear,' said Sir Condy, 'we shall part as good friends as we met; so all's right.'

I was greatly rejoiced to hear this, and went out of the parlour to report it all to the kitchen. The next morning my lady and Mrs Jane set out for Mount Juliet's town in the jaunting car: many wondered at my lady's choosing to go away, considering all things, upon the jaunting car, as if it was only a party of pleasure; but they did not know, till I told them, that the coach was all broke in the journey down, and no other vehicle but the car to be had; besides, my lady's friends were to send their coach to meet her at the cross roads; so it was all done very proper.

My poor master was in great trouble after my lady left us. The execution came down; and every thing at Castle Rackrent was seized by the gripers,[36] and my son Jason, to his shame be it spoken, amongst them. I wondered, for the life of me, how he could harden himself to do it; but then he had been studying the law, and had made himself attorney Quirk; so he brought down at once a heap of accounts upon my master's head. To cash lent, and to ditto, and to ditto, and to ditto, and oats, and bills paid at the milliner's and linen draper's, and many dresses for the fancy balls in Dublin for my lady, and all the bills to the workmen and tradesmen for the scenery of the theatre, and the chandler's and grocer's bills, and tailor's besides butcher's and baker's, and worse than all, the old one at that base wine merchant's, that wanted to arrest my poor master for the amount on the election day, for which amount Sir Condy afterwards passed his note of hand, bearing lawful interest from the date thereof; and the interest and compound interest was now mounted to a terrible deal on many other notes and bonds for money borrowed, and there was besides hush money to the sub-sheriffs, and sheets upon sheets of old and new attorneys' bills, with heavy balances, *as per former account furnished*, brought forward with interest thereon; then there was a powerful deal due to the crown for sixteen years' arrear of quit-rent of the town-lands of Carrickshaughlin, with driver's fees, and a compliment to the receiver every year for letting the quit-rent run on, to oblige Sir Condy, and Sir Kit afore him. Then there were bills for spirits and ribands at the election time, and the gentlemen of the committee's accounts unsettled, and their subscription never gathered; and there were cows to be paid for, with the smith and farrier's bills to be set against the rent of the demesne, with calf and hay money; then there was all the servants' wages, since I don't know when, coming due to them, and sums advanced for them by my son Jason for clothes, and boots, and whips, and odd moneys for sundries expended by them in journeys to town and elsewhere, and pocket-money for the master continually, and messengers and postage before his being a parliament man; I can't myself tell you what besides; but this I know, that when the evening came on the which Sir Condy had appointed to settle all with my son Jason, and when he comes into the parlour, and sees the sight of bills and load of papers all gathered on the great dining-table for him, he puts his hands before both his eyes, and cried out, 'Merciful Jasus! what is it I see before me?' Then I sets an arm-chair at the table for him, and with a deal of difficulty he sits him down, and my son Jason hands him over the pen and ink to sign to this man's bill and t'other man's bill, all which he did without making the least objections. Indeed, to give him his due, I never *seen* a man more fair and honest, and easy in all his dealings, from first to last, as Sir Condy, or more willing to pay every man his own as far as he was able, which is as much as any one can do. 'Well,' says he, joking like with Jason, 'I wish we could settle it all with a stroke of my grey goose quill. What signifies making me wade through all this ocean of papers here; can't you now, who understand drawing out an account, debtor and creditor, just sit down here at the corner of the table, and get it done out for me, that I may have a clear view of the balance, which is all I need be talking about, you know?' 'Very true, Sir Condy; nobody understands business better than yourself,' says Jason. 'So I've a right to do, being born and bred to the bar,' says Sir Condy. 'Thady, do step out and see are they bringing in the things for the punch, for we've just done all we have to do for this evening.' I goes out accordingly, and when I came back, Jason was pointing to the balance, which was a terrible sight to my poor master. 'Pooh! pooh! pooh!' says he, 'here's so many noughts they dazzle my eyes, so they do, and put me in mind of all I suffered, larning of my numeration table, when I was a boy at the day-school along with you, Jason – units, tens, hundreds, tens of hundred. Is the punch ready, Thady?' says he, seeing me. 'Immediately; the boy has the jug in his hand; it's coming up stairs, please your honour, as fast as possible,' says I, for I saw his honour was tired out of his life; but Jason, very short and cruel, cuts me off with – 'Don't be talking of punch yet a while; it's no time for punch yet a bit – units, tens, hundreds,' goes he on, counting over the master's shoulder, units, tens, hundreds, thousands. 'A-a-ah! hold your hand,' cries my master; 'where in this wide world am I to find hundreds, or units itself, let alone thousands?' 'The balance has been running on too long,' says

Jason, sticking to him as I could not have done at the time, if you'd have given both the Indies and Cork to boot; 'the balance has been running on too long, and I'm distressed myself on your account, Sir Condy, for money, and the thing must be settled now on the spot, and the balance cleared off,' says Jason. 'I'll thank you if you'll only show me how,' says Sir Condy. 'There's but one way,' says Jason, 'and that's ready enough: when there's no cash, what can a gentleman do, but go to the land?' 'How can you go to the land, and it under custodiam to yourself already,' says Sir Condy, 'and another custodiam hanging over it? and no one at all can touch it, you know, but the custodees.' 'Sure, can't you sell, though at a loss? sure you can sell, and I've a purchaser ready for you,' says Jason. 'Have ye so?' said Sir Condy; 'that's a great point gained; but there's a thing now beyond all, that perhaps you don't know yet, barring Thady has let you into the secret.' 'Sarrah[37] bit of a secret, or any thing at all of the kind, has he learned from me these fifteen weeks come St John's eve,' says I; 'for we have scarce been upon speaking terms of late; but what is it your honour means of a secret?' 'Why, the secret of the little keepsake I gave my lady Rackrent the morning she left us, that she might not go back empty-handed to her friends.' 'My lady Rackrent, I'm sure, has baubles and keepsakes enough, as those bills on the table will show,' says Jason; 'but whatever it is,' says he, taking up his pen, 'we must add it to the balance, for to be sure it can't be paid for.' 'No, nor can't till after my decease,' said Sir Condy; 'that's one good thing.' Then colouring up a good deal, he tells Jason of the memorandum of the five hundred a year jointure he had settled upon my lady; at which Jason was indeed mad, and said a great deal in very high words, that it was using a gentleman, who had the management of his affairs, and was moreover his principal creditor, extremely ill, to do such a thing without consulting him, and against his knowledge and consent. To all which Sir Condy had nothing to reply, but that upon his conscience, it was in a hurry and without a moment's thought on his part, and he was very sorry for it, but if it was to do over again he would do the same; and he appealed to me, and I was ready to give my evidence, if that would do, to the truth of all he said.

So Jason with much ado was brought to agree to a compromise. 'The purchaser that I have ready,' says he, 'will be much displeased, to be sure, at the incumbrance on the land, but I must see and manage him; here's a deed ready drawn up; we have nothing to do but to put in the consideration money and our names to it.' 'And how much am I going to sell? – the lands of O'Shaughlin's town, and the lands of Gruneaghoolaghan, and the lands of Crookaghna-waturgh,' says he, just reading to himself, – 'and – Oh, murder, Jason! sure you won't put this in – the castle, stable, and appurtenances of Castle Rackrent.' 'Oh, murder!' says I, clapping my hands, 'this is too bad, Jason.' 'Why so?' said Jason, 'when it's all, and a great deal more to the back of it, lawfully mine, was I to push for it.' 'Look at him,' says I, pointing to Sir Condy, who was just leaning back in his arm-chair, with his arms falling beside him like one stupified; 'is it you, Jason, that can stand in his presence, and recollect all he has been to us, and all we have been to him, and yet use him so at the last?' 'Who will you find to use him better, I ask you?' said Jason; 'if he can get a better purchaser, I'm content; I only offer to purchase, to make things easy and oblige him: though I don't see what compliment I am under, if you come to that; I have never had, asked, or charged more than sixpence in the pound, receiver's fees; and where would he have got an agent for a penny less?' 'Oh, Jason! Jason! how will you stand to this in the face of the county and all who know you?' says I; 'and what will people think and say, when they see you living here in Castle Rackrent, and the lawful owner turned out of the seat of his ancestors, without a cabin to put his head into, or so much as a potato to eat?' Jason, whilst I was a saying this, and a great deal more, made me signs, and winks, and frowns; but I took no heed; for I was grieved and sick at heart for my poor master, and couldn't but speak.

'Here's the punch,' says Jason, for the door opened; 'here's the punch!' Hearing that, my master starts up in his chair, and recollects himself, and Jason uncorks the whiskey. 'Set down the jug here,' says he, making room for it beside the papers opposite to Sir Condy, but still not stirring the deed that was to make over all. Well, I was in great hopes he had some touch of mercy about him when I saw him making the punch, and my master took a glass; but Jason put it back as he was going to fill again, saying, 'No, Sir Condy, it sha'n't be said of me, I got your signature to this deed when you were half-seas over: you know your name and handwriting in that condition would not, if brought before the courts, benefit me a straw; wherefore let us settle all before we go deeper into the punch-bowl.' 'Settle all as you will,' said Sir Condy, clapping his hands to his ears; 'but let me hear no more; I'm bothered to death this night.' 'You've only to sign,' said Jason, putting the pen to him. 'Take all, and be content,' said my master. So he signed; and the man who brought in the punch witnessed it, for I was not able, but crying like a child; and besides, Jason said, which I was glad of, that I was no fit witness, being so old and doting. It was so bad with me, I could not taste a drop of the punch itself, though my master himself, God bless him! in the midst of his trouble, poured out a glass for me, and brought it up to my lips. 'Not a drop, I thank your honour's honour as much as if I took it though,' and I just set down the glass as it was, and went out, and when I got to the street-door, the neighbour's childer, who were playing at marbles there, seeing me in great trouble, left their play, and gathered about me to know what ailed me; and I told them all, for it was a great relief to me to speak to these poor childer, that seemed to have some natural feeling left in them: and when they were made sensible that Sir Condy was going to leave Castle Rackrent for good and all, they set up a whillalu that could be heard to the farthest end of the street; and one fine boy he was, that my master had given an apple to that morning, cried the loudest, but they all were the same sorry, for Sir Condy was greatly beloved amongst the childer,[38] for letting them go a nutting in the demesne, without saying a word to them, though my lady objected to them. The people in the town, who were the most of them standing at their doors, hearing the childer cry, would know the reason of it; and when the report was made known, the people one and all gathered in great anger against my son Jason, and terror at the notion of his coming to be landlord over them, and they cried, 'No Jason! no Jason! Sir Condy! Sir Condy! Sir Condy Rackrent for ever!' and the mob grew so great and so loud, I was frightened, and made my way back to the house to warn my son to make his escape, or hide himself for fear of the consequences. Jason would not believe me till they came all round the house, and to the windows with great shouts: then he grew quite pale, and asked Sir Condy what had he best do? 'I'll tell you what you'd best do,' said Sir Condy, who was laughing to see his fright; 'finish your glass first, then let's go to the window and show ourselves, and I'll tell 'em, or you shall, if you please, that I'm going to the Lodge for change of air for my health, and by my own desire, for the rest of my days.' 'Do so,' said

Jason, who never meant it should have been so, but could not refuse him the Lodge at this unseasonable time. Accordingly Sir Condy threw up the sash, and explained matters, and thanked all his friends, and bid 'em look in at the punch-bowl, and observe that Jason and he had been sitting over it very good friends; so the mob was content, and he sent 'em out some whiskey to drink his health, and that was the last time his honour's health was ever drunk at Castle Rackrent.

The very next day, being too proud, as he said, to me, to stay an hour longer in a house that did not belong to him, he sets off to the Lodge, and I along with him not many hours after. And there was great bemoaning through all O'Shaughlin's town, which I stayed to witness, and gave my poor master a full account of when I got to the Lodge. He was very low and in his bed when I got there, and complained of a great pain about his heart, but I guessed it was only trouble, and all the business, let alone vexation, he had gone through of late; and knowing the nature of him from a boy, I took my pipe, and, whilst smoking it by the chimney, began telling him how he was beloved and regretted in the county, and it did him a deal of good to hear it. 'Your honour has a great many friends yet, that you don't know of, rich and poor, in the county,' says I; 'for as I was coming along the road, I met two gentlemen in their own carriages, who asked after you, knowing me, and wanted to know where you was and all about you, and even how old I was: think of that.' Then he wakened out of his doze, and began questioning me who the gentlemen were. And the next morning it came into my head to go, unknown to any body, with my master's compliments, round to many of the gentlemen's houses, where he and my lady used to visit, and people that I knew were his great friends, and would go to Cork to serve him any day in the year, and I made bold to try to borrow a trifle of cash from them. They all treated me very civil for the most part, and asked a great many questions very kind about my lady, and Sir Condy, and all the family, and were greatly surprised to learn from me Castle Rackrent was sold, and my master at the Lodge for health; and they all pitied him greatly, and he had their good wishes, if that would do, but money was a thing they unfortunately had not any of them at this time to spare. I had my journey for my pains, and I, not used to walking, nor supple as formerly, was greatly tired, and had the satisfaction of telling my master, when I got to the Lodge, all the civil things said by high and low.

'Thady,' says he, 'all you've been telling me brings a strange thought into my head; I've a notion I shall not be long for this world any how, and I've a great fancy to see my own funeral afore I die.' I was greatly shocked, at the first speaking, to hear him speak so light about his funeral, and he, to all appearance, in good health, but recollecting myself, answered, 'To be sure, it would be as fine a sight as one could see, I dared to say, and one I should be proud to witness, and I did not doubt his honour's would be as great a funeral as ever Sir Patrick O'Shaughlin's was, and such a one as that had never been known in the county afore or since.' But I never thought he was in earnest about seeing his own funeral himself, till the next day he returns to it again. 'Thady,' says he, 'as far as the wake *[39G] goes, sure I might without any great trouble have the satisfaction of seeing a bit of my own funeral.' 'Well, since your honour's honour's so bent upon it,' says I, not willing to cross him, and he in trouble, 'we must see what we can do.' So he fell into a sort of a sham disorder, which was easy done, as he kept his bed, and no one to see him; and I got my shister, who was an old woman very handy about the sick, and very skilful, to come up to the Lodge, to nurse him; and we gave out, she knowing no better, that he was just at his latter end, and it answered beyond any thing; and there was a great throng of people, men, women, and childer, and there being only two rooms at the Lodge, except what was locked up full of Jason's furniture and things, the house was soon as full and fuller than it could hold, and the heat, and smoke, and noise wonderful great; and standing amongst them that were near the bed, but not thinking at all of the dead, I was started by the sound of my master's voice from under the great coats that had been thrown all at top, and I went close up, no one noticing. 'Thady,' says he, 'I've had enough of this; I'm smothering, and can't hear a word of all they're saying of the deceased.' 'God bless you, and lie still and quiet,' says I, 'a bit longer, for my shister's afraid of ghosts, and would die on the spot with fright, was she to see you come to life all of a sudden this way without the least preparation.' So he lays him still, though well nigh stifled, and I made all haste to tell the secret

---

* A wake in England is a meeting avowedly for merriment; in Ireland it is a nocturnal meeting avowedly for the purpose of watching and bewailing the dead; but, in reality, for gossiping and debauchery.

of the joke, whispering to one and t'other, and there was a great surprise, but not so great as we had laid out it would. 'And aren't we to have the pipes and tobacco, after coming so far to-night?' said some; but they were all well enough pleased when his honour got up to drink with them, and sent for more spirits from a shebean-house,* where they very civilly let him have it upon credit. So the night passed off very merrily, but, to my mind, Sir Condy was rather upon the sad order in the midst of it all, not finding there had been such a great talk about himself after his death as he had always expected to hear.

The next morning, when the house was cleared of them, and none but my shister and myself left in the kitchen with Sir Condy, one opens the door, and walks in, and who should it be but Judy M'Quirk herself! I forgot to notice, that she had been married long since, whilst young Captain Moneygawl lived at the Lodge, to the captain's huntsman, who after a while listed and left her, and was killed in the wars. Poor Judy fell off greatly in her good looks after her being married a year or two; and being smoke-dried in the cabin, and neglecting herself like, it was hard for Sir Condy himself to know her again till she spoke; but when she says, 'It's Judy M'Quirk, please your honour, don't you remember her?' 'Oh, Judy, is it you?' says his honour; 'yes, sure, I remember you very well; but you're greatly altered, Judy.' 'Sure it's time for me,' says she; 'and I think your honour, since I *seen* you last, – but that's a great while ago, – is altered too.' 'And with reason, Judy,' says Sir Condy, fetching a sort of a sigh; 'but how's this, Judy?' he goes on; 'I take it a little amiss of you, that you were not at my wake last night.' 'Ah, don't be being jealous of that,' says she; 'I didn't hear a sentence of your honour's wake till it was all over, or it would have gone hard with me but I would have been at it sure; but I was forced to go ten miles up the country three days ago to a wedding of a relation of my own's, and didn't get home till after the wake was over; but,' says she, 'it won't be so, I hope, the next time,† please your honour.' 'That we shall see, Judy,' says his honour, 'and may be sooner than you think for, for I've been very unwell this while past, and don't

---

* *Shebean-house*, a hedge-alehouse. Shebean properly means weak small-beer, taplash.[40]
† At the coronation of one of our monarchs, the king complained of the confusion which happened in the procession. The great officer who presided told his majesty, 'That it should not be so next time.'

reckon any way I'm long for this world.' At this, Judy takes up the corner of her apron, and puts it first to one eye and then to t'other, being to all appearance in great trouble; and my shister put in her word, and bid his honour have a good heart, for she was sure it was only the gout, that Sir Patrick used to have flying about him, and he ought to drink a glass or a bottle extraordinary to keep it out of his stomach; and he promised to take her advice, and sent out for more spirits immediately; and Judy made a sign to me, and I went over to the door to her, and she said, 'I wonder to see Sir Condy so low! has he heard the news?' 'What news?' says I. 'Didn't ye hear it, then?' says she; 'my lady Rackrent that was is kilt^G and lying for dead, and I don't doubt but it's all over with her by this time.' 'Mercy on us all,' says I; 'how was it?' 'The jaunting car it was that ran away with her,' says Judy. 'I was coming home that same time from Biddy M'Guggin's marriage, and a great crowd of people too upon the road, coming from the fair of Crookaghnawaturgh, and I sees a jaunting car standing in the middle of the road, and with the two wheels off and all tattered. "What's this?" says I. "Didn't ye hear of it?" says they that were looking on; "it's my lady Rackrent's car, that was running away from her husband, and the horse took fright at a carrion that lay across the road, and so ran away with the jaunting car, and my lady Rackrent and her maid screaming, and the horse ran with them against a car that was coming from the fair, with the boy asleep on it, and the lady's petticoat hanging out of the jaunting car caught, and she was dragged I can't tell you how far upon the road, and it all broken up with the stones just going to be pounded, and one of the road-makers, with his sledge-hammer in his hand, stops the horse at the last; but my lady Rackrent was all kilt* and smashed, and they lifted her into a cabin hard by, and the maid was found after, where she had been thrown, in the gripe of the ditch, her cap and bonnet all full of bog water, and they say my lady can't live any way." Thady, pray now is it true what I'm told

---

* *Kilt and smashed.* – Our author is not here guilty of an anti-climax. The mere English reader, from a similarity of sound between the words *kilt* and *killed*, might be induced to suppose that their meanings are similar, yet they are not by any means in Ireland synonymous terms. Thus you may hear a man exclaim, 'I'm kilt and murdered!' but he frequently means only that he has received a black eye, or a slight contusion. – *I'm kilt all over* means that he is in a worse state than being simply *kilt*. Thus, *I'm kilt with the cold* is nothing to *I'm kilt all over with the rheumatism.*^G

for sartain, that Sir Condy has made over all to your son Jason?'
'All,' says I. 'All entirely?' says she again. 'All entirely,' says I.
'Then,' says she, 'that's a great shame, but don't be telling Jason
what I say.' 'And what is it you say?' cries Sir Condy, leaning over
betwixt us, which made Judy start greatly. 'I know the time when
Judy M'Quirk would never have stayed so long talking at the door,
and I in the house.' 'Oh!' says Judy, 'for shame, Sir Condy; times
are altered since then, and it's my lady Rackrent you ought to be
thinking of.' 'And why should I be thinking of her, that's not thinking of me now?' says Sir Condy. 'No matter for that,' says Judy,
very properly; 'it's time you should be thinking of her, if ever you
mean to do it at all, for don't you know she's lying for death?' 'My
lady Rackrent!' says Sir Condy, in a surprise; 'why it's but two days
since we parted, as you very well know, Thady, in her full health
and spirits, and she and her maid along with her going to Mount
Juliet's town on her jaunting car.' 'She'll never ride no more on her
jaunting car,' said Judy, 'for it has been the death of her, sure
enough.' 'And is she dead, then?' says his honour. 'As good as dead,
I hear,' says Judy; 'but there's Thady here has just learnt the whole
truth of the story as I had it, and it is fitter he or any body else
should be telling it you than I, Sir Condy: I must be going home to
the childer.' But he stops her, but rather from civility in him, as I
could see very plainly, than any thing else, for Judy was, as his
honour remarked at her first coming in, greatly changed, and little
likely, as far as I could see – though she did not seem to be clear of it
herself – little likely to be my lady Rackrent now, should there be a
second toss-up to be made. But I told him the whole story out of the
face, just as Judy had told it to me, and he sent off a messenger with
his compliments to Mount Juliet's town that evening, to learn the
truth of the report, and Judy bid the boy that was going call in at
Tim M'Enerney's shop in O'Shaughlin's town and buy her a new
shawl. 'Do so,' said Sir Condy, 'and tell Tim to take no money from
you, for I must pay him for the shawl myself.' At this my shister
throws me over a look, and I·says nothing, but turned the tobacco
in my mouth, whilst Judy began making a many words about it,
and saying how she could not be beholden for shawls to any gentleman. I left her there to consult with my shister, did she think there
was any thing in it, and my shister thought I was blind to be asking
her the question, and I thought my shister must see more into it

than I did; and recollecting all past times and every thing, I changed my mind, and came over to her way of thinking, and we settled it that Judy was very like to be my lady Rackrent after all, if a vacancy should have happened.

The next day, before his honour was up, somebody comes with a double knock at the door, and I was greatly surprised to see it was my son Jason. 'Jason, is it you?' said I; 'what brings you to the Lodge?' says I; 'is it my lady Rackrent? we know that already since yesterday.' 'May be so,' says he, 'but I must see Sir Condy about it.' 'You can't see him yet,' says I; 'sure he is not awake.' 'What then,' says he, 'can't he be wakened? and I standing at the door.' 'I'll not be disturbing his honour for you, Jason,' says I; 'many's the hour you've waited in your time, and been proud to do it, till his honour was at leisure to speak to you. His honour,' says I, raising my voice, at which his honour wakens of his own accord, and calls to me from the room to know who it was I was speaking to. Jason made no more ceremony, but follows me into the room. 'How are you, Sir Condy?' says he; 'I'm happy to see you looking so well; I came up to know how you did to-day, and to see did you want for any thing at the Lodge.' 'Nothing at all, Mr Jason, I thank you,' says he; for his honour had his own share of pride, and did not choose, after all that had passed, to be beholden, I suppose, to my son; 'but pray take a chair and be seated, Mr Jason.' Jason sat him down upon the chest, for chair there was none, and after he had sat there some time, and a silence on all sides, 'What news is there stirring in the country, Mr Jason M'Quirk?' says Sir Condy very easy, yet high like. 'None that's news to you, Sir Condy, I hear,' says Jason: 'I am sorry to hear of my lady Rackrent's accident.' 'I'm much obliged to you, and so is her ladyship, I'm sure,' answered Sir Condy, still stiff; and there was another sort of a silence, which seemed to lie the heaviest on my son Jason.

'Sir Condy,' says he at last, seeing Sir Condy disposing himself to go to sleep again, 'Sir Condy, I dare say you recollect mentioning to me the little memorandum you gave to Lady Rackrent about the £500 a-year jointure.' 'Very true,' said Sir Condy; 'it is all in my recollection.' 'But if my lady Rackrent dies, there's an end of all jointure,' says Jason. 'Of course,' says Sir Condy. 'But it's not a matter of certainty that my lady Rackrent won't recover,' says Jason. 'Very true, sir,' says my master. 'It's a fair speculation, then, for you to consider what the chance of the jointure on those lands, when out of custodiam, will be to you.' 'Just five hundred a-year, I take it, without any speculation at all,' said Sir Condy. 'That's supposing the life dropt, and the custodiam off, you know; begging your pardon, Sir Condy, who understands business, that is a wrong calculation.' 'Very likely so,' said Sir Condy; 'but, Mr Jason, if you have any thing to say to me this morning about it, I'd be obliged to you to say it, for I had an indifferent night's rest last night, and wouldn't be sorry to sleep a little this morning.' 'I have only three words to say, and those more of consequence to you, Sir Condy, than me. You are a little cool, I observe; but I hope you will not be offended at what I have brought here in my pocket,' and he pulls out two long rolls, and showers down golden guineas upon the bed. 'What's this?' said Sir Condy; 'it's long since' – but his pride stops him. 'All these are your lawful property this minute, Sir Condy, if you please,' said Jason. 'Not for nothing, I'm sure,' said Sir Condy, and laughs a little – 'nothing for nothing, or I'm under a mistake with you, Jason.' 'Oh, Sir Condy, we'll not be indulging ourselves in any unpleasant retrospects,' says Jason; 'it's my present intention to behave, as I'm sure you will, like a gentleman in this affair. Here's two hundred guineas, and a third I mean to add, if you should think proper to make over to me all your right and title to those lands that you know of.' 'I'll consider of it,' said my master; and a great deal more, that I was tired listening to, was said by Jason, and all that, and the sight of the ready cash upon the bed worked with his honour; and the short and the long of it was, Sir Condy gathered up the golden guineas, and tied them up in a handkerchief, and signed some paper Jason brought with him as usual, and there was an end of the business; Jason took himself away, and my master turned himself round and fell asleep again.

I soon found what had put Jason in such a hurry to conclude this business. The little gossoon we had sent off the day before with my master's compliments to Mount Juliet's town, and to know how my lady did after her accident, was stopped early this morning, coming back with his answer through O'Shaughlin's town, at Castle Rackrent, by my son Jason, and questioned of all he knew of my lady from the servant at Mount Juliet's town; and the gossoon told him my lady Rackrent was not expected to live over night; so Jason thought it high time to be moving to the Lodge, to make his bargain with my master about the jointure afore it should be too late, and afore the little gossoon should reach us with the news. My master was greatly vexed, that is, I may say, as much as ever I *seen* him, when he found how he had been taken in; but it was some comfort to have the ready cash for immediate consumption in the house, any way.

And when Judy came up that evening, and brought the childer to see his honour, he unties the handkerchief, and, God bless him! whether it was little or much he had, 'twas all the same with him, he gives 'em all round guineas a-piece. 'Hold up your head,' says my shister to Judy, as Sir Condy was busy filling out a glass of punch for her eldest boy – 'Hold up your head, Judy; for who knows but we may live to see you yet at the head of the Castle Rackrent estate?' 'May be so,' says she, 'but not the way you are thinking of.' I did not rightly understand which way Judy was looking when she makes this speech, till a-while after. 'Why, Thady, you were telling me yesterday, that Sir Condy had sold all entirely to Jason, and where then does all them guineas in the handkerchief come from?' 'They are the purchase-money of my lady's jointure,' says I. 'A penny for your thoughts, Judy,' says my shister; 'hark, sure Sir Condy is drinking her health.' He was at the table in *the room*,* drinking with the exciseman and the gauger,[41] who came up to see his honour, and we were standing over the fire in the kitchen. 'I don't much care is he drinking my health or not,' says Judy; 'and it is not Sir Condy I'm thinking of, with all your jokes, whatever he is of me.' 'Sure you wouldn't refuse to be my lady Rackrent, Judy, if you had the offer?' says I. 'But if I could do better!' says she. 'How better?' says I and my shister both at once. 'How better?' says she; 'why, what signifies it to be my lady Rackrent, and no castle? sure what good is the car, and no horse to draw it?' 'And where will ye get the horse, Judy?' says I. 'Never mind that,' says she; 'may be it is your own son Jason might find that.' 'Jason!' says I; 'don't be trusting to him, Judy. Sir Condy, as I have good reason to know, spoke well of you, when Jason spoke very indifferently of you, Judy.' 'No matter,' says Judy; 'it's often men speak the contrary just to what they think of us.' 'And you the same way of them, no doubt,' answers I. 'Nay, don't be denying it, Judy, for I think the better of ye for it, and shouldn't

* *The room* – the principal room in the house.

be proud to call ye the daughter of a shister's son of mine, if I was to hear ye talk ungrateful, and any way disrespectful of his honour.' 'What disrespect,' says she, 'to say I'd rather, if it was my luck, be the wife of another man?' 'You'll have no luck, mind my words, Judy,' says I; and all I remembered about my poor master's goodness in tossing up for her afore he married at all came across me, and I had a choaking in my throat that hindered me to say more. 'Better luck, any how, Thady,' says she, 'than to be like some folk, following the fortunes of them that have none left.' 'Oh! King of Glory!' says I, 'hear the pride and ungratitude of her, and he giving his last guineas but a minute ago to her childer, and she with the fine shawl on her he made her a present of but yesterday!' 'Oh, troth, Judy, you're wrong now,' says my shister, looking at the shawl. 'And was not he wrong yesterday, then,' says she, 'to be telling me I was greatly altered, to affront me?' 'But, Judy,' says I, 'what is it brings you here then at all in the mind you are in; is it to make Jason think the better of you?' 'I'll tell you no more of my secrets, Thady,' says she, 'nor would have told you this much, had I taken you for such an unnatural fader as I find you are, not to wish your own son preferred to another.' 'Oh, troth, *you* are wrong now, Thady,' says my shister. Well, I was never so put to it in my life: between these womens, and my son and my master, and all I felt and thought just now, I could not, upon my conscience, tell which was the wrong from the right. So I said not a word more, but was only glad his honour had not the luck to hear all Judy had been saying of him, for I reckoned it would have gone nigh to break his heart; not that I was of opinion he cared for her as much as she and my shister fancied, but the ungratitude of the whole from Judy might not plase him; and he could never stand the notion of not being well spoken of or beloved like behind his back. Fortunately for all parties concerned, he was so much elevated at this time, there was no danger of his understanding any thing, even if it had reached his ears. There was a great horn at the Lodge, ever since my master and Captain Moneygawl was in together, that used to belong originally to the celebrated Sir Patrick, his ancestor; and his honour was fond often of telling the story that he learned from me when a child, how Sir Patrick drank the full of this horn without stopping, and this was what no other man afore or since could without drawing breath. Now Sir Condy challenged the gauger, who seemed to think little of the horn, to swallow the contents, and had it filled to the brim with punch; and the gauger said it was what he could not do for nothing, but he'd hold Sir Condy a hundred guineas he'd do it. 'Done,' said my master; 'I'll lay you a hundred golden guineas to a tester* you don't.' 'Done,' says the gauger; and done and done's enough between two gentlemen. The gauger was cast, and my master won the bet, and thought he'd won a hundred guineas, but by the wording it was adjudged to be only a tester than was his due by the exciseman. It was all one to him; he was as well pleased, and I was glad to see him in such spirits again.

The gauger, bad luck to him! was the man that next proposed to my master to try himself could he take at a draught the contents of the great horn. 'Sir Patrick's horn!' said his honour; 'hand it to me: I'll hold you your own bet over again I'll swallow it.' 'Done,' says the gauger; 'I'll lay ye any thing at all you do no such thing.' 'A hundred guineas to sixpence I do,' says he: 'bring me the handkerchief.' I was loth, knowing he meant the handkerchief with the gold in it, to bring it out in such company, and his honour not very able to reckon it. 'Bring me the handkerchief, then, Thady,' says he, and stamps with his foot; so with that I pulls it out of my great coat pocket, where I had put it for safety. Oh, how it grieved me to see the guineas counting upon the table, and they the last my master had! Says Sir Condy to me, 'Your hand is steadier than mine to-night, old Thady, and that's a wonder; fill you the horn for me.' And so, wishing his honour success, I did; but I filled it, little thinking of what would befall him. He swallows it down, and drops like one shot. We lifts him up, and he was speechless, and quite black in the face. We put him to bed, and in a short time he wakened, raving with a fever on his brain. He was shocking either to see or hear. 'Judy! Judy! have you no touch of feeling? won't you stay to help us nurse him?' says I to her, and she putting on her shawl to go out of the house. 'I'm frightened to see him,' says she, 'and wouldn't nor couldn't stay in it; and what use? he can't last till the morning.' With that she ran off. There was none but my sister and myself left near him of all the many friends he had. The fever came and went, and came and went, and lasted five days, and the sixth he was

* *Tester* – sixpence; from the French word tête, a head: a piece of silver stamped with a head, which in old French was called 'un testion', and which was about the value of an old English sixpence. Tester is used in Shakspeare.

sensible for a few minutes, and said to me, knowing me very well. 'I'm in burning pain all withinside of me, Thady.' I could not speak, but my shister asked him would he have this thing or t'other to do him good? 'No,' says he, 'nothing will do me good no more,' and he gave a terrible screech with the torture he was in – then again in a minute's ease – 'brought to this by drink,' says he; 'where are all the friends? – where's Judy? – Gone, hey? Ay, Sir Condy has been a fool all his days,' said he; and there was the last word he spoke, and died. He had but a very poor funeral, after all.

If you want to know any more, I'm not very well able to tell you; but my lady Rackrent did not die, as was expected of her, but was only disfigured in the face ever after by the fall and bruises she got; and she and Jason, immediately after my poor master's death, set about going to law about that jointure; the memorandum not being on stamped paper, some say it is worth nothing, others again it may do; others say, Jason won't have the lands at any rate. Many wishes it so: for my part, I'm tired wishing for any thing in this world, after all I've seen in it – but I'll say nothing; it would be a folly to be getting myself ill-will in my old age. Jason did not marry, nor think of marrying Judy, as I prophesied and I am not sorry for it; who is? As for all I have here set down from memory and hearsay of the family, there's nothing but truth in it from beginning to end: that you may depend upon; for where's the use of telling lies about the things which every body knows as well as I do?

The Editor could have readily made the catastrophe of Sir Condy's history more dramatic and more pathetic, if he thought it allowable to varnish the plain round tale of faithful Thady. He lays it before the English reader as a specimen of manners and characters, which are, perhaps, unknown in England. Indeed, the domestic habits of no nation in Europe were less known to the English than those of their sister country, till within these few years.

Mr Young's picture of Ireland, in his tour through that country, was the first faithful portrait of its inhabitants.[42] All the features in the foregoing sketch were taken from the life, and they are characteristic of that mixture of quickness, simplicity, cunning, carelessness, dissipation, disinterestedness, shrewdness, and blunder, which, in different forms, and with various success, has been brought upon the stage, or delineated in novels.

It is a problem of difficult solution to determine, whether an Union will hasten or retard the melioration of this country. The few gentlemen of education, who now reside in this country, will resort to England: they are few, but they are in nothing inferior to men of the same rank in Great Britain. The best that can happen will be the introduction of British manufacturers in their places.

Did the Warwickshire militia, who were chiefly artisans, teach the Irish to drink beer? or did they learn from the Irish to drink whiskey?[43]

1800.

Some friends, who have seen Thady's history since it has been printed, have suggested to the Editor that many of the terms and idiomatic phrases, with which it abounds, could not be intelligible to the English reader without further explanation. The Editor has therefore furnished the following Glossary. [45]

Page 65. *Monday morning.* – Thady begins his memoirs of the Rackrent Family by dating *Monday morning*, because no great undertaking can be auspiciously commenced in Ireland on any morning but *Monday morning.* 'O, please God we live till Monday morning, we'll set the slater to mend the roof of the house. On Monday morning we'll fall to, and cut the turf. On Monday morning we'll see and begin mowing. On Monday morning, please your honour, we'll begin and dig the potatoes,' &c.

All the intermediate days, between the making of such speeches and the ensuing Monday, are wasted: and when Monday morning comes, it is ten to one that the business is deferred to *the next* Monday morning. The Editor knew a gentleman, who, to counteract this prejudice, made his workmen and labourers begin all new pieces of work upon a Saturday.

Page 66. *Let alone the three kingdoms itself.* – *Let alone*, in this sentence, means *put out of consideration*. The phrase, *let alone*, which is now used as the imperative of a verb, may in time become a conjunction, and may exercise the ingenuity of some future etymologist. The celebrated Horne Tooke has proved most satisfactorily, that the conjunction *but* comes from the imperative of the Anglo-Saxon verb (*bouant*) *to be out;* also that *if* comes from *gift,* the imperative of the Anglo-Saxon verb which signifies *to give,* &c. [46]

Page 68. *Whillaluh*. – Ullaloo, Gol, or lamentation over the dead –

> 'Magnoque ululante tumultu.' – VIRGIL.

> 'Ululatibus omne
> Implevere nemus.' – OVID.

A full account of the Irish Gol, or Ullaloo, and of the Caoinan or Irish funeral song, with its first semichorus, second semichorus, full chorus of sighs and groans, together with the Irish words and music, may be found in the fourth volume of the transactions of the Royal Irish Academy. For the advantage of *lazy* readers, who would rather read a page than walk a yard, and from compassion, not to say sympathy, with their infirmity, the Editor transcribes the following passages:

'The Irish have been always remarkable for their funeral lamentations, and this peculiarity has been noticed by almost every traveller who visited them; and it seems derived from their Celtic ancestors, the primæval inhabitants of this isle . . .

'It has been affirmed of the Irish, that to cry was more natural to them than to any other nation, and at length the Irish cry became proverbial . . .

'Cambrensis in the twelfth century says, the Irish then musically expressed their griefs; that is, they applied the musical art, in which they excelled all others, to the orderly celebration of funeral obsequies, by dividing the mourners into two bodies, each alternately singing their part, and the whole at times joining in full chorus . . . The body of the deceased, dressed in grave clothes, and ornamented with flowers, was placed on a bier, or some elevated spot. The relations and keepers (*singing mourners*) ranged themselves in two divisions, one at the head, and the other at the feet of the corpse. The bards and croteries had before prepared the funeral Caoinan. The chief bard of the head chorus began by singing the first stanza in a low, doleful tone, which was softly accompanied by the harp; at the conclusion, the foot semichorus began the lamentation, or Ullaloo, from the final note of the preceding stanza, in which they were answered by the head semichorus; then both united in one general chorus. The chorus of the first stanza being ended, the chief bard of the foot semichorus began the second Gol or lamentation, in which he was answered by that of the head; and then, as before, both united in the general full chorus. Thus alternately were the song and choruses performed during the night. The genealogy, rank, possessions, the virtues and vices of the dead were rehearsed, and a number of interrogations were addressed to the deceased; as, Why did he die? If married, whether his wife was faithful to him, his sons dutiful, or good hunters or warriors? If a woman, whether her daughters were fair or chaste? If a young man, whether he had been crossed in love; or if the blue-eyed maids of Erin treated him with scorn?'[47]

We are told, that formerly the feet (the metrical feet) of the Caoinan were much attended to; but on the decline of the Irish bards these feet were gradually neglected, and the Caoinan fell into a sort of slipshod metre amongst women. Each province had different Caoinans, or at least different imitations of the original. There was the Munster cry, the Ulster cry, &c. It became an extempore performance, and every set of keepers varied the melody according to their own fancy.

It is curious to observe how customs and ceremonies degenerate. The present Irish cry, or howl, cannot boast of such melody, nor is the funeral procession conducted with much dignity. The crowd of people who assemble at these funerals sometimes amounts to a thousand, often to four or five hundred. They gather as the bearers of the hearse proceed on their way, and when they pass through any village, or when they come near any houses, they begin to cry – Oh! Oh! Oh! Oh! Oh! Agh! Agh! raising their notes from the first *Oh!* to the last *Agh!* in a kind of mournful howl. This gives notice to the inhabitants of the village that a *funeral is passing*, and immediately they flock out to follow it. In the province of Munster it is a common thing for the women to follow a funeral, to join in the universal cry with all their might and main for some time, and then to turn and ask – 'Arrah! who is it that's dead? – who is it we're crying for?' Even the poorest people have their own burying-places, that is, spots of ground in the church-yards, where they say that their ancestors have been buried ever since the wars of Ireland; and if these burial-places are ten miles from the place where a man dies, his friends and neighbours take care to carry his corpse thither. Always one priest, often five or six priests, attend these funerals; each priest repeats a mass, for which he is paid, sometimes a shilling, sometimes half-a-crown, sometimes half-a-guinea, or a guinea, according to their circumstances, or, as they say, according to the *ability* of the deceased. After the burial of any very poor man, who has left a widow or children, the priest makes what is called a *collection* for the widow; he goes round to every person present, and each contributes sixpence or a shilling, or what they please. The reader will find in the note upon the word *Wake*, p. 137, more particulars respecting the conclusion of the Irish funerals.

Certain old women, who cry particularly loud and well, are in great request, and, as a man said to the Editor, 'Every one would wish and be proud to have such at his funeral, or at that of his friends.' The lower Irish are wonderfully eager to attend the funerals of their friends and relations, and they make their relationships branch out to a great extent. The proof that a poor man has been well beloved during his life is his having a crowded funeral. To attend a neighbour's funeral is a cheap proof of humanity, but it does not, as some imagine, cost nothing. The time spent in attending funerals may be safely valued at half a million to the Irish nation; the Editor thinks that double that sum would not be too high an estimate. The habits of profligacy and drunkenness, which are acquired at *wakes*, are here put out of the question. When a labourer, a carpenter, or a smith, is not at his work, which frequently happens, ask where he is gone, and ten to one the answer is – 'Oh faith, please your honour, he couldn't do a stroke to-day, for he's gone to *the* funeral.'

Even beggars, when they grow old, go about begging *for their own funerals;* that is, begging for money to buy a coffin, candles, pipes and tobacco. For the use of the candles, pipes, and tobacco, see *Wake*.

Those who value customs in proportion to their antiquity, and nations in proportion to their adherence to ancient customs, will, doubtless, admire the Irish *Ullaloo*, and the Irish nation, for persevering in this usage from time immemorial. The Editor, however, has observed some alarming symptoms, which seem to prognosticate the declining taste for the Ullaloo in Ireland. In a comic theatrical entertainment, represented not long since on the Dublin stage, a chorus of old women was introduced, who set up the Irish howl round the relics of a physician, who is supposed to have fallen under the wooden sword of Harlequin. After the old women have continued their Ullaloo for a decent time, with all the necessary accompaniments of wringing their hands, wiping or rubbing their eyes with the corners of their gowns or aprons, &c. one of the mourners suddenly suspends her lamentable cries, and, turning to her neighbour, asks, 'Arrah now, honey, who is it we're crying for?'

Page 68. *The tenants were sent away without their whiskey.* – It is usual with some landlords to give their inferior tenants a glass of whiskey when they pay their rents. Thady calls it *their* whiskey; not that the whiskey is actually the property of the tenants, but that it becomes their *right* after it has been often given to them. In this general mode of reasoning respecting *rights* the lower Irish are not singular, but they are peculiarly quick and tenacious in claiming these rights. 'Last year your honour gave me some straw for the roof of my house, and I *expect* your honour will be after doing the same this year.' In this manner gifts are frequently turned into tributes. The high and low are not always dissimilar in their habits. It is said, that the Sublime Ottoman Porte is very apt to claim gifts as tributes: thus it is dangerous to send the Grand Seignor a fine horse on his birthday one year, lest on his next birthday he should expect a similar present, and should proceed to demonstrate the reasonableness of his expectations.

Page 68. *He demeaned himself greatly* – means, he lowered or disgraced himself much.

Page 69. *Duty fowls, and duty turkies, and duty geese.* – In many leases in Ireland, tenants were *formerly* bound to supply an inordinate quantity of poultry to their landlords. The Editor knew of thirty turkies[48] being reserved in one lease of a small farm.

Page 69. *English tenants.* – An English tenant does not mean a tenant who is an Englishman, but a tenant who pays his rent the day that it is due. It is a common prejudice in Ireland, amongst the poorer classes of people, to believe that all tenants in England pay their rents on the very day when they become due. An Irishman, when he goes to take a farm, if he wants to prove to his landlord that he is a substantial man, offers to become an *English tenant*. If a tenant disobliges his landlord by voting against him, or against his opinion, at an election, the tenant is immediately informed by the agent, that he must become an *English tenant*. This threat does not imply that he is to change his language or his country, but that he must pay all the arrear of rent which he owes, and that he must thenceforward pay his rent on that day when it becomes due.

Page 69. *Canting* – does not mean talking or writing hypocritical nonsense, but selling substantially by auction.

Page 70. *Duty work*. – It was formerly common in Ireland to insert clauses in leases, binding tenants to furnish their landlords with labourers and horses for several days in the year. Much petty tyranny and oppression have resulted from this feudal custom. Whenever a poor man disobliged his landlord, the agent sent to him for his duty work, and Thady does not exaggerate when he says, that the tenants were often called from their own work to do that of their landlord. Thus the very means of earning their rent were taken from them: whilst they were getting home their landlord's harvest, their own was often ruined, and yet their rents were expected to be paid as punctually as if their time had been at their own disposal. This appears the height of absurd injustice.

In Esthonia, amongst the poor Sclavonian race of peasant slaves, they pay tributes to their lords, not under the name of duty work, duty geese, duty turkies, &c., but under the name of *righteousnesses*. The following ballad is a curious specimen of Esthonian poetry: –

> This is the cause that the country is ruined,
> And the straw of the thatch is eaten away,
> The gentry are come to live in the land –
> Chimneys between the village,
> And the proprietor upon the white floor!
> The sheep brings forth a lamb with a white forehead,
>   This is paid to the lord for a *righteousness sheep*.
> The sow farrows pigs,
> They go to the spit of the lord.
> The hen lays eggs,
> They go into the lord's frying-pan.
> The cow drops a male calf,
> That goes into the lord's herd as a bull.
> The mare foals a horse foal,
> That must be for my lord's nag.

The boor's wife has sons,
They must go to look after my lord's poultry.[49]

Page 70. *Out of forty-nine suits which he had, he never lost one but seventeen.* – Thady's language in this instance is a specimen of a mode of rhetoric common in Ireland. An astonishing assertion is made in the beginning of a sentence, which ceases to be in the least surprising, when you hear the qualifying explanation that follows. Thus a man who is in the last stage of staggering drunkenness will, if he can articulate, swear to you – 'Upon his conscience now, and may he never stir from the spot alive if he is telling a lie, upon his conscience he has not tasted a drop of any thing, good or bad, since morning at-all-at-all, but half a pint of whiskey, please your honour.'

Page 71. *Fairy mounts* – Barrows. It is said that these high mounts were of great service to the natives of Ireland when Ireland was invaded by the Danes. Watch was always kept on them, and upon the approach of an enemy a fire was lighted to give notice to the next watch, and thus the intelligence was quickly communicated through the country. *Some years ago*, the common people believed that these barrows were inhabited by fairies, or, as they called them, by the *good people*. 'O troth, to the best of my belief, and to the best of my judgement and opinion,' said an elderly man to the Editor, 'it was only the old people that had nothing to do, and got together, and were telling stories about them fairies, but to the best of my judgement there's nothing in it. Only this I heard myself not very many years back from a decent kind of a man, a grazier, that as he was coming just *fair and easy* (*quietly*) from the fair, with some cattle and sheep, that he had not sold, just at the church of —, at an angle of the road like, he was met by a good-looking man, who asked him where he was going? And he answered, "Oh, far enough, I must be going all night." "No, that you mustn't nor won't (says the man), you'll sleep with me the night, and you'll want for nothing, nor your cattle nor sheep neither, nor your *beast* (*horse*); so come along with me." With that the grazier *lit* (*alighted*) from his horse, and it was dark night; but presently he finds himself, he does not know in the wide world how, in a fine house, and plenty of every thing to eat and drink; nothing at all wanting that he could wish for or think of. And he does not *mind* (*recollect* or *know*) how at last he falls asleep;

and in the morning he finds himself lying, not in ever a bed or a house at all, but just in the angle of the road where first he met the strange man: there he finds himself lying on his back on the grass, and all his sheep feeding as quiet as ever all round about him, and his horse the same way, and the bridle of the beast over his wrist. And I asked him what he thought of it; and from first to last he could think of nothing, but for certain sure it must have been the fairies that entertained him so well. For there was no house to see any where nigh hand, or any building, or barn, or place at all, but only the church and the *mote* (*barrow*). There's another odd thing enough that they tell about this same church, that if any person's corpse, that had not a right to be buried in that church-yard, went to be burying there in it, no, not all the men, women, or childer in all Ireland could get the corpse any way into the church-yard; but as they would be trying to go into the church-yard, their feet would seem to be going backwards instead of forwards; ay, continually backwards the whole funeral would seem to go; and they would never set foot with the corpse in the church-yard. Now they say that it is the fairies do all this; but it is my opinion it is all idle talk, and people are after being wiser now.'

The country people in Ireland certainly *had* great admiration mixed with reverence, if not dread, of fairies. They believed that beneath these fairy-mounts were spacious subterraneous palaces, inhabited by *the good people*, who must not on any account be disturbed. When the wind raises a little eddy of dust upon the road, the poor people believe that it is raised by the fairies, that it is a sign that they are journeying from one of the fairies' mounts to another, and they say to the fairies, or to the dust as it passes, 'God speed ye, gentlemen; God speed ye.' This averts any evil that *the good people* might be inclined to do them. There are innumerable stories told of the friendly and unfriendly feats of these busy fairies; some of these tales are ludicrous, and some romantic enough for poetry. It is a pity that poets should lose such convenient, though diminutive machinery. By-the-bye, Parnell,[50] who showed himself so deeply 'skilled in faerie lore', was an Irishman; and though he has presented his faeries to the world in the ancient English dress of 'Britain's isle, and Arthur's days', it is probable that his first acquaintance with them began in his native country.

Some remote origin for the most superstitious or romantic popular illusions or vulgar errors may often be discovered. In Ireland, the old churches and church-yards have been usually fixed upon as the scenes of wonders. Now the antiquarians tell us, that near the ancient churches in that kingdom caves of various constructions have from time to time been discovered, which were formerly used as granaries or magazines by the ancient inhabitants, and as places to which they retreated in time of danger. There is (p. 84 of the R.I.A. Transactions for 1789) a particular account of a number of these artificial caves at the west end of the church of Killossy, in the county of Kildare. Under a rising ground, in a dry sandy soil, these subterraneous dwellings were found: they have pediment roofs, and they communicate with each other by small apertures. In the Brehon laws these are mentioned, and there are fines inflicted by those laws upon persons who steal from the subterraneous granaries. All these things show that there was a real foundation for the stories which were told of the appearance of lights, and of the sounds of voices near these places. The persons who had property concealed there very willingly countenanced every wonderful relation that tended to make these places objects of sacred awe or superstitious terror.

Page 71. *Weed ashes.* – By ancient usage in Ireland, all the weeds on a farm belonged to the farmer's wife, or to the wife of the squire who holds the ground in his own hands. The great demand for alkaline salts in bleaching rendered these ashes no inconsiderable perquisite.

Page 71. *Sealing money.* – Formerly it was the custom in Ireland for tenants to give the squire's lady from two to fifty guineas as a perquisite upon the sealing of their leases. The Editor not very long since knew of a baronet's lady accepting fifty guineas as sealing money, upon closing a bargain for a considerable farm.

Page 71. *Sir Murtagh grew mad.* – Sir Murtagh grew angry.

Page 72. *The whole kitchen was out on the stairs* – means that all the inhabitants of the kitchen came out of the kitchen, and stood upon the stairs. These, and similar expressions, show how much the Irish are disposed to metaphor and amplification.

Page 74. *Fining down the yearly* [*year's*] rent. – When an Irish gentleman, like Sir Kit Rackrent, has lived beyond his income, and finds himself distressed for ready money, tenants obligingly offer to take his land at a rent far below the value, and to pay him a small sum of money in hand, which they call fining down the yearly rent. The temptation of this ready cash often blinds the landlord to his future interest.

Page 74. *Driver*. – A man who is employed to drive tenants for rent; that is, to drive the cattle belonging to tenants to pound. The office of driver is by no means a sinecure.

Page 74. *I thought to make him a priest*. – It was customary amongst those of Thady's rank in Ireland, whenever they could get a little money, to send their sons abroad to St Omer's, or to Spain, to be educated as priests. Now they are educated at Maynooth.[51] The Editor has lately known a young lad, who began by being a post-boy, afterwards turn into a carpenter, then quit his plane and work-bench to study his *Humanities*, as he said, at the college of Maynooth; but after he had gone through his course of Humanities, he determined to be a soldier instead of a priest.

Page 76. *Flam*. – Short for flambeau.

Page 77. *Barrack-room*. – Formerly it was customary, in gentlemen's houses in Ireland, to fit up one large bedchamber with a number of beds for the reception of occasional visitors. These rooms were called Barrack-rooms.

Page 77. *An innocent* – in Ireland, means a simpleton, and idiot.

Page 82. *The Curragh* – is the Newmarket of Ireland.[52]

Page 82. *The cant*. – The auction.

Page 86. *And so should cut him off for ever, by levying a fine, and suffering a recovery to dock the entail*. – The English reader may perhaps be surprised at the extent of Thady's legal knowledge, and at the fluency with which he pours forth law-terms; but almost every poor man in Ireland, be he farmer, weaver, shopkeeper, or steward, is, beside his other occupations, occasionally a lawyer. The nature of processes, ejectments, custodiams, injunctions, replevins, &c. is perfectly known to them, and the terms as familiar to them as to any attorney. They all love law. It is a kind of lottery, in which every man, staking his own wit or cunning against his neighbour's property, feels that he has little to lose, and much to gain.

'I'll have the law of you, so I will!' is the saying of an Englishman who expects justice. 'I'll have you before his honour' is the threat of an Irishman who hopes for partiality. Miserable is the life of a justice of the peace in Ireland the day after a fair, especially if he resides near a small town. The multitude of the *kilt* (*kilt* does not mean *killed*, but hurt) and wounded who come before his honour with black eyes or bloody heads is astonishing: but more astonishing is the number of those who, though they are scarcely able by daily labour to procure daily food, will nevertheless, without the least reluctance, waste six or seven hours of the day lounging in the yard or hall of a justice of the peace, waiting to make some complaint about – nothing. It is impossible to convince them that *time is money*. They do not set any value upon their own time, and they think that others estimate theirs at less than nothing. Hence they make no scruple of telling a justice of the peace a story of an hour long about a *tester* (sixpence); and if he grows impatient, they attribute it to some secret prejudice which he entertains against them.

Their method is to get a story completely by heart, and to tell it, as they call it, *out of the face*, that is, from the beginning to the end, without interruption.

'Well, my good friend, I have seen you lounging about these three hours in the yard; what is your business?'

'Please your honour, it is what I want to speak one word to your honour.'

'Speak then, but be quick – What is the matter?'

'The matter, please your honour, is nothing at-all-at-all, only just about the grazing of a horse, please your honour, that this man here sold me at the fair of Gurtishannon last Shrove fair, which lay down three times with myself, please your honour, and *kilt* me; not to be telling your honour of how, no later back than yesterday night, he lay down in the house there within, and all the childer standing round, and it was God's mercy he did not fall a-top of them, or into the fire to burn himself. So, please your honour, to-day I took him back to this man, which owned him, and after a great deal to do I got the mare again I *swopped* (*exchanged*) him for; but he won't pay the grazing of the horse for the time I had him, though he promised to pay the grazing in case the horse didn't answer; and he never did a day's work, good or bad, please your honour, all the time he was with me, and I had the doctor to him five times any how. And so, please your honour, it is what I expect your honour will stand my friend, for I'd sooner come to your honour for justice than to any other in all Ireland. And so I brought him here before your honour, and expect your honour will make him pay me the grazing, or tell me, can I process him for it at the next assizes, please your honour?'

The defendant now turning a quid of tobacco with his tongue into some secret cavern in his mouth, begins his defence with –

'Please your honour, under favour, and saving your honour's presence, there's not a word of truth in all this man has been saying from beginning to end, upon my conscience, and I wouldn't, for the value of the horse itself, grazing and all, be after telling your honour a lie. For, please your honour, I have a dependence upon your honour that you'll do me justice, and not be listening to him or the like of him. Please your honour, it's what he has brought me before your honour, because he had a spite against me about some oats I sold your honour, which he was jealous of, and a shawl his wife got at my shister's shop there without, and never paid for; so I offered to set the shawl against the grazing, and give him a receipt in full of all demands, but he wouldn't out of spite, please your honour; so he brought me before your honour, expecting your honour was mad with me for cutting down the tree in the horse park, which was none of my doing, please your honour – ill luck to them that went and belied me to your honour behind my back! So if your honour is pleasing, I'll tell you the whole truth about the horse that he swopped against my mare out of the face. Last Shrove fair I met this man, Jemmy Duffy, please your honour, just at the corner of the road, where the bridge is broken down, that your honour is to have the presentment for this year – long life to you for it! And he was at that time coming from the fair of Gurtishannon, and I the same way, "How are you, Jemmy?" says I. "Very well, I thank ye, kindly, Bryan," says he; "shall we turn back to Paddy Salmon's and take a naggin[53] of whiskey to our better acquaintance?" "I don't care if I did, Jemmy," says I; "only it is what I can't take the whiskey, because I'm under an oath against it for a month." Ever since, please your honour, the day your honour met me on the road, and observed to me I could hardly stand, I had taken so much; though upon my conscience your honour wronged me greatly that same time – ill luck to them that belied me behind my back to your honour! Well, please your honour, as I was telling you, as he was taking the whiskey, and we talking of one thing or t'other, he makes me an offer to swop his mare that he couldn't sell at the fair of Gurtishannon, because nobody would be troubled with the beast, please your honour, against my horse, and to oblige him I took the mare – sorrow take her! and him along with her! She kicked me a new car, that was worth three pounds ten, to tatters the first time I ever put her into it, and I expect your honour will make him pay me the price of the car, any how, before I pay the grazing, which I've no right to pay at-all-at-all, only to oblige him. But I leave it all to your honour; and the whole grazing he ought to be charging for the beast is but two and eightpence halfpenny, any how, please your honour. So I'll abide by what your honour says, good or bad. I'll leave it all to your honour.'

I'll leave *it* all to your honour – literally means, I'll leave all the trouble to your honour.

The Editor knew a justice of the peace in Ireland, who had such a dread of *having it all left to his honour*, that he frequently gave the complainants the sum about which they were disputing, to make peace between them, and to get rid of the trouble of hearing their stories *out of the face*. But he was soon cured of this method of buying off disputes, by the increasing multitude of those who, out of pure regard to his honour, came 'to get justice from him, because they would sooner come before him than before any man in all Ireland'.

Page 95. *A raking pot of tea.* – We should observe, this custom has long since been banished from the higher orders of Irish gentry. The mysteries of a raking pot of tea, like those of the Bona Dea,[54] are supposed to be sacred to females; but now and then it has happened, that some of the male species, who were either more audacious or more highly favoured than the rest of their sex, have been admitted by stealth to these orgies. The time when the festive ceremony begins varies according to circumstances, but it is never earlier than twelve o'clock at night; the joys of a raking pot of tea depending on its being made in secret, and at an unseasonable hour. After a ball, when the more discreet part of the company has departed to rest, a few chosen female spirits, who have footed it till they can foot it no longer, and till the sleepy notes expire under the slurring hand of the musician, retire to a bedchamber, call the favourite maid, who alone is admitted, bid her *put down the kettle*, lock the door, and amidst as much giggling and scrambling as possible, they get round a tea-table, on which all manner of things are huddled together. Then begin mutual railleries and mutual confidences amongst the young ladies, and the faint scream and the loud laugh is heard, and the romping for letters and pocket-books begins, and gentlemen are called by their surnames, or by the general name of fellows! pleasant fellows! charming fellows! odious fellows! abominable fellows! and then all prudish decorums are forgotten, and then we might be convinced how much the satirical poet was mistaken when he said,

'There is no woman where there's no reserve.'[55]

The merit of the original idea of a raking pot of tea evidently belongs to the washerwoman and the laundry-maid. But why should not we have *Low life above stairs as well as High life below stairs?*[56]

Page 96.[57] *We gained the day by this piece of honesty.* – In a dispute which occurred some years ago in Ireland, between Mr E. and Mr M., about the boundaries of a farm, an old tenant of Mr M.'s cut a *sod* from Mr M.'s land, and inserted it in a spot prepared for its reception in Mr E.'s land; so nicely was it inserted, that no eye could detect the junction of the grass. The old man, who was to give his evidence as to the property, stood upon the inserted sod when the *viewers* came, and swore that the ground he *then stood upon* belonged to his landlord, Mr M.

The Editor had flattered himself that the ingenious contrivance which Thady records, and the similar subterfuge of this old Irishman, in the dispute concerning boundaries, were instances of *'cuteness* unparalleled in all but Irish story: an English friend, however, has just mortified the Editor's national vanity by an account of the following custom, which prevails in part of Shropshire. It is discreditable for women to appear abroad after the birth of their children till they have been *churched*. To avoid this reproach, and at the same time to enjoy the pleasure of gadding, whenever a woman goes abroad before she has been to church, she takes a tile from the roof of her house, and puts it upon her head: wearing this panoply all the time she pays her visits, her conscience is perfectly at ease; for she can afterwards safely declare to the clergyman, that she 'has never been from under her own roof till she came to be churched'.

Page 98. *Carton, or half carton.* – Thady means cartron, or half cartron. 'According to the old record in the black book of Dublin, a *cantred* is said to contain 30 *villatas terras*, which are also called *quarters* of land (quarterons, *cartrons*); every one of which quarters must contain so much ground as will pasture 400 cows, and 17 plough-lands. A knight's fee was composed of 8 hydes, which amount to 160 acres, and that is generally deemed about a *plough-land*.'

The Editor was favoured by a learned friend with the above extract, from a MS. of Lord Totness's in the Lambeth library.

Page 112.[58] *Wake.* – A wake in England means a festival held upon the anniversary of the saint of the parish. At these wakes, rustic games, rustic conviviality, and rustic courtship, are pursued with all the ardour and all the appetite which accompany such pleasures as occur but seldom. In Ireland a wake is a midnight meeting, held professedly for the indulgence of holy sorrow, but usually it is converted into orgies of unholy joy. When an Irish man or woman of the lower order dies, the straw which composed the bed, whether it has been contained in a bag to form a mattress, or simply spread upon the earthen floor, is immediately taken out of the house, and burned before the cabin door, the family at the same time setting up the death howl. The ears and eyes of the neighbours being thus alarmed, they flock to the house of the deceased, and by their vociferous sympathy excite and at the same time soothe the sorrows of the family.

It is curious to observe how good and bad are mingled in human institutions. In countries which were thinly inhabited, this custom prevented private attempts against the lives of individuals, and formed a kind of coroner's inquest upon the body which had recently expired, and burning the straw upon which the sick man lay became a simple preservative against infection. At night the dead body is waked, that is to say, all the friends and neighbours of the deceased collect in a barn or stable, where the corpse is laid upon some boards, or an unhinged door, supported upon stools, the face exposed, the rest of the body covered with a white sheet. Round the body are stuck in brass candlesticks, which have been borrowed perhaps at five miles' distance, as many candles as the poor person can beg or borrow, observing always to have an odd number. Pipes and tobacco are first distributed, and then, according to the *ability* of the deceased, cakes and ale, and sometimes whiskey, are *dealt* to the company:

> Deal on, deal on, my merry men all,
>> Deal on your cakes and your wine,
> For whatever is dealt at her funeral to-day
>> Shall be dealt to-morrow at mine.[59]

After a fit of universal sorrow, and the comfort of a universal dram, the scandal of the neighbourhood, as in higher circles, occupies the company. The young lads and lasses romp with one another, and when the father and mothers are at last overcome with sleep and whiskey (*vino et somno*), the youth become more enterprising, and are frequently successful. It is said, that more matches are made at wakes than at weddings.

Page 114. *Kilt.* – This word frequently occurs in the preceding pages, where it means not *killed*, but much *hurt*. In Ireland, not only cowards, but the brave 'die many times before their death'. – There *killing is no murder*.

ENNUI

or, Memoirs of the Earl of Glenthorn

Tutta la gente in lieta fronte udiva
Le graziose e finte istorielle,
Ed i difetti altrui tosto scopriva
Ciascuno, e non i proprj espressi in quelle;
O se de' proprj sospettava, ignoti
Credeali a ciascun altro, e a sé sol noti.[1]

PREFACE*

My daughter asks me for a Preface to the following volumes; from a pardonable weakness she calls upon me for parental protection: but, in fact, the public judges of every work, not from the sex, but from the merit of the author.

What we feel, and see, and hear, and read, affects our conduct from the moment when we begin till the moment when we cease to think. It has therefore been my daughter's aim to promote, by all her writings, the progress of education from the cradle to the grave.

Miss Edgeworth's former works consist of tales for children – of stories for young men and women – and of tales suited to that great mass which does not move in the circles of fashion. The present volumes are intended to point out some of those errors to which the higher classes of society are disposed.

All the parts of this series of moral fictions bear upon the faults and excellencies of different ages and classes; and they have all arisen from that view of society which we have laid before the public in more didactic works on education. In the PARENT'S ASSISTANT, in MORAL and in POPULAR TALES, it was my daughter's aim to exemplify the principles contained in PRACTICAL EDUCATION. In these volumes, and in others which are to follow, she endeavours to disseminate, in a familiar form, some of the ideas that are unfolded in ESSAYS ON PROFESSIONAL EDUCATION.

The first of these stories is called

ENNUI. – The causes, curses, and cure of this disease are exemplified, I hope, in such a manner, as not to make the remedy worse than the disease. Thiebauld tells us, that a prize-essay on Ennui was read to the Academy of Berlin, which put all the judges to sleep.

THE DUN – is intended as a lesson against the common folly of

* This is the Preface to *Tales of Fashionable Life*, 1st series, 1809.

believing that a debtor is able by a few cant phrases to alter the nature of right and wrong. We had once thoughts of giving to these books the title of FASHIONABLE TALES: alas! the Dun could never have found favour with fashionable readers.

MANŒUVRING – is a vice to which the little great have recourse, to show their second-rate abilities. Intrigues of gallantry upon the continent frequently lead to political intrigue: amongst us the attempts to introduce this *improvement* of our manners have not yet been successful; but there are, however, some, who, in every thing they say or do, show a predilection for 'left-handed wisdom'. It is hoped that the picture here represented of a *manoeuvrer* has not been made alluring.

ALMERIA – gives a view of the consequences which usually follow the substitution of the gifts of fortune in the place of merit; and shows the meanness of those who imitate manners and haunt company above their station in society.

Difference of rank is a continual excitement to laudable emulation; but those who consider the being admitted into circles of fashion as the summit of human bliss and elevation, will here find how grievously such frivolous ambition may be disappointed and chastised.

I may be permitted to add a word on the respect with which Miss Edgeworth treats the public – their former indulgence has not made her careless or presuming. The dates subjoined to these stories show, that they have not been hastily intruded upon the reader.

RICHARD LOVELL EDGEWORTH
Edgeworthstown,
March 1809.

ENNUI

'Que faites-vous à Potzdam?' demandois-je un jour au prince Guillaume. 'Monsieur,' me répondit-il, 'nous passons notre vie à conjuguer tous le même verbe; *Je m'ennuie, tu t'ennuies, il s'ennuie, nous nous ennuyons, vous vous ennuyez, ils s'ennuient; je m'ennuyois, je m'ennuierai,' &c.

THIEBAULD, Mém. de Frederick le Grand.[2]

CHAPTER I

Bred up in luxurious indolence, I was surrounded by friends who seemed to have no business in this world but to save me the trouble of thinking or acting for myself; and I was confirmed in the pride of helplessness by being continually reminded that I was the only son and heir of the Earl of Glenthorn. My mother died a few weeks after I was born; and I lost my father when I was very young. I was left to the care of a guardian, who, in hopes of winning my affection, never controlled my wishes or even my whims: I changed schools and masters as often as I pleased, and consequently learned nothing. At last I found a private tutor who suited me exactly, for he was completely of my own opinion, 'that every thing which the young Earl of Glenthorn did not know by the instinct of genius was not worth his learning'. Money could purchase a reputation for talents, and with money I was immoderately supplied; for my guardian expected to bribe me with a part of my own fortune, to forbear inquiring what had become of a certain deficiency in the remainder. This tacit compact I perfectly understood: we were consequently on the most amicable terms imaginable, and the most confidential; for I thought it better to deal with my guardian than with Jews. Thus at an age when other young men are subject to some restraint, either from the necessity of their circumstances, or the discretion of their friends, I became completely master of myself and of my fortune. My companions envied me; but even their envy was not sufficient to make me happy. Whilst yet a boy, I began to feel the dreadful symptoms of that mental malady which baffles the skill of medicine, and for which wealth can purchase only temporary alleviation. For this complaint there is no precise English name; but, alas! the foreign term is now naturalized in England. Among the higher classes, whether in the wealthy or the fashionable world, who is unacquainted with *ennui*? At first I was unconscious of being subject to this disease; I felt that something was the matter with me, but I did not know what: yet the symptoms were sufficiently marked. I was afflicted with frequent fits of fidgeting, yawning, and stretching, with a constant restlessness of mind and body; an aversion to the place I was in, or the thing I was doing, or rather to that which was passing before my eyes, for I was never doing any thing; I had an utter abhorrence and an incapacity of voluntary exertion. Unless roused by external stimulus, I sank into that kind of apathy, and vacancy of ideas, vulgarly known by the name of *a brown study*. If confined in a room for more than half an hour by bad weather or other contrarieties, I would pace backwards and forwards, like the restless *cavia* in his den, with a fretful, unmeaning pertinacity. I felt an insatiable longing for something new, and a childish love of locomotion.

My physician and my guardian, not knowing what else to do with me, sent me abroad. I set out upon my travels in my eighteenth year, attended by my favourite tutor as my *companion*. We perfectly agreed in our ideas of travelling; we hurried from place to place as fast as horses and wheels, and curses and guineas, could carry us. Milord Anglois[3] rattled over half the globe without getting one inch farther from his ennui. Three years were to be consumed before I should be of age. What sums did I spend during this interval in expedition-money to Time! but the more I tried to hasten him, the slower the rogue went. I lost my money and my temper.

At last the day for which I had so long panted arrived – I was twenty-one! and I took possession of my estate. The bells rang, the bonfires blazed, the tables were spread, the wine flowed, huzzas resounded, friends and tenants crowded about me, and nothing but the voice of joy and congratulation was to be heard. The bustle of my situation kept me awake for some weeks; the pleasure of property was new, and, as long as the novelty lasted, delightful. I cannot say that I was satisfied; but my mind was distended by the sense of the magnitude of my possessions. I had large estates in England; and in one of the remote maritime counties of Ireland, I was lord over an immense territory, annexed to the ancient castle of Glenthorn; – a noble pile of antiquity! worth ten degenerate castles of modern days. It was placed in a bold romantic situation; at least as far as I could judge of it by a picture, said to be a striking likeness, which hung in my hall at Sherwood Park in England. I was born in Ireland, and nursed, as I was told, in an Irish cabin; for my father had an idea that this would make me hardy: he left me with my Irish nurse till I was two years old, and from that time forward neither he nor I ever revisited Ireland. He had a dislike to that country, and I grew up in his prejudices. I declared that I would always reside in England. Sherwood Park, my English country-seat, had but one fault; it was completely finished. The house was magnificent, and in the modern taste; the furniture fashionably elegant, and in all the gloss of novelty. Not a single luxury omitted; not a fault could be found by the most fastidious critic. My park, my grounds, displayed all the beauties of nature and of art, judiciously combined. Majestic woods, waving their dark foliage, overhung – But I will spare my readers the description, for I remember falling asleep myself whilst a poet was reading to me an ode on the beauties of Sherwood Park. These beauties too soon became familiar to my eye; and even the idea of being the proprietor of this enchanting place soon palled upon my vanity. Every casual visitor, all the strangers, even the common people, who were allowed once a week to walk in my pleasure-grounds, enjoyed them a thousand times more than I could. I remember, that, about six weeks after I came to Sherwood Park, I one evening escaped from the crowds of *friends* who filled my house, to indulge myself in a solitary, melancholy walk. I saw at some distance a party of people, who were coming to admire the place; and to avoid meeting them I took shelter under a fine tree, the branches of which, hanging to the ground, concealed me from the view of passengers. Thus seated, I was checked in the middle of a desperate yawn, by hearing one among the party of strangers exclaiming –

'How happy the owner of this place must be!'

Yes, had I known how to enjoy the goods of life, I might have been happy; but want of occupation, and antipathy to exertion, rendered me one of the most miserable men upon earth. Still I imagined that the cause of my discontent proceeded from some external circumstance. Soon after my coming of age, business of various sorts required my attention; papers were to be signed, and lands were to be let: these things appeared to me terrible difficulties. Not even that minister of state, who so feelingly describes his horror at the first appearance of the secretary with the great portfolio, ever experienced sensations so oppressive as mine were, when my steward began to talk to me of my own affairs. In the peevishness of my indolence, I declared that I thought the pains overbalanced the pleasures of property. Captain Crawley, a friend – a sort of a friend – a humble companion of mine, a gross, unblushing, thorough-going flatterer, happened to be present when I made this declaration: he kindly undertook to stand between me and the shadow of trouble. I accepted this offer.

'Ay, Crawley,' said I, 'do see and settle with these people.'

I had not the slightest confidence in the person into whose hands, to save myself from the labour of thinking, I thus threw all my affairs; but I satisfied my understanding, by resolving that, when I should have leisure, I would look out for an agent upon whom I could depend.

I had now been nearly two months at Sherwood Park; too long a time, I thought, to remain in any place, and I was impatient to get away. My steward, who disliked the idea of my spending my summers at home, found it easy to persuade me that the water on my estate had a brackish unwholesome taste. The man who told me this stood before me in perfect health, though he had drunk this insalubrious water all his life: but it was too laborious a task for my intellects to compare the evidence of my different senses, and I found it most easy to believe what I heard, though it was in direct opposition to what I saw. Away I hurried to a *watering-place*, after the example of many of my noble contemporaries, who leave their delightful country-seats, to pay, by the inch, for being squeezed up in lodging houses, with all imaginable inconvenience, during the hottest months in summer. I whiled away my time at Brighton, cursing the heat of the weather, till the winter came, and then cursing the cold, and longing for the London winter.

The London winter commenced; and the young Earl of Glenthorn, and his entertainments, and his equipages, and extravagance, were the conversation of all the world, and the joy of the newspapers. The immense cost of the fruit at my desserts was recorded; the annual expence of the vast nosegays of hot-house flowers worn daily by the footmen who clung behind my coach was calculated; the hundreds of wax lights, which burned nightly in my house, were numbered by the idle admirers of folly; and it was known by every body that Lord Glenthorn suffered nothing but wax to be burned in his stables; that his servants drank nothing but claret and champagne; that his liveries, surpassing the imagination of ambassadors, vied with regal magnificence, whilst their golden trappings could have stood even the test of Chinese curiosity. My coachmaker's bill for this year, if laid before the public, would amuse and astonish sober-minded people, as much as some charges which have lately appear in our courts of justice for *extraordinary coaches* and *very extraordinary landaus*.[4] I will not enter into the detail of my extravagance in minor articles of expence; these, I thought, could never be felt by such a fortune as that of the Earl of Glenthorn; but, for the information of those who have the same course to run or to avoid, I should observe, that my diurnal visits to jewellers' shops amounted, in time, to sums worth mentioning. Of the multitude of baubles that I bought, the rings, the seals, the chains, I will give no account; it would pass the belief of man, and the imagination of woman. Those who have the least value for their time have usually the greatest number of watches, and are the most anxious about the exactness of their going. I and my repeaters[5] were my own plagues, and the profit of all the fashionable watchmakers, whose shops I regularly visited for a *lounge*. My history, at this period, would be a complete lounger's journey; but I will spare my readers this diary. I wish, however, as I have had ample experience, to impress it on the minds of all whom it may concern, that a lounger of fortune *must* be extravagant. I went into shops merely to pass an idle hour, but I could not help buying something; and I was ever at the mercy of tradesmen, who took advantage of my indolence, and who thought my fortune inexhaustible. I really had not any taste for expence; but I let all who dealt with me, especially my servants, do as they pleased, rather than be at the trouble of making them do as they ought. They assured me, that Lord Glenthorn must have such and such things, and must do so and so; and I quietly submitted to this imaginary necessity.

All this time I was the envy of my acquaintance; but I was more deserving of their compassion. Without anxiety or exertion, I possessed every thing they wanted; but then I had no motive – I had nothing to desire. I had an immense fortune, and I was the Earl of Glenthorn: my title and wealth were sufficient distinctions; how could I be anxious about my boots, or the cape of my coat, or any of those trifles which so happily interest and occupy the lives of fashionable young men, who have not the misfortune to possess large estates? Most of my companions had some real or imaginary grievance, some old uncle or father, some *cursed* profession to complain of; but I had none. They had hopes and fears; but I had none. I was on the pinnacle of glory, which they were endeavouring to reach; and I had nothing to do but to sit still, and enjoy the barrenness of the prospect.

In this recital I have communicated, I hope, to my readers some portion of that ennui which I endured; otherwise they cannot form an adequate idea of my temptation to become a gambler. I really had no vice, nor any of those propensities which lead to vice; but ennui produced most of the effects that are usually attributed to strong passions or a vicious disposition.

CHAPTER II

> *O! ressource assurée,*
> *Viens ranimer leur langueur desœuvrée:*
> *Leur âme vide est du moins amusée*
> *Par l'avarice en plaisir déguisée.*[6]

Gaming relieved me from that insuperable listlessness by which I was oppressed. I became interested – I became agitated; in short, I found a new kind of stimulus, and I indulged in it most intemperately. I grew immoderately fond of that which supplied me with sensations. My days and nights were passed at the gaming-table. I remember once spending three days and three nights in the hazard-room of a well-known house in St James's-street;[7] the shutters were closed, the curtains down, and we had candles the whole time; even in the adjoining rooms we had candles, that when our doors were opened to bring in refreshments, no obtrusive gleam of daylight might remind us how the hours had passed. How human nature supported the fatigue, I know not. We scarcely allowed ourselves a moment's pause to take the sustenance our bodies required. At last, one of the markers, who had been in the room with us the whole time, declared that he could hold out no longer, and that sleep he must. With difficulty he obtained an hour's truce: the moment he got out of the room he fell asleep, absolutely at the very threshold of our door. By the rules of the house he was entitled to a bonus on every transfer of property at the hazard-table: and he had made, in the course of these three days, upwards of three hundred pounds. Sleep and avarice had struggled to the utmost, but, with his vulgar habits, sleep prevailed. We were wide awake: I shall never forget the figure of one of my noble associates, who sat holding his watch, his eager eyes fixed upon the minute-hand, whilst he exclaimed continually, 'This hour will never be over!' Then he listened to discover whether his watch had stopped; then cursed the lazy fellow for falling asleep, protesting that, for his part, he never would again consent to such waste of time. The very instant the hour was ended, he ordered '*that dog*' to be awakened, and to work we went. At this sitting £35,000 were lost and won. I was very fortunate, for I lost a mere trifle – ten thousand pounds; but I could not expect to be always so lucky. – Now we come to the old story of being ruined by play. My English John-o'-the-Scales warned me that he could *advance* no more money; my Irish agent, upon whom my drafts had indeed been unmerciful, could not *oblige* me any longer, and he threw up his agency, after having made his fortune at my expence. I railed, but railing would not pay my debts of honour. I inveighed against my grandfather for having tied me up so tight; I could neither mortgage nor sell: my Irish estate would have been sold instantly, had it not been settled upon a Mr Delamere. The pleasure of abusing him, whom I had never seen, and of whom I knew nothing but that he was to be my heir, relieved me wonderfully. He died, and left only a daughter, a mere child. My chance of possessing the estate in fee-simple[8] increased: I sold this increased value to the Jews, and gamed on. Miss Delamere, some time afterwards, had the small-pox. Upon the event of her illness I laid bets to an amazing amount.

She recovered. No more money could be raised, and my debts were to be paid. In this dilemma I recollected that I once had a guardian, and that I had never settled accounts with him. Crawley, who continued to be my factotum and flatterer in ordinary and extraordinary, informed me, upon looking over these accounts, that there was a mine of money due to me, if I could but obtain it by law or equity. To law I went: and the anxiety of a lawsuit might have, in some degree, supplied the place of gambling, but that all my business was managed for me by Crawley, and I charged him never to mention the subject to me till a verdict should be obtained.

A verdict was obtained against me. It was proved in open court, by my own witnesses, that I was a fool; but as no judge, jury, or chancellor, could believe that I was so great a fool as my carelessness indicated, my guardian stood acquitted in equity of being so great a rogue as he really was. What was now to be done? I saw my doom. As a highwayman knows that he must come to the gallows at last, and acts accordingly, so a fashionably extravagant youth knows that, sooner or later, he must come to matrimony. No one could have more horror of this catastrophe than I felt; but it was in vain to oppose my destiny. My opinion of women had been formed from the commonplace jests of my companions, and from my own acquaintance with the worst part of the sex. I had never felt the passion of love, and, of course, believed it to be something that might have existed in former ages, but that it was in our days quite obsolete, at least, among the *knowing* part of the world. In my imagination young women were divided into two classes; those who were to be purchased, and those who were to purchase. Between these two classes, though the division was to be marked externally by a certain degree of ceremony, yet I was internally persuaded, that there was no essential difference. In my feelings towards them there was some distinction; of the first class I was tired, and of the second I was afraid. Afraid! Yes – afraid of being taken in. With these fears, and these sentiments, I was now to choose a wife. I chose her by the numeration table: Units, tens, hundreds, thousands, tens of thousands, hundreds of thousands. I was content, in the language of the newspapers, *to lead to the Hymeneal altar* any fashionable fair one whose fortune came under the sixth place of figures. No sooner were my *dispositions* known than the friends of a young heiress, who wanted to purchase a coronet, settled a match between us. My bride had one hundred wedding-dresses, elegant as a select committee of dressmakers and milliners, French and English, could devise. The least expensive of these robes, as well as I remember, cost fifty guineas: the most admired came to about five hundred pounds, and was thought, by the best judges in these matters, to be wonderfully cheap, as it was of lace such as had never before been trailed in

English dust, even by the lady of a nabob. These things were shown in London as a *spectacle* for some days, by the dress-maker, who declared that she had lost many a night's rest in contriving how to make such a variety of dresses sufficiently magnificent and *distinguished*. The jewellers also requested and obtained permission to exhibit the different sets of jewels: these were so numerous that Lady Glenthorn scarcely knew them all. One day, soon after her marriage, somebody at court, observing that her diamonds were prodigiously fine, asked where she bought them. 'Really,' said she, 'I cannot tell. I have so many sets, I declare I don't know whether *it's* my Paris, or my Hamburgh, or my London set.'

Poor young creature! I believe her chief idea of happiness in marriage was the possession of the jewels and paraphernalia of a countess – I am sure it was the only hope she could have, that was likely to be realized, in marrying me. I thought it manly and fashionable to be indifferent, if not contemptuous to my wife: I considered her only as an incumbrance, that I was obliged to take along with my fortune. Beside the disagreeable ideas generally connected with the word *wife*, I had some peculiar reasons for my aversion to my lady Glenthorn. Before her friends would suffer me to take possession of her fortune, they required from me a solemn oath against gambling: so I was compelled to abjure the hazard-table and the turf, the only two objects in life that could keep me awake. This extorted vow I set down entirely to my bride's account; and I therefore became even more averse to her than men usually are who marry for money. Yet this dislike subsided. Lady Glenthorn was only childish – I, of an easy temper. I thought her ridiculous, but it was too much trouble to tell her so continually. I let the occasions pass, and even forgot her ladyship, when she was not absolutely in my way. She was too frivolous to be hated, and the passion of hatred was not to be easily sustained in my mind. The habit of ennui was stronger than all my passions put together.

CHAPTER III

Or realize what we think fabulous,
I' th' bill of fare of Eliogabalus.[9]

After my marriage, my old malady rose to an insupportable height. The pleasures of the table were all that seemed left to me in life. Most of the young men of any *ton*, either were, or pretended to be, *connoisseurs* in the science of good eating. Their *talk* was of sauces and of cooks, what dishes each cook was famous for; whether his *forte* lay in white sauces or brown, in soups, *lentilles*, *fricandeaus*, *bechemele*, *matelotes*, *daubes*, &c. Then the history and genealogy of the cooks came after the discussion of the merit of the works; whom my lord C—'s cook lived with formerly – what my lord D— gave his cook – where they met with these great geniuses, &c. I cannot boast that our conversation at these select dinners, from which the ladies were excluded, was very entertaining; but true good eaters detest wit at dinner-time, and sentiment at all times. I think I observed that amongst these cognoscenti there was scarcely one to whom the delicacy of taste did not daily prove a source of more pain than pleasure. There was always a cruel something that spoiled the rest; or if the dinner were excellent, beyond the power of the most fastidious palate to condemn, yet there was the hazard of being placed far from the favourite dish, or the still greater danger of being deputed to carve at the head or foot of the table. How I have seen a heavy nobleman, of this set, dexterously manoeuvre to avoid the dangerous honour of carving a haunch of venison! 'But, good Heavens!' said I, when a confidential whisper pointed out this first to my notice, 'why does he not like to carve? – he would have it in his power to help himself to his mind, which nobody else can do so well.' – 'No! if he carves, he must give the *nice bits* to others; every body here understands them as well as he – each knows what is upon his neighbour's plate, and what ought to be there, and what must be in the dish.' I found that it was an affair of calculation – a game at which nobody can cheat without being discovered and disgraced. I emulated, and soon equalled my experienced friends. I became a perfect epicure, and gloried in the character, for it could be supported without any intellectual exertion, and it was fashionable. I cannot say that I could ever eat as much as some of my companions. One of them I once heard to exclaim, after a monstrous dinner, 'I wish my digestion was equal to my appetite.' I would not be thought to exaggerate, therefore I shall not recount the wonders I have seen performed by these capacious heroes of the table. After what I have beheld, to say nothing of what I have achieved, I can believe any thing that is related of the capacity of the human stomach. I can credit even the account of the dinner which Madame de Bavière affirms she saw eaten by Lewis the Fourteenth; *viz*, 'quatre assiettes des différentes soupes; un faisan tout entier; un perdrix; une grande assiette pleine de salade; du mouton coupé dans son jus avec de l'ail; deux bons morceaux de jambon; une assiette pleine de pâtisserie; du fruit et des confitures!'[10] Nor can I doubt the accuracy of the historian, who assures me that a Roman emperor,* one of the most moderate of those imperial gluttons, *took* for his breakfast, 500 figs, 100 peaches, 10 melons, 100 beccaficoes, and 400 oysters.[11]

Epicurism was scarcely more prevalent during the decline of the Roman empire than it is at this day amongst some of the wealthy and noble youths of Britain. Not one of my select dinner-party but would have been worthy of a place at the *turbot consultation* immortalized by the Roman satirist.[12] A friend of mine, a bishop, one day went into his kitchen, to look at a large turbot, which the cook was dressing. The cook had found it so large that he had cut off the fins: 'What a shame!' cried the bishop; and immediately calling for the cook's apron, he spread it before his cassock, and actually sewed the fins again to the turbot with his own episcopal hands.

If I might judge from my own experience, I should attribute fashionable epicurism in a great measure to ennui. Many affect it, because they have nothing else to do; and sensual indulgences are all that exist for those who have not sufficient energy to enjoy intellectual pleasures. I dare say, that if Heliogabalus could be brought in evidence in his own case, and could be made to understand the meaning of the word ennui, he would agree with me in opinion, that it was the cause of half his vices. His offered reward for the discovery of a new pleasure is stronger evidence than any confession he could make.[13] I thank God that I was not born an emperor, or I might have become a monster. Though not in the least inclined to cruelty, I might

---

* Clodius Albinus.

have acquired the taste for it, merely for desire of the emotion which real tragedies excite. Fortunately, I was only an earl and an epicure.

My indulgence in the excesses of the table injured my health; violent bodily exercise was necessary to counteract the effects of intemperance. It was my maxim, that a man could never eat or drink too much, if he would but take exercise enough. I killed fourteen horses,* and survived; but I grew tired of killing horses, and I continued to eat immoderately. I was seized with a nervous complaint, attended with extreme melancholy. Frequently the thoughts of putting an end to my existence occurred; and I had many times determined upon the means; but very small, and apparently inadequate and ridiculous motives, prevented the execution of my design. Once I was kept alive by a *piggery*, which I wanted to see finished. Another time, I delayed destroying myself, till a statue, which I had just purchased at a vast expence, should be put up in my Egyptian *salon*.[14] By the awkwardness of the unpacker, the statue's thumb was broken. This broken thumb saved my life; it converted ennui into anger. Like Montaigne and his sausage,[15] I had now something to complain of, and I was happy. But at last my anger subsided, the thumb would serve me no longer as a subject of conversation, and I relapsed into silence and black melancholy. I was 'a'weary of the sun;'[16] my old thoughts recurred. At this time I was just entering my twenty-fifth year. Rejoicings were preparing for my birthday. My lady Glenthorn had prevailed upon me to spend the summer at Sherwood Park, because it was new to her. She filled the house with company and noise; but this only increased my discontent. My birthday arrived – I wished myself dead – and I resolved to shoot myself at the close of the day. I put a pistol into my pocket, and stole out towards the evening, unobserved by my jovial companions. Lady Glenthorn and her set were dancing, and I was tired of these sounds of gaiety. I took the private way to the forest, which was near the house; but one of my grooms met me with a fine horse, which an old tenant had just sent as a present on my birthday. The horse was saddled and bridled; the groom held the stirrup, and up I got. The fellow told me the private gate was

---

*I was not the nobleman, who laid a wager, that he could ride a fine horse to death in fifteen minutes. Indeed, I must do myself the justice to say, that I rejoiced at this man's losing his bet. He *blew* the horse in four minutes, and killed it; but it did not die within the time prescribed by the bet.

locked, and I turned as he pointed to go through the grand entrance. At the outside of the gate sat upon the ground, huddled in a great red cloak, an old woman, who started up and sprang forwards the moment she saw me, stretching out her arms and her cloak with one and the same motion.

'Ogh! is it you I see?' cried she, in a strong Irish tone.

At this sound and this sight, my horse, who was shy, backed a little. I called to the woman to stand out of my way.

'Heaven bless your sweet face! I'm the nurse that suckled *yees* when ye was a baby in Ireland. Many's the day I've been longing to see you,' continued she, clasping her hands, and standing her ground in the middle of the gateway, regardless of my horse, which I was pressing forward.

'Stand out of the way, for God's sake, my good woman, or I shall certainly ride over you. So! so! so!' said I, patting my restless horse.

'Oh! he's only shy, God bless him! he's as *quite* now as a lamb; and kiss one or other of *yees*, I must,' cried she, throwing her arms about the horse's neck.

The horse, unaccustomed to this mode of salutation, suddenly plunged, and threw me. My head fell against the pier of the gate. The last sound I heard was the report of a pistol; but I can give no account of what happened afterwards. I was stunned by my fall, and senseless. When I opened my eyes, I found myself stretched on one of the cushions of my landau, and surrounded by a crowd of people, who seemed to be all talking at once; in the buzz of voices I could not distinguish any thing that was said, till I heard Captain Crawley's voice above the rest, saying.

'Send for a surgeon instantly: but it's all over! it's all over! Take the body the back way to the banqueting-house; I must run to Lady Glenthorn.'

I perceived that they thought me dead. I did not at this moment feel that I was hurt. I was curious to know what they would all do; so I closed my eyes again before any one perceived that I had opened them. I lay motionless, and they proceeded with me, according to Captain Crawley's orders, to the banqueting-house. When we arrived there, my servants laid me on one of the Turkish sofas; and the crowd, after having satisfied their curiosity, dropped off one by one, till I was left with a single footman and my steward.

'I don't believe he's quite dead,' said the footman, 'for his heart beats.'

'Oh, he's the same as dead, for he does not stir hand or foot, and his skull, they say, is fractured for certain; but it will all be seen when the surgeon comes. I am sure he will never do. Crawley will have every thing his own way now, and I may as well decamp.'

'Ay; and among them,' said the footman, 'I only hope I may get my wages.'

'What a fool that Crawley made of my lord!' said the steward.

'What a fool my lord made of himself,' said the footman, 'to be ruled, and let all his people be ruled, by such an upstart! With your leave, Mr Turner, I'll just run to the house to say one word to James, and be back immediately.'

'No, no, you must stay, Robert, whilst I step home to lock my places, before Crawley begins to rummage.'

The footman was now left alone with me. Scarcely had the steward been gone two minutes, when I heard a low voice near me saying, in a tone of great anxiety, 'Is he dead?'

I half opened my eyes to see who it was that spoke. The voice came from the door which was opposite to me; and whilst the footman turned his back. I raised my head, and beheld the figure of the old woman, who had been the cause of my accident. She was upon her knees on the threshold – her arms crossed over her breast. I never shall forget her face, it was so expressive of despair.

'Is he dead?' she repeated.

'I tell you yes,' replied the footman.

'For the love of God, let me come in, if he is here,' cried she.

'Come in, then, and stay here whilst I run to the house.'*

The footman ran off; and my old nurse, on seeing me, burst into an agony of grief. I did not understand one word she uttered, as she spoke in her native language; but her lamentations went to my heart, for they came from hers. She hung over me, and I felt her tears dropping upon my forehead. I could not refrain from whispering, 'Don't cry – I am alive.'

'Blessings on him!' exclaimed she, starting back: she then dropped

*If any one should think it impossible that a man of Lord Glenthorn's consequence should, at the supposed moment of his death, thus be neglected, let them recollect the scenes that followed the death of Tiberius – of Henry the Fourth of France – of William Rufus, and of George the Second.

down on her knees to thank God. Then calling me by every fondling name that nurses use to their children, she begged my forgiveness, and alternately cursed herself and prayed for me.

The strong affections of this poor woman touched me more than anything I had ever yet felt in my life; she seemed to be the only person upon earth who really cared for me; and in spite of her vulgarity, and my prejudice against the tone in which she spoke, she excited in my mind emotions of tenderness and gratitude. 'My good woman, if I live, I will do something for you: tell me what I can do,' said I. 'Live! live! God bless you, live; that's all in the wide world I want of you, my jewel; and, till you are well, let me watch over you at nights, as I used to do when you were a child, and I had you in my arms all to myself, dear.'

Three or four people now ran into the room, to get before Captain Crawley, whose voice was heard at this instant at a distance. I had only time to make the poor woman understand that I wished to appear to be dead; she took the hint with surprising quickness. Captain Crawley came up the steps, talking in the tone of a master to the steward and people who followed.

'What is this old hag doing here? Where is Robert? Where is Thomas? I ordered them to stay till I came. Mr Turner, why did not you stay? What! has not the coroner been here yet? The coroner must see the body, I tell you. Good God! What a parcel of blockheads you all are! How many times must I tell you the same thing? Nothing can be done till the coroner has seen him; then we'll talk about the funeral, Mr Turner – one thing at a time. Every thing shall be done properly, Mr Turner. Lady Glenthorn trusts every thing to me – Lady Glenthorn wishes that I should order every thing.'

'To be sure – no doubt – very proper – I don't say against that.'

'But,' continued Crawley, turning towards the sofa upon which I lay, and seeing Ellinor kneeling beside me, 'what keeps this old Irish witch here still? What business have you here, pray; and who are you, or what are you?'

'Plase your honour, I was his nurse formerly, and so had a nat'ral longing to see him once again before I would die.'

'And did you come all the way from Ireland on this wise errand?'

'Troth I did – every inch of the way from his own sweet place.'

'Why, you are little better than a fool, I think,' said Crawley.

'Little better, plase your honour; but I was always so about them *childer* that I nursed.'

'*Childer*! Well, get along about your business now; you see your nursing is not wanted here.'

'I'll not stir out of this, while he is here,' said my nurse, catching hold of the leg of the sofa, and clinging to it.

'You'll not stir, you say,' cried Captain Crawley: 'Turn her out!'

'Oh, sure you would not have the cru'lty to turn his old nurse out before he's even *cowld*. And won't you let me see him buried?'

'Out with her! out with her! the old Irish hag! We'll have no howling here. Out with her, John!' said Crawley to my groom.

The groom hesitated, I fancy; for Crawley repeated the order more imperiously: 'Out with her! or go yourself.'

'May be it's you that will go first yourself,' said she.

'Go first myself!' cried Captain Crawley, furiously: 'Are you insolent to *me*?'

'And are not you cru'l to me, and to my child I nursed, that lies all as one as dead before you, and was a good friend to you in his day, no doubt?'

Crawley seized hold of her: but she resisted with so much energy, that she dragged along with her the sofa to which she clung, and on which I lay.

'Stop!' cried I, starting up. There was sudden silence. I looked round, but could not utter another syllable. Now, for the first time, I was sensible that I had been really hurt by the fall. My head grew giddy, and my stomach sick. I just saw Crawley's fallen countenance, and him and the steward looking at one another; they were like hideous faces in a dream. I sank back.

'Ay, lie down, my darling; don't be disturbing yourself for such as them,' said my nurse. 'Let them do what they will with me; it's little I'd care for them, if you were but once in safe hands.'

I beckoned to the groom, who had hesitated to turn out Ellinor, and bid him go to the housekeeper, and have me put to bed. 'She,' added I, pointing to my old nurse, 'is to sit up with me at night.' It was all I could say. What they did with me afterwards, I do not know; but I was in my bed, and a bandage was round my temples, and my poor nurse was kneeling on one side of the bed, with a string of beads in her hand; and a surgeon and physician, and Crawley and my lady Glenthorn were on the other side, whispering together.

The curtain was drawn between me and them; but the motion I made on wakening was instantly observed by Crawley, who immediately left the room. Lady Glenthorn drew back my curtain, and began to ask me how I did: but when I fixed my eyes upon her, she sunk upon the bed, trembling violently, and could not finish her sentence. I begged her to go to rest, and she retired. The physician ordered that I should be kept quiet, and seemed to think I was in danger. I asked what was the matter with me? and the surgeon, with a very grave face, informed me that I had an ugly contusion on my head. I had heard of a concussion of the brain; but I did not know distinctly what it was, and my fears were increased by my ignorance. The life which, but a few hours before, I had been on the point of voluntarily destroying, because it was insupportably burdensome, I was now, the moment it was in danger, most anxious to preserve; and the interest which I perceived others had in getting rid of me increased my desire to recover. My recovery was, however, for some time doubtful. I was seized with a fever, which left me in a state of alarming debility. My old nurse, whom I shall henceforward call by her name of Ellinor, attended me with the most affectionate solicitude during my illness;* she scarcely stirred from my bedside, night or day; and, indeed, when I came to the use of my senses, she was the only person whom I really liked to have near me. I knew that she was sincere; and, however unpolished her manners, and however awkward her assistance, the good-will with which it was given, made me prefer it to the most delicate and dexterous attentions which I believed to be interested. The very want of a sense of propriety, and the freedom with which she talked to me, regardless

---

* 'For fostering, I did never hear or read, that it was in use or reputation in any country, barbarous or civil, as it hath been, and yet is, in Ireland ... In the opinion of this people, fostering hath always been a stronger alliance than blood; and the foster-children do love and are beloved of their foster-fathers and their sept (or *clan*) more than of their natural parents and kindred; and do participate of their means more frankly, and do adhere unto them, in all fortunes, with more affection and constancy ... Such a general custom in a kingdom, in giving and taking children to foster, making such a firm alliance as it doth in Ireland, was never seen or heard of in any other country of the world beside.' – DAVIES.[17]

See in Lodge's Peerage of Ireland an account of an Irish nurse, who went from Kerry to France, and from France to Milan, to see her foster-son, the lord Thomas Fitzmaurice; and to warn him that his estate was in danger from an heir-at-law, who had taken possession of it in his absence. The nurse, being very old, died on her return home.[18]

of what was suited to her station, or due to my rank, instead of off-ending or disgusting me, became agreeable; besides, the novelty of her dialect, and of her turn of thought, entertained me as much as a sick man could be entertained. I remember once her telling me, that, 'if it *plased* God, she would like to die on a Christmas-day, of all days; *becaase* the gates of Heaven, they say, will be open all that day; and who knows but a body might slip in *unknownst?*' When she sat up with me at nights, she talked on eternally; for she assured me there was nothing like talking, as she had found, to put one *asy asleep*. I listen-ed or not, just as I liked; *any way* she was *contint*. She was inexhaustible in her anecdotes of my ancestors, all tending to the honour and glory of the family; she had also an excellent memory for all the insults, or traditions of insults, which the Glenthorns had received for many ages back, even to the times of the old kings of Ireland; long and long before they stooped to be *lorded*; when their 'names, which it was a pity and a murder, and moreover a burning shame, to change, was O'Shaugh-nessy'. She was well stored with histories of Irish and Scottish chiefs. The story of O'Neill, the Irish black-beard,[19] I am sure I ought to remember, for Ellinor told it to me at least six times. Then she had a large assortment of fairies and *shadowless* witches, and *banshees*; and besides, she had legions of spirits and ghosts, and haunted castles without end, my own castle of Glenthorn not excepted, in the descrip-tion of which she was extremely eloquent; she absolutely excited in my mind some desire to see it. For many a long year, she said, it had been her nightly prayer, that she might live to see me in my own castle; and often and often she was coming over to England to tell me so, only her husband, as long as he lived, would not let her set out on what he called a fool's errand: but it pleased God to take him to himself last fair day, and then she resolved that nothing should hinder her to be with her own child against his birthday: and now, could she see me in my own Castle Glenthorn, she would die *contint* – and what a pity but I should be in it! I was only a lord, as she said, in England; but I could be all as one as a king in Ireland.

Ellinor impressed me with the idea of the sort of feudal power I should possess in my vast territory, over tenants who were almost vassals, and amongst a numerous train of dependants. We resist the efforts made by those who, we think, exert authority or employ artifice to change our determinations; whilst the perverse mind insen-sibly yields to those, who appear not to have power, or reason, or address, sufficient to obtain a victory. I should not have heard any human being with patience try to persuade me to go to Ireland, except this ignorant poor nurse, who spoke, as I thought, merely from the instinct of affection to me and to her native country. I promised her that I would, *sometime or other*, visit Glenthorn Castle: but this was only a vague promise, and it was but little likely that it should be accomplished. As I regained my strength, my mind turned, or rather was turned, to other thoughts.

CHAPTER IV

One morning – it was the day after my physicians had pronounced me out of all danger – Crawley sent me a note by Ellinor, congratulating me upon my recovery, and begging to speak to me for half an hour. I refused to see him; and said, that I was not yet well enough to do business. The same morning Ellinor came with a message from Turner, my steward, who, with his humble duty, requested to see me for five minutes, to communicate to me something of importance. I consented to see Turner. He entered with a face of suppressed joy and affected melancholy.

'Sad news I am bound in duty to be the bearer of, my lord. I was determined, whatever came to pass, however, not to speak till your honour was out of danger, which, I thank Heaven, is now the case, and I am happy to be able to congratulate your lordship upon looking as well as—'

'Never mind my looks. I will excuse your congratulations, Mr Turner,' said I, impatiently; for the recollection of the banqueting-house, and the undertaker, whom Turner was so eager to introduce, came full into my mind. 'Go on, if you please; five minutes is all I am at present able to give to any business, and you sent me word you had something of importance to communicate.'

'True, my lord; but in case your lordship is not at present well enough, or not so disposed, I will wait your lordship's leisure.'

'Now or never, Mr Turner. Speak, but speak at once.'

'My lord, I would have done so long ago, but was loth to make mischief; and besides, could not believe what I heard whispered, and would scarce believe what I verily saw; though now, as I cannot reasonably have a doubt, I think it would be a sin, and a burden upon my conscience, not to speak; only that I am unwilling to shock your lordship too much, when but just recovering, for that is not the time one would wish to tell or to hear disagreeable things,'

'Mr Turner, either come to the point at once, or leave me; for I am not strong enough to bear this suspense.'

'I beg pardon, my lord: why then, my lord, the point is Captain Crawley.'

'What of him? I never desire to hear his name again.'

'Nor I, I am sure, my lord; but there are some in the house might not be of our opinion.'

'Who? you sneaking fellow; speak out, can't you?"

'My lady – my lord – Now it is out. She'll go off with him this night, if not prevented.'

My surprise and indignation were as great as if I had always been the fondest and the most attentive of husbands. I was at length roused from that indifference and apathy into which I had sunk; and though I had never loved my wife, the moment I knew she was lost to me for ever was exquisitely painful. Astonishment, the sense of disgrace, the feeling of rage against that treacherous parasite by whom she had been seduced, all combined to overwhelm me. I could command my voice only enough to bid Turner leave the room, and tell no one that he had spoken to me on this subject. 'Not a soul,' he said, 'should be told, or could guess it.'

Left to my own reflections, as soon as the first emotions of anger subsided, I blamed myself for my conduct to Lady Glenthorn. I considered that she had been married to me by her friends, when she was too young and too childish to judge for herself; that from the first day of our marriage I had never made the slightest effort to win her affections, or to guide her conduct; that, on the contrary, I had shown her marked indifference, if not aversion. With fashionable airs, I had professed, that provided she left me at liberty to spend the large fortune which she brought me, and in consideration of which she enjoyed the title of Countess of Glenthorn, I cared for nothing farther. With the consequences of my neglect I now reproached myself in vain. Lady Glenthorn's immense fortune had paid my debts, and had for two years supplied my extravagance, or rather my indolence: little remained, and she was now, in her twenty-third year, to be consigned to public disgrace, and to a man whom I knew to be destitute of honour and feeling. I pitied her, and resolved to go instantly and make an effort to save her from destruction.

Ellinor, who watched all Crawley's motions, informed me, that he was gone to a neighbouring town, and had left word that he should not be home till after dinner. Lady Glenthorn was in her dressing-room, which was at a part of the house farthest from that which I now inhabited. I had never left my room since my illness, and had scarcely walked farther than from my bed to my arm-chair; but I was so much roused by my feelings at this instant, that, to Ellinor's great astonishment, I started from my chair, and, forbidding her to follow me, walked without any assistance along the corridor, which led to the back-stairs, and to Lady Glenthorn's apartment. I opened the private door of her dressing-room suddenly – the room was in great disorder – her woman was upon her knees packing a trunk: Lady Glenthorn was standing at a table, with a parcel of open letters before her, and a diamond necklace in her hand. She started at the sight of me as if she had beheld a ghost: the maid screamed, and ran to a door at the farther end of the room, to make her escape, but that was bolted. Lady Glenthorn was pale and motionless, till I approached; and then, recollecting herself, she reddened all over, and thrust the letters into her table-drawer. Her woman, at the same instant, snatched a casket of jewels, swept up in her arms a heap of clothes, and huddled them altogether into the half-packed trunk.

'Leave the room,' said I to her sternly. She locked the trunk, pocketed the key, and obeyed.

I placed a chair for Lady Glenthorn, and sat down myself. We were almost equally unable to stand. We were silent for some moments. Her eyes were fixed upon the ground and she leaned her head upon her hand in an attitude of despair. I could scarcely articulate; but making an effort to command my voice, I at last said –

'Lady Glenthorn, I blame myself more than you for all that has happened.'

'For what?' said she, making a feeble attempt at evasion, yet at the same time casting a guilty look towards the drawer of letters.

'You have nothing to conceal from me,' said I.

'Nothing!' said she, in a feeble voice.

'Nothing,' said I; 'for I know every thing' – she started – 'and am willing to pardon every thing.'

She looked up in my face astonished. 'I am conscious,' continued I, 'that you have not been well treated by me. You have had much reason to complain of my neglect. To this I attribute your error. Forget the past – I will set you the example. Promise me never to see the man more, and what has happened shall never be known to the world.'

She made me no answer, but burst into a flood of tears. She seemed incapable of decision, or even of thought. I felt suddenly inspired with energy.

'Write this moment,' continued I, placing a pen and ink before her, 'write to forbid him ever to return to this house, or ever more to appear in your presence. If he appears in mine, I know how to chastise him, and to vindicate my own honour. To preserve your reputation, I refrain, upon these conditions, from making my contempt of him public.'

I put a pen into Lady Glenthorn's hand; but she trembled so that she could not write. She made several ineffectual attempts, then tore the paper; and again giving way to tears, exclaimed, 'I cannot write – I cannot think – I do not know what to say. Write what you will, and I will sign it.'

'*I* write to Captain Crawley! Write what *I* will! Lady Glenthorn, it must be your will to write, not mine. If it be not your will, say so.'

'Oh! I do not say so – <u>I</u> do not say *that*. Give me a moment's time. I do not know what I say. I have been very foolish – very wicked. You are very good – but it is too late: it will all be known. Crawley will betray me; he will tell it to Mrs Mattocks: so whichever way I turn, I am undone. Oh! what *will* become of me?'

She wrung her hands and wept, and was for an hour in this state, in all the indecision and imbecility of a child. At last, she wrote a few scarcely legible lines to Crawley, forbidding him to see or think of her more. I despatched the note, and she was full of penitence, and gratitude, and tears. The next morning, when I wakened, I in my turn received a note from her ladyship.

'Since I saw you Captain Crawley has convinced me that I am his wife, *in the eye of Heaven*, and I therefore desire a divorce, as much as your *whole conduct*, since my marriage, convinces me you must in your *heart*, whatever may be your motives to *pretend* otherwise. Before you receive this I shall be *out of your way* and *beyond your reach*; so do not think of pursuing one who is no longer

Yours,

A. CRAWLEY

After reading this note, I thought not of pursuing or saving Lady Glenthorn. I was as anxious for a divorce as she could be. Some months afterwards the affair was brought to a public trial. When the cause came on, so many circumstances were brought in mitigation of damages, to prove my utter carelessness respecting my wife's conduct, that a suspicion of collusion arose. From this imputation I was clear in the opinion of all who really knew me; and I repelled the charge publicly, with a degree of indignation that surprised all who knew the usual apathy of my temper. I must observe, that during the whole time my divorce-bill was pending, and whilst I was in the greatest possible anxiety, my health was perfectly good. But no sooner was the affair settled, and a decision made in my favour, than I relapsed into my old nervous complaints.

CHAPTER V

> *'Twas doing nothing was his curse; —*
> *Is there a vice can plague us worse?*
> *The wretch who digs the mine for bread,*
> *Or ploughs, that others may be fed,*
> *Feels less fatigue than that decreed*
> *To him who cannot think or read.* [20]

Illness was a sort of occupation to me, and I was always sorry to get well. When the interest of being in danger ceased, I had no other to supply its place. I fancied that I should enjoy my liberty after my divorce; but 'even freedom grew tasteless'. I do not recollect any thing that wakened me from my torpor, during two months after my divorce, except a violent quarrel between all my English servants and my Irish nurse. Whether she assumed too much, upon the idea that she was a favourite, or whether national prejudice was alone the cause of the hatred that prevailed against her, I know not; but they one and all declared that they could not, and would not, live with her. She expressed the same dislike to *consorting* with them; 'but would *put up* with worse, ay, with the devils themselves, to oblige my honour, and to lie under the same roof *wid* my honour'.

The rest of the servants laughed at her blunders. This she could bear with good-humour; but when they seriously affected to reproach her with having, by her uncouth appearance, at her first presenting herself at Sherwood Park, endangered my life, she retorted, 'And who cared for him in the wide world but I, amongst you all, when he lay for dead? I ask you that,' said she.

To this there was no reply; and they hated her the more for their having been silenced by her shrewdness. I protected her as long as I could; but, for the sake of peace, I at last yielded to the combined forces of the steward's room and the servants' hall, and despatched Ellinor to Ireland, with a renewal of the promise that I would visit Glenthorn Castle this year or the next. To comfort her at parting, I would have made her a considerable present; but she would take only a few guineas, to bear her expences back to her native place. The sacrifice I made did not procure me a peace of any continuance in my own house: – ruined by indulgence, and by my indolent, reckless temper, my servants were now my masters. In a large, ill-regulated establishment, domestics become, like spoiled children, discontented, capricious, and the tyrants over those who have not the sense or steadiness to command. I remember one delicate puppy *parted with me*, because, as he informed me, the curtains of his bed did not close at the foot; he had never been used to such a thing, and had told the housekeeper so three times, but could obtain no redress, which necessitated him to beg my permission to retire from the service.

In his stead another coxcomb came to offer himself, who, with an incomparable easy air, begged to know whether I wanted *a man of figure* or *a man of parts*? For the benefit of those to whom this fashionable classification of domestics may not be familiar, I should observe, that the department of *a man of figure* is specially and solely to announce company on gala days; the business of *the man of parts* is multifarious: to write cards of invitation, to speak to impertinent tradesmen, to carry confidential messages, et cetera. Now, where there is an et cetera in an agreement, there is always an opening for dispute. The functions of *the man of parts* not being accurately defined, I unluckily required from him some service which was not in his bond; I believe it was to go for my pocket handkerchief: 'He could not possibly do it, because it was not his business;' and I, the laziest of mortals, after waiting a full quarter of an hour, whilst they were settling whose business it was to obey me, was forced to get up and go for what I wanted. I comforted myself by the recollection of the poor king of Spain and *le brasier*. [21] With a regal precedent I could not but be satisfied. All great people, said I to myself, are obliged to submit to these inconveniences. I submitted with so good a grace, that my submission was scarcely felt to be a condescension. My *bachelor's* house soon exhibited in perfection 'High Life below Stairs'. [22]

It is said that a foreign nobleman permitted his servants to take their own way so completely, that one night he and his guests being kept waiting an unconscionable time for supper, he at last went down stairs to inquire into the cause of the delay: he found the servant, whose business it was to take up supper, quietly at cards with a large party of his friends. The man coolly remonstrated, that it was impossible to leave his game unfinished. The master candidly acknowledged the force of his plea; but insisted upon the man's going up stairs to lay the cloth for supper, whilst he took his cards, sat down, and finished the game for him.

The suavity of my temper never absolutely reached this degree of complaisance. My home was disagreeable to me: I had not the resolution to remove the causes of the discontents. Every day I swore I would part with all these rascals the next morning; but still they staid. Abroad I was not happier than at home. I was disgusted with my former companions: they had convinced me, the night of my accident at Sherwood Park, that they cared not whether I was alive or dead; and ever since that time I had been more and more struck with their selfishness as well as folly. It was inexpressibly fatiguing and irksome to me to keep up a show of good fellowship and joviality with these people, though I had not sufficient energy to make the attempt to quit them. When these *dashers* and *loungers* found that I was not always at their disposal, they discovered that Glenthorn had always something *odd* about him; that Glenthorn had always a melancholy turn; that it ran in the family, &c. Satisfied with these phrases, they let me take my own way, and forgot my existence. Public amusements had lost their charm; I had sufficient steadiness to resist the temptation to game: but, for want of stimulus, I could hardly endure the *tedium* of my days. At this period of my life, ennui was very near turning into misanthropy. I balanced between becoming a misanthrope and a democrat.

Whilst I was in this critical state of ineptitude, my attention was accidentally roused by the sight of a boxing-match. My feelings were so much excited, and the excitation was so delightful, that I was now in danger of becoming an amateur of the pugilistic art. It did not occur to me, that it was beneath the dignity of a British nobleman to learn the vulgar terms of the boxing *trade*. I soon began to talk very *knowingly* of *first-rate bruisers, game men*, and *pleasing* fighters; *making play – beating a man under the ropes – sparring – rallying – sawing* – and *chopping*. What farther proficiency I might have made in this language, or how long my interest in these feats of prize-fighters might have continued, had I been left to myself, I cannot determine; but I was unexpectedly seized with a fit of national shame, on hearing a foreigner of rank and reputation express astonishment at our taste for these savage spectacles. It was in vain that I repeated the arguments of some of the parliamentary panegyrists of boxing and bull-baiting;[23] and asserted, that these diversions render a people hardy and courageous. My opponent replied, that he did not perceive the necessary connexion between cruelty and courage; that he did not comprehend how the standing by in safety to see two men bruise each other almost to death could evince or inspire heroic sentiments or warlike dispositions. He observed, that the Romans were most eager for the fights of gladiators during the reigns of the most effeminate and cruel emperors, and in the decline of all public spirit and virtue. These arguments would have probably made but a feeble impression on an understanding like mine, unaccustomed to general reasoning, and on a temper habituated to pursue, without thought of consequences, my immediate individual gratification; but it happened that my feelings were touched at this time by the dreadful sufferings of one of the pugilistic combatants. He died a few hours after the battle. He was an Irishman: most of the spectators being English, and triumphing in the victory of their countryman, the poor fellow's fate was scarcely noticed. I spoke to him a little while before he died, and found that he came from my own county. His name was Michael Noonan. He made it his dying request, that I would carry half-a-guinea, the only money he possessed, to his aged father, and a silk handkerchief he had worn round his neck, to his sister. Pity for this unfortunate Irishman recalled Ireland to my thoughts. Many small reasons concurred to make me now desirous of going to that country. I should get rid at once of a tormenting establishment, and of servants, without the odium of turning them away; for most of them declined going into banishment, as they called it. Beside this, I should leave my companions, with whom I was disgusted. I was tired of England, and wanted to see something new, even if it were to be worse than what I had seen before. These were not my ostensible reasons: I professed to have more exalted motives for my journey. It was my duty, I said, to visit my Irish estate, and to encourage my tenantry, by residing some time among them. Duties often spring up to our view at a convenient opportunity. Then my promise to poor Ellinor; it was impossible for a man of honour to break a promise, even to an old woman: in short, when people are determined upon any action, they seldom fail to find arguments capable of convincing them that their resolution is reasonable. Mixed motives govern the conduct of half mankind; so I set out upon my journey to Ireland.

CHAPTER VI

> *Es tu contente à la fleur de tes ans?*
> *As tu des goûts et des amusemens?*
> *Tu dois mener une assez douce vie.*
> *L'autre en deux mots repondait ' Je m'ennuie.'*
> *C'est un grand mal, dit la fée, et je croi*
> *Qu'un beau secret est de rester chez soi.*[24]

I was detained six days by contrary winds at Holyhead.[25] Sick of that miserable place, in my ill-humour I cursed Ireland, and twice resolved to return to London: but the wind changed, my carriage was on board the packet; so I sailed and landed safely in Dublin. I was surprised by the excellence of the hotel at which I was lodged. I had not conceived that such accommodation could have been found in Dublin. The house had, as I was told, belonged to a nobleman: it was fitted up and appointed with a degree of elegance, and even magnificence, beyond what I had been used to in the most fashionable hotels in London.[26]

'Ah! sir,' said an Irish gentleman, who found me in admiration upon the staircase, 'this is all very good, very fine, but it is too good and too fine to last; come here again in two years, and I am afraid you will see all this going to rack and ruin. This is too often the case with us in Ireland: we can project, but we can't calculate; we must have every thing upon too large a scale. We mistake a grand beginning for a good beginning. We begin like princes, and we end like beggars.'

I rested only a few days in a capital, in which, I took it for granted, there could be nothing worth seeing by a person who was just come from London. In driving through the streets, I was, however, surprised to see buildings, which my prejudices could scarcely believe to be Irish. I also saw some things, which recalled to my mind the observations I had heard at my hotel. I was struck with instances of grand beginnings and lamentable want of finish, with mixture of the magnificent and the paltry; of admirable and execrable taste. Though my understanding was wholly uncultivated, these things struck my eye. Of all the faculties of my mind, my taste had been most exercised, because its exercise had given me least trouble.

Impatient to see my own castle, I left Dublin. I was again astonished by the beauty of the prospects, and the excellence of the roads. I had in my ignorance believed that I was never to see a tree in Ireland, and that the roads were almost impassable. With the promptitude of credulity, I now went from one extreme to the other: I concluded that we should travel with the same celerity as upon the Bath road; and I expected, that a journey for which four days had been allotted might be performed in two. Like all those who have nothing to do any where, I was always in a prodigious hurry to get from place to place; and I ever had a noble ambition to go over as much ground as possible in a given space of time. I travelled in a light barouche, and with my own horses. My own man (an Englishman), and my cook (a Frenchman), followed in a hackney chaise; I cared not how, so that they kept up with me; the rest was their affair. At night, my gentleman complained bitterly of the Irish post carriages, and besought me to let him follow at an easier rate the next day; but to this I could by no means consent: for how could I exist without my own man and my French cook? In the morning, just as I was ready to set off, and had thrown myself back in my carriage, my Englishman and Frenchman came to the door, both in so great a rage, that the one was inarticulate and the other unintelligible. At length the object of their indignation spoke for itself. From the inn yard came a hackney chaise, in a most deplorable crazy state; the body mounted up to a prodigious height, on unbending springs, nodding forwards, one door swinging open, three blinds up, because they could not be let down, the perch tied in two places, the iron of the wheels half off, half loose, wooden pegs for linch-pins, and ropes for harness. The horses were worthy of the harness; wretched little dog-tired creatures, that looked as if they had been driven to the last gasp, and as if they had never been rubbed down in their lives; their bones starting through their skin; one lame, the other blind; one with a raw back, the other with a galled breast; one with his neck poking down over his collar, and the other with his head dragged forward by a bit of a broken bridle, held at arm's length by a man dressed like a mad beggar, in half a hat and half a wig, both awry in opposite directions; a long tattered great-coat, tied round his waist by a hay-rope; the jagged rents in the skirts of his coat showing his bare legs marbled of many colours; while something like stockings hung loose about his ankles. The noises he made by way of threatening or encouraging his steeds, I pretend not to describe.

In an indignant voice I called to the landlord, 'I hope these are not the horses – I hope this is not the chaise, intended for my servants.'

The innkeeper, and the pauper who was preparing to officiate as postilion, both in the same instant exclaimed, '*Sorrow* better chaise in the county!'[27]

'*Sorrow!*' said I; 'what do you mean by sorrow?'

'That there's no better, plase your honour, can be seen. We have two more, to be sure; but one has no top, and the other no bottom. Any way there's no better can be seen than this same.'*

'And these horses!' cried I; 'why, this horse is so lame he can hardly stand.'

'Oh, plase your honour, tho' he can't stand, he'll *go* fast enough. He has a great deal of the rogue in him, plase your honour. He's always that way at first setting out.'

'And that wretched animal with the galled breast!'

'He's all the better for it, when once he warms; it's he that will go with the speed of light, plase your honour. Sure, is not he Knock-ecroghery? and didn't I give fifteen guineas for him, barring the

*Verbatim.[28]

luck penny, at the fair of Knockecroghery, and he rising four year old at the same time?'

I could not avoid smiling at this speech: but my *gentleman*, maintaining his angry gravity, declared, in a sullen tone, that he would be cursed if he went with such horses; and the Frenchman, with abundance of gesticulation, made a prodigious chattering, which no mortal understood.

'Then I'll tell you what you'll do,' said Paddy; 'you'll take four, as becomes gentlemen of your quality, and you'll see how we'll powder along.'

And straight he put the knuckle of his fore-finger in his mouth, and whistled shrill and strong; and, in a moment, a whistle somewhere out in the fields answered him.

I protested against these proceedings, but in vain; before the first pair of horses were fastened to the chaise, up came a little boy with the others *fresh* from the plough. They were quick enough in putting these to; yet how they managed it with their tackle, I know not. 'Now we're fixed handsomely,' said Paddy.

'But this chaise will break down the first mile.'

'Is it this chaise, plase your honour? I'll engage it will go the world's end. The universe wouldn't break it down now; sure it was mended but last night.'

Then seizing his whip and reins in one hand, he clawed up his stockings with the other: so with one easy step he got into his place, and seated himself, coachman-like, upon a well-worn bar of wood, that served as a coach-box. 'Throw me the loan of a trusty Bartly, for a cushion,' said he. A frieze coat was thrown up over the horses' heads – Paddy caught it. 'Where are you, Hosey?' cried he. 'Sure I'm only rowling a wisp of straw on my leg,' replied Hosey. 'Throw me up,' added this paragon of postilions, turning to one of the crowd of idle bystanders. 'Arrah, push me up, can't ye?'

A man took hold of his knee, and threw him upon the horse: he was in his seat in a trice; then clinging by the mane of his horse, he scrambled for the bridle, which was under the other horse's feet – reached it, and, well satisfied with himself, looked round at Paddy, who looked back to the chaise-door at my angry servants, 'secure in the last event of things'. In vain the Englishman in monotonous anger, and the Frenchman in every note of the gamut, abused Paddy: necessity and wit were on Paddy's side; he parried all that was said against his chaise, his horses, himself, and his country, with invincible comic dexterity, till at last, both his adversaries, dumbfoundered, clambered into the vehicle, where they were instantly shut up in straw and darkness. Paddy, in a triumphant tone, called to *my* postilions, bidding them 'get on, and not be stopping the way any longer'.

Without uttering a syllable, they drove on; but they could not, nor could I, refrain from looking back to see how those fellows would manage. We saw the fore-horses make towards the right, then to the left, and every way but straight forwards; whilst Paddy bawled to Hosey – 'Keep the middle of the road, can't ye? I don't want ye to draw a pound at-all-at-all.'

At last, by dint of whipping, the four horses were compelled to set off in a lame gallop; but they stopped short at a hill near the end of the town, whilst a shouting troop of ragged boys followed, and pushed them fairly to the top. Half an hour afterwards, as we were putting on our drag-chain to go down another steep hill, – to my utter astonishment, Paddy, with his horses in full gallop, came rattling and *chehupping* past us. My people called to warn him that he had no *drag*: but still he cried 'Never fear!' and shaking the long reins, and stamping with his foot, on he went thundering down the hill. My Englishmen were aghast.

'The turn yonder below, at the bottom of the hill, is as sharp and ugly as ever I see,' said my postilion, after a moment's stupified silence. 'He will break their necks, as sure as my name is John.'

Quite the contrary: when we had dragged and undragged, and came up with Paddy, we found him safe on his legs, mending some of his tackle very quietly.

'If that had broke as you were going down the steep hill,' said I, 'it would have been all over with you, Paddy.'

'That's true, plase your honour: but it never happened me going down hill – nor never will, by the blessing of God, if I've any luck.'

With this mixed confidence in a special providence, and in his own good luck, Paddy went on, much to my amusement. It was his glory to keep before us; and he rattled on till he came to a narrow part of the road, where they were rebuilding a bridge. Here there was a dead stop. Paddy lashed his horses, and called them all manner of names; but the wheel-horse, Knockecroghery, was restive, and at last began to kick most furiously. It seemed inevitable that the first kick which should reach the splinter-bar, at which it was aimed, must demolish it instantly. My English gentleman and my Frenchman both put their heads out of the only window which was pervious, and called most manfully to be let out. 'Never fear,' said Paddy. To open the door for themselves was beyond their force or skill. One of the hind wheels, which had belonged to another carriage, was too high to suffer the door to be opened, and the blind at the other side prevented their attempts, so they were close prisoners. The men who had been at work on the broken bridge came forward, and rested on their spades to see the battle. As my carriage could not pass, I was also compelled to be a spectator of this contest between man and horse.

'Never fear,' reiterated Paddy; 'I'll engage I'll be up wid him. Now for it, Knockecroghery! Oh the rogue, he thinks he has me at a *nonplush*, but I'll show him the *differ*.'

After this brag of war, Paddy whipped, Knockecroghery kicked; and Paddy seemingly unconscious of danger, sat within reach of the kicking horse, twitching up first one of his legs, then the other, and shifting as the animal aimed his hoofs, escaping every time as it were by miracle. With a mixture of temerity and presence of mind, which made us alternately look upon him as a madman and a hero, he gloried in the danger, secure of success, and of the sympathy of the spectators.

'Ah! didn't I *compass* him cleverly then? Oh the villain, to be browbating me! I'm too cute for him yet. See there, now, he's come to; and I'll be his bail he'll go *asy* enough wid me. Ogh! he has a fine spirit of his own, but it's I that can match him: 'twould be a poor case if a man like me cou'dn't match a horse any way, let alone a mare, which this is, or it never would be so vicious.'

After this hard-fought battle, and suitable rejoicing for the victory, Paddy walked his subdued adversary on a few yards to allow us to pass him; but, to the dismay of my postilions, a hay-rope was at this instant thrown across the road, before our horses, by the road-makers, who, to explain this proceeding, cried out, 'Plase your honour, the road is so dry, we'd expect a trifle to wet it.'

'What do these fellows mean?' said I.

'It's only a tester or a hog they want, your honour, to give 'em to drink your honour's health,' said Paddy.

'A hog to drink my health?'

'Ay, that is a thirteen, plase your honour; all as one as an English shilling.'[29]

I threw them a shilling: the hay-rope was withdrawn, and at last we went on. We heard no more of Paddy till evening. He came in two hours after us, and expected to be doubly paid *for driving my honour's gentlemen so well.*

I must say that on this journey, though I met with many delays and disasters; though one of my horses was lamed in shoeing by a smith, who came home drunk from a funeral; and though the back pannel of my carriage was broken by the pole of a chaise; and though one day I went without my dinner at a large desolate inn, where nothing was to be had but whiskey; and though one night I lay in a little smoky den, in which the meanest of my servants in England would have thought it impossible to sleep; and though I complained bitterly, and swore it was impracticable for a gentleman to travel in Ireland; yet I never remember to have experienced, on any journey, less ennui.* I was out of patience twenty times a day,

---

*Since Lord Glenthorn's Memoirs were published, the editor has received letters and information from the east, west, north, and south of Ireland, on the present state of posting in that country. The following is one of the many, which is vouched by indisputable authority as a true and recent anecdote, given in the very words in which it was related to the editor . . . Mr —, travelling in Ireland, having got into a hackney chaise, was surprised to hear the driver knocking at each side of the carriage. 'What are you doing?' – 'A'n't I nailing your honour up?' – 'Why do you nail me up? I don't wish to be nailed up.' – 'Augh! would your honour have the doors fly off the hinges?' When they came to the end of the stage, Mr — begged the man to unfasten the doors. 'Ogh! what would I be taking out the nails for, to be racking the doors?' – 'How shall I get out then?' – 'Can't your honour get out of the window like any other *jantleman?*' Mr — began the operation; but, having forced his head and shoulder out, could get no farther, and called again to the postilion. 'Augh! did any one ever see any one get out of a chay head foremost? Can't your honour put out your feet first, like a Christian?'

Another correspondent from the south relates, that when he refused to go on till one of the four horses, who wanted a shoe, was shod, his two postilions in his hearing commenced thus: 'Paddy, where *will* I get a shoe, and no smith nigh hand?' – 'Why don't you see yon *jantleman's* horse in the field; can't you go and unshoe him?' – 'True for ye,' said Jem; 'but that horse's shoe will never fit him.' – 'Augh! you can but try it,' said Paddy. – So the gentleman's horse was actually unshod, and his shoe put upon the hackney horse; and, fit or not fit, Paddy went off with it.

Another gentleman, travelling in the north of Ireland in a hackney chaise during a storm of wind and rain, found that two of the windows were broken, and two could not by force or art of man be pulled up: he ventured to complain to his Paddy of the inconvenience he suffered from the storm pelting in his face. His consolation was, 'Augh! God bless your honour, and can't you get out and *set* behind the carriage, and you'll not get a drop at all, I'll engage.'[30]

but I certainly felt no ennui; and I am convinced that the benefit some patients receive from a journey is in an inverse proportion to the ease and luxury of their mode of travelling. When they are compelled to exert their faculties, and to use their limbs, they forget their nerves, as I did. Upon this principle I should recommend to wealthy hypochondriacs a journey in Ireland, preferably to any country in the civilized world. I can promise them, that they will not only be moved to anger often enough to make their blood circulate briskly, but they will even, in the acme of their impatience, be thrown into salutary convulsions of laughter, by the comic con-comitants of their disasters: besides, if they have hearts, their best feelings cannot fail to be awakened by the warm, generous hospital-ity, they will receive in this country, from the cabin to the castle.

Late in the evening of the fourth day, we came to an inn on the verge of the county where my estate was situate. It was one of the wildest parts of Ireland. We could find no horses, nor accommoda-tions of any sort, and we had several miles farther to go. For our only comfort, the dirty landlady, who had married the hostler, and wore gold drop ear-rings, reminded us, that, 'Sure, if we could but wait an hour, and take a fresh egg, we should have a fine moon.'

After many fruitless imprecations, my French cook was obliged to mount one of my saddle-horses; my groom was left to follow us the next day; I let my gentleman sit on the barouche box, and proceeded with my own tired horses. The moon, which my landlady had promised me, rose, and I had a full view of the face of the country. As we approached my maritime territories, the cottages were thinly scattered, and the trees had a stunted appearance; they all slanted one way, from the prevalent winds that blew from the ocean. Our road presently stretched along the beach, and I saw nothing to vary the prospect but rocks, and their huge shadows upon the water. The road being sandy, the feet of the horses made no noise, and nothing interrupted the silence of the night but the hissing sound of the carriage-wheels passing through the sand.

'What o'clock is it now, think you, John?' said one of my postilions to the other.

'Past twelve, for *sartain*,' said John; 'and this *bees* a strange Irish place,' continued he, in a drawling voice; 'with no possible way o' getting at it, as I see.' John, after a pause, resumed, 'I say, Timothy, to the best of my opinion, this here road is leading *on* us into the sea.' John replied, 'that he did suppose there might be such a thing as a boat farther on, but where he could not say for *sartain*'. Dismayed and helpless, they at last stopped to consult whether they had come the right road to the house. In the midst of their consultation there came up an Irish carman, whistling as he walked beside his horse and car.

'Honest friend, is this the road to Glenthorn Castle?'

'To Glenthorn, sure enough, your honour.'

'Whereabouts is the castle?'

'Forenent you, if you go on to the turn.'

'*Forenent* you!' As the postilions pondered upon this word, the carman, leaving his horse and car, turned back to explain by action what he could not make intelligible by words.

'See, isn't here the castle?' cried he, darting before us to the turn of the road, where he stood pointing at what we could not possibly see, as it was hid by a promontory of rock. When we reached the spot where he was stationed, we came full upon the view of Glenthorn Castle: it seemed to rise from the sea, abrupt and insulated, in all the gloomy grandeur of ancient times, with turrets and battlements, and a huge gateway, the pointed arch of which receded in perspective between the projecting towers.

'It's my lord himself, I'm fond to believe!' said our guide, taking off his hat; 'I had best step on and tell 'em at the castle.'

'No, my good friend, there is no occasion to trouble you farther; you had better go back to your horse and car, which you have left on the road.'

'Oh! they are used to that, plase your honour; they'll go on very *quite*, and I'll run like a redshank with the news to the castle.'

He ran on before us with surprising velocity, whilst our tired horses dragged us slowly through the sand. As we approached, the gateway of the castle opened, and a number of men, who appeared to be dwarfs when compared with the height of the building, came out with torches in their hands. By their bustle, and the vehemence with which they bawled to one another, one might have thought that the whole castle was in flames; but they were only letting down a drawbridge. As I was going over this bridge, a casement window opened in the castle; and a voice, which I knew to be old Ellinor's, exclaimed, 'Mind the big hole in the middle of the bridge, God bless *yees!*'

I passed over the broken bridge, and through the massive gate, under an arched way, at the farthest end of which a lamp had just been lighted: then I came into a large open area, the court of the castle. The hollow sound of the horses' feet, and of the carriage rumbling over the drawbridge, was immediately succeeded by the strange and eager voices of the people, who filled the court with a variety of noises, contrasting, in the most striking manner, with the silence in which we had travelled over the sands. The great effect that my arrival instantaneously produced upon the multitude of servants and dependants, who issued from the castle, gave me an idea of my own consequence beyond any thing which I had ever felt in England. These people seemed 'born for my use': the officious precipitation with which they ran to and fro; the style in which they addressed me; some crying, 'Long life to the Earl of Glenthorn!' some blessing me for coming to reign over them; all together gave more the idea of vassals than of tenants, and carried my imagination centuries back to feudal times.

The first person I saw on entering the hall of my castle was poor Ellinor: she pushed her way up to me –

"'Tis himself!' cried she. Then turning about suddenly, 'I've seen him in his own castle – I've seen him; and if it pleases God this minute to take me to himself, I would die with pleasure.'

'My good Ellinor,' said I, touched to the heart by her affection, 'my good Ellinor, I hope you will live many a happy year; and if I can contribute –'

'And himself to speak to me so kind before them all!' interrupted she. 'Oh! this is too much – quite too much!' She burst into tears; and, hiding her face with her arm, made her way out of the hall.

The flights of stairs which I had to ascend, and the length of galleries through which I was conducted, before I reached the apartment where supper was served, gave me a vast idea of the extent of my castle; but I was too much fatigued to enjoy fully the gratifications of pride. To the simple pleasures of appetite I was more sensible: I ate heartily of one of the most profusely hospitable suppers that ever was prepared for a noble baron, even in the days when oxen were roasted whole. Then I grew so sleepy, that I was impatient to be shown to my bed. I was ushered through another suite of chambers and galleries; and, as I was traversing one of these, a door of some strange dormitory opened, and a group of female heads were thrust out, in the midst of which I could distinguish old Ellinor's face; but, as I turned my head, the door closed so quickly, that I had no time to speak: I only heard the words 'Blessings on him! that's he!'

I was so sleepy, that I rejoiced having escaped an occasion where I might have been called upon to speak, yet I was really grateful to my poor nurse for her blessing. The state tower, in which, after reiterated entreaties, I was at last left alone to repose, was hung with magnificent, but ancient tapestry. It was so like a room in a haunted castle, that if I had not been too much fatigued to think of any thing, I should certainly have thought of Mrs Radcliffe. I am sorry to say that I have no mysteries, or even portentous omens, to record of this night; for the moment that I lay down in my antiquated bed, I fell into a profound sleep.

CHAPTER VII

When I awoke, I thought that I was on shipboard; for the first sound I heard was that of the sea booming against the castle walls. I arose, looked out of the window of my bedchamber, and saw that the whole prospect bore an air of savage wildness. As I contemplated the scene, my imagination was seized with the idea of remoteness from civilized society: the melancholy feeling of solitary grandeur took possession of my soul.

From this feeling I was relieved by the affectionate countenance of my old nurse, who at this instant put her head half in at the door.

'I only just made bold to look in at the fire, to see did it burn, because I lighted it myself, and would not be blowing of it for fear of wakening you.'

'Come in, Ellinor, come in,' said I. 'Come quite in.'

'I will, since you've nobody with you that I need be afraid of,' said she, looking round satisfied, when she saw my own man was not in the room.

'You need never be afraid of any body, Ellinor, whilst I am alive,' said I; 'for I will always protect you. I do not forget your conduct, when you thought I was dead in the banqueting-room.'

'Oh! don't be talking of that; thanks be to God there was nothing in it! I see you well now. Long life to you! Sure you must have been tired to death last night, for this morning early you lay so *quite*, sleeping like an angel; and I could see a great likeness in *yees* to what you were when you were a child in my arms.'

'But sit down, sit down, my good Ellinor,' said I, 'and let us talk a little of your own affairs.'

'And are not these my own affairs?' said she, rather angrily.

'Certainly; but I mean, that you must tell me how you are going on in the world, and what I can do to make you comfortable and happy.'

'There's one thing would make me happy,' said she.

'Name it,' said I.

'To be let light your fire myself every morning, and open your shutters, dear.'

I could not help smiling at the simplicity of the request. I was going to press her to ask something of more consequence, but she heard a servant coming along the gallery, and, starting from her chair, she ran and threw herself upon her knees before the fire, blowing it with her mouth with great vehemence.

The servant came to let me know that Mr M'Leod, my agent, was waiting for me in the breakfast-room.

'And will I be let light your fire then every morning?' said Ellinor eagerly, turning as she knelt.

'And welcome,' said I.

'Then you won't forget to speak about it for me,' said she, 'else may be I won't be let up by them English. God bless you, and don't forget to speak for me.'

'I will remember to speak about it,' said I; but I went down stairs and forgot it.

Mr M'Leod, whom I found reading the newspaper in the breakfast-room, seemed less affected by my presence than any body I had seen since my arrival. He was a hard-featured, strong-built, perpendicular man, with a remarkable quietness of deportment: he spoke with deliberate distinctness, in an accent slightly Scotch; and, in speaking, he made use of no gesticulation, but held himself surprisingly still. No part of him but his eyes moved, and they had an expression of slow, but determined good sense. He was sparing of his words; but the few that he used said much, and went directly to the point. He pressed for the immediate examination and settlement of his accounts: he enumerated several things of importance, which he had done for my service: but he did this without pretending the slightest attachment to me; he mentioned them only as proofs of his having done his duty to his employer, for which he neither expected nor would accept of thanks. He seemed to be cold and upright in his mind as in his body. I was not influenced in his favour even by his striking appearance of plain-dealing, so strong was the general abhorrence of agents which Crawley's treachery had left in my mind. The excess of credulity, when convinced of its error, becomes the extreme of suspicion. Persons not habituated to reason often argue absurdly, because, from particular instances, they deduce general conclusions, and extend the result of their limited experience of individuals indiscriminately to whole classes. The labour of thinking was so great to me, that having once come to a conclusion upon any subject, I would rather persist in it, right or wrong, than be at the trouble of going over the process again to revise and rectify my judgement.

Upon this occasion national prejudice heightened the prepossession which circumstances had raised. Mr M'Leod was not only an agent, but a Scotchman; and I had a notion that all Scotchmen were crafty: therefore I concluded that his blunt manner was assumed, and his plain-dealing but a more refined species of policy.

After breakfast he laid before me a general statement of my affairs; obliged me to name a day for the examination of his accounts; and then, without expressing either mortification or displeasure at the coldness of my behaviour, or at my evident impatience of his presence, he, unmoved of spirit, rang for his horse, wished me a good morning, and departed.

By this time my castle-yard was filled with a crowd of 'greatcoated suitors', who were all *come to see – could they see my lordship?* or *waiting just to say two words to my honour*. In various lounging attitudes, leaning against the walls, or pacing backwards and forwards before the window, to catch my eye, they, with a patience passing the patience of courtiers, waited, hour after hour, the live-long day, for their turn, or their chance, of an audience. I had promised myself the pleasure of viewing my castle this day, and of taking a ride through my grounds; but that was totally out of the question. I was no longer a man with a will of my own, or with time at my own disposal.

'*Long may you live to reign over us!*' was the signal that I was now to live, like a prince, only for the service of my subjects. How these subjects of mine had contrived to go on for so many years in my absence, I was at a loss to conceive; for, the moment I was present, it seemed evident that they could not exist without me.

One had a wife and six *childer*, and not a spot in the wide world to live in, if my honour did not let him live under me, in any bit of a skirt of the estate that would feed a cow.

Another had a brother in jail, who could not be *got out* without me.

Another had three lives dropped in a *lase* for ever; another wanted a renewal; another a farm; another a house; and one *expected* my lard would make his son an exciseman; and another that I would make him a policeman; and another was *racked*, if I did not settle the *mearing* between him and Corny Corkran; and half a hundred had given in *proposals* to the agent for lands that would be out next May; and half a hundred more came with legends of traditionary *promises from the old lord, my lordship's father that was*: and for hours I was forced to listen to long stories *out of the face*, in which there was such a perplexing and provoking mixture of truth and fiction, involved in language so figurative, and tones so new to my English ears, that, with my utmost patience and strained attention, I could comprehend but a very small portion of what was said to me.[31]

Never were my ears so weary any day of my life as they were this day. I could not have endured the fatigue, if I had not been supported by the agreeable idea of my own power and consequence; a power seemingly next to despotic. This new stimulus sustained me for three days that I was kept a state-prisoner in my own castle, by the crowds who came to do me homage, and to claim my favour and protection. In vain every morning was my horse led about saddled and bridled: I never was permitted to mount. On the fourth morning, when I felt sure of having despatched all my tormentors, I was in astonishment and despair on seeing my levée crowded with a fresh succession of petitioners. I gave orders to my people to say that I was going out, and absolutely could see nobody. I supposed that they did not understand what my English servants said, for they never stirred from their posts. On receiving a second message, they acknowledged that they understood the first; but replied, that they could wait there till my honour came back from my ride. With difficulty I mounted my horse, and escaped from the closing ranks of my persecutors. At night I gave directions to have the gates kept shut, and ordered the porter not to admit any body at his peril. When I got up, I was delighted to see the coast clear; but the moment I went out, lo! at the outside of the gate, the host of besiegers were posted, and in my lawn, and along the road, and through the fields: they pursued me; and when I forbade them to speak to me when I was on horseback, the next day I found parties in ambuscade, who laid wait for me in silence, with their hats off, bowing and bowing, till I could not refrain from saying, 'Well, my good friend, what do you stand bowing there for?' Then I was fairly prisoner, and held by the bridle for an hour.

In short, I found that I was now placed in a situation where I could hope neither for privacy nor leisure; but I had the joys of power, my rising passion for which would certainly have been extinguished in a short time by my habitual indolence, if it had not been kept alive by jealousy of Mr M'Leod.

One day, when I refused to hear an importunate tenant, and declared that I had been persecuted with petitioners ever since my arrival, and that I was absolutely tired to death, the man answered, 'True, *for ye*, my lard; and it's a shame to be troubling you this way. Then, may be, it's to Mr M'Leod I'll go? Sure the agent will do as well, and no more about it. Mr M'Leod will do every thing the same way as usual.'

'Mr M'Leod will do every thing!' said I, hastily: 'no, by no means.'

'Who will we speak to, then?' said the man.

'To myself,' said I, with as haughty a tone as Louis XIV could have assumed, when he announced to his court his resolution to be his own minister. After this intrepid declaration to act for myself, I could not yield to my habitual laziness. So much had my pride been hurt, as well as my other feelings, by Captain Crawley's conduct, that I determined to show the world I was not to be duped a second time by an agent.

When, on the day appointed, Mr M'Leod came to settle accounts with me, I, with an air of self-important capability, as if I had been all my life used to look into my own affairs, sat down to inspect the papers; and, incredible as it may appear, I went through the whole at a sitting, without a single yawn; and, for a man who never before had looked into an account, I understood the nature of debtor and creditor wonderfully well: but, with my utmost desire to evince my arithmetical sagacity, I could not detect the slightest error in the accounts; and it was evident that Mr M'Leod was not Captain Crawley; yet, rather than believe that he could be both an agent and an honest man, I concluded, that if he did not cheat me out of my money, his aim was to cheat me out of power; and, fancying that he wished to be a man of influence and consequence in the county, I transferred to him instantly the feelings that were passing in my own mind, and took it for granted that he must be actuated by a love of power in every thing that he did apparently for my service.

About this time I remember being much disturbed in my mind, by a letter which Mr M'Leod received in my presence, and of which he read to me only a part: I never rested till I saw the whole. The epistle proved well worth the trouble of deciphering: it related merely to the paving of my chicken-yard. Like the King of Prussia,* who was said to be so jealous of power, that he wanted to regulate all the mouse-traps in his dominions,[32] I soon engrossed the management of a perplexing multiplicity of minute insignificant details. Alas! I discovered to my cost, that trouble is the inseparable attendant upon power: and many times, in the course of the first ten days of my reign, I was ready to give up my dignity from excessive fatigue.

CHAPTER VIII

Early one morning, after having passed a feverish night, tortured in my dreams by the voices and faces of the people who had surrounded me the preceding day, I was awakened by the noise of somebody lighting my fire. I thought it was Ellinor; and the idea of the disinterested affection of this poor woman came full into my mind, contrasted in the strongest manner with the recollection of the selfish encroaching people by whom, of late, I had been worried.

'How do you do, my good Ellinor?' said I; 'I have not seen any thing of you this week past.'

'It's not Ellinor at all, my lard,' said a new voice.

'And why so? Why does not Ellinor light my fire?'

* Mirabeau – Secret Memoirs.

'Myself does not know, my lard.'

'Go for her directly.'

'She's gone home these three days, my lard.'

'Gone! is she sick?'

'Not as I know *on*, my lard. Myself does not know what ailed her, except she would be jealous of my lighting the fire. But I can't say what ailed her; for she went away without a word good or bad, when she seen me lighting this fire, which I did by the housekeeper's orders.'

I now recollected poor Ellinor's request, and reproached myself for having neglected to fulfil my promise, upon an affair which, however trifling in itself, appeared of consequence to her. In the course of my morning's ride I determined to call upon her at her own house, and make my apologies: but first I satisfied my curiosity about a prodigious number of *parks* and *towns* which I had heard of upon my estate. Many a ragged man had come to me, with the modest request that I would let him *one of the parks near the town*. The horse-park, the deer-park, the cow-park, were not quite sufficient to answer the ideas I had attached to the word *park*: but I was quite astonished and mortified when I beheld the bits and corners of land near the town of Glenthorn, on which these high-sounding titles had been bestowed: – just what would feed a cow is sufficient in Ireland to constitute a park.

When I heard the names of above a hundred towns on the Glenthorn estate, I had an exalted idea of my own territories; and I was impatient to make a progress through my dominions: but, upon visiting a few of these places, my curiosity was satisfied. Two or three cabins gathered together were sufficient to constitute a town, and the land adjoining thereto is called a town-land. The denominations of these town-lands having continued from generation to generation, according to ancient surveys of Ireland, it is sufficient to show the boundaries of a town-land, to prove that there must be a town; and a tradition of a town continues to be satisfactory, even when only a single cabin remains. I turned my horse's head away in disgust from one of these traditionary towns, and desired a boy to show me the way to Ellinor O'Donoghoe's house.

'So I will, plase your honour, my lard; sure I've a right to know, for she's my own granny.'

The boy, or, as he was called, the *gossoon*, ran across some fields where there was abundance of fern and of rabbits. The rabbits, sitting quietly at the entrance of their holes, seemed to consider themselves as proprietors of the soil, and me and my horse as intruders. The boy apologized for the number of rabbit-holes on this part of the estate: 'It would not be so, my lard, if I had a gun allowed me by the gamekeeper, which he would give me if he knew it would be plasing to your honour.' The ingenuity with which even the young boys can introduce their requests in a favourable moment sometimes provoked me, and sometimes excited my admiration. This boy made his just at the time he was rolling out of my way a car that stopped a gap in the hedge; and he was so hot and out of breath with running in my service, that I could not refuse him *a token to the gamekeeper that he might get a gun* as soon as I understood what it meant.

We came to Ellinor's house, a wretched-looking, low, and mud-walled cabin; at one end it was propped by a buttress of loose stones, upon which stood a goat reared on his hind legs, to browse on the grass that grew on the house-top. A dunghill was before the only window, at the other end of the house, and close to the door was a puddle of the dirtiest of dirty water, in which ducks were dabbling. At my approach there came out of the cabin a pig, a calf, a lamb, a kid, and two geese, all with their legs tied; followed by turkeys, cocks, hens, chickens, a dog, a cat, a kitten, a beggar-man, a beggar-woman with a pipe in her mouth, children innumerable, and a stout girl with a pitchfork in her hand; all together more than I, looking down upon the roof as I sat on horseback, and measuring the superficies with my eye, could have possibly supposed the mansion capable of containing. I asked if Ellinor O'Donoghoe was at home; but the dog barked, the geese cackled, the turkeys gobbled, and the beggars begged, with one accord, so loudly, that there was no chance of my being heard. When the *girl* had at last succeeded in appeasing them all with her pitchfork, she answered, that Ellinor O'Donoghoe was at home, but that she was out with the potatoes; and she ran to fetch her, after calling to *the boys, who was within in the room smoking*, to come out to his honour. As soon as they had crouched under the door, and were able to stand upright, they welcomed me with a very good grace, and were proud to see me in *the kingdom*. I asked if they were all Ellinor's sons?

'All entirely,' was the first answer.

'Not one but one,' was the second answer. The third made the other two intelligible.

'Plase your honour, we are all her sons-in-law, except myself, who am her lawful son.'

'Then you are my foster-brother?'

'No, plase your honour, it's not me, but my brother, and he's *not in it*.'

'*Not in it?*'

'No, plase your honour; becaase he's in the forge up *abow*.'

'Abow!' said I; 'what does he mean?'

'Sure he's the blacksmith, my lard.'

'And what are you?'

'I'm Ody, plase your honour; the short for Owen.'

'And what is your trade?'

'Trade, plase your honour, I was bred to none, more than another; but expects, only that my mother's not willing to part me, to go into the militia next month; and I'm sure she'd let me, if your honour's lordship would spake a word to the colonel, to see to get me made a serjeant *immediately*.'

As Ody made his request, all his companions came forward in sign of sympathy, and closed round my horse's head to make me *sinsible* of their expectations: but at this instant Ellinor came up, her old face colouring all over with joy when she saw me.

'So, Ellinor,' said I, 'you were affronted, I hear, and left the castle in anger?'

'In anger! And if I did, more shame for me – but anger does not last long with me any way; and against you, my lord, dear, how could it? Oh, think how good he is, coming to see me in such a poor place!'

'I will make it a better place for you, Ellinor,' said I. Far from being eager to obtain promises, she still replied, that 'all was good enough for her'. I desired that she would come and live with me at the castle, till a better house than her present habitation could be built for her; but she seemed to prefer this hovel. I assured her that she should be permitted to light my fire.

'Oh, it's better for me not,' said she; 'better keep out of the way. I could not be asy if I got any one ill-will.'

I assured her that she should be at liberty to do just as she liked: and whilst I rode home I was planning a pretty cottage for her near the porter's lodge. I was pleased with myself for my gratitude to this poor woman. Before I slept, I actually wrote a letter, which obtained for Ody the honour of being made a serjeant in the — militia; and Ellinor, dazzled by this military glory, was satisfied that he should leave home, though he was her favourite.

'Well, let him leave me then,' said she; 'I won't stand in his light. I never thought of my living to see Ody a serjeant. Now, Ody, have done being wild, honey-dear, and be a credit to your family, and to his honour's commendation – God bless him for ever for it! From the very first I knew it was he that had the kind heart.'

I am not sure that it was a very good action to get a man made a serjeant, of whom I knew nothing but that he was son to my nurse. Self-complacency, however, cherished my first indistinct feelings of benevolence. Though not much accustomed to reflect upon my own sensations, I think I remember, at this period, suspecting that the feeling of benevolence is a greater pleasure than the possession of *barouches*, and horses, and castles, and parks – greater even than the possession of power. Of this last truth, however, I had not as yet a perfectly clear conception. Even in my benevolence I was as impatient and unreasonable as a child. Money, I thought, had the power of Aladdin's lamp, to procure with magical celerity the gratification of my wishes. I expected that a cottage for Ellinor should rise out of the earth at my command. But the slaves of Aladdin's lamp were not Irishmen. The delays, and difficulties, and blunders, in the execution of my orders, provoked me beyond measure; and it would have been difficult for a cool spectator to decide, whether I or my workmen were most in fault; they for their dilatory habits, or I for my impatient temper.

'Well, *plase* your honour, when the *pratees* are set, and the turf cut, we'll *fall-to* at Ellinor's house.'

'Confound the potatoes and the turf! you must *fall-to*, as you call it, directly.'

'Is it without the lime, and plase your honour? Sure that same is not drawn yet, nor the stones quarried, since it is of stone it will be – nor the foundations itself dug, and the horses were all putting out dung.'

Then after the bog and the potatoes came funerals and holidays innumerable. The masons were idle one week waiting for the mortar, and the mortar another week waiting for the stones, and then they were at a stand for the carpenter when they came to the door-case, and the carpenter was looking for the sawyer, and the sawyer was gone to have the saw mended. Then there was a *stop* again at the window-sills for the stone-cutter, and he was at the quarter-sessions, processing his brother for *tin and tinpence, hay-money*. And when, in spite of all delays and obstacles, the walls reached their destined height, the roof was a new plague; the carpenter, the slater, and the nailer, were all at variance, and I cannot tell which was the most provoking rogue of the three. At last, however, the house was roofed and slated: then I would not wait till the walls were dry before I plastered, and papered, and furnished it. I fitted it up in the most elegant style of English cottages; for I was determined that Ellinor's habitation should be such as had never been seen in this part of the world. The day when it was finished, and when I gave possession of it to Ellinor, paid me for all my trouble; I tasted a species of pleasure that was new to me, and which was the sweeter from having been earned with some difficulty. And now, when I saw a vast number of my tenants assembled at a rural feast which I gave on Ellinor's *installation*, my benevolence enlarged, even beyond the possibility of its gratification, and I wished to make all my dependents happy, provided I could accomplish it without much trouble. The method of doing good, which seemed to require the least exertion, and which I, therefore, most willingly practised, was giving away money. I did not wait to inquire, much less to examine into the merits of the claimants; but, without selecting proper objects, I relieved myself from the uneasy feeling of pity, by indiscriminate donations to objects apparently the most miserable.

I was quite angry with Mr M'Leod, my agent, and considered him as a selfish, hard-hearted miser, because he did not seem to sympathize with me, or to applaud my generosity. I was so much irritated by his cold silence, that I could not forbear pressing him to say something.

'*I doubt*, then,' said he, 'since you desire me to speak my mind, my lord, *I doubt* whether the best way of encouraging the industrious is to give premiums to the idle.'

'But, idle or not, these poor wretches are so miserable, that I cannot refuse to give them something; and, surely, when one can do it so easily, it is right to relieve misery. Is it not?'

'Undoubtedly, my lord; but the difficulty is, to relieve present misery, without creating more in future. Pity for one class of beings sometimes makes us cruel to others. I am told that there are some

Indian Brahmins so very compassionate, that they hire beggars to let fleas feed upon them: I doubt whether it might not be better to let the fleas starve.'

I did not in the least understand what Mr M'Leod meant: but I was soon made to comprehend it, by crowds of eloquent beggars, who soon surrounded me: many who had been resolutely struggling with their difficulties, slackened their exertions, and left their labour for the easier trade of imposing upon my credulity. The money I had bestowed was wasted at the dram-shop, or it became the subject of family-quarrels; and those whom I had *relieved* returned to *my honour*, with fresh and insatiable expectations. All this time my in-dustrious tenants grumbled, because no encouragement was given to them; and, looking upon me as a weak, good-natured fool, they combined in a resolution to ask me for long leases, or reduction of rent.

The rhetoric of my tenants succeeded in some instances; and again I was mortified by Mr M'Leod's silence. I was too proud to ask his opinion. I ordered, and was obeyed. A few leases for long terms were signed and sealed; and when I had thus my own way completely, I could not refrain from recurring to Mr M'Leod's opinion.

'I doubt, my lord,' said he, 'whether this measure may be as advantageous as you hope. These fellows, these middle-men, will underset the land, and live in idleness, whilst they *rack* a parcel of wretched under-tenants.'

'But they said they would keep the land in their own hands, and improve it; and that the reason why they could not afford to improve before was, that they had not long leases.'

'It may be doubted whether long leases alone will make improving tenants; for in the next county to us, there are many farms of the dowager Lady Ormsby's land let at ten shillings an acre, and her tenantry are beggars: and the land now, at the end of the leases, is worn out, and worse than at their commencement.'

I was weary listening to this cold reasoning, and resolved to apply no more for explanations to Mr M'Leod; yet in my indolence I wanted the support of his approbation, at the very time I was jealous of his interference.

At one time I had a mind to raise the wages of labour; but Mr M'Leod said, '*It might be doubted* whether the people would not work less, when they could with less work have money enough to support them.'

I was puzzled: and then I had a mind to lower the wages of labour, to force them to work or starve. Still provoking Mr M'Leod said, '*It might be doubted* whether it would not be better to leave them alone.'

I gave marriage-portions to the daughters of my tenants, and rewards to those who had children; for I had always heard that legislators should encourage population.

Still Mr M'Leod hesitated to approve; he observed, 'that my estate was so populous, that the complaint in each family was, that they had not land for the sons. *It might be doubted* whether, if a farm could support but ten people, it were wise to encourage the birth of twenty. *It might be doubted* whether it were not better for ten to live, and be well fed, than for twenty to be born, and to be half-starved.'

To encourage manufactures in my town of Glenthorn, I proposed putting a clause in my leases, compelling my tenants to buy stuffs and linens manufactured at Glenthorn, and nowhere else. Stubborn M'Leod, as usual, began with, '*I doubt* whether that will not encourage the manufacturers at Glenthorn to make bad stuffs and bad linen, since they are sure of a sale, and without danger of competition.'

At all events, I thought my tenants would grow rich and *independent*, if they made every thing *at home* that they wanted: yet Mr M'Leod perplexed me by his 'doubt whether it would not be better for a man to buy shoes, if he could buy them cheaper than he could make them'. He added something about the division of labour, and Smith's Wealth of Nations; to which I could only answer – 'Smith's a Scotchman.'

I cannot express how much I dreaded Mr M'Leod's *I doubt* – and – *It may be doubted*.

From the pain of doubt, and the labour of thought, I was soon most agreeably reprieved by the company of a Mr Hardcastle, whose visits I constantly encouraged by a most gracious reception. Mr Hardcastle was the agent of the dowager Lady Ormsby, who had a large estate in my neighbourhood: he was the very reverse of my Mr M'Leod in his deportment and conversation. Talkative, self-sufficient, peremptory, he seemed not to know what it was *to doubt*; he considered doubt as a proof of ignorance, imbecility, or cowardice.

'*Can any man doubt?*' was his usual beginning. On every subject of human knowledge, taste, morals, politics, economy, legislation; on all affairs, civil, military, or ecclesiastical, he decided at once in the most confident tone. Yet he 'never read, not he!' he had nothing to do with books; he consulted only his own eyes and ears, and appealed only to common sense. As to theory, he had no opinion of theory; for his part, he only pretended to understand practice and experience – and his practice was confined steadily to his own practice, and his experience uniformly to what he had tried at New-town-Hardcastle.

At first I thought him a mighty clever man, and I really rejoiced to see my *doubter* silenced. After dinner, when he had finished speaking in this decisive manner, I used frequently to back him with a – *Very true – very fair – very clear* – though I understood what he said as little as he did himself; but it was an ease to my mind to have a disputed point settled – and I filled my glass with an air of triumph, whilst M'Leod never contradicted my assertions, nor controverted Mr Hardcastle's arguments. There was still an air of content and quiet self-satisfaction in M'Leod's very silence, which surprised and vexed me.

One day, when Hardcastle was laying down the law upon several subjects in his usual dictatorial manner, telling us how he managed his people, and what order he kept them in, I was determined that M'Leod should not enjoy the security of his silence, and I urged him to give us his general opinion, as to the means of improving the poor people in Ireland.

'I doubt,' said M'Leod, 'whether any thing effectual can be done, till they have a better education.'

'Education! – Pshaw! – There it is now – these book-men,' cried Hardcastle: 'Why, my dear sir, can any man alive, who knows this country, doubt that the common people have already too much education, as it is called – a vast deal too much? Too many of them know how to read, and write, and cipher, which I presume is all you mean by education.'

'Not entirely,' said M'Leod; 'a good education comprehends something more.'

'The more the worse,' interrupted Hardcastle. 'The more they know, the worse they are, sir, depend on that; I know the people of this country, sir; I have *a good right* to know them, sir, being born amongst them, and bred amongst them; so I think I may speak with some confidence on these matters. And I give it as my decided humble opinion, founded on irrefragable experience, which is what I always build upon, that the way to ruin the poor of Ireland would be to educate them, sir. Look at the poor scholars, as they call themselves; and what are they? a parcel of young vagabonds in rags, with a book under their arm instead of a spade or a shovel, sir. And what comes of this? that they grow up the worst-disposed, and the most troublesome seditious rascals in the community. I allow none of them about New-town-Hardcastle – none – banished them all. Useless vagrants – hornets – vipers, sir: and show me a quieter, better-managed set of people than I have made of mine. I go upon experience, sir; and that's the only thing to go upon; and I'll go no farther than New-town-Hardcastle: if that won't bring conviction home to you, nothing will.'

'I never was at New-town-Hardcastle,' said M'Leod, drily.

'Well, sir, I hope it will not be the case long. But in the mean time, my good sir, do give me leave to put it to your own common sense, what can reading or writing do for a poor man, unless he is to be a bailiff or an excisemen? and you know all men can't expect to be bailiffs or excisemen. Can all the book-learning in the world, sir, dig a poor man's potatoes for him, or plough his land, or cut his turf? Then, sir, in this country, where's the advantage of education, I humbly ask? No, sir, no, trust me – keep the Irish common people ignorant, and you keep 'em quiet; and that's the only way with them; for they are too quick and smart, as it is, naturally. Teach them to read and write, and it's just adding fuel to fire – fire to gunpowder, sir. Teach them any thing, and directly you *set them up*: now it's our business to *keep them down*, unless, sir, you'd wish to have your throat cut. Education, sir! Lord bless your soul, sir! they have a great deal too much; they know too much already, which makes them so refractory to the laws, and so idle. I will go no farther than New-town-Hardcastle, to prove all this. So, my good sir,' concluded he, triumphantly, 'education, I grant you, is necessary for the rich; but tell me, if you can, what's the use of education to the poor?'

'Much the same, I apprehend, as to the rich,' answered M'Leod. 'The use of education, as I understand it, is to teach men to see clearly, and to follow steadily, their real interests. All morality, you know, is comprised in this definition; and –'

'Very true, sir; but all this can never apply to the poor in Ireland.'

'Why, sir; are they not men?'

'Men, to be sure; but not like men in Scotland. The Irish know nothing of their interests; and as to morality, that's out of the question: they know nothing about it, my dear sir.'

'That is the very thing of which I complain,' said M'Leod. 'They know nothing, because they have been taught nothing.'

'They cannot be taught, sir.'

'Did you ever try?'

'I *did*, sir, no later than last week. A fellow that I caught stealing my turf, instead of sending him to jail, I said to him, with a great deal of lenity, My honest fellow, did you never hear of the eighth commandment, "Thou shalt not steal?" He confessed he had; but did not know it was the eighth. I showed it to him, and counted it to him myself; and set him, for a punishment, to get his whole catechism. Well, sir, the next week I found him stealing my turf again! and when I caught him by the wrist in the fact, he said, it was because the priest would not let him learn the catechism I gave him, because it was a Protestant one. Now you see, sir, there's a bar for ever to all education.'

Mr M'Leod smiled, said something about time and patience, and observed, 'that one experiment was not conclusive against a whole nation'. Any thing like a general argument, Mr Hardcastle could not comprehend. He knew every blade of grass within the reach of his tether, but could not reach an inch beyond. Any thing like an appeal to benevolent feelings was lost upon him; for he was so frank in his selfishness, that he did not even pretend to be generous. By sundry self-complacent motions he showed whilst his adversary spoke, that he disdained to listen almost as much as to read: but, as soon as M'Leod paused, he said, 'What you observe, sir, may possibly be very true; but I have made up my mind.' Then he went over and over again his assertions, in a louder and a louder voice, ending with a tone of interrogation that seemed to set all answer at defiance, 'What have you to answer to me now, sir? – Can any man alive doubt this, sir?'

M'Leod was perfectly silent. The company broke up; and, as we were going out of the room, I maliciously asked M'Leod, why he, who could say so much in his own defence, had suffered himself to be so completely silenced? He answered me, in his low deliberate voice, in the words of Molière – '"Qu'est-ce que la raison avec un filet de voix contre une gueule comme celle-là?'[33] At some other time,' added Mr M'Leod, 'my sentiments shall be at your lordship's disposal.'

Indolent persons love positive people, when they are of their own opinion; because they are saved the trouble of developing their thoughts, or supporting their assertions: but the moment the positive differs in sentiment from the indolent man, there is an end of the friendship. The indolent man then hates his pertinacious adversary as much as he loved his sturdy friend. So it happened between Mr Hardcastle and me. This gentleman was a prodigious favourite with me, so long as his opinions were not in opposition to my own; but an accident happened, which brought his love of power and mine into direct competition, and then I found his peremptory mode of reasoning and his ignorance absurd and insufferable.

Before I can do justice to my part of this quarrel, I must explain the cause of the interest which I took in behalf of the persons aggrieved. During the time that my first hot fit of benevolence was on me, I was riding home one evening after dining with Mr Hardcastle, and I was struck with the sight of a cabin, more wretched than any I had ever before beheld: the feeble light of a single rush-candle through the window revealed its internal misery.

'Does any body live in that hovel?' said I.

'Ay, sure, does there: the Noonans, plase your honour,' replied a man on the road. Noonans! I recollected the name to be that of the pugilist, who had died in consequence of the combat at which I had been present in London; who had, with his dying breath, besought me to convey his only half-guinea and his silk handkerchief to his poor father and sister. I alighted from my horse, asking the man, at the same time, if the son of this Noonan had not died in England.

'He had, sir, a son in England, Mick Noonan, who used to send him odd guineas, *I mind*, and was a *good lad to his father*, though wild; and there's been no account of him at-all-at-all this long while: but the old man has another boy, a sober lad, who's abroad with the army in the East Indies; and it's he that is the hope of the family. And there's the father – and old as he is, and poor, and a cripple, I'd engage there is not a happier man in the three counties at this very time speaking: for it is just now I seen young Jemmy Riley, the daughter's *bachelor*, go by with a letter. What news? says I. Great news! says he: a letter from Tom Noonan to his father; and I'm going in to read it for him.'

By the time my voluble informant had come to this period, I had reached the cabin door. Who could have expected to see smiles and hear exclamations of joy under such a roof?

I saw the father, with his hands clasped in ecstasy, and looking up to heaven, with the strong expression of delight in his aged countenance. I saw every line of his face; for the light of the candle was full upon it. The daughter, a beautiful girl, kneeling beside him, held the light for the young man, who was reading her brother's letter. I was sorry to interrupt them.

'Your honour's kindly welcome,' said the old man, making an attempt to rise.

'Pray, don't let me disturb you.'

'It was only a letter from a boy of mine that's over the seas we was reading,' said the old man. 'A better boy to an ould father, that's good for nothing now in this world, never was, plase your honour. See what he has sent me: a draught here for ten guineas out of the little pay he has. God for ever bless him! – as he surely will.'

After a few minutes' conversation, the old man's heart was so much opened towards me, that he talked as freely as if he had known me for years. I led to the subject of his other son Michael, who was mentioned in the letter as a wild chap. 'Ah! your honour, that's what lies heaviest on my heart, and will to my dying day, that Mick, before he died, which they say he did surely a twelvemonth ago, over there in England, never so much as sent me one line, good or bad, or his sister a token to remember him by even!'

'Had he but sent us the least bit of a word, or the least token in life, I had been content,' said the sister, wiping her eyes: 'we don't so much as know how he died.'

I took this moment to relate the circumstances of Michael Noonan's death; and when I told them of his dying request about the half-guinea and the silk handkerchief, they were all so much touched, that they utterly forgot the ten-guinea draught, which I saw on the ground, in the dirt, under the old man's feet, whilst he contemplated the half-guinea which his *poor Michael* had sent him: repeating, 'Poor fellow! poor fellow! 'twas all he had in the world. God bless him! – Poor Michael! he was a wild chap! but none better to his parents than he while the life was in him. Poor Michael!'

In no country have I found such strong instances of filial affection as in Ireland. Let the sons go where they may, let what will befall them, they never forget their parents at home: they write to them constantly the most affectionate letters, and send them a share of whatever they earn.

When I asked the daughter of this Noonan, why she had not married? the old man answered, 'That's her own fault – if it be a fault to abide by an old father. She wastes her youth here, in the way your honour sees, tending him who has none other to mind him.'

'Oh! let alone *that*,' said the girl, with a cheerful smile; 'we be too poor to think of marrying yet, by a great deal! so, father dear, you're no hinderance any way. For don't I know, and doesn't Jemmy there know, that it's a sin and a shame, as my mother used to say, for them that have nothing to marry and set up house-keeping, like the rogue that ruined my father?'

'That's true,' said the young man, with a heavy sigh; 'but times will mend, or we'll strive and mend them, with the blessing of God.'

I left this miserable hut in admiration of the generosity of its inhabitants. I desired the girl to come to Glenthorn Castle the next day, that I might give her the silk handkerchief which her poor brother had sent her. The more I inquired into the circumstances of this family, the more cause I found for pity and approbation. The old man had been a good farmer in his day, as the traditions of the aged, and the memories of the young, were ready to witness; but he was unfortunately joined in *copartnership* with a drunken rogue, who ran away, and left an arrear of rent, which ruined Noonan. Mr Hardcastle, the agent, called upon him to pay it, and sold all that the old man possessed; and this being insufficient to discharge the debt, he was forced to give up his farm, and retire, with his daughter, to this hovel; and soon afterwards he lost the use of his side by a paralytic stroke.

I was so much pleased with the goodness of these poor people, that, in despite of my indolent disposition, I bestirred myself the very next day to find a better habitation for them on my own estate. I settled them, infinitely to their satisfaction, in a small farm; and the girl married her lover, who undertook to manage the farm for the old man. To my utter surprise, I found that Mr Hardcastle was affronted by the part I took in this affair. He complained that I had behaved in a very ungentlemanlike manner, and had spirited the tenants away from Lady Ormsby's estate, against the regulation which he had laid down for all *the* tenants not to *emigrate* from *the estate*. Jemmy Riley, it seems, was one of the *cotters* on the Ormsby estate, a circumstance with which I was unacquainted; indeed I scarcely at that time understood what was meant by a *cotter*. Mr Hardcastle's complaint, in matter and manner, was unintelligible to me; but I was quite content to leave off visiting him, as he left off visiting me – but here the matter did not stop. This over-wise and over-busy gentleman took upon him, amongst other offices, the regulation of the markets in the town of Ormsby; and as he apprehended, for reasons best and only known to himself, a year of scarcity, he thought fit to keep down the price of oats and potatoes. He would allow none to be sold in the market of Ormsby but at the price which he stipulated. The poor people grumbled, and, to remedy the injustice, made private bargains with each other. He had information of this, and seized the corn that was selling above the price he had fixed. Young Riley, Noonan's son-in-law, came to me to complain, that *his little oats were seized and detained*. I remonstrated – Hardcastle resented the appeal to me, and bid him wait and be damned. The young man, who was rather of a hasty temper, and who did not much like either to wait or be damned, seized his own oats, and was marching off, when they were recaptured by Hardcastle's bailiff, whom young Riley knocked down; and who, as soon as he got up again, went *straight* and swore examinations against Riley. Then I was offended, as I had a right to be, by the custom of the country, with the magistrate who took an examination against my tenant without writing first to me. Then there was a race between the examinations of *my* justice of peace and *his* justice of peace. My indolence was conquered by my love of power: I supported the contest: the affair came before our grand jury: I conquered, and Mr Hardcastle was ever after, of course, my enemy. To English ears the possessive pronouns *my* and *his* may sound extraordinary, prefixed to a justice of peace; but, in many parts of Ireland, this language is perfectly correct. A great man talks of *making* a justice of the peace with perfect confidence; a very great man talks with as much certainty of *making* a sheriff; and a sheriff makes the jury; and the jury makes the law. We must not forget, however, that, in England, during the reign of Elizabeth, a member of parliament defined a justice of peace to be 'an animal, who for half a dozen chickens will dispense with half a dozen penal statutes'.[34] Time is necessary to

enforce the sanctions of legislation and civilization – But I am antici-
pating reflections which I made at a much later period of my life.
To return to my history.

My benevolence was soon checked by slight disappointments.
Ellinor's cottage, which I had taken so much pains to build, became
a source of mortification to me. One day I found my old nurse
sitting at her wheel, in the midst of the wreck and litter of all sorts of
household furniture, singing her favourite song of

> 'There was a lady lov'd a swine:
> Honey! says she,
> I'll give ye a silver trough.
> *Hunk!* says he!'[35]

Ellinor seemed, alas! to have as little taste for the luxuries with
which I had provided her as the pig had for the silver trough. What
I called conveniences were to her encumbrances: she had not been
used to them; she was put out of her way; and it was a daily torment
to one of her habits, to keep her house clean and neat.

There may be, as some philosophers assure us that there is, an
innate love of order in the human mind; but of this instinctive
principle my poor Ellinor was totally destitute. Her ornamented
farm-house became, in a wonderfully short time, a scene of dirt,
rubbish, and confusion. There was a partition between two rooms,
which had been built with turf or peat, instead of bricks, by the wise
economy I had employed. Of course, this was pulled down to get at
the turf. The stairs also were pulled down and burned, though there
was no scarcity of firing. As the walls were plastered and papered
before they were quite dry, the paper grew mouldy, and the plaster
fell off. In the hurry of finishing, some of the woodwork had but one
coat of paint. In Ireland they have not faith in the excellent Dutch
proverb, '*Paint costs nothing.*' I could not get my workmen to give a
second coat of paint to any of the sashes, and the wood decayed:
divers panes of glass in the windows were broken, and their places
filled up with shoes, an old hat, or a bundle of rags. Some of the
slates were blown off one windy night: the slater lived at ten miles
distance, and before the slates were replaced, the rain came in, and
Ellinor was forced to make a bedchamber of the parlour, and then
of the kitchen, retreating from corner to corner as the rain pursued, till, at last, when 'it *would* come *every way* upon her bed', she

petitioned me to let her take the slates off and thatch the house; for a slated house, she said, was never so warm as a *tatched cabin*; and as there was no smoke, she was *kilt* with the *cowld*.

In my life I never felt so angry. I was ten times more angry than when Crawley ran away with my wife. In a paroxysm of passion, I reproached Ellinor with being a savage, an Irishwoman, and an ungrateful fool.

'Savage I am, for any thing I know; and *fool* I am, that's certain; but ungrateful I am not,' said she, bursting into tears. She went home and took to her bed; and the next thing I heard from her son was 'that she was *lying in the rheumatism*, which had kept her awake many a long night, before she would come to complain to my honour of the house, in dread that I should blame myself for *sending of* her into it *afore* it was dry'.

The rheumatism reconciled me immediately to Ellinor; I let her take her own way, and thatch the house, and have as much smoke as she pleased, and she recovered. But I did not entirely recover my desire to do good to my poor tenants. After forming, in the first enthusiasm of my benevolence, princely schemes for their advantage, my ardour was damped, and my zeal discouraged, by a few slight disappointments.

I did not consider, that there is often, amongst uncultivated people, a mixture of obstinate and lazy content, which makes them despise the luxuries of their richer neighbours; like those mountaineers, who, proud of their own hard fare,* out of a singular species of contempt, call the inhabitants of the plains *mange-rôtis*, 'eaters of roast meat'. I did not consider, that it must take time to change local and national habits and prejudices; and that it is necessary to raise a taste for comforts, before they can be properly enjoyed.

In the pettishness of my disappointment, I decided that it was in vain to attempt to improve and civilize such people as the Irish. I did not recollect, perhaps at that time I did not know, that even in the days of the great queen Elizabeth, 'the greatest part of the buildings in the cities and good towns of England consisted only of timber, cast over with thick clay to keep out the wind. The new houses of the nobility were indeed either of brick or stone; and glass

---

* See Philosophical Transactions, vol. lxvii, part 2, Sir George Shuckburgh's observations to ascertain the height of mountains – for a full account of the cabin of a couple of Alpine shepherdesses.[36]

windows were then beginning to be used in England:'*³⁷ and clean rushes were strewed over the dirty floors of the royal palace. In the impatience of my zeal for improvement, I expected to do the work of two hundred years in a few months: and because I could not accelerate the progress of refinement in this miraculous manner, I was out of humour with myself and with a whole nation. So easily is the humanity of the rich and great disgusted and discouraged! as if any people could be civilized in a moment, and at the word of command of ignorant pride or despotic benevolence.

CHAPTER IX

He saw – and but that admiration
Had been too active, too like passion,
Or had he been to ton *less true,*
Cupid had shot him through and through.

I have not thought it necessary to record every visit that I received from all my country neighbours; but I must now mention one, which led to important consequences; a visit from Sir Harry Ormsby, a very young dashing man of fortune, who, in expectation of the happy moment when he should be of age, resided with his mother, the dowager Lady Ormsby. Her ladyship had heard that there had been some disagreement between her agent, Mr Hardcastle, and *my people*; but she took the earliest opportunity of expressing her wishes, that our families should be on an amicable footing.

Lady Ormsby was just come to the country, with a large party of her fashionable friends – some Irish, some English: Lord and Lady Kilrush; my lady Kildangan, and her daughter the Lady Geraldine —; the knowing widow O'Connor; the English *dasher*, Lady Hauton; the interesting Mrs Norton, *separated* but not *parted* from her husband; the pleasant Miss Bland; the three Miss Ormsbys, better known by the name of the Swanlinbar Graces; two English aides-de-camp from the Castle, and a brace of brigadiers; beside other men of inferior note.

* See Harrison.

I perceived that Sir Harry Ormsby took it for granted that I must be acquainted with the pretensions of all these persons to celebrity; his talkativeness and my taciturnity favoured me so fortunately, that he never discovered the extent of my ignorance. He was obligingly impatient to make me personally acquainted 'with those of whom I must have heard so much in England'. Observing that Ormsby Villa was too far from Glenthorn Castle for a morning visit, he pressed me to waive ceremony, and to do Lady Ormsby and him the honour of spending a week with them, as soon as I could make it convenient. I accepted this invitation, partly from a slight emotion of curiosity, and partly from my habitual inability to resist any reiterated importunity.

Arrived at Ormsby Villa, and introduced to this crowd of people, I was at first disappointed by seeing nothing extraordinary. I expected that their manners would have been as strange to me as some of their names appeared: but whether it was from my want of the powers of discrimination, or from the real sameness of the objects, I could scarcely, in this fashionable flock, discern any individual marks of distinction. At first view, the married ladies appeared much the same as those of a similar class in England, whom I had been accustomed to see. The young ladies I thought, as usual, 'best distinguished by black, brown, and fair': but I had not yet seen Lady Geraldine—; and a great part of the conversation, the first day I was at Ormsby Villa, was filled with lamentations on the unfortunate tooth-ache, which prevented her ladyship from appearing. She was talked of so much, and as a person of such importance, and so essential to the amusement of society, that I could not help feeling a slight wish to see her. The next day at breakfast she did not appear; but, five minutes before dinner, her ladyship's humble companion whispered, 'Now Lady Geraldine is coming, my lord.' I was always rather displeased to be called upon to attend to any thing or any body, yet as Lady Geraldine entered, I gave one involuntary glance of curiosity. I saw a tall, finely shaped woman, with the commanding air of a woman of rank; she moved well; not with feminine timidity, but with ease, promptitude, and decision. She had fine eyes and a fine complexion, yet no regularity of feature. The only thing that struck me as really extraordinary was her indifference when I was introduced to her. Every body had seemed extremely desirous that I should see her ladyship, and that her ladyship should see me; and I was rather surprised by her unconcerned air. This piqued me, and fixed my attention. She turned from me and began to converse with others. Her voice was agreeable:[38] she did not speak with the Irish accent; but, when I listened maliciously, I detected certain Hibernian inflections; nothing of the vulgar Irish idiom, but something that was more interrogative, more exclamatory, and perhaps more rhetorical, than the common language of English ladies, accompanied with much animation of countenance and demonstrative gesture. This appeared to me peculiar and unusual, but not affected. She was uncommonly eloquent, and yet, without action, her words were not sufficiently rapid to express her ideas. Her manner appeared foreign, yet it was not quite French. If I had been obliged to decide, I should, however, have pronounced it rather more French than English. To determine what it was, or whether I had ever seen any thing similar, I stood considering her ladyship with more attention than I had ever bestowed on any other woman. The words *striking– fascinating–bewitching*, occurred to me as I looked at her and heard her speak. I resolved to turn my eyes away, and shut my ears; for I was positively determined not to like her, I dreaded so much the idea of a second Hymen. I retreated to the farthest window, and looked out very soberly upon a dirty fish-pond. Dinner was announced. I observed Lady Kildangan manoeuvring to place me beside her daughter Geraldine, but Lady Geraldine counteracted this movement. I was again surprised and piqued. After yielding the envied position to one of the Swanlinbar Graces, I heard Lady Geraldine whisper to her next neighbour, 'Baffled, mamma!'

It was strange to me to feel piqued by a young lady's not choosing to sit beside me. After dinner, I left the gentlemen as soon as possible, because the conversation wearied me. Lord Kilrush, the chief orator, was a courtier, and could talk of nothing but Dublin Castle, and my lord lieutenant's levées.[39] The moment that I went to the ladies, I was seized upon by the officious Miss Bland: she could not speak of any thing but Lady Geraldine, who sat at so great a distance, and who was conversing with such animation herself, that she could not hear her *prôneuse*,[40] Miss Bland, inform me that 'her friend, Lady Geraldine, was extremely clever; so clever, that many people were at first a little afraid of her; but that there was not the least occasion; for that, where she liked, nobody could be more affable and engaging'. This judicious friend, a minute afterwards, told me, as a very great secret, that Lady Geraldine was an admirable mimic; that she could draw or *speak* caricatures; that she was also wonderfully happy in the invention of agnomens and cognomens,[41] so applicable to the persons, that they could scarcely be forgotten or forgiven. I was a little anxious to know whether her ladyship would honour me with an agnomen. I could not learn this from Miss Bland, and I was too prudent to betray my curiosity: I afterwards heard it, however. Pairing me and Mr M'Leod, whom she had seen together, her ladyship observed, that *Sawney* and *Yawnée* were made for each other; and she sketched, in strong caricature, my relaxed elongation of limb, and his rigid rectangularity. A slight degree of fear of Lady Geraldine's powers kept my attention alert. In the course of the evening, Lady Kildangan summoned her daughter to the music-room, and asked me to come and hear an Irish song. I exerted myself so far as to follow immediately; but though summoned, Lady Geraldine did not obey. Miss Bland tuned the harp, and opened the music-books on the piano; but no Lady Geraldine appeared. Miss Bland was sent backwards and forwards with messages; but Lady Geraldine's ultimatum was, that she could not possibly sing, because she was afraid of the tooth-ache. God knows, her mouth had never been shut all the evening. 'Well, but,' said Lady Kildangan, 'she can play for us, cannot she?' No; her ladyship was afraid of the cold in the music-room. 'Do, my lord Glenthorn, go and tell the dear capricious creature, that we are very warm here.'

Very reluctantly I obeyed. The Lady Geraldine, with her circle round her, heard and answered me with the air of a princess.

'Do you the honour to play for you, my lord! Excuse me: I am no professor – I play so ill, that I make it a rule never to play but for my own amusement. If you wish for music, there is Miss Bland; she plays incomparably, and I dare say will think herself happy to oblige your lordship.' I never felt so silly, or so much abashed, as at this instant. 'This comes,' thought I, 'of acting out of character. What possessed me to exert myself to ask a lady to play? I, that have been tired to death of music! Why did I let myself be sent ambassador, when I had no interest in the embassy?'

To convince myself and others of my apathy, I threw myself on a sofa, and never stirred or spoke the remainder of the night. I presume I appeared fast asleep, else Lady Geraldine would not have said, within my hearing, 'Mamma wants me to catch somebody, and to be caught by somebody; but that will not be; for, do you know, I think somebody is nobody.'

I was offended as much as it was in my nature to be offended, and I began to meditate apologies for shortening my visit at Ormsby Villa: but, though I was shocked by the haughtiness of Lady Geraldine, and accused her, in my own mind, of want of delicacy and politeness, yet I could not now suspect her of being an accomplice with her mother in any matrimonial designs upon me. From the moment I was convinced of this, my conviction was, I suppose, visible to her ladyship's penetrating eyes, and from that instant she showed me that she could be polite and agreeable. Now, soothed to a state of ease and complacency, I might have sunk to indifference and ennui, but fresh singularities in this lady struck me, and kept my attention awake and fixed upon her character. If she had treated me with tolerable civility at first, I never should have thought about her. High-born and high-bred, she seemed to consider more what she thought of others than what others thought of her. Frank, candid, and affable, yet opinionated, insolent, and an egotist, her candour and affability appeared the effect of a naturally good temper, her insolence and egotism only those of a spoiled child. She seemed to talk of herself purely to oblige others, as the most interesting possible topic of conversation; for such it had always been to her fond mother, who idolized her ladyship as an only daughter, and the representative of an ancient house. Confident of her talents, conscious of her charms, and secure of her station, Lady Geraldine gave free scope to her high spirits, her fancy, and her turn for ridicule. She looked, spoke, and acted, like a person privileged to think, say, and do, what she pleased. Her raillery, like the raillery of princes, was without fear of retort. She was not ill-natured, yet careless to whom she gave offence, provided she produced amusement; and in this she seldom failed; for, in her conversation, there was much of the raciness of Irish wit, and the oddity of Irish humour. The singularity that struck me most about her ladyship was her indifference to flattery. She certainly preferred frolic. Miss Bland was her humble companion; Miss Tracey her *butt*. Her ladyship appeared to consider Miss Bland as a necessary appendage to her rank and person, like her dress or her shadow; and she seemed to think no more of the one than of the other. She suffered Miss Bland to follow her; but she would go in quest of Miss Tracey. Miss Bland was allowed to speak;

but her ladyship listened to Miss Tracey. Miss Bland seldom obtained an answer; but Miss Tracey never opened her lips without a repartee.

In describing Miss Tracey, Lady Geraldine said, 'Poor simpleton! she cannot help imitating all she sees us do; yet, would you believe it, she really has starts of common sense, and some tolerable ideas of her own. Spoiled by bad company! In the language of the bird-fanciers, she has a few notes nightingale, and all the rest rubbish.'

It was one of Lady Geraldine's delights to humour Miss Tracey's rage for imitating the fashions of fine people.

'Now you shall see Miss Tracey appear at the ball to-morrow, in every thing that I have sworn to her is fashionable. Nor have I cheated her in a single article: but the *tout ensemble* I leave to her better judgement; and you shall see her, I trust, a perfect monster, formed of every creature's best: Lady Kilrush's feathers, Mrs Moore's wig, Mrs O'Connor's gown, Mrs Lighton's sleeves, and all the necklaces of all the Miss Ormsbys. She has no taste, no judgement; none at all, poor thing! but she can imitate as well as those Chinese painters, who, in their drawings, give you the flower of one plant stuck on the stalk of another, and garnished with the leaves of a third.'

Miss Tracey's appearance the ensuing night justified all Lady Geraldine's predictions, and surpassed her ladyship's most sanguine hopes. Even I, albeit unused to the laughing mood, could not forbear smiling at the humour and ease with which her ladyship played off this girl's credulous vanity.

At breakfast the next morning, Lord Kilrush, in his grave manner (always too solemn by half for the occasion), declared, 'that no man was more willing than himself to enter into a jest in proper time, and season, and measure, and so forth; but that it was really, positively, morally unjustifiable, in *his* apprehension, *the making* this poor girl so publicly ridiculous'.

'My good lord,' replied Lady Geraldine, 'all the world are ridiculous some way or other: some in public, some in private. Now,' continued she, with an appealing look to the whole company, 'now, after all, what is there more extravagant in my Miss Tracey's delighting, at sixteen, in six yards of pink riband, than in your courtier sighing, at sixty, for three yards of blue riband? or what is there more ridiculous in her coming simpering into a ball-room, fancying herself the mirror of fashion, when she is a figure for a print-shop, than in the courtier rising solemnly in the House of Lords, believing himself an orator, and expecting to make a vast reputation, by picking up, in every debate, the very worst arguments that every body else let fall? There would be no living in this world, if we were all to see and expose one another's *ridicules*. My plan is much the best – to help my friends to expose themselves, and then they are infinitely obliged to me.'

Satisfied with silencing all opposition, and seeing that the majority was with her, Lady Geraldine persisted in her course; and I was glad she was incorrigible, because her faults entertained me. As to love, I thought I was perfectly safe; because, though I admired her quickness and cleverness, yet I still, at times, perceived, or fancied I perceived, some want of polish, and elegance, and *tact*. She was not exactly cut out according to my English pattern of a woman of fashion; so I thought I might amuse myself without danger, as it was partly at her ladyship's expence. But about this time I was alarmed for myself by a slight twinge of jealousy. As I was standing lounging upon the steps at the hall-door, almost as ennuyé as usual, I saw a carriage at a distance, between the trees, driving up the *approach*; and, at the same instant, I heard Lady Geraldine's eager voice in the hall, 'Oh! they are coming; he is coming; they are come. Run, Miss Bland, run, and give Lord Craiglethorpe my message before he gets out of the carriage – before any body sees him.'

Afraid of hearing what I should not hear, I walked down the steps deliberately, and turned into a shrubbery-walk, to leave the coast clear. Out ran Miss Bland: and then it was that I felt the twinge – very slight, however. 'Who is this Lord Craiglethorpe, with whom Lady Geraldine is on such favourable terms? I wonder what kind of looking man he is; and what could *the message* mean? – but, at all events, it cannot concern me; yet I am curious to see this Lord Craiglethorpe. I wonder any woman can like a man with so strange a name: but does she like him, after all? – Why do I plague myself about it?'

As I returned from my saunter, I was met by Miss Bland.

'A charming day, ma'am,' said I, endeavouring to pass on.

'A charming day, my lord! But I must stop your lordship a moment. Oh, I am so out of breath – I went the wrong way –'

'The wrong way! Indeed! I am sorry. I am concerned you should have had so much trouble.'

'No trouble in the world. Only I want to beg you'll keep our secret – my lady Geraldine's secret.'

'Undoubtedly, madam – a man of honour – Lady Geraldine cannot doubt – her ladyship's secret is perfectly safe.'

'But do you know it? You don't know it yet, my lord.'

'Pardon me; I was on the steps just now. I thought you saw me.'

'I did, my lord – but I don't understand –'

'Nor I, neither,' interrupted I, half laughing; for I began to think I was mistaken in my suspicions; 'pray explain yourself, my dear Miss Bland: I was very rude to be so quick in interrupting you.'

Miss Bland then made me the confidant of a charming scheme of Lady Geraldine's for quizzing Miss Tracey.

'She has never in her life seen Lord Craiglethorpe, who is an English lord travelling through Ireland,' continued Miss Bland. 'Now, you must know, that Miss Tracey is passionately fond of lords, let them be what they may. Now. Lord Craiglethorpe, this very morning, sent his groom with a note and excuse to Lady Ormsby, for not coming to us to-day; because, he said, he was bringing down in the chaise with him a surveyor, to survey his estate *near here*; and he could not possibly think of bringing the surveyor, who is a low man, to Ormsby Villa. But Lady Ormsby would take no apology, and wrote by the groom to beg that Lord Craiglethorpe would make no scruple of bringing the surveyor; for you know she is so polite and accommodating, and all that. Well, the note was scarcely gone, before Lady Geraldine thought of her charming scheme, and regretted, *of all things*, she had not put *it* into it.'

'*It into it!*' repeated I to myself. 'Ma'am,' said I, looking a little bewildered.

'But,' continued my clear narrator, 'I promised to remedy *all that*, by running to meet the carriage, which was what I ran for when you saw me, my lord, in such a hurry.'

I bowed – and was as wise as ever.

'So, my lord, you comprehend, that the surveyor, whose name, whose odious name, is Gabbitt, is to be my lord Craiglethorpe, and my lord Craiglethorpe is to be passed for Mr Gabbitt upon Miss Tracey; and, you will see, Miss Tracey will admire Mr Gabbitt prodigiously, and call him vastly genteel, when she thinks him a lord. Your lordship will keep our secret; and she is sure Lord Craiglethorpe will do any thing to oblige her, because he is a near connexion of hers. But, I assure you, it is not every body could get Lord Craiglethorpe to join in a joke; for he is very stiff, and cold, and high. Of course your lordship will know which is the real lord at first sight. He is a full head taller than Gabbitt.'

Never was explanation finally more satisfactory: and whether the jest was really well contrived and executed, or whether I was put into a humour to think so, I cannot exactly determine; but, I confess, I was amused with the scenes that followed, though I felt that they were not quite justifiable even in jest.

The admiration of Miss Tracey for *the false Craiglethorpe*, as Lady Geraldine called Mr Gabbitt; the awkwardness of Mr Gabbitt with his title, and the awkwardness of Lord Craiglethorpe without it, were fine subjects of her ladyship's satirical humour.

In another point of view, Lord Craiglethorpe afforded her lady-ship amusement; as an English traveller, full of English prejudices against Ireland and every thing Irish. Whenever Miss Tracey was out of the room, Lady Geraldine allowed Lord Craiglethorpe to be himself again; but he did not fare the better for this restoration to his honours. Lady Geraldine contrived to make him as ridiculous in his real as in his assumed character. Lord Craiglethorpe was, as Miss Bland had described him, very stiff, cold, and *high*. His manners were in the extreme of English reserve, and his ill-bred show of contempt for the Irish was sufficient provocation and justification of Lady Geraldine's ridicule. He was much in awe of his fair and witty cousin: she could easily put him out of countenance, for he was extremely bashful.

His lordship had that sort of bashfulness which makes a man surly and obstinate in his taciturnity; which makes him turn upon all who approach him, as if they were going to assault him; which makes him answer a question as if it were an injury, and repel a compliment as if it were an insult. Once, when he was out of the room, Lady Geraldine exclaimed, 'That cousin Craiglethorpe of mine is scarcely an agreeable man: the awkwardness of *mauvaise honte* might be pitied and pardoned, even in a nobleman,' continued her ladyship, 'if it really proceeded from humility; but here, when I know it is con-nected with secret and inordinate arrogance, 'tis past all endurance. Even his ways of sitting and standing provoke me, they are so self-sufficient. Have you observed how he stands at the fire? Oh, the caricature of "*the English fire-side*" outdone! Then, if he sits, we hope that change of posture may afford our eyes transient relief: but worse again; bolstered up, with his back against his chair, his hands in his pockets, and his legs thrown out, in defiance of all passengers and all decorum, there he sits, in magisterial silence, throwing a gloom upon all conversation. As the Frenchman said of the Englishman, for whom even his politeness could not find another compliment, 'Il faut avouer que ce monsieur a un grand talent pour le silence";[42] he holds his tongue, till the people actually believe that he has something to say; a mistake they could never fall into if he would but speak.'

Some of the company attempted to interpose a word or two in favour of Lord Craiglethorpe's timidity, but the vivacious and merciless lady went on.

'I tell you, my good friends, it is not timidity, – it is all pride. I would pardon his dullness, and even his ignorance; for one, as you say, might be the fault of his nature, and the other of his education: but his self-sufficiency is his own fault, and that I will not, and cannot, pardon. Somebody says, that nature may make a fool, but a coxcomb is always of his own making. Now, my cousin – (as he is my cousin, I may say what I please of him) – my cousin Craiglethorpe is a solemn coxcomb, who thinks, because his vanity is not talkative and sociable, that it's not vanity. What a mistake! his silent superciliousness is to me more intolerable than the most garrulous egotism that ever laid itself open to my ridicule.'

Miss Bland and Miss Ormsby both confessed that Lord Craiglethorpe was vastly too silent.

'For the honour of my country,' continued Lady Geraldine, 'I am determined to make this man talk, and he shall say all that I know he thinks of us poor Irish savages. If he would but speak, one could answer him: if he would find fault, one might defend: if he would laugh, one might perhaps laugh again: but here he comes to hospitable, open-hearted Ireland; eats as well as he can in his own country; drinks better than he can in his own country; sleeps as well as he can in his own country; accepts all our kindness without a word or a look of thanks, and seems the whole time to think, that "Born for his use, we live but to oblige him."[43] There he is at this instant: look at him, walking in the park, with his note-book in his hand, setting down our faults, and conning them by rote. We are even with him. I understand, Lady Kilrush, that my bright cousin Craiglethorpe means to write a book, a great book, upon Ireland.'

Lady Kilrush replied, that she understood Lord Craiglethorpe had it in contemplation to publish a Tour through Ireland, or a View of Ireland, or something of that nature.[44]

'He! with his means of acquiring information!' exclaimed Lady Geraldine. 'Posting from one great man's house to another, what can he see or know of the manners of any rank of people but of the class of gentry, which in England and Ireland is much the same? As to the lower classes, I don't think he ever speaks to them; or, if he does, what good can it do him? for he can't understand their modes of expression, nor they his: if he inquire about a matter of fact, I defy him to get the truth out of them, if they don't wish to tell it; and, for some reason or other, they will, nine times in ten, not wish to tell it to an Englishman. There is not a man, woman, or child, in any cabin in Ireland, who would not have wit and *cuteness* enough to make *my lard* believe just what they please. So, after posting from Dublin to Cork, and from the Giants' Causeway to Killarney; after travelling east, west, north, and south, my wise cousin Craiglethorpe will know just as much of the lower Irish as the cockney who has never been out London, and who has never, *in all his born days*, seen an Irishman but on the English stage; where the representations are usually as like the originals, as the Chinese pictures of lions, drawn from description, are to the real animal.'

'Now! now! look at his lordship!' cried Miss Bland; 'he has his note-book out again.'

'Mercy on us!' said Miss Callwell, 'how he is writing!'

'Yes, yes, write on, my good cousin Craiglethorpe,' pursued Lady Geraldine, 'and fill the little note-book, which will soon turn to a ponderous quarto. I shall have a copy, bound in morocco, no doubt, *from the author*, if I behave myself prettily; and I will earn it, by supplying valuable information. You shall see, my friends, how I'll deserve well of my country, if you'll only keep my counsel and your own countenances.'

Presently Lord Craiglethorpe entered the room, walking very pompously, and putting his note-book up as he advanced.

'O, my dear lord, open the book again; I have a bull for you.'

Lady Geraldine, after putting his lordship in good humour by this propitiatory offering of a bull, continued to supply him, either directly or indirectly, by some of her confederates, with the most absurd anecdotes, incredible *facts*, stale jests, and blunders, such as were never made by true-born Irishmen; all which my lord Craig-lethorpe took down with an industrious sobriety, at which the specta-tors could scarcely refrain from laughing. Sometimes he would pause, and exclaim, 'A capital anecdote! a curious fact! May I give my authority? may I quote your ladyship?'

'Yes, if you'll pay me a compliment in the preface,' whispered Lady Geraldine; 'and now, dear cousin, do go up stairs *and put it all in ink*.'

When she had despatched the noble author, her ladyship indulged her laughter. 'But now,' cried she, 'only imagine a set of sober English readers studying my cousin Craiglethorpe's New View of Ireland, and swallowing all the nonsense it will contain!'

When Lord Kilrush remonstrated against the cruelty of letting the man publish such stuff, and represented it as a fraud upon the public, Lady Geraldine laughed still more, and exclaimed, 'Surely you don't think I would use the public and my poor cousin so ill. No, I am doing him and the public the greatest possible service. Just when he is going to leave us, when the writing-box is packed, I will step up to him, and tell him the truth. I will show him what a farrago of nonsense he has collected as materials for his quarto; and convince him at once how utterly unfit he is to write a book, at least a book on Irish affairs. Won't this be deserving well of my country and of my cousin?'

Neither on this occasion, nor on any other, were the remonstrances of my lord Kilrush of power to stop the course of this lady's flow of spirits and raillery.

Whilst she was going on in this manner with the real Lord Craig-lethorpe, Miss Tracey was taking charming walks in the park with Mr Gabbitt, and the young lady began to be seriously charmed with her false lord. This was carrying the jest farther than Lady Geraldine had intended or foreseen; and her good-nature would probably have disposed her immediately to dissolve the enchant-ment, had she not been provoked by the interference of Lord Kilrush, and the affected sensibility of Miss Clementina Ormsby, who, to give me an exalted opinion of her delicacy, expostulated incessantly in favour of the deluded fair-one.

'But, my dear Lady Geraldine, I do assure you, it really hurts my feelings. This is going too far – when it comes to the heart. I can't laugh, I own – the poor girl's affections will be engaged – she is really falling in love with this odious surveyor.'

'But now, my dear Clementina, I do assure you, it really hurts my feelings to hear you talk so childishly. "When it comes to the heart!" "affections engaged!" You talk of falling in love as if it were a terrible fall: for my part, I should pity a person much more for falling down stairs. Why, my dear, where is the mighty height from which Miss Tracey could fall? She does not live in the clouds, Clementina, as you do. No ladies live there now; for the best of all possible reasons, because there are no men there. So, my love, make haste and come down, before you are out of your teens, or you may chance to be left there till you are an angel or an old maid. Trust me, my dear, I, who have tried, tell you, there is no such thing as falling in love, nowadays: you may slip, slide, or stumble; but to fall in love, I defy you.'

I saw Lady Kildangan's eyes fix upon me as her daughter pronounced the last sentence.

'Geraldine, my dear, you do not know what you are talking about,' said her ladyship. 'Your time may come, Geraldine. Nobody should be too courageous. Cupid does not like to be defied.'

Lady Kildangan walked away, as she spoke, with a very well-satisfied air, leaving a party of us young people together. Lady Geraldine looked haughtily vexed. When in this mood, her wit gave no quarter; spared neither sex nor age.

'Every body says,' whispered she, 'that mamma is the most artful woman in the world; and I should believe it, only that every body says it: now, if it were true, nobody would know it.'

Lady Geraldine's air of disdain towards me was resumed. I did not quite understand. Was it pride? was it coquetry? She certainly blushed deeply, and for the first time that I ever saw her blush, when her mother said, 'Your time may come, Geraldine.'

My week being now at an end, I resolved to take my leave. When I announced this resolution, I was assailed with the most pressing entreaties to stay a few days longer – one day longer. Lady Ormsby and Sir Harry said every thing that could be said upon the occasion: indeed, it seemed a matter of general interest to all, except to Lady Geraldine. She appeared wholly indifferent, and I was not even gratified by any apparent affectation of desiring my departure. Curiosity to see whether this would be sustained by her ladyship to the last gave me resolution sufficient to resist the importunities of Sir Harry; and I departed, rejoicing that my indifference was equal to her ladyship's. As Tasso said of some fair one, whom he met at the carnival of Mantua, *I ran some risk of falling in love*. I had been so far roused from my habitual apathy, that I actually made some reflections. As I returned home, I began to perceive that there was some difference between woman and woman, beside the distinctions of rank, fortune, and figure. I think I owe to Lady Geraldine my first relish for wit, and my first idea that a woman might be, if not a reasonable, at least a companionable animal. I compared her ladyship with the mere puppets and parrots of fashion, of whom I had been wearied; and I began to suspect, that one might find, in a lady's 'lively nonsense', a relief from ennui. These reflections, however, did not prevent me from sleeping the greatest part of the morning on my way home; nor did I dream of any thing that I can remember.

At the porter's lodge I saw Ellinor sitting at her spinning-wheel; and my thoughts took up my domestic affairs just where I had left them the preceding week.

CHAPTER X

In vain I attempted to interest myself in my domestic affairs; the silence and solitude of my own castle appeared to me intolerably melancholy, after my return from Ormsby Villa. There was a blank in my existence during a week, in which I can remember nothing that I did, said, or thought, except what passed during one ride, which Mr M'Leod compelled my politeness to take with him. He came with the same face to see me, and the same set of ideas, as those he had before I went to Ormsby Villa. He began to talk of my schemes for improving my tenantry, and of my wish that he should explain his notions relative to the education of the poor of Ireland, which, he said, as I now seemed to be at leisure, he was ready to do as concisely as possible. *As concisely as possible* were the only words of his address that I heard with satisfaction; but of course I bowed, said I was much obliged, and should be happy to have the advantage of Mr M'Leod's opinions and sentiments. What these were I cannot recollect, for I settled myself in a reverie soon after his voice began to sound upon my ear; but I remember at last he wakened me, by proposing that I should ride with him to see a school-house and some cottages, which he had built on a little estate of his own in my neighbourhood: 'for,' said he, ''tis better, my lord, to show you what can be done with these people, than to talk of what might be effected.'

'Very true,' said I, agreeing readily; because I wanted to finish a conversation that wearied me, and to have a refreshing ride. It was a delightful evening; and when we came on M'Leod's estate, I really could not help being pleased and interested. In an unfavourable situation, with all nature, vegetable and animal, against him, he had actually created a paradise amid the wilds. There was nothing wonderful in any thing I saw around me; but there was such an air of neatness and comfort, order and activity, in the people and in their cottages, that I almost thought myself in England; and I could not forbear exclaiming, – 'How could all this be brought about in Ireland!'

'Chiefly by not doing and not expecting too much at first,' said M'Leod. 'We took time, and had patience. We began by setting them the example of some very slight improvements, and then, lured on by the sight of success, they could make similar trials themselves. My wife and I went among them, and talked to them in their cottages, and took an interest in their concerns, and did not want to have every thing our own way; and when they saw that, they began to consider which way was best; so by degrees we led where we could not have driven; and raised in them, by little and little, a taste for conveniences and comforts. Then the business was done; for the moment the taste and ambition were excited, to work the people went to gratify them; and according as they exerted themselves, we helped them. Perhaps it was best for them and for us, that we were not rich; for we could not do too much at a time, and were never tempted to begin grand schemes that we could not finish. There,' said M'Leod, pointing to a cottage with a pretty porch covered with woodbine, and a neat garden, in which many children were busily at work, 'that house and that garden were the means of doing all the rest; that is our school-house. We could not expect to do much with the old, whose habits were fixed; but we tried to give the young children better notions, and it was a long time before we could bring that to bear. Twenty-six years we have been at this work; and in that time if we have done any thing, it was by beginning with the children: a race of our own training has now grown up, and they go on in the way they were taught, and prosper to our hearts' content, and, what is better still, to their hearts' content.'

M'Leod, habitually grave and taciturn, seemed quite enlivened and talkative this day; but I verily believe that not the slightest ostentation or vanity inspired him, for I never before or since heard him talk or allude to his own good deeds: I am convinced his motive was to excite me to persevere in my benevolent projects, by showing what had been done by small means. He was so truly in earnest that he never perceived how tired I was; indeed he was so little in the habit of expecting sympathy or applause, that he never missed even the ordinary expressions of concurrent complaisance.

'Religion,' continued he, 'is the great difficulty in Ireland. We make no difference between protestants and catholics; we always have admitted both into our school. The priest comes on Saturday morning, and the parish minister on Saturday evening, to hear the children belonging to each church their catechisms, and to instruct them in the tenets of their faith. And as we keep to our word, and never attempt making proselytes, nor directly or indirectly interfere with their religious opinions, the priests are glad to let us instruct the catholic children in all other points, which they plainly see must advance their temporal interests.'

Mr M'Leod invited me to go in and look at the school. 'In a hedge or ditch school,' said he, 'which I once passed on this road, and in which I saw a crowd of idle children, I heard the schoolmaster cry out, "Rehearse! rehearse! there's company going by;" and instantly all the boys snatched up their books, and began gabbling as fast as ever they could, to give an idea to the passenger of their diligence in repeating their lessons. But here, my lord,' continued M'Leod, 'you will not see any exhibitions *got up* for company. I hate such tricks. Walk in, my lord, if you please.'

I walked in; but am ashamed to say, that I observed only that every thing looked as if it had been used for many years, and yet not worn out; and the whole school appeared as if all were in their places, and occupied and intent upon their business: but this general recollection is all I have retained. The enthusiasm for improvement had subsided in my mind; and though I felt a transient pleasure in the present picture of the happiness of these poor people and their healthy children, yet, as I rode home, the images faded away like a dream. I resolved, indeed, at some future period, to surpass all that Mr M'Leod had done, or all that with his narrow income he could ever accomplish; and to this resolution I was prompted by jealousy of this man, rather than by benevolence. Before I had arranged, even in imagination, my plans, young Ormsby came one morning, and pressed me to return with him to Ormsby Villa. I yielded to his solicitations and to my own wishes. When I arrived, the ladies were all at their toilettes, except Miss Bland, who was in the book-room with the gentlemen, ready to receive me with her perpetual smile. Wherever Miss Bland went, she was always *l'amie de la maison*, accustomed to share with the lady of the house the labour of entertaining her guests. This *double* of Lady Ormsby talked to me most courteously of all the nothings of the day, and informed me of the changes which had taken place in the ever-varying succession of company at Ormsby Villa. The two brigadiers and one of the aides-de-camp were gone; but Captain Andrews, another castle aide-de-camp, was come, and my lord O'Toole had arrived. Then followed a by-conversation between Miss Bland and some of the gentlemen, about the joy and sorrow which his lordship's arrival would create in the hearts of two *certain ladies*; one of whom, as I gathered from the innuendoes, was Lady Hauton, and the other Lady O'Toole. As I knew nothing of Dublin intrigues and scandal, I was little attentive to all this. Miss Bland, persisting in entertaining me, proceeded to inform me, that my lord O'Toole had brought down with him Mr Cecil Devereux, who was a wit and a poet, very handsome and gallant, and one of the most fashionable young men in Dublin. I determined not to like him – I always hated a flourish of trumpets; whoever enters, announced in this parading manner, appears to disadvantage. Mr Cecil Devereux entered just as the flourish ceased. He was not at all the sort of person I was prepared to see: though handsome, and with the air of a man used to good company, there was nothing of a coxcomb in his manner; on the contrary, there was such an appearance of carelessness about himself, and deference towards others, that, notwithstanding the injudicious praise that had been bestowed on him, and my consequent resolution to dislike him, I was pleased and familiar with him before I had been ten minutes in his company. Lord Kilrush introduced him to me, with great pomposity, as a gentleman of talents, for whom he and his brother O'Toole interested themselves much. This air of patronage, I saw, disgusted Mr Devereux; and instead of suffering himself to be *shown off*, he turned the conversation from his own poems to general subjects. He asked me some questions about a curious cavern, or subterraneous way, near Glenthorn Castle, which stretched from the sea-shore to a considerable distance under the rock, and communicated with an old abbey near the castle. Mr Devereux said that such subterraneous places had been formerly used in Ireland as granaries by the ancient inhabitants; but a gentleman of the neighbourhood who was present observed, that the caverns on this coast had, within his memory, been used as hiding-places by smugglers: on this hint Lord Kilrush began a prosing dissertation upon smugglers and contraband traders, and talked to me a prodigious deal about exports and imports, and bounties, and the balance of trade. Not one word he said did I comprehend, and I question whether his lordship understood the subjects upon which he spoke so dictatorially; but he thought he succeeded in giving me an opinion of his wisdom and information. His brother O'Toole appeared next: he did not look like a man of gallantry, as I had been taught to expect from the hints thrown out respecting Lady Hauton; his lordship's whole soul seemed devoted to ambition, and he talked so much of great men, and state affairs, and court intrigues, and honours and preferments, that I began to fancy I had been buried alive, because I knew little of these things. I was tired of hearing him, yet mortified that I could not speak exactly in the same manner, and with the same air of being the best possible authority. I began to wish that I also had some interest at court. The cares and troubles of the ambitious man, so utterly repugnant to the indolence of my disposition, vanished in this moment of infatuation from my view, and I thought only of the pleasures of power. Such is the infectious nature of ambition!

Mr Devereux helped me to throw off this dangerous contagion, before it did me any injury. He happened to stay in the room with me a quarter of an hour after the other gentlemen went to dress. Though not often disposed to conversation with a stranger, yet I was won by this gentleman's easy address: he politely talked of the English fashionable world, with which he knew that I was well acquainted; I, with equal politeness, recurred to the Irish great world; we fastened together upon Lord O'Toole, who took us to Dublin Castle; and I began to express my regret that I had not yet been at the Irish court, and that I had not earlier in life made myself of political consequence. 'Ambition,' said I, 'might help to keep a man awake and alive; all common pleasures have long since ceased to interest me – they really cannot make me stir.'

'My lord,' said Mr Devereux, 'you would do better to sit or lie still all your life than to toil for such vain objects.

> Full little knowest thou that hast not tried,
> What hell it is in sueing long to bide:

Your lordship may remember Spenser's description of that hell?'

'Not exactly,' said I, unwilling to lower the good opinion this gentleman seemed to have taken for granted of my literature. He took Spenser's poems out of the book-case, and I actually rose from my seat to read the passage; for what trouble will not even the laziest of mortals take to preserve the esteem of one by whom he sees that he is over-valued. I read the following ten lines without yawning!

> Full little knowest thou that hast not tried,
> What hell it is in sueing long to bide;
> To lose good days, that might be better spent,
> To waste long nights in pensive discontent,
> To speed to-day, to be put back to-morrow,
> To feed on hope, to pine with fear and sorrow,
> To fret thy soul with crosses and with cares,
> To eat thy heart through comfortless despairs,
> To fawn, to crouch, to wait, to ride, to run,
> To spend, to give, to want, to be undone.[45]

'Very strong, indeed,' said I, with a competent air, as if used to judge of poetry.

'And it comes with still greater force, when we consider by whom it was written. A man, you know, my lord, who had been secretary to a lord lieutenant.'

I felt my nascent ambition die away within me. I acknowledged it was better to spend an easy life. My determination was confirmed at this instant by the appearance of Lady Geraldine. Ambition and love, it is said, are incompatible passions. Neither of them had yet possession of my heart; but love and Lady Geraldine had perhaps a better chance than ambition and Lord O'Toole. Lady Geraldine appeared in high spirits; and, though I was not a vain man, I could not help fancying that my return to Ormsby Villa contributed to her charming vivacity. This gratified me secretly and soberly, as much as it visibly delighted her mother. Miss Bland, to pay her court to Lady Kildangan, observed that Lady Geraldine was in uncommonly fine spirits this evening. Lady Geraldine threw back a haughty frown over her left shoulder: this was the only time I ever saw her notice, in any manner, any thing that fell from her obsequious friend. To avert the fair one's displeasure, I asked for Miss Tracey and Mr Gabbitt.

'Mr Gabbitt,' said her ladyship, resuming her good-humour instantly; 'Mr Gabbitt is gone off the happiest man in Ireland, with the hopes of surveying my lord O'Toole's estate; a good job, which I was bound in honour to obtain for him, as a reward for taking a good joke. After mocking him with the bare imagination of a feast, you know the Barmecide in the Arabian Tales gave poor Shakabac a substantial dinner, a full equivalent for the jest.'[46]

'And Miss Tracey,' said I, 'what did your ladyship do for her?'

'I persuaded her mamma that the sweet creature was falling into an atrophy. So she carried the forlorn damsel post haste to the Black Rock for the recovery of her health, or her heart. Clementina, my dear, no reproachful looks; in your secret soul do not you know, that I could not do a young lady a greater favour than to give her a plausible excuse for getting away from home?'

I was afraid that Lady Geraldine would feel the want of her butt; however, I found that Miss Tracey's place was supplied by Captain Andrews, one of the castle's aides-de-camp; and when Captain Andrews was out of the way, Lord Kilrush and his brother O'Toole were *good marks*. High and mighty as these personages thought themselves, and respectfully, nay obsequiously, as they were treated by most others, to this lady their characters appeared only a good *study*; and to laugh at them seemed only a *good practice*.

'Perhaps, my lord,' said she to me, 'you do not yet know my lord O'Toole?'

'I have had the honour to be introduced to him.'

'That's well; for he thinks that,

Not to know him, argues yourself unknown.[47]

But as your lordship is a stranger in this country, you may be pardoned; and I will make you better acquainted with him. I suppose you know there are many Tooles in Ireland; some very ancient, respectable, and useful: this, however, is but a mere political tool, and the worst of all tools, a cat's paw. There's one thing to the credit of these brothers, they agree vastly well; for one delights in being always on the stage, and the other always behind the scenes. These brothers, with Captain Andrews – I hope they are none of them within hearing – form a charming trio, all admirable in their way. My lord O'Toole is – artifice without art. My lord Kilrush – importance without power. And Captain Andrews – pliability without ease. Poor Andrews! he's a defenceless animal – safe in impenetrable armour. Give him but time – as a man said, who once showed me a land-tortoise – give him but time to draw his head into his shell, and a broad-wheeled waggon may go over him without hurting him. Lord Glenthorn, did you ever observe Captain Andrews's mode of conversation?'

'No; I never heard him converse.'

'Converse! nor I indeed; but you have heard him talk.'

'I have heard him say – *Very true* – and *Of course*.'

'Lord Glenthorn is quite severe this evening,' said Mrs O'Connor.

'But though your lordship,' continued Lady Geraldine, 'may have observed Captain Andrews's wonderful economy of words, do you know whence it arises? Perhaps, you think from his perception of his own want of understanding.'

'Not from his perception of the want,' said I.

'Again! again!' said Mrs O'Connor, with an insulting tone of surprise; 'Lord Glenthorn's quite witty this evening.'

Lady Geraldine looked as if she were fully sensible of the want of politeness in Mrs O'Connor's mode of praising. 'But, my lord,' pursued she, 'you wrong Captain Andrews, if you attribute his monosyllabic replies either to stupidity or timidity. You have not guessed the reason why he never gives on any subject more than half an opinion.'

'It was in the diplomatic school he was taught that art,' said Mr Devereux.

'You must know,' pursued Lady Geraldine, 'that Captain Andrews is only an aide-de-camp till a diplomatic situation can be found for him; and to do him justice, he has been so well trained in the diplomatic school, that he will not hazard an assertion on any subject; he is not certain of any thing, not even of his own identity.'

'He assuredly wants,' said Devereux, 'the only proof of existence which Descartes would admit – *I think*, therefore I am.'

'He has such a holy horror of committing himself,' continued Lady Geraldine, 'that if you were to ask him if the sun rose this morning, he would answer with his sweet smile – *So I am told* – or – *So I am informed.*'

'Begging your ladyship's pardon,' cried Mr Devereux, 'that is much too affirmative. In the pure diplomatic style, impersonal verbs must ever be used in preference to active or passive. *So I am told*, lays him open to the dangerous questions, Who told you? or, By whom were you informed? Then he is forced into the imprudence of giving up his authorities; whereas he is safe in the impersonality of *So it is said*, or, *So it is reported.*'

'How I should like to see a meeting between two perfectly finished diplomatists!' cried Lady Geraldine.

'That is demonstrably impossible,' said Mr Devereux; 'for in certain political, as well as in certain geometrical lines, there is a continual effort to approach, without a possibility of meeting.'

Lady Geraldine's raillery, like all other things, would, perhaps, soon have become tiresome to me; but that there was infinite variety in her humour. At first I had thought her merely superficial, and intent solely upon her own amusement; but I soon found that she had a taste for literature, beyond what could have been expected in one who lived so dissipated a life; a depth of reflection that seemed inconsistent with the rapidity with which she thought; and, above all, a degree of generous indignation against meanness and vice, which seemed incompatible with the selfish character of a fine lady, and which appeared quite incomprehensible to the imitating tribe of her fashionable companions.

I mentioned a Mrs Norton and Lady Hauton amongst the company of Ormsby Villa. These two English ladies, whom I had never met in any of the higher circles in London, who were persons of no consequence and of no marked character in their own country, made, it seems, a prodigious *sensation* when they came over to Ireland, and turned the heads of half Dublin by the extravagance of their dress, the impertinence of their airs, and the audacity of their conduct. Fame flew before them to the remote parts of the country; and when they arrived at Ormsby Villa, all the country gentlemen and ladies were prepared to admire these celebrated fashionable belles. All worshipped them present, and abused them absent, except Lady Geraldine, who neither joined in the admiration nor inquired into the scandal. One morning Mrs Norton and Lady Hauton had each collected her votaries round her: one group begging patterns of dress from Lady Hauton, who stood up in the midst of them, to have every thing she wore examined and envied; the other group sat on a sofa apart, listening to Mrs Norton, who, *sotto voce*, was telling interesting anecdotes of an English crim. con., which then occupied the attention of the fashionable world. Mrs Norton had letters *from the best authorities* in London, which she was entreated by her auditors to read to them. Mrs Norton went to look for the letters, Lady Hauton to direct her woman to furnish some patterns of I know not what articles of dress; and, in the mean time, all the company joined in canvassing the merits and demerits of the dress and characters of the two ladies who had just left the room. Lady Geraldine, who had kept aloof, and who was examining some prints at the farther end of the room, at this instant laid down her book, and looked upon the whole party with an air of magnanimous disdain; then smiling, as in scorn, she advanced towards them, and in a tone of irony addressing one of the Swanlinbar graces, 'My dear Theresa,' said her ladyship, 'you are absolutely ashamed, I see, of not being quite naked; and you, my good Bess, will, no doubt, very soon be equally scandalized, at the imputation of being a perfectly modest woman. Go on, my friends; go on, and prosper; beg and borrow all the patterns and precedents you can collect of the newest fashions of folly and vice. Make haste, make haste; they don't reach our remote island fast enough. We Irish might live in innocence half a century longer, if you didn't expedite the progress of profligacy; we might escape the plague that rages in neighbouring countries, if we didn't, without any quarantine, and with open arms, welcome every *suspected* stranger; if we didn't encourage the importation of whole bales of tainted fineries, that will spread the contagion from Dublin to Cork, and from Cork to Galway!'

'La!' said Miss Ormsby, 'how severe your ladyship is; and all only for one's asking for a pattern!'

'But you know,' pursued Mrs O'Connor, 'that Lady Geraldine is too proud to take pattern from any body.'

'Too proud am I? Well, then, I'll be humble; I'll abase myself— shall I?

Proud as I am, I'll put myself to school;[48]

and I'll do what the ladies Hauton and Norton shall advise, to heighten my charms and preserve my reputation. I must begin, must not I, Mrs O'Connor, by learning not to blush? for I observed you were ashamed for me yesterday at dinner, when I blushed at something said by one of our fair missionaries. Then, to whatever lengths flirtations and gallantry may go between unmarried or married people, I must look on. I may shut my eyes, if I please, and look down; but not from shame – from affectation I may as often as I please, or to show my eyelashes. Memorandum – to practise this before Clementina Ormsby, my mirror of fashion. So far, so good, for my looks; but now for my language. I must reform my barbarous language, and learn from Mrs Norton, with her pretty accommodating voice, to call an intrigue *an arrangement*, and a crim. con. *an affair in Doctor's Commons*, or *that business before the Lords*.

We never mention Hell to ears polite.[49]

How virtuous we shall be when we have no name for vice! But stay, I must mind my lessons – I have more, much more to learn. From the dashing Lady Hauton I may learn, if my head be but strong, and my courage intrepid enough, "to touch the brink of all we hate",[50] without tumbling headlong into the gulf; and from the interesting Mrs Norton, as I hear it whispered amongst you ladies, I may learn how, with the assistance of a Humane-society,[51] to save a half-drowned reputation. It is, I understand, the glory of one class of fashionable females, to seem worse than they are; and of another class the privilege, to be worse than they seem.'

Here clamorous voices interrupted Lady Geraldine – some justifying, some attacking, Lady Hauton and Mrs Norton.

'O! Lady Geraldine, I assure you, notwithstanding all that was said about General—and Mrs Norton, I am convinced there was nothing in it.'

'And, my dear Lady Geraldine, though Lady Hauton does go great lengths in coquetting with a certain lord, you must see that there's *nothing wrong*; and that she means nothing, but to provoke his lady's jealousy. You know his lordship is not a man to fall in love with.'

'So, because Lady Hauton's passion is hatred instead of love, and because her sole object is to give pain to a poor wife, and to make mischief in families, all her sins are to be forgiven! Now, if I were forced to forgive any ill-conducted female, I would rather excuse the woman who is hurried on by love than she who is instigated by hatred.'

Miss Bland now began to support her ladyship's opinion, that 'Lady Hauton was much the worst of the two'; and all the scandal that was in circulation was produced by the partisans of each of these ladies.

'No matter, no matter, which is the worst,' cried Lady Geraldine; 'don't let us waste our time in repeating or verifying scandalous stories of either of them. I have no enmity to these ladies; I only despise them, or, rather, their follies and their faults. It is not the sinner, but the sin we should reprobate. O! my dear countrywomen,' cried Lady Geraldine, with increasing animation of countenance and manner – 'O! my dear countrywomen, let us never stoop to admire and imitate these second-hand airs and graces, follies and vices. Let us dare to be ourselves!'

My eyes were fixed upon her animated countenance, and, I believe, I continued gazing even after her voice ceased. Mrs O'Connor pointed this out, and I was immediately embarrassed. Miss Bland accounted for my embarrassment by supposing, that what Lady Geraldine had said of English crim. cons. had affected me. From a look and a whisper among the ladies, I guessed this; but Lady Geraldine was too well-bred to suppose I could suspect her of ill-breeding and ill-nature, or that I could apply to myself what evidently was not intended to allude to my family misfortunes. By an openness of manner and sweetness of expression, which I cannot forget, she, in one single look, conveyed all this to me; and then resuming her conversation, 'Pray, my lord,' said she, 'you who have lived so much in the great world in England, say, for you can, whether I am right or wrong in my suspicion, that these ladies, who have made such a noise in Ireland, have been little heard of in England?'

I confirmed her ladyship's opinion by my evidence. The faces of the company changed. Thus, in a few seconds, the empire of Lady Hauton and of Mrs Norton seemed shaken to the foundation, and never recovered from this shock.

The warmth of Lady Geraldine's expressions on this and many other occasions wakened dormant feelings in my heart, and made me sensible that I had a soul, and that I was superior to the puppets with whom I had been classed.

One day Lady Kilrush, in her mixed mode, with partly the graces of a fine lady and partly the airs of a *bel esprit*, was talking of Mr Devereux, whom she affected to patronise and *produce*.

'Here, Devereux!' cried she; 'Cecil Devereux! What can you be thinking of? I am talking to you. Here's this epitaph of Francis the First upon Petrarch's Laura, that you showed me the other day: do you know, I dote upon it. I must have it translated: nobody can do it so well as you. I have not time; but I shall not sleep to-night if it is not done: and you are so quick: so sit down here, there's a dear man, and do it in your elegant way for me, whilst I go to my toilette. Perhaps you did not know that my name was Laura,' said she, leaving the room with a very sentimental air.

'What will become of me!' cried Devereux. 'Never was a harder task set by cruel patroness. I would rather "turn a Persian tale for half-a-crown". Read this, my lord, and tell me whether it will be easy to turn my Lady Kilrush into Petrarch's Laura.'

'This sonnet, to be sure, is rather difficult to translate, or at least to modernize, as bespoke,' said Lady Geraldine, after she had perused the sonnet;* 'but I think, Mr Devereux, you brought this difficulty upon yourself. How came you to show these lines to such an amateur, such a fetcher and carrier of bays as Lady Kilrush? You might have been certain that, had they been trash, with the name of Francis the First, and with your fashionable approbation, and something to say about Petrarch and Laura, my Lady Kilrush would talk for ever, *et se pâmerait d'affectation*.'

'Mr Devereux,' said I, 'has only to abide by the last lines, as a good and sufficient apology to Lady Kilrush for his silence:

> "Qui te pourra louer qu'en se taisant?
> Car la parole est toujours réprimée
> Quand le sujet surmonte le disant."'

---

* En petit compris vous pouvez voir
Ce qui comprend beaucoup par renommé
Plume, labeur, la langue, et le devoir
Furent vaincus par l'amans de l'aimée
O gentille ame, etant toute estimée
Qui te pourra louer qu'en se taisant?
Car la parole est toujours réprimée
Quand le sujet surmonte le disant.[52]

226

'There is no way to get out of my difficulties,' said Mr Devereux, with a very melancholy look; and with a deep sigh he sat down to attempt the translation of the poem. In a few minutes, however, he rose and left the room, declaring that he had the bad habit of not being able to do any thing in company.

Lady Geraldine now, with much energy of indignation, exclaimed against the pretensions of rich amateurs, and the mean and presumptuous manner in which some would-be great people affect to patronize genius.

'O! the baseness, the emptiness of such patronizing ostentation!' cried she. 'I am accused of being proud myself; but I hope – I believe – I am sure, that my pride is of another sort. Persons of any elevation or generosity of mind never have this species of pride; but it is your mean, second-rate folk, who imagine that people of talent are a sort of raree-show for their entertainment. At best, they consider men of genius only as artists formed for their use, who, if not in a situation to be paid with money, are yet to be easily recompensed by praise – by their praise – *their* praise! Heavens! what conceit! And these amateur-patrons really think themselves judges, and presume to advise and direct genius, and employ it to their petty purposes! Like that Pietro de Medicis, who, at some of his entertainments set Michael Angelo to make a statue of snow.⁵³ My lord, did you ever happen to meet with Les Mémoires de Madame de Staël?'

'No: I did not know that they were published.'

'You mistake me: I mean Madame de Staël of Louis the Fourteenth and the Regent's time, Mademoiselle de Launay.'

I had never heard of such a person, and I blushed for my ignorance.

'Nay, I met with them myself only yesterday,' said Lady Geraldine: 'I was struck with the character of the Duchesse de la Ferté, in which this kind of proud patronizing ignorance is admirably painted from the life. It is really worth your while, my lord, to look at it. There's the book on that little table; here is the passage. You see, this Duchesse de la Ferté showing off to a sister-duchess a poor girl of genius, like a puppet or an ape.

'"Allons, mademoiselle, parlez – Madame, vous allez voir comme elle parle – Elle vit que j'hesitois à repondre, et pensa qu'il falloit m'aider comme une chanteuse à qui l'on indique ce qu'on désire d'entendre – Parlez un peu de religion, mademoiselle, vous direz ensuite autre chose."[54]

'This speech, Mr Devereux tells me, has become quite proverbial in Paris,' continued Lady Geraldine; 'and it is often quoted, when any one presumes in the Duchess de la Ferté's style.'

'Ignorance, either in high or low life, is equally self-sufficient, I believe,' said I, exerting myself to illustrate her ladyship's remarks. 'A gentleman of my acquaintance lately went to buy some razors at Packwood's. Mrs Packwood alone was *visible*. Upon the gentleman's complimenting her on the infinite variety of her husband's ingenious and poetical advertisements, she replied, "La! sir, and do you think husband has time to write them there things his-self? Why, sir, we keeps a poet to do all that there work."'[55]

Though Lady Geraldine spoke only in general of amateur-patrons and of men of genius, yet I could not help fancying, from the warmth with which she expressed herself, and from her dwelling on the subject so long, that her feelings were peculiarly interested for some individual of this description. Thus I discovered that Lady Geraldine had a heart; and I suspected that her ladyship and Mr Devereux had also made the same discovery. This suspicion was strengthened by a slight incident, which occurred the following evening.

Lady Geraldine and Cecil Devereux, as we were drinking coffee, were in a recessed window, while some of the company stood round them, amused by their animated conversation. They went on, repartee after repartee, as if inspired by each other's spirits.

'You two,' said a little girl of six years old, who was playing in the window, 'go on singing to one another like two nightingales; and this shall be your cage,' added she, drawing the drapery of the window-curtains across the recessed window. 'You shall live always together in this cage: will you, pretty birds?'

'No, no; some birds cannot live in a cage, my dear,' cried Lady Geraldine, playfully struggling to get free, whilst the child held her prisoner.

'Mr Devereux seems tolerably quiet and contented in his cage,' said the shrewd Mrs O'Connor.

'I can't get out! I can't get out!' cried Devereux, in the melancholy tone of the starling in the Sentimental Journey.[56]

'What is all this?' said my lady Kildangan, sailing up to us.

'Only two birds,' the child began.

'Singing-birds,' interrupted Lady Geraldine, catching the little girl up in her arms, and stopping her from saying more, by beginning to sing most charmingly.

Lady Kildangan returned to the sofa without comprehending one word of what had passed. For my part, I now felt almost certain of the justice of my suspicions: I was a little vexed, but not by any means in that despair into which a man heartily in love would have been thrown by such a discovery.

Well, thought I, it is well it is no worse: it was very lucky that I did not fall quite in love with this fair lady, since it seems that she has given her heart away. But am I certain of this? I was mistaken once. Let me examine more carefully.

Now I had a new motive to keep my attention awake.

CHAPTER XI

To preserve the continuity of my story, and not to fatigue the reader with the journals of my comings and goings from Ormsby Villa to Glenthorn Castle, and from Glenthorn Castle to Ormsby Villa, I must here relate the observations I made, and the incidents that occurred, during various visits at Sir Harry Ormsby's in the course of the summer.

After the incident of the birds and cage, my sagacity was for some time at fault. I could not perceive any further signs of intelligence between the parties: on the contrary, all communication seemed abruptly to cease. As I was not well versed in such affairs, this quieted my suspicions, and I began to think that I had been entirely mistaken. Cecil Devereux spent his days shut up in his own apartment, immersed, as far as I could understand, in the study of the Persian language.[57] He talked to me of nothing but his hopes of an appointment, which Lord O'Toole had promised to procure for him in India. When he was not studying, he was botanizing or *mineralogizing* with O'Toole's chaplain. I did not envy him his new mode of life. Lady Geraldine took no notice of it. When they did meet, which happened as seldom as possible, there was an air of haughty displeasure on her part; on his, steady and apparently calm respect and self-satisfaction. Her spirits were exuberant, but variable; and, at times, evidently forced: his were not high, but even and certain. Towards me, her ladyship's manners were free from coquetry, yet politely gratifying, as she marked, by the sort of conversation she addressed to me, her opinion that I was superior in ability and capability to what she had at first thought me, and to what I had always thought myself.

Mr Devereux, though with more effort, treated me with distinction, and showed a constant desire to cultivate my friendship. On every occasion he endeavoured to raise my opinion of myself: to give me ambition and courage to cultivate my mind. Once, when I was arguing in favour of natural genius, and saying that I thought no cultivation could make the abilities of one man equal to those of another, he, without seeming to perceive that I was apologizing at once for my own indolence and my intellectual inferiority, answered in general terms, 'It is difficult to judge what are the natural powers of the mind, they appear so different in different circumstances. You can no more judge of a mind in ignorance than of a plant in darkness. A philosophical friend told me, that he once thought he had discovered a new and strange plant growing in a mine. It was common sage; but so degenerated and altered, that he could not know it: he planted it in the open air and in the light, and gradually it resumed its natural appearance and character.'

Mr Devereux excited, without fatiguing, my mind by his conversation; and I was not yet sufficiently in love to be seriously jealous. I was resolved, however, to sound him upon the subject of Lady Geraldine. I waited for a good opportunity: at length, as we were looking together over the prints of Buerger's Lenore, he led to the sort of conversation that I desired, by telling me an anecdote relative to the poet, which he had lately heard from a German baron.

Buerger was charmed with a sonnet, which an unknown fair one addressed to him, in praise of his poetry; he replied in equal strains: and they went on flattering one another, till both believed themselves in love: without ever having met, they determined to marry: they at length met, and married: they quarrelled and parted: in other words, the gentleman was terribly disappointed in his unknown mistress; and she consoled herself by running away from him with another lover.[58]

The imprudence of this poetic couple led us to reflections on love and marriage in general. Keeping far away from an allusion to Lady Geraldine, I rallied Mr Devereux about the fair Clementina, who was evidently a romantic admirer of his.

'Who, except Cupid, would barter his liberty for a butterfly?' said he; 'and Cupid was a child. Men nowadays are grown too wise to enslave themselves for women. Love occupies a vast space in a woman's thoughts, but fills a small portion in a man's life. Women are told, that "The great, th'important business of their life, is love"; but men know that they are born for something better than to sing mournful ditties to a mistress's eyebrow.[59] As to marriage, what a serious, terrible thing! Some quaint old author says, that man is of too smooth and oily a nature to climb up to heaven, if, to make him less slippery, there be not added to his composition the vinegar of marriage.[60] This may be; but I will keep as long as possible from the vinegar.'

'Really, Devereux,' said I, smiling, 'you talk so like a cynic and an old bachelor, and you look so little like either, that it is quite ridiculous.'

'A man must be ridiculous sometimes,' said he, 'and bear to be thought so. No man ever distinguished himself, who could not bear to be laughed at.'

Mr Devereux left the room singing.

> 'No more for Amynta fresh garlands I wove;
> Ambition, I said, will soon cure me of love.'[61]

I was uncertain what to think of all this. I inclined to believe that ambition was his ruling passion, notwithstanding the description of that Hell which he showed me in Spenser. His conduct to his patron-lords, by which a surer judgement of his character could be formed than by his professions, was not, however, that of a man merely intent upon rising in the world.

I remember once hearing Lord O'Toole attack a friend of this gentleman's, calling him, in a certain tone, *a philosopher*. Mr Devereux replied, 'that he could not consider that as a term of reproach; that where a false or pretended philosopher was meant, some other name should be used, equivalent to the Italian term of reproach, *filoso-fastro*'.

Lord O'Toole would by no means admit of this Italianism: he

would make no distinctions: he deemed philosophers altogether a race of beings dangerous and inimical to states.[62]

'For states read statesmen,' said Devereux, who persisted in the vindication of his friend till Lord O'Toole grew pale with anger, while Captain Andrews smiled with ineffable contempt at the political *bévue*:[63] Lady Geraldine glowed with generous indignation.

Afterwards, in speaking to me of Lord O'Toole, Devereux said, 'His lordship's classification of men is as contracted as the savage's classification of animals:[64] he divides mankind into two classes, knaves and fools; and when he meets with an honest man, he does not know what to make of him.'

My esteem for Mr Devereux was much increased by my daily observations upon his conduct: towards Lady Geraldine, I thought it particularly honourable: when her displeasure evidently merged in esteem, when her manners again became most winning and attractive, his continued uniformly the same; never passing the bounds of friendly respect, or swerving, in the slightest degree, from the line of conduct which he had laid down for himself. I thought I now understood him perfectly. That he liked Lady Geraldine I could scarcely doubt; but I saw that he refrained from aiming at the prize which he knew he ought not to obtain; that he perceived her ladyship's favourable disposition towards him, yet denied himself not only the gratification of his vanity, but the exquisite pleasure of conversing with her, lest he should stand in the way of her happier prospects. He frequently spoke to me of her ladyship in terms of the warmest approbation. He said, that all the world saw and admired her talents and beauty, but that he had had opportunities, as a relation, of studying her domestic life. 'With all her vivacity, she has a heart formed for tenderness,' said he; 'a high sense of duty, the best security for a woman's conduct; and in generosity and magnanimity, I never found her superior in either sex. In short, I never saw any woman whose temper and disposition were more likely to make a man of sense and feeling supremely happy.'

I could not forbear smiling, and asking Cecil Devereux how all this accorded with his late professions of hatred to marriage.

'My professions were sincere,' said he. 'It would be misery to me to marry any inferior woman, and I am not in circumstances to marry as I could wish. I could not think of Lady Geraldine without a breach of trust, of which your lordship, I hope, cannot suspect me.

Her mother places confidence in me. I am not only a relation, but treated as a friend of the family. I am not in love with Lady Geraldine. I admire, esteem, respect her ladyship; and I wish to see her united to a man, if such a man there be, who may deserve her. We understand one another now. Your lordship will have the goodness never more to speak to me on this subject.' He spoke with much emotion, but with steadiness, and left me penetrated with feelings that were entirely new to me.

Much as I admired his conduct, I was yet undecided as to my own: my aversion to a second marriage was not yet conquered: – I was amused, I was captivated by Lady Geraldine; but I could not bring myself to think of making a distinct proposal. Captain Andrews himself was not more afraid of being committed than I was upon this tender subject. To gain time, I now thought it necessary to verify all the praises Mr Devereux had bestowed on her ladyship. Magnanimity was a word that particularly struck my ear as extraordinary when applied to a female. However, by attending carefully to this lady, I thought I discovered what Mr Devereux meant. Lady Geraldine was superior to manoeuvring little arts and petty stratagems to attract attention: she would not stoop, even to conquer. From gentlemen she seemed to expect attention as her right, as the right of her sex; not to beg or accept of it as a favour: if it were not paid, she deemed the gentleman degraded, not herself. Far from being mortified by any preference shown to other ladies, her countenance betrayed only a sarcastic sort of pity for the bad taste of the men, or an absolute indifference and look of haughty absence. I saw that she beheld with disdain the paltry competitions of the young ladies her companions: as her companions, indeed, she hardly seemed to consider them; she tolerated their foibles, forgave their envy, and never exerted any superiority, except to show her contempt of vice and meanness. To be in any degree excepted from the common herd; to be in any degree distinguished by a lady so proud, and with so many good reasons to be proud, was flattering to my self-love. She gave me no direct encouragement; but I never advanced far enough to require encouragement, much less to justify repulse. Sometimes I observed, or I fancied, that she treated me with more favour when Mr Devereux was present than at other times; perhaps – for she was a woman, not an angel – to pique Devereux, and try if she could move him from the settled purpose of his soul. He bore it all with surprising constancy: his spirits, however, and his health, began visibly to decline.

'If I do not intrude too much on your valuable time, Mr Devereux,' said her ladyship to him one evening, in her most attractive manner, 'may I beg you to read to us some of these beautiful poems of Sir William Jones?'[65]

There was a seat beside her ladyship on the sofa: the book was held out by the finest arm in the world.

'Nay,' said Lady Geraldine, 'do not look so respectfully miserable; if you have any other engagements, you have only to say so: or if you cannot speak you may bow: a bow, you know, is an answer to every thing. And here is my Lord Glenthorn ready to supply your place: pray, do not let me detain you prisoner. You shall not a second time say, *I can't get out.*'

Devereux made no further effort to escape, but took the book and his dangerous seat. He remained with us, contrary to his custom, the whole evening. Afterwards, as if he felt that some apology was necessary to me for the pleasure in which he had indulged himself, 'Perhaps, my lord,' said he, 'another man in my situation, and with my feelings, would think it necessary to retreat, and prudent to secure his safety by flight; but flight is unworthy of him who can combat and conquer: the man who is sure of himself does not sculk away to avoid danger, but advances to meet it, armed secure in honesty.'

This proud and rash security in his own courage, strength of mind, and integrity, was the only fault of Cecil Devereux. He never prayed not to be led into temptation, he thought himself so sure of avoiding evil. Unconscious of his danger, even though his disease was at its height, he now braved it most imprudently: he was certain that he should never pass the bounds of friendship; he had proved this to himself, and was satisfied: he told me, that he could with indifference, nay, with pleasure, see Lady Geraldine mine. In the mean time, upon the same principle that he deemed flight inglorious, he was proud to expose himself to the full force of Love's artillery. He was with us now every day, and almost all day, and Lady Geraldine was more charming than ever. The week was fixed for her departure. Still I could not decide. I understood that her ladyship would pass the ensuing winter in Dublin, where she would probably meet with new adorers; and even if Mr Devereux should not succeed, some adventurous knight might win and wear the prize. This was an alarming thought. It almost decided me to hazard the fatal declaration: but then I recollected that I might follow her ladyship to town the next winter, and that if the impression did not, as might be hoped, wear off during the intervening autumn, it would be time enough to *commit* myself when I should meet my fair one in Dublin. This was at last my fixed resolution. Respited from the agonies of doubt, I now waited very tranquilly for that moment to which most lovers look forward with horror, the moment of separation. I was sensible that I had accustomed myself to think about this lady so much, that I had gradually identified my existence with hers, and I thus found my *spirit of animation* much increased. I dreaded the departure of Lady Geraldine less than the return of ennui.

In this frame of mind I was walking one morning in the pleasure-grounds with Lady Geraldine, when a slight accident made me act in direct contradiction to all my resolutions, and, I think, inconsistently with my character. But such is the nature of man! and I was doomed to make a fool of myself, even in the very temple of Minerva. Among the various ornamental buildings in the grounds at Ormsby Villa, there was a temple dedicated to this goddess, from which issued a troop of hoyden young ladies, headed by the widow O'Connor and Lady Kilrush, all calling to us to come and look at some charming discovery which they had just made in the temple of Minerva. Thither we proceeded, accompanied by the merry troop. We found in the temple only a poetical inscription of Lady Kilrush's, pompously engraved on a fine marble tablet. We read the lines with all the attention usually paid to a lady's poetry in the presence of the poetess. Lady Geraldine and I turned to pay some compliments on the performance, when we found that Lady Kilrush and all her companions were gone.

'Gone! all gone!' said Lady Geraldine; 'and there they are, making their way very fast down to the temple of Folly! Lady Kilrush, you know, is so ba-a-ashful, she could not possibly stay to receive *nos hommages*. I love to laugh at affectation. Call them back, do, my lord, and you shall see the *fair author* go through all the evolutions of mock humility, and end by yielding quietly to the notion that she is the tenth Muse. But run, my lord, or they will be out of our reach.'

I never was seen to run on any occasion; but to obey Lady Geraldine I walked as fast as I could to the door, and, to my surprise, found it fastened.

'Locked, I declare! Some of the witty tricks of the widow O'Conner, or the hoyden Miss Callwells!'

'How I hate hoydens!' cried Lady Geraldine: 'but let us take patience; they will be back presently. If young ladies must perform practical jokes, because quizzing is the fashion, I wish they would devise something new. This locking-up is so stale a jest. To be sure it has lately to boast the authority of high rank in successful practice: but these bungling imitators never distinguish between cases the most dissimilar imaginable. Silly creatures! We have only to be wise and patient.'

Her ladyship sat down to re-peruse the tablet. I never saw her look so beautiful. – The dignified composure of her manner charmed me; it was so unlike the paltry affectation of some of the fashionable ladies by whom I had been disgusted. I recollected the precedent to which she alluded. I recollected that the locking-up ended in matrimony; and as Lady Geraldine made some remarks upon the verses, I suppose my answers showed my absence of mind.

'Why so grave, my lord? why so absent? I assure you I do not suspect your lordship of having any hand in this vulgar manoeuvre. I acquit you honourably; therefore you need not stand any longer like a criminal.'

What decided me at this instant I cannot positively tell: whether it was the awkwardness of my own situation, or the grace of her ladyship's manner; but all my prudential arrangements were forgotten, all my doubts vanished. Before I knew that the words passed my lips, I replied, 'That her ladyship did me justice by such an acquittal; but that though I had no part in the contrivance, yet I felt irresistibly impelled to avail myself of the opportunity it afforded of declaring my real sentiments.' I was at her ladyship's feet, and making very serious love, before I knew where I was. In what words my long-delayed declaration was made I cannot recollect, but I well remember Lady Geraldine's answer.

'My lord, I assure you that you do not know what you are saying: you do not know what you are doing. This is all a mistake, as you will find half an hour hence. I will not be so cruelly vain as to suppose you serious.'

'Not serious! no man ever was more serious.'

'No, no – No, no, no.'

I swore, of course, most fervently.

'O! rise, rise, I beseech you, my lord, and don't look so like a hero; though you have done an heroical action, I grant. How you ever brought yourself to it, I cannot imagine. But now, for your comfort, you are safe – Vous voilà quitte pour la peur! Do not, however, let this encourage you to venture again in the same foolish manner. I know but few, very few young ladies, to whom Lord Glenthorn could offer himself with any chance or reasonable hope of being refused. So take warning: never again expect to meet with such another as my whimsical self.'

'Never, never can I expect to meet with any thing resembling your charming self,' cried I. This was a new text for a lover's rhapsody. It is not necessary, and might not be *generally* interesting to repeat all the ridiculous things I said, even if I could remember them.

Lady Geraldine listened to me, and then very calmly replied, 'Granting you believe all that you are saying at this minute, which I must grant from common gratitude, and still more common vanity; nevertheless, permit me to assure you, my lord, that this is not love; it is only a fancy – only the nettle-rash, not the plague. You will not die this time. I will ensure your life. So now jump out of the window as fast as you can, and unlock the door – you need not be afraid of breaking your neck – you know your life is ensured. Come, take the lover's leap, and get rid of your passion at once.'

I grew angry.

'Only a cloud,' said Lady Geraldine – 'it will blow over.'

I became more passionate – I did not know the force of my own feelings, till they met with an obstacle; they suddenly rose to a surprising height.

'Now, my lord,' cried Lady Geraldine with a tone and look of comic vexation, 'this is really the most provoking thing imaginable; you have no idea how you distress me, nor of what exquisite pleasures you deprive me – all the pleasures of coquetry; legitimate pleasures, in certain circumstances, as I am instructed to think them by one of the first moral authorities. There is a case – I quote from memory, my lord; for my memory, like that of most other people, on subjects where I am deeply interested, is tolerably tenacious – there is a case, says the best of fathers, in his Legacy to the best of daughters – there is a case, where a woman may coquet justifiably to the utmost verge which her conscience will allow. It is where a gentleman purposely declines making his addresses, till such time as he thinks himself perfectly sure of her consent.[66] Now, my lord, if you had had the goodness to do so, I might have made this delightful case my own; and what charming latitude I might have allowed my conscience! But now, alas! it is all over, and I must be as frank as you have been, under pain of forfeiting what I value more even than admiration – my own good opinion.'

She paused, and was silent for a few moments; then suddenly changing her manner, she exclaimed, in a serious, energetic tone, 'Yes, I must, I will be sincere; let it cost me what it may. I will be sincere. My lord, I never can be yours. My lord, you will believe me, even from the effort with which I speak:' her voice softened, and her face suffused with crimson, as she spoke. 'I love another – my heart is no longer in my own possession: whether it will ever be in my power, consistently with my duty and his principles, to be united with the man of my choice, is doubtful – more than doubtful – but this is certain, that with such a prepossession, such a conviction in my mind, I never could nor ought to think of marrying any other person.'

I pleaded, that however deserving of her preference the object of her favour might be, yet that if there were, as her own prudence seemed to suggest, obstacles, rendering the probability of her union with that person more than doubtful, it might be possible that her superior sense and strength of mind, joined to the persevering affection of another lover, who would spare no exertions to render himself worthy of her, might, perhaps, in time –

'No, no,' said she, interrupting me; 'do not deceive yourself. I will not deceive you. I give you no hopes that my sentiments may change. I know my own mind – it will not change. My attachment is founded on the firm basis of esteem; my affection has grown from the intimate knowledge of the principles and conduct of the man I love. No other man, let his merits be what they may, could have these advantages in my opinion. And when I say that the probability of our being united is more than doubtful, I do not mean to deny, that I have distant hope that change of circumstances might render love and duty compatible. Without hope I know love cannot long exist. You see I do not talk romantic nonsense to you. All that you say of prudence, and time, and the effect of the attentions of another admirer, would be perfectly just and applicable, if my attachment were a fancy of yesterday – if it were a mere young lady's common-place first love; but I am not a *very* young lady, nor is this, though a first love, commonplace. I do not, you see, in the usual style, tell you that the man I adore is an angel, and that no created form ever did, or ever can, resemble this *angel in green and gold*; but, on the contrary, do justice to your lordship's merit: and believing, as I do, that you are capable of a real love; still more, believing that such an attachment would rouse you to exertion, and bring to life and light a surprising number of good qualities; yet I should deceive you unpardonably, fatally for my own peace of mind, if not for yours, were I not frankly and decidedly to assure you, that I never could reward or return your affection. My attachment to – I trust entirely where I trust at all – my attachment to Mr Devereux is for life.'

'He deserves it – deserves it all,' cried I, struggling for utterance; 'that is as much as a rival can say.'

'Not more than I expected from you, my lord.'

'But your ladyship says there is a hope of duty and love being compatible. *Would* Lady Kildangan *ever* consent?'

She looked much disturbed.

'No, certainly; not unless – Lord O'Toole has promised – not that I depend on courtiers' promises – but Lord O'Toole is a relation of ours, and he has promised to obtain an appointment abroad, in India, for Mr Devereux. If that were done, he might appear of more consequence in the eyes of the world. My mother might then, perhaps, be propitious. My lord, I give you the strongest proof of my esteem, by speaking with such openness. I have had the honour of your lordship's acquaintance only a few months; but without complimenting my own penetration, I may securely trust to the judgement of Mr Devereux, and his example has taught me to feel confidence in your lordship. Your conduct now will, I trust, justify my good opinion, by your secrecy; and by desisting from useless pursuit you will entitle yourself to my esteem and gratitude. These, I presume, you will think worth securing.'

My soul was so completely touched, that I could not articulate.

'Mr Devereux is right – I see, my lord, that you have a soul that can be touched.'

'Kissing hands, I protest!' exclaimed a shrill voice at the window. We turned, and saw Mrs O'Connor and a group of tittering faces peeping in. 'Kissing hands, after a good hour's tête-à-tête! O pray,

Lady Kildangan, make haste here,' continued Mrs O'Connor; 'make haste, before Lady Geraldine's blushes are over.'

'Were you ever detected in the crime of blushing, in your life, Mrs O'Connor?' said I.

'I never was found out locked up with so fine a gentleman,' replied Mrs O'Connor.

'Then it hurts your conscience only to be found out, like all the rest of the vast family of the Surfaces,'[67] said Lady Geraldine, resuming her spirit.

'Found out! – Locked up! – Bless me! bless me! What is all this?' cried Lady Kildangan, puffing up the hill. 'For shame! young ladies; for shame!' continued her ladyship, with a decent suppression of her satisfaction, when she saw, or thought she saw how matters stood. 'Unlock the door, pray. Don't be vexed, my Geraldine. Fie! fie! Mrs O'Connor. But quizzing is now so fashionable – nobody can be angry with any body. My Geraldine, consider we are all friends.'

The door unlocked, and as we were going out, Lady Geraldine whispered to me – 'For mercy's sake, my lord, don't break my poor mother's heart! Never let her know, that a coronet has been within my grasp, and that I have not clutched it.'

Lady Kildangan, who thought that all was now approaching that happy termination she so devoutly wished, was so full of her own happy presentiments, that it was impossible for me to undeceive her ladyship. Even when I announced before her, to Sir Harry Ormsby, that I was obliged to return home immediately on particular business, she was, I am sure, persuaded that I was going to prepare matters for marriage-settlements. When I mounted my horse, Mr Devereux pressed through a crowd assembled on the steps at the hall-door, and offered me his hand, with a look and manner that seemed to say – Have you sufficient generosity to be still my friend? 'I know the value of your friendship, Mr Devereux,' said I, 'and I hope to deserve it better every year that I live.'

For the effort which it cost me to say this I was rewarded. Lady Geraldine, who had retired behind her companions, at this instant approached with an air of mingled grace and dignity, bowed her head, and gave me a smile of grateful approbation. This is the last image left on my mind, the last look of the charming Geraldine – I never saw her again.

After I got home I never shaved for two days, and scarcely ever spoke. I should have taken to my bed to avoid seeing any human creature; but I knew that if I declared myself ill, no power would keep my old nurse Ellinor from coming to moan over me; and I was not in a humour to listen to stories of the Irish Black Beard, or the ghost of king O'Donoghoe; nor could I, however troublesome, have repulsed the simplicity of her affection. Instead of going to bed, therefore, I continued to lie stretched upon a sofa, ruminating sweet and bitter thoughts, after giving absolute orders that I should not be disturbed on any account whatever. Whilst I was in this state of reverie, one of my servants – an odd Irish fellow, who, under pretence of being half-witted, took more liberties than his companions – bolted into my presence.

'Plase your lordship, I thought it my duty, in spite of 'em all below, to come up to advertise to your lordship of the news that's going through the country. That they are all upside down at Ormsby Villa, all mad entirely – fighting and setting off through the kingdom, every one their own way; and, they say, it's all on account of something that Miss Clemmy Ormsby told, that Lady Geraldine said about my lord O'Toole being no better than a cat's paw, or something that way, which made his lordship quite mad; and he said, in the presence of Captain Andrews, and my lady Kildangan, and Lady Geraldine, and all that were in it, something that vexed Lady Geraldine, which made Mr Cecil Devereux mad next; and he said something smart in reply, that Lord O'Toole could not digest, he said, which made his lordship madder than ever, and he discharged Mr Devereux from his favour, and he is not to get that place that was vacant, the lord-lieutenancy of some place in the Indies that he was to have had; this made Lady Geraldine mad, and it was found out she was in love with Mr Devereux, which made her mother mad, the maddest of all, they say, so that none can hold her, and she is crying night and day how her daughter might have had the first coronet in the kingdom, *maning* you, my lard, if it had not been that she *prefarred* a beggar-man, *maning* Mr Cecil Devereux, who is as poor, they say, as a Connaughtman – and he's forbid to think of her, and she's forbid, under pain of bread and water, ever to set her eyes upon him the longest day ever she lives; so the horses and coaches are ordered, and they are all to be off with the first light for Dublin: and that's all, my lard; and all truth, not a word of lies I'm telling.'

I was inclined not to credit a story so oddly told; but, upon inquiry, I found it true in its material points. My own words to Mr Devereux, and the parting look of Lady Geraldine, were full in my recollection; I was determined, by an unexpected exertion, to surprise both the lovers, and to secure for ever their esteem and gratitude. The appointment, which Mr Devereux desired, was not yet given away; the fleet was to sail in a few days. I started up from my sofa – ordered my carriage instantly – shaved myself – sent a courier on before to have horses ready at every stage to carry me to Dublin – got there in the shortest time possible – found Lord O'Toole but just arrived. Though unused to diplomatic language and political negociation, I knew pretty well on what they all *hinge*. I went directly to the point, and showed that it would be the interest of the party concerned to grant my request. By expressing a becoming desire that my boroughs, upon a question where a majority was required, should *strengthen the hands of government*, I obtained for my friend the favour he *deserved*. Before I quitted Lord O'Toole, his secretary, Captain Andrews, was instructed to write a letter, announcing to Mr Devereux his appointment. A copy of the former letter of refusal now lay before me; it was in his lordship's purest diplomatic style – as follows:

Private

Lord O'Toole is concerned to inform Mr Devereux that he cannot feel himself justified in encouraging Mr D., under the existing circumstances, to make any direct application relative to the last conversation his lordship had the honour to hold with Mr Devereux.

To Cecil Devereux, Esq.
    &c.   Thursday —

The letter which I obtained, and of which I took possession, ran as follows:

Private

Lord O'Toole is happy to have it in command to inform Mr Devereux, that his lordship's representations on the subject of their last conversation have been thought sufficient, and that

an official notification of the appointment to India, which Mr
D. desired, will meet the wishes of Mr Devereux.

Captain Andrews has the honour to add his congratulations.

To Cecil Devereux, Esq.
&c.   Thursday —

Having despatched this business with a celerity that surprised all
the parties concerned, and most myself, I called at the lodgings of
Mr Devereux, delivered the letter to his servant, and left town. I
could not bear to see either Mr Devereux or Lady Geraldine. I had
the pleasure to hear, that the obtaining this appointment was followed by Lady Kildangan's consent to their marriage. Soon after
my return to Glenthorn Castle, I received a letter of warm thanks
from Devereux, and a polite postscript from Lady Geraldine, declaring that, though she felt much pleasure, she could feel no surprise in
seeing her opinion of Lord Glenthorn justified: persuaded, as she
and Mr Devereux had always been, that only motive and opportunity were wanting to make his lordship's superior qualities known to
the world, and, what is still more difficult, to himself. They left
Ireland immediately afterwards, in consequence of their appointment in India.

I was raised in my own estimation – I revelled a short time in my
self-complacent reflections; but when nothing more remained to be
done, or to be said – when the hurry of action, the novelty of
generosity, the glow of enthusiasm, and the freshness of gratitude,
were over, I felt that, though large motives could now invigorate my
mind, I was still a prey to habitual indolence, and that I should
relapse into my former state of apathy and disease.

CHAPTER XII

I remember to have heard, in some epilogue to a tragedy, that the
tide of pity and of love, whilst it overwhelms, fertilizes the soul. That
it may deposit the seeds of future fertilization, I believe; but some
time must elapse before they germinate: on the first retiring of the

tide, the prospect is barren and desolate. I was absolutely inert, and almost imbecile for a considerable time, after the extraordinary stimulus, by which I had been actuated, was withdrawn. I was in this state of apathy when the rebellion broke out in Ireland;[68] nor was I roused in the least by the first news of the disturbances. The intelligence, however, so much alarmed my English servants, that, with one accord, they left me; nothing could persuade them to remain longer in Ireland. The parting with my English gentleman affected my lethargic selfishness a little. His loss would have been grievous to such a helpless being as I was, had not his place been immediately supplied by that half-witted Irishman, Joe Kelly, who had ingratiated himself with me by a mixture of drollery and simplicity, and by suffering himself to be continually my laughing-stock; for, in imitation of Lady Geraldine, I thought it necessary to have a butt. I remember he first caught my notice by a strange answer to a very simple question. I asked, 'What noise is that I hear?' 'My lard,' said he, 'it is only the singing in my ears; I have had it these six months.' Another time, when I reproached him for having told me a lie, he answered, 'Why, now indeed, and plase your honour, my lard, I tell as few lies as possibly I can.' This fellow, the son of a bricklayer, had originally been intended for a priest, and he went, as he told me, to the College of Maynooth, to study his *humanities*; but, unluckily, the charms of some Irish Heloise came between him and the altar. He lived in a cabin of love, till he was weary of his smoke-dried Heloise, and then thought it *convanient* to turn *sarving* man, as he could play on the flute, and brush a coat remarkably well, which he *larned* at Maynooth, by brushing the coats of the superiors. Though he was willing to be laughed at, Joe Kelly could in his turn laugh; and he now ridiculed, without mercy, the pusillanimity of the English *renegadoes*, as he called the servants who had just left my service. He assured me that, to his knowledge, there was no manner of danger, *excepted a man prefarred being afraid of his own shadow, which some did, rather than have nothing to talk of, or enter into resolutions about, with some of the spirited men in the chair.*

Unwilling to be disturbed, I readily believed all that lulled me in my security. I would not be at the trouble of reading the public papers; and when they were read to me, I did not credit any paragraph that militated against my own opinion. Nothing could awaken me. I remember, one day, lying yawning on my sofa, repeating to Mr M'Leod, who endeavoured to open my eyes to the situation of the country, 'Pshaw, my dear sir; there is no danger, be assured – none at all – none at all. For mercy's sake! talk to me of something more diverting, if you would keep me awake; time enough to think of these things when they come nearer to us.'

Evils that were not immediately near me had no power to affect my imagination. My tenantry had not yet been contaminated by the epidemic infection, which broke out soon after with such violence as to threaten the total destruction of all civil order. I had lived in England – I was unacquainted with the causes and the progress of the disease, and I had no notion of my danger; all I knew was, that some houses had been robbed of arms, and that there was a set of desperate wretches called *defenders*; but I was *annoyed* only by the rout that was now made about them. Having been used to the regular course of justice which prevailed in England, I was more shocked at the summary proceedings of my neighbours than alarmed at the symptoms of insurrection. Whilst my mind was in this mood, I was provoked by the conduct of some of the violent party, which wounded my personal pride, and infringed upon my imagined consequence. My foster-brother's forge was searched for pikes, his house ransacked, his bed and *bellows*, as possible hiding places, were cut open; by accident, or from private malice, he received a shot in his arm; and, though not the slightest cause of suspicion could be found against him, the party left him with a broken arm, and the consolation of not being sent to jail as a defender. Without making any allowance for the peculiar circumstances of the country, my indignation was excited in the extreme, by the injury done to my foster-brother; his sufferings, the tears of his mother, the taunts of Mr (now *Captain*) Hardcastle, and the opposition made by his party, called forth all the faculties of my mind and body. The poor fellow, who was the subject of this contest, showed the best disposition imaginable; he was excessively grateful to me for interesting myself to *get* him justice; but as soon as he found that parties ran high against me, he earnestly dissuaded me from persisting.

'Let it drop, and *plase* your honour; my lord, let it drop, and don't be making of yourself *inimies* for the likes of me. Sure, what signifies my arm? and, before the next assizes, sha'n't I be as well as ever, arm and all?' continued he, trying to appear to move the arm without pain. 'And there's the new bellows your honour has *give* me; it does my heart good to look at 'em, and it won't be long before I will be blowing them again as stout as ever; and so God bless your honour, my lord, and think no more about it – let it drop entirely, and don't be bringing yourself into trouble.'

'Ay, don't be bringing yourself into trouble, dear,' added Ellinor, who seemed half distracted between her feelings for her son and her fears for me; 'it's a shame to think of the way they've treated Christy – but there's no help now, and it's best not to be making bad worse; and so, as Christy says, let the thing drop, jewel, and don't be bringing yourself into trouble; you don't know the *natur* of them people, dear – you are *too innocent* for them entirely, and myself does not know the mischief they might do *yees*.'

'True for ye,' pursued Christy; 'I wouldn't for the best cow ever I see that your honour ever larnt a sentence about me or my arm; and it is not for such as we to be minding every little accident – so God lend you long life, and don't be plaguing yourself to death! Let it drop, and I'll sleep well the night, which I did not do the week, for thinking of all the trouble you got, and would get, God presarve ye!'

This generous fellow's eloquence produced an effect directly contrary to what was intended; both my feelings and my pride were now more warmly interested in his cause. I insisted upon his swearing examinations before Mr M'Leod, who was a justice of the peace. Mr M'Leod behaved with the utmost steadiness and impartiality; and in this trying moment, when 'it was infamy to seem my friend', he defended my conduct calmly, but resolutely, in private and in public, and gave his unequivocal testimony, in few but decided words, in favour of my injured tenant. I should have respected Mr M'Leod more, if I had not attributed this conduct to his desire of being returned for one of my boroughs at the approaching election. He endeavoured, with persevering goodness, to convince me of the reality of the danger in the country. My eyes were with much difficulty forced open so far as to perceive that it was necessary to take an active part in public affairs to vindicate my loyalty, and to do away the prejudices that were entertained against me; nor did my incredulity, as to the magnitude of the peril, prevent me from making exertions essential to the defence of my own character, if not to that of the nation. How few act from purely patriotic and rational motives! At all events I acted, and acted with energy; and certainly at this period of my life I felt no ennui. Party spirit is an effectual cure for ennui; and perhaps it is for this reason that so many are addicted to its intemperance. All my passions were roused, and my mind and body kept in continued activity. I was either galloping, or haranguing, or fearing, or hoping, or fighting; and so long as it was said that I could not sleep in my bed, I slept remarkably well, and never had so good an appetite as when I was in hourly danger of having nothing to eat. *The rebels were up*, and *the rebels were down* – and Lord Glenthorn's spirited conduct in the chair, and indefatigable exertions in the field, were the theme of daily eulogium amongst my convivial companions and immediate dependants. But, unfortunately, my sudden activity gained me no credit amongst the violent party of my neighbours, who persisted in their suspicions; and my reputation was now still more injured, by the alternate charge of being a trimmer or a traitor. Nay, I was further exposed to another danger, of which, from my ignorance of the country, I could not possibly be aware. The disaffected themselves, as I afterwards found, really believed, that, as I had not begun by persecuting the poor, I must be a favourer of the rebels; and all that I did to bring the guilty to justice, they thought was only to give a *colour to the thing*, till the proper moment should come for my declaring myself. Of this absurd and perverse mode of judging I had not the slightest conception; and I only laughed when it was hinted to me. My treating the matter so lightly confirmed suspicion on both sides. At this time all objects were so magnified and distorted by the mist of prejudice, that no inexperienced eye could judge of their real proportions. Neither party could believe the simple truth, that my tardiness to act arose from the habitual *inertia* of my mind and body.

Whilst prepossessions were thus strong, the time, the important time, in Ireland the most important season of the year, the assizes, arrived. My foster-brother's cause, or, as it was now generally called, *Lord Glenthorn's* cause, came on to be tried. I spared no expence, I spared no exertions; I fee'd the ablest counsel; and not content with leaving them to be instructed by my attorney, I explained the affair to them myself with indefatigable zeal. One of the lawyers, whom I had seen, or by whom I had been seen, in my former inert state of existence, at some watering-place in England, could not refrain from expressing his astonishment at my change of character; he could scarcely believe that I was the same Lord Glenthorn, of whose indolence and ennui he had formerly heard and seen so much.

Alas! all my activity, all my energy, on the present occasion, proved ineffectual. After a dreadful quantity of false swearing, the jury professed themselves satisfied; and, without retiring from the box, acquitted the persons who had assaulted my foster-brother. The mortification of this legal defeat was not all that I had to endure; the victorious party mobbed me, as I passed some time afterwards through a neighbouring town, where Captain Hardcastle and his friends had been carousing. I was hooted, and pelted, and narrowly escaped with my life – *I* who, but a few months ago, had imagined myself possessed of nearly despotic power: but opinions had changed; and on opinion almost all power is founded. No individual, unless he possess uncommon eloquence, joined to personal intrepidity, can withstand the combination of numbers, and the force of prejudice.

Such was the result of my first public exertions! Yet I was now happier and better satisfied with myself than I had ever been before. I was not only conscious of having acted in a manly and generous manner; but the alarms of the rebels, and of the French, and of the loyalists; and the parading, and the galloping, and the quarrelling, and the continual agitation in which I was kept, whilst my character and life were at stake, relieved me effectually from the intolerable burden of ennui.

CHAPTER XIII

And, for the book of knowledge fair,
Presented with an universal blank
Of Nature's works, to me expunged and rased.[69]

Unfortunately for me, the rebellion in Ireland was soon quelled; the nightly scouring of our county ceased; the poor people returned to their duty and their homes; the occupation of upstart and ignorant *associators* ceased, and their consequence sunk at once. Things and persons settled to their natural level. The influence of men of property, and birth, and education, and character, once more prevailed. The spirit of party ceased to operate; my neighbours wakened, as if from a dream, and wondered at the strange injustice with which I had been treated. Those who had lately been my combined enemies were disunited, and each was eager to assure me that he had *always been privately my friend*, but that he was compelled to conceal his sentiments: each exculpated himself, and threw the blame on others: all apologized to me, and professed to be my most devoted humble servants. My popularity, my power, and my prosperity were now at their zenith, *unfortunately for me*; because my adversity had not lasted long enough to form and season my character. I had been driven to exertion by a mixture of pride and generosity; my understanding being uncultivated, I had acted from the virtuous impulse of the moment, but never from rational motive, which alone can be permanent in its operation. When the spur of the occasion pressed upon me no longer, I relapsed into my former inactivity. When the great interests and strong passions, by which I had been impelled to exertion, subsided, all other feelings, and all less objects, seemed stale, flat, and unprofitable. For the tranquillity which I was now left to enjoy I had no taste; it appeared to me a dead calm, most spiritless and melancholy.

I remember hearing, some years afterwards, a Frenchman, who had been in imminent danger of been guillotined by Robespierre, and who at last was one of those who arrested the tyrant, declare, that when the bustle and horror of the revolution were over, he could hardly keep himself awake; and that he thought it very insipid to live in quiet with his wife and family. He further summed up the catalogue of Robespierre's crimes, by exclaiming, 'D'ailleurs c'étoit un grand philantrope!' I am not conscious of any disposition to cruelty, and I heard this man's speech with disgust; yet upon a candid self-examination, I must confess, that I have felt, though from different causes, some degree of what he described. Perhaps *ennui* may have had a share in creating revolutions. A French author pronounces ennui to be 'a moral indigestion, caused by a monotony of situations'!

I had no wife or family to make domestic life agreeable: nor was I inclined to a second marriage, my first had proved so unfortunate, and the recollection of my disappointment with Lady Geraldine was so recent. Even the love of power no longer acted upon me: my power was now undisputed. My jealousy and suspicions of my agent, Mr M'Leod, were about this time completely conquered, by his behaviour at a general election. I perceived that he had no underhand design upon my boroughs; and that he never attempted or wished to interfere in my affairs, except at my particular desire. My confidence in him became absolute and unbounded; but this was really a misfortune to me, for it became the cause of my having still less to do. I gave up all business, and from all manner of trouble I was now free: yet I became more and more unhappy, and my nervous complaints returned. I was not aware that I was taking the very means to increase my own disease. The philosophical Dr Cullen observes, that 'Whatever aversion to application of any kind may appear in hypochondriacs, there is nothing more pernicious to them than absolute idleness, or a vacancy from all earnest pursuit. It is owing to wealth admitting of indolence, and leading to the pursuit of transitory and unsatisfying amusements, or exhausting pleasures only, that the present times exhibit to us so many instances of hypochondriacism.'[70]

I fancied that change of air and change of place would do me good; and, as it was fine summer weather, I projected various parties of pleasure. The Giants' Causeway, and the Lake of Killarney, were the only things I had ever heard mentioned as worth seeing in Ireland. I suffered myself to be carried into the county of Antrim, and I saw the Giants' Causeway. From the description given by Dr Hamilton of some of these wonders of nature, the reader may judge how much I *ought* to have been astonished and delighted.

In the bold promontory of Bengore, you behold, as you look up from the sea, a gigantic colonnade of basaltes, supporting a black mass of irregular rock, over which rises another range of pillars, 'forming all together a perpendicular height of one hundred and seventy feet, from the base of which the promontory, covered over with rock and grass, slopes down to the sea, for the space of two hundred feet more: making, in all, a mass of near four hundred feet in height, which, in the beauty and variety of its colouring, in elegance and novelty of arrangement, and in the extraordinary magnificence of its objects, cannot be rivalled'.[71]

Yet I was seized with a fit of yawning, as I sat in my pleasure-boat, to admire this sublime spectacle. I looked at my watch, observed that we should be late for dinner, and grew impatient to be rowed back to the place where we were to dine; not that I was hungry, but I wanted to be again set in motion. Neither science nor taste expanded my view; and I saw nothing worthy of my admiration, or capable of giving me pleasure. The watching a straw floating down the tide was the only amusement I recollect to have enjoyed upon this excursion.

I was assured, however, by Lady Ormsby, that I could not help being enchanted with the lake of Killarney. The party was arranged by this lady, who, having the preceding summer seen me captivated by Lady Geraldine, and pitying my disappointment, had formed the obliging design of restoring my spirits, and marrying me to one of her near relations. She calculated that as I had been charmed by Lady Geraldine's vivacity, I must be enchanted with the fine spirits of Lady Jocunda Lawler. So far were the thoughts of marriage from my imagination, that I only was sorry to find a young lady smuggled into our party, because I was afraid she would be troublesome: but I resolved to be quite passive upon all occasions, where attentions to the fair sex are sometimes expected. My arm, or my hand, or my assistance, in any manner, I was determined not to offer: the lounging indifference, which some fashionable young men affect towards ladies, I really felt; and, besides, nobody minds unmarried women! This fashion was most convenient to my indolence. In my state of torpor I was not, however, long left in peace. Lady Jocunda was a high-bred romp, who made it a rule to say and do whatever she pleased. In a hundred indirect ways I was called upon to admire her charming spirits: but the rattling voice, loud laughter, flippant wit, and hoyden gaiety, of Lady Jocunda, disgusted me beyond expression. A thousand times on my journey I wished myself quietly asleep in my own castle. Arrived at Killarney, such blowing of horns, such boating, such seeing of prospects, such prosing of guides, all telling us what to admire! Then such exclamations, and such clambering! I was walked and talked till I was half-dead. I wished the rocks, and the hanging-woods and the glens, and the water-falls, and the arbutus, and the myrtles, and the upper and lower lakes, and the islands, and Mucruss, and Mucruss Abbey, and the purple mountain, and the eagle's nest, and the Grand Turk, and the lights and the shades, and the echoes, and, above all, the Lady Jocunda, fairly at the devil.

A nobleman in the neighbourhood had the politeness to invite us to see a stag-hunt upon the water. The account of this diversion, which I had met with in my Guide to the Lakes,*[72] promised well. I

---

* 'The stag is roused from the woods that skirt Glenaa mountain, in which there are

consented to stay another day: that day I really was revived by this spectacle, for it was new. The sublime and the beautiful had no charms for me: novelty was the only power that could waken me from my lethargy; perhaps there was in this spectacle something more than novelty. The Romans had recourse to shows of wild beasts and gladiators to relieve their ennui. At all events, I was kept awake this whole morning, though I cannot say that I felt in *such ecstasies as to be in any imminent danger of jumping out of the boat.*

Of our journey back from Killarney I remember nothing, but my being discomfited by Lady Jocunda's practical jests and overpowering gaiety. When she addressed herself to me, my answers were as constrained and as concise as possible; and, as I was afterwards told, I seemed, at the close of my reply to each interrogative of her ladyship's, to answer with Odin's prophetess,

> Now my weary lips I close;
> Leave me, leave me to repose.[73]

This she never did till we parted; and at that moment, I believe, my satisfaction appeared so visible, that Lady Ormsby gave up all hopes of me. Arrived at my own castle, I threw myself on my bed quite exhausted. I took three hours' additional sleep every day for a week,

many of these animals that run wild; the bottoms and sides of the mountains are covered with woods and the declivities are so long and steep that no horse could either make his way to the bottom, or climb these impracticable hills. It is impossible to follow the hunt, either by land or on horseback. The spectator enjoys the diversion on the lake, where the cry of hounds, the harmony of the horn, resounding from the hills on every side, the universal shouts of joy along the valleys and mountains, which are often lined with foot-people, who come in vast numbers to partake and assist at the diversion, re-echo from hill to hill, and give the highest glee and satisfaction that the imagination can conceive possible to arise from the chase, and perhaps can nowhere be enjoyed with that spirit and sublime elevation of soul, that a thorough-bred sportsman feels at a stag-hunt on the lake of Killarney. There is, however, one imminent danger which awaits him; that in his raptures and ecstasies he may forget himself and jump out of the boat. When hotly pursued, and weary with the constant difficulty of making his way with his ramified antlers through the woods, the stag, terrified at the cry of his open-mouthed pursuers, almost at his heels, now looks toward the lake as his last resource – then pauses and looks upwards; but the hills are insurmountable, and the woods refuse to shelter him – the hounds roar with redoubled fury at the sight of their victim – he plunges into the lake. He escapes but for a few minutes from one merciless enemy to fall into the hands of another – the shouting boatmen surround their victim, – throw cords round his majestic antlers – he is haltered and dragged to shore; while the big tears roll down his face, and his heaving sides and panting flanks speak his agonies, the keen searching knife drinks his blood, and savages exult at his expiring groan.'

to recruit my strength, and rest my nerves, after all that I had been made to suffer by this young lady's prodigious animal spirits.

CHAPTER XIV

I could now boast that I had travelled all over Ireland, from north to south; but, in fact, I had seen nothing of the country or of its inhabitants. In these commodious parties of pleasure, every thing had been provided to prevent the obstacles that roused my faculties. Accustomed by this time to the Hibernian tone, I fancied that I knew all that could be known of the Irish character; familiarized with the comic expressions of the lower class of people, they amused me no longer. On this journey, however, I recollect making one observation, and once laughing at what I thought a practical bull. We saw a number of labourers at work in a bog, on a very hot day, with a fire lighted close to them. When I afterwards mentioned, before Mr M'Leod, this circumstance, which I had thought absurd, he informed me that the Irish labourers often light fires, that the smoke may drive away or destroy those myriads of tiny flies, called *midges*, by which they are often tormented so much, that without this remedy, they would, in hot and damp weather, be obliged to abandon their work. Had I been sufficiently active during my journey to pen a journal, I should certainly, without further inquiry, have noted down, that the Irish labourers *always* light fires in the hottest weather to cool themselves; and thus I should have added one more to the number of cursory travellers, who expose their own ignorance, whilst they attempt to ridicule local customs, of which they have not inquired the cause, or discovered the utility.

A foreigner, who has lately written Letters on England, has given a laughable instance of this promptitude of misapprehension. He says, he had heard much of the venality of the British parliament, but he had no idea of the degree to which it extended, till he actually was an eye-witness of the scene. The moment the minister entered the House, all the members ran about exclaiming, 'Places! places!' which means, Give us places – give us places.[74]

My heavy indolence fortunately preserved me from exposing

myself, like these volatile tourists. I was at least secure from the danger of making mistakes in telling what I never saw.

As to the mode of living of the Irish, their domestic comforts or grievances, their habits and opinions, their increasing or decreasing ambition to better their condition, the proportion between the population and the quantity of land cultivated or capable of cultivation, the difference between the profits of the husbandman and the artificer, the relation between the nominal wages of labour and the actual command over the necessaries of life: – these were questions wholly foreign to my thoughts, and, at this period of my life, absolutely beyond the range of my understanding. I had travelled through my own country without making even a single remark upon the various degrees of industry and civilization visible in different parts of the kingdom. In fact, it never occurred to me that it became a British nobleman to have some notion of the general state of that empire, in the legislation of which he has a share; nor had I the slightest suspicion that political economy was a study requisite or suitable to my rank in life or situation in society. Satisfied with having seen all that is worth seeing in Ireland, the Giants' Causeway, and the Lake of Killarney, I was now impatient to return to England. During the rebellion, I could not, with honour, desert my post; but now that tranquillity was apparently restored; I determined to quit a country of which my partial knowledge had in every respect been unfortunate. This resolution of mine to leave Ireland threw Ellinor into despair, and she used all her eloquence to dissuade me from the journey. I was quite surprised by the agony of grief into which she was thrown by the dread of my departure. I felt astonished that one human being could be so attached to another, and I really envied her sensibility. My new man, Joe Kelly, also displayed much reluctance at the thoughts of leaving his native country; and this sentiment inclined Ellinor to think more favourably of him, though she could not quite forgive him for being a Kelly of Ballymuddy.

'Troth,' said she to him one day, in my presence, 'none of them Kellys of Ballymuddy but what are a bad clan! Joey, is not there you own *broder's* uncle lying in the jail of—at this present time for the murder of a woman?' – 'Well,' replied Joe, 'and if he was so unfortunate to be *put up*, which was not *asy* done neither, is it not better and more *creditabler* to lie in a jail for murder than a robbery, I ask you?' This new scale of crimes surprised me; but Joe spoke what was the sense of many of his countrymen at that period.

By various petty attentions, this man contrived to persuade me of the sincerity of his attachment: chiefly by the art of appearing to be managed by me in all things, he insensibly obtained power over my pride; and, by saving me daily trouble, secured considerable influence over my indolence. More than any one whom I had ever seen, he had the knack of seeming half-witted – too simple to overreach, and yet sufficiently acute and droll to divert his master. I liked to have him about me, as uncultivated kings like to have their fools.[75] One of our ancient monarchs is said to have given three parishes to his *joculator*; I gave only three farms to mine. I had a sort of mean pride in making my favourite an object of envy: besides, I fell into the common mistake of the inexperienced great, who fancy that attachment can be purchased, and that gratitude can be secured, by favours disproportioned to deserts. Joe Kelly, by sundry manoeuvres too minute for description, contrived to make me delay, from day to day, the preparations for my journey to England. From week to week it was put off till the autumn was far advanced. At length Kelly had nothing left to *suggest*, but that it would be best to wait for answers from my English steward to the letters that had been written to inquire whether every thing was ready for my reception. During this interval, I avoided every human creature (except Joe Kelly), and was in great danger of becoming a misanthrope from mere indolence. I did not hate my fellow-creatures, but I dreaded the trouble of talking to them. My only recreation, at this period, was sauntering out in the evening beside the sea-shore. It was my regular practice to sit down upon a certain large stone, at the foot of a rock, to watch the ebbing of the tide. There was something in the contemplation of the sea and of the tides which was fascinating to my mind. I could sit and look at the ocean whole hours together; for, without any exertion of my own, I beheld a grand operation of nature, accompanied with a sort of vast monotony of motion and sound, which lulled me into reverie.

Late one evening, as I was seated on my accustomed stone, my attention was slightly diverted from the sea by the sight of a man descending the crag above me, in rather a perilous manner.

With one end of a rope coiled round his body, and the other fastened to a stake driven into the summit of the rock, he let himself half-way down the terrible height. One foot now rested on a projecting point, one hand held the rope, and hanging thus midway in the air, he seemed busy searching in the crevices of the rock, for the eggs of water-fowl. This dangerous trade I had seen frequently plied on this coast, so that I should scarcely have regarded the man if he had not turned, from time to time, as if to watch me. When he saw that he had fixed my eye, he threw down, as I thought, a white stone, which fell nearly at my feet. I stooped to examine it; the man waited till he saw it in my hands, then coiled himself swiftly up his rope to the summit of the rock, and disappeared. I found a paper tied round the stone, and on this paper, in a hand-writing that seemed to be feigned, were written these words:

> Your life and caracter, one or t'other – say both, is in danger. Don't be walking here any more late in the evening, near them caves, nor don't go near the old abbey, any time – And don't be trusting to Joe Kelly any way – Lave the kingdom entirely; the wind sarves.

> So prays your true well-wisher.

> P.S. Lave the castle the morrow, and say nothing of this to Joe Kelly, or you'll repent when it's all over wid you.

I was startled a little by this letter at first, but in half an hour I relapsed into my apathy. Many gentlemen in the country had received anonymous letters: I had been tired of hearing of them during the rebellion. This, I thought, might be only a *quiz*, or a trick to hurry me out of the kingdom, contrived by some of those who desired my absence. In short, the labour of *thinking* about the matter fatigued me. I burned the letter as soon as I got home, and resolved not to puzzle or plague myself about it any more. My steward's answer came the next morning from England; Kelly made no difficulty, when I ordered him to be ready to set out in three days. This confirmed me in my opinion that the letter was malicious, or a jest. Mr M'Leod came to take leave of me. I mentioned the circumstances to him slightly, and in general terms: he looked very serious, and said, 'All these things are little in themselves, but are to be heeded, as marking the unsettled minds of the people – straws that show which way the wind blows. I apprehend we shall have a rough winter again, though we have had so still a summer. The people about us are too *hush* and too prudent – it is not their natures – there's something contriving among them: they don't break one another's heads at fairs as they used to do; they keep from whiskey; there must be some strong motive working this change upon them – good or bad, 'tis hard to say which. My lord, if we consider the condition of these poor people, and if we consider the causes –'

'Oh! for Heaven's sake, do not let us consider any more about it now; I am more than half asleep already,' said I, yawning; 'and our considering about it can do no good, to *me* at least; for you know I am going out of the kingdom; and when I am gone, M'Leod, you, in whom I have implicit confidence, must manage as you always used to do, you know, and as well as you can.'

'True,' said M'Leod, calmly, 'that is what I shall do, indubitably; for that is my duty, and, since your lordship has implicit confidence in me, my pleasure. – I wish your lordship a good night and a good journey.'

'I shall not set out in the morning; not till the day after to-morrow, I believe,' said I, 'for I feel consumedly tired to-night: they have plagued me about so many things to-day; so much business always before one can get away from a place; and then Joe Kelly has no head.'

'Have a care he has not too much head, my lord, as your anonymous correspondent hints – he may be right there: I told you from the first I would not go security for Joe Kelly's honesty; and where there is not strict honesty, I conceive there ought not to be implicit confidence.'

'O, hang it! as to honesty, they are none of them honest; I know that: but would you have me plague myself till I find a strictly honest servant? Joe's as honest as his neighbours, I dare say: the fellow diverts me, and is attached to me, and that's all I can expect. I must submit to be cheated, as all men of large fortunes are, more or less.'

Mr M'Leod listened with stubborn patience, and replied, that if I thought it necessary to submit to be cheated he could make no objection, except where it might come under his cognizance, and then he must take the liberty to remonstrate, or to give up his agency to some of the many, who could play better than he could the part of the dog in the fable, *pretending* to guard his master's meat.[76]

The cold ungracious integrity of this man, even in my own cause, at once excited my spleen and commanded my respect. After shaking my leg, as I sat for two minutes in silence, I called after M'Leod, who moved towards the door, 'Why, what can I do, Mr M'Leod? What would you have me do? Now, don't give me one of your dry answers, but let me have your notions as a friend: you know, M'Leod, I cannot help having the most perfect confidence in you.'

He bowed, but rather stiffly.

'I am proud to hear you can't help that, my lord,' said he. 'As to a friend, I never considered myself upon that footing till now: but, as you at present honour me so far as to ask my counsel, I am free to give it. Part with Joe Kelly to-night; and, whether you go or stay, you are safer without him. Joe's a rogue: he can do no good, and may do harm.'

'Then,' said I, 'you are really frightened by this anonymous letter?'

'Cannot a man take prudent precautions without he is frightened?' said M'Leod.

'But have you any particular reason to believe – in short to – to think, there can be any real danger for my life?'

'No particular reason, my lord; but the general reasons I have mentioned, the symptoms among the common people lead me to apprehend there may be fresh *risings* of the people soon; and you, as a man of fortune and rank, must be in danger. Captain Hardcastle says, that he has had informations of seditious meetings; but, he being a prejudiced man, I don't trust altogether to what he says.'

'Trust altogether to what he says!' exclaimed I; 'no, surely; for my part, I do not trust a word he says; and his giving it as his opinion that the people are ill-inclined would decide me to believe the exact contrary.'

'It would hardly be safe to judge that way either,' said M'Leod; 'for that method of judging by contraries might make another's folly the master of one's own sense.'

'I don't comprehend you now. Safe way of judging or not, Captain

Hardcastle's opinion shall never lead mine. When I asked for your advice, Mr M'Leod, it was because I have a respect for your under-standing; but I cannot defer to Captain Hardcastle's. I am now decided in my own opinion, that the people in this neighbourhood are perfectly well-disposed; and as to this anonymous letter, it is a mere trick, depend upon it, my good sir. I am surprised that a man of your capacity should be the dupe of such a thing; I should not be surprised if Hardcastle himself, or some of his people, wrote it.'

'I should,' said M'Leod, coolly.

'You should!' cried I, warmly. 'Why so? And why do you pro-nounce so decidedly, my good friend? Have not I the same means of judging as you have? unless, indeed, you have some private reason with which I am unacquainted. Perhaps,' cried I, starting half up from the sofa on which I lay, charmed with a bright idea, which had just struck me, 'perhaps, M'Leod, you wrote the letter yourself for a jest. Did you?'

'That's a question, my lord,' said M'Leod, growing suddenly red, and snatching up his hat with a quicker motion than I ever saw from him before, 'that's a question, my lord, which I must take leave not to answer; a question, give me leave to add, my lord Glenthorn,' continued he, speaking in a broader Scotch accent than I had ever heard from him before, 'which I should knock my equal *doon* for putting to me. A M'Leod, my lord, in jest or in earnest, would scorn to write to any man breathing that letter to which he would not put his name; and more, a M'Leod would scorn to write or to say that thing, to which he ought not to put his name. Your humble servant, my lord Glenthorn,' said he, and, making a hasty bow, departed.

I called after him, and even followed him to the head of the stairs, to explain and apologize; but in vain: I never saw him angry before.

'It's very weel, my lord, it's very weel; if you say you meant nothing offensive, it's very weel; but, if you think fit, my lord, we will sleep upon it before we talk any more. I am a wee bit warmer than I could wish, and your lordship has the advantage of me, in being cool. A M'Leod is apt to grow warm, when he's touched on the point of honour; and there's no wisdom in talking when a man's not his own master.'

'My good friend,' said I, seizing his hand as he was buttoning up his coat, 'I like you the better for this warmth; but I won't let you sleep upon your wrath: you must shake hands with me before that hall-door is opened to you.'

'Then so I do, for there's no standing against this frankness; and, to be as frank with you, my lord, I was wrong myself to be so testy – I ask pardon, too. A M'Leod never thought it a disgrace to crave a pardon when he was wrong.'

We shook hands, and parted better friends than ever. I spoke the exact truth when I said that I liked him the better for his warmth: his anger wakened me, and gave me something to think of, and some emotion for a few minutes. Joe Kelly presently afterwards came, with the simplest face imaginable, to inquire what I had determined about the journey.

'To put it off till the day after to-morrow,' said I. 'Light me to bed.'

He obeyed; but observed, that 'it was not his fault now if there was puttings-off; for his share every thing was ready, and he was willing and ready to follow me, at a moment's warning, to the world's end, as he had a good right to do, let alone inclination; for, parting me, he could never be right in himself: and though loth to part his country, he had rather part that *nor** me'.

Then, without dwelling upon these expressions of attachment, he changed to a merry mood, and by his drolleries diverted me all the time I was going to bed, and at last fairly talked me asleep.

CHAPTER XV

When the first grey light of morning began to make objects indistinctly visible, I thought I saw the door of my apartment open very softly. I was broad awake, and kept my eyes fixed upon it – it opened by very slow degrees; my head was so full of visions, that I expected a ghost to enter – but it was only Ellinor.

'Ellinor!' cried I; 'is it you at this time in the morning?'

'Hush! hush!' said she, shutting the door with great precaution, and then coming on tiptoe close to my bedside; 'for the love of God, speak softly, and make no stir to awake them that's asleep near and

* Than.

too near you. It's unknown to all that I come up; for may be, when them people are awake and about, I might not get the opportunity to speak, or they might guess I knew something by my looks.'

Her looks were full of terror – I was all amazement and expectation. Before she would say a word more, she searched the closets carefully and looked behind the tapestry, as if she apprehended that she might be overheard: satisfied that we were alone, she went on speaking, but still in a voice that, with my utmost strained attention, I could but just hear.

'As you hope to live and breathe,' said she, 'never go again after night-fall any time walking in that lone place by the sea-shore. It's a mercy you escaped as you did; but if you go again you'll never come back alive – for never would they get you to do what they want, and to be as wicked as themselves – the wicked villains!'

'Who?' said I – 'What wicked villains? I do not understand you; are you in your right senses?'

'That I am, and wish you was as much in yours; but it's time yet, by the blessing of God! What wicked villains am I talking of? Of three hundred that have sworn to make you their captain, or, in case you refuse, to have your life this night. What villains am I talking of? Of him, the wickedest of all, who is now living in the very house with you, that is now lying in the very next room to you.'

'Joe Kelly?'

'That same – from the first minute I saw him in the castle, I should have hated him, but for his causing you for to put off the journey to England. I never could abide him; but that blinded me, or I am sure I would have found him out long ago.'

'And what have you found out concerning him?'

'That he is (speaking very low) a *united-man*,[77] and stirring up the *rubbles* again here; and they have their meetings at night in the great cave, where the smugglers used to hide formerly, under the big rock, opposite the old abbey – and there's a way up into the abbey, that you used to be so fond of walking to, dear.'

'Good Heavens! can this be true?'

'True it is, and too true, dear.'

'But how did you find all this out, Ellinor?'

'It was none of I found it, nor ever could any such things have come into my head – but it pleased God to make the discovery of all by one of the *childer* – my own grandson – the boy you gave the gun to, long and long ago, to shoot them rabbits. He was after a hare yesterday, and it took him a chase over that mountain, and down it went and took shelter in the cave, and in went the boy after it, and as he was groping about, he lights on an old great coat; and if he did he brought it home with him, and was showing it, as I was boiling the potatoes for their dinner yesterday, to his father forenent me; and turning the pockets inside out, what should come up but the broken head of a pike; then he *sarches* in the other pocket, and finds a paper written all over – I could not read it – thank God, I never could read none of them wicked things, nor could the boy – by very great luck he could not, being no scholar, or it would be all over the country before this.'

'Well, well! but what was in the paper after all? Did any body read it?'

'Ay, did they – that is, Christy read it – none but Christy – but he would not tell us what was in it – but said it was no matter, and he'd not be wasting his time reading an old song – so we thought no more, and he sent the boy up to the castle with a bill for smith's work, as soon as we had eat the potatoes, and I thought no more about any thing's being going wrong, no more than a child; and in the evening Christy said he must go to the funeral of a neighbour, and should not be home till early in the morning, may be; and it's not two hours since he came home and wakened me, and told me where he had been, which was not to the funeral at all, but to the cave where the coat was found; and he put the coat and the broken head of the pike, and the papers all in the pockets, just as we found it, in the cave – and the paper was a list of the names of them *rubbles* that met there, and a letter telling how they would make Lord Glenthorn their captain, or have his life; this was what made Christy to try and find out more – so he hid hisself in a hole in the side of the cave, and built hisself up with rubbish, only just leaving a place for hisself to breathe – and there he staid till nightfall; and then on till midnight, God help us! so sure enough, them villains all come filling fast into the cave. He had good courage, God bless him for it – but he always had – and there he heard and saw all – and this was how they were talking: – First, one began by saying, how they must not be delaying longer to show themselves; they must make a rising in the country – then named the numbers in other parts that would join, and that they would not be put down so *asy* as afore, for they would have good leaders – then some praised you greatly, and said they was sure you favoured them in your heart, by all the ill-will you got in the county the time of the last 'ruction. But, again, others said you was milk and water, and did not go far enough, and never would, and that it was not *in* you, and that you was a sleepy man, and not the true thing at all, and neither beef nor *vael*. Again, thim that were for you spoke and said you would show yourself soon – and the others made reply, and observed you must now spake out, or never spake more; you must either head 'em, or be tramped under foot along with the rest, so it did not signify talking, and Joey Kelly should not be fribbling any more about it; and it was a wonder, said they, he was not the night at the meeting. And what was this about your being going off for England – what would they do when you was gone, with M'Leod the Scotchman, to come in over them again agent, who was another guess sort of man from you, and never slept at all, and would scent 'em out, and have his corps after 'em, and that once M'Leod was master, there would be no making any head again his head; so, not to be tiring you too much with all they said, backward and forward, one that was a captain, or something that way, took the word, and bid 'em all hold their peace, for they did not know what they was talking on, and said that Joey Kelly and he had settled it all, and that the going to England was put off by Joe, and all a sham, and that when you would be walking out to-morrow at nightfall, in those lone places by the sea-side or the abbey, he and Joe was to seize upon you, and when you would be coming back near the abbey, to have you down through the trap-door into the cave, and any way they would swear you to join and head them, and if you would not, out with you, and shove you into the sea, and no more about it, for it would be give out you drown' yourself in a fit of the melancholy lunacy, which none would question, and it would be proved too you made away wid yourself, by your hat and gloves lying on the bank – Lord save us! What are you laughing at in that, when it is truth every word, and Joe Kelly was to find the body, after a great search. Well, again, say you would swear and join them, and head them, and do whatever they pleased, still that would not save you in the end; for they would quarrel with you at the first turn, because you would not be ruled by them as captain, and then they would shoot or pike you (God save the mark, dear), and give the castle to Joe Kelly, and the plunder all among 'em entirely. So it was all laid out, and they are all to meet in the cave to-morrow evening – they will go along bearing a funeral, seemingly to the abbey-ground. And now you know the whole truth, and the Lord preserve you! And what will be done? My poor head has no more power to think for you no more than an infant's, and I'm all in a tremble ever since I heard it, and afraid to meet any one lest they should see all in my face. Oh, what will become of *yees* now – they will be the death of you, whatever you do!'

By the time she came to these last words, Ellinor's fears had so much overpowered her, that she cried and sobbed continually, repeating – 'What will be done now! What will be done! They'll surely be the death of you, whatever you do.' As to me, the urgency of the danger wakened my faculties: I rose instantly, wrote a note to Mr M'Leod, desiring to see him immediately on particular business. Lest my note should by any accident be intercepted or opened, I couched it in the most general and guarded terms; and added a request, that he would bring his last settlement of accounts with him; so that it was natural to suppose my business with him was of a pecuniary nature. I gradually quieted poor Ellinor by my own appearance of composure; I assured her, that we should take our measures so as to prevent all mischief – thanked her for the timely warning she had given me – advised her to go home before she was observed, and charged her not to speak to any one this day of what had happened. I desired that as soon as she should see Mr M'Leod coming through the gate, she would send Christy after him to the castle, to get his bill paid; so that I might then, without exciting suspicion, talk to him in private, and we might learn from his own lips the particulars of what he saw and heard in the cavern.

Ellinor returned home, promising to obey me exactly, especially as to my injunction of secrecy – to make sure of herself she said 'she would go to bed straight, and have the rheumatism very bad all day; so as not to be in a way to talk to none who would call in'. The note to M'Leod was despatched by one of my grooms, and I, returning to bed, was now left at full leisure to finish my morning's nap.

Joe Kelly presented himself at the usual hour in my room; I turned my head away from him, and, in a sleepy tone, muttered that I had passed a bad night, and should breakfast in my own apartment.

Some time afterwards Mr M'Leod arrived, with an air of sturdy pride, and produced his accounts, of which I suffered him to talk, till the servant who waited upon us had left the room; I then explained the real cause of my sending for him so suddenly. I was rather vexed, that I could not produce in him, by my wonderful narrative, any visible signs of agitation or astonishment. He calmly observed – 'We are lucky to have so many hours of daylight before us. The first thing we have to do is to keep the old woman from talking.'

I answered for Ellinor.

'Then the next thing is for me, who am a magistrate, to take the examinations of her son, and see if he will swear to the same that he says.'

Christy was summoned into our presence, and he came with his *bill for smith's work done*; so that the servants could have no suspicion of what was going forward. His examinations were taken and sworn to in a few minutes; his evidence was so clear and direct, that there was no possibility of doubting the truth. The only variation between his story and his mother's report to me was as to the numbers he had seen in the cavern – her fears had turned thirteen into three hundred.

Christy assured us that there were but thirteen at this meeting, but that they said there were three hundred ready to join them.

'You were a very bold fellow, Christy,' said I, 'to hazard yourself in the cave with these villains; if you had been found out in your hiding-place, they would have certainly murdered you.'

'True for me,' said Christy; 'but a man must die some way, please your honour; and where's the way I could die better? Sure, I could not but remember how good you was to me that time I was shot, and all you suffered for it! It would have been bad indeed if I would stay quiet, and let 'em murder you after all. No, no, Christy O'Donoghoe would not do that – any way. I hope, if there's to be any fighting, your honour would not wrong me so much as not to give me a blunderbush, and let me fight a bit along wid de rest for yees.'

'We are not come to that yet, my good fellow,' said Mr M'Leod, who went on methodically; 'if you are precipitate, you will spoil all. Go home to your forge, and work as usual, and leave the rest to us; and I promise that you shall have your share, if there is any fighting.'

Very reluctantly Christy obeyed. Mr M'Leod then deliberately settled our plan of operations. I had a fishing-lodge at a little distance, and a pleasure-boat there: to this place M'Leod was to go, as if on a fishing-party with his nephew, a young man, who often went there to fish. They were to carry with them some yeomen[78] in coloured clothes, as their attendants, and more were to come as their guests to dinner. At the lodge there was a small four-pounder, which had been frequently used in times of public rejoicing; a naval victory, announced in the papers of the day, afforded a plausible pretence for bringing it out. We were aware that the rebels would be upon the watch, and therefore took every precaution to prevent their suspecting that we had made any discovery. Our fishing-party was to let the mock-funeral pass them quietly, to ask some trifling questions, and to give money for pipes and tobacco. Towards evening the boat, with the four-pounder on board, was to come under shore, and at a signal given by me was to station itself opposite to the mouth of the cave.

At the same signal a trusty man on the watch was to give notice to a party hid in the abbey, to secure the trap-door above. The signal was to be my presenting a pistol to the captain of the rebels, who intended to meet and seize me on my return from my evening's walk. Mr M'Leod at first objected to my hazarding a meeting with this man; but I insisted upon it, and I was not sorry to give a public proof of my loyalty, and my personal courage. As to Joe Kelly, I also undertook to secure him.

Mr M'Leod left me, and went to conduct his fishing-party. As soon as he was gone, I sent for Joe Kelly to play on the flute to me. I guarded my looks and voice as well as I could, and he did not see or suspect any thing – he was too full of his own schemes. To disguise his own plots he affected great gaiety; and to divert me, alternately played on the flute, and told me *good* stories all the morning. I would not let him leave me the whole day. Towards evening I began to talk of my journey to England, proposed setting out the next morning, and sent Kelly to look for some things in what was called *the strong closet* – a closet with a stout door and iron-barred windows, out of which no mortal could make his escape. Whilst he was busy searching in a drawer, I shut the door upon him, locked it, and put the key into my pocket. As I left the castle, I said in a jesting tone to some of the servants who met me – 'I have locked Joe

Kelly up in the strong room; if he calls to you to let him out never mind him; he will not get out till I come home from my walk – I owe him this trick.' The servants thought it was some jest, and I passed on with my loaded pistols in my pocket. I walked for some time by the sea-shore, without seeing any one. At last I espied our fishing-boat, just peering out, and then keeping close to the shore. I was afraid that the party would be impatient at not seeing my signal, and would come out to the mouth of the cave, and show themselves too soon. If Mr M'Leod had not been their commander, this, as I afterwards learned, would have infallibly happened; but he was so punctual, cool, and peremptory, that he restrained the rest of the party, declaring that, if it were till midnight, he would wait till the signal agreed upon was given. At last I saw a man creeping out of the cave – I sat down upon my wonted stone, and yawned as naturally as I could; then began to describe figures in the sand with my stick, as I was wont to do, still watching the image of the man in the water as he approached. He was muffled up in a frieze great coat; he sauntered past, and went on to a turn in the road, as if looking for some one. I knew well for whom he was looking. As no Joe Kelly came to meet him, he returned in a few minutes towards me. I had my hand upon the pistol in my pocket.

'You are my lard Glenthorn, I presume,' said he.

'I am.'

'Then you will come with me, if you plase, my lard,' said he.

'Make no resistance, or I will shoot you instantly,' cried I, presenting my pistol with one hand, and seizing him by the collar with the other. I dragged him (for I had force enough, now my energy was roused) to the spot appointed for my signal. The boat appeared opposite the mouth of the cave. Every thing answered my expectation.

'There,' said I, pointing to the boat, 'there are my armed friends; they have a four-pounder – the match is ready lighted – your plot is discovered. Go in to your confederates in that cave; tell them so. The trap-door is secured above; there is no escape for them: bid them surrender: if they attempt to rush out, the grape-shot will pour upon them, and they are dead men.'

I cannot say that my rebel captain showed himself as stout as I could have wished, for the honour of my victory. The surprise disconcerted him totally: I felt him tremble under my grasp. He obeyed my orders – went into the cave to bring his associates to submission. His parley with them, however, was not immediately successful: I suppose there were some braver fellows than he amongst them, whose counsel might be for open war. In the mean time our yeomen landed, and surrounded the cave on all sides, so that there was no possibility of escape for those within. At last they yielded themselves our prisoners. I am sorry I have no bloody battle for the entertainment of such of my readers as like horrors; but so it was, that they yielded without a drop of blood being spilled, or a shot fired. We let them out of their hiding-place one by one, searching each as he issued forth, to be secure that they had no concealed weapons. After they had given up the arms which were concealed in the cave, the next question was, what to do with our prisoners. As it was now late, and they could not all be examined and committed with due legal form to the county gaol, Mr M'Leod advised that we should detain them in the place they had chosen for themselves till morning. Accordingly, in the cave we again stowed them, and left a guard at each entrance to secure them for the night. We returned to the castle. I stopped at the gate to tell Ellinor and Christy that I was safe. They were sitting up watching for the news. The moment Ellinor saw me, she clasped her hands in an ecstasy of joy, but could not speak. Christy was voluble in his congratulations; but, in the midst of his rejoicing, he could not help reproaching me with forgetting to give him the *blunderbush*, and to let him have a bit of the fighting. 'Upon my honour,' said I, 'there was none, or you should have been there.'

'O, don't be plaguing and gathering round him now,' said Ellinor: 'sure, he is tired, and look how hot – no wonder – let him get home and to bed: I'll run and warm it with the pan myself, and not be trusting them.'

She would not be persuaded that I did not desire to have my bed warmed, but, by some short cut, got in before us. On entering the castle-hall, I found her, with the warming-pan in her hand, held back by the inquisitive servants, who were all questioning her about the news, of which she was the first, and not very intelligible enunciator.

I called for bread and water for my prisoner in the strong-room, and then I heard various exclamations of wonder.

'Ay, it is all true! it is no jest! Joe is at the bottom of all. *I* never liked Joe Kelly – *I* always knew Joe was not the right thing – and *I* always said so; and I, and I, and I. And it was but last week I was saying so: and it was but yesterday *I* said so and so.'

I passed through the gossiping crowd with bread and water for my culprit. M'Leod instantly saw and followed me.

'I will make bold to come with you,' said he; 'a pent rat's a dangerous animal.' – I thanked him, and acquiesced; but there was no need for the precaution. When we opened the door, we found the conscience or terror-struck wretch upon his knees, and, in the most abject terms, he implored our mercy. From the windows of the room, which looked into the castle-yard, he had heard enough to guess all that had happened. I could not bear to look at him. After I had set down his food, he clung to my knees, crying and whining in a most unmanly manner. M'Leod, with indignation, loosened him from me, threw him back, and locked the door.

'Cowardice and treachery,' said he, 'usually go together.'

'And courage and sincerity,' said I. 'And now we'll go to supper, my good friends. I hope you are all as hungry as I am.'

I never did eat any meal with so much appetite.

''Tis a pity, my lord,' said M'Leod, 'but that there was a conspiracy against you every day of your life, it seems to do you so much good.'

CHAPTER XVI

'What new wonders? What new misfortunes, Ellinor?' said I, as Ellinor, with a face of consternation, appeared again in the morning in my room, just as I was going down to breakfast: 'what new misfortunes, Ellinor?'

'Oh! the worst that could befall me!' cried she, wringing her hands; 'the worst, the very worst! – to be the death of my own child!' said she, with inexpressible horror. 'Oh! save him! save him! for the love of Heaven, dear, save him! If you don't save him, 'tis I shall be his death.'

She was in such agony, that she could not explain herself farther for some minutes.

'It was I gave the information against them all to you. But how could I ever have thought Owen was one of them? My son, my own son, the unfortunate cratur; I never thought but what he was with the militia far away. And how could it ever come into my head that Owen could have any hand in a thing of the kind!'

'But I did not see him last night,' interrupted I.

'Oh! he was there! One of his own friends, one of the military that went with you, saw him among the prisoners, and came just now to tell me of it. That Owen should be guilty of the like! – Oh! what could have come over him! He must have been out of his *rason*. And against you to be plotting! That's what I never will believe, if even I'd hear it from himself. But he's among them that were taken last night. And will I live to see him go to gaol? – and will I live to see – No, I'd rather die first, a thousand and a thousand times over. Oh! for mercy's sake!' said she, dropping on her knees at my feet, 'have pity on me, and don't let the blood of my own child be upon me in my old days.'

'What would you have me do, Ellinor?' said I, much moved by her distress.

'There is but one thing to do,' said she. 'Let him off: sure a word from you would be enough for the soldiers that are over them on guard. And Mr M'Leod has not yet seen him; and if he was just let escape, there would be no more about it; and I'd engage he shall fly the country, the unfortunate cratur! and never trouble you more. This is all I ask: and sure, dear, you can't refuse it to your own Ellinor; your old nurse, that carried ye in her arms, and fed ye with her milk, and watch'd over ye many's the long night, and loved ye; ay, none ever loved, or could love ye so well.'

'I am sensible of it; I am grateful,' interrupted I; 'but what you ask of me, Ellinor, is impossible – I cannot let him escape; but I will do my utmost.'

'Troth, nothing will save him, if you would not say the word for him now. Ah! why cannot you let him off, then?'

'I should lose my honour; I should lose my character. You know that I have been accused of favouring the rebels already – you saw the consequences of my protecting your other son, though he was innocent and injured, and bore an excellent character.'

'Christy; ay, true: but poor Owen, unlucky as he is, and misguided, has a better claim upon you.'

'How can that be? Is not the other my foster-brother, in the first place?'

'True, for him.'

'And had not I proofs of his generous conduct and attachment to me?'

'Owen is naturally fonder of you by a great deal,' interrupted she; 'I'll answer for that.'

'What! when he has just been detected in conspiring against my life?'

'That's what I'll never believe,' cried Ellinor vehemently: 'that he might be drawn in, may be, when out of his *rason* – he was always a wild boy – to be a united-man, and to hope to get you for his captain, might be the case, and bad enough that; but, jewel, you'll find he did never conspire against you: I'd lay down my life upon that.'

She threw herself again at my feet, and clung to my knees.

'As you hope for mercy yourself in this world, or the world to come, show some now, and do not be so hard-hearted as to be the death of both mother and son.'

Her supplicating looks and gestures, her words, her tears, moved me so much, that I was on the point of yielding; but recollecting what was due to justice and to my own character, with an effort of what I thought virtuous resolution I repeated, 'It is impossible: my good Ellinor, urge me no farther: ask any thing else, and it shall be granted, but this is impossible.'

As I spoke, I endeavoured to raise her from the ground; but with the sudden force of angry despair, she resisted.

'No, you shall not raise me,' cried she. 'Here let me lie, and break my heart with your cruelty! 'Tis a judgement upon me – it's a judgement, and it's fit I should feel it as I do. But you shall feel too, in spite of your hard heart. Yes, your heart is harder than the marble: you want the natural touch, you do; for your mother has knelt at your feet, and you have denied her prayer.'

'My mother!'

'And what was her prayer? – to save the life of your brother.'

'My brother! Good heavens! what do I hear?'

'You hear the truth: you hear that I am your lawful mother. Yes, you are my son. You have forced that secret from me, which I thought to have carried with me to my grave. And now you know all: and now you know how wicked I have been, and it was all for you; for you that refused me the only thing ever I asked, and that, too, in my greatest distress, when my heart was just breaking: and all this time too, there's Christy – poor good Christy; he that I've wronged, and robbed of his rightful inheritance, has been as a son, a dutiful good son to me, and never did he deny me any thing I could ask; but in you I have found no touch of tenderness. Then it's fit I should tell you again, and again, and again, that he who is now slaving at the forge, to give me the earnings of his labour; he that lives, and has lived all his days, upon potatoes and salt, and is content; he who has the face and the hands so disguised with the smoke and the black, that yourself asked him t'other day did he ever wash his face since he was born – I tell ye, he it is who should live in this castle, and sleep on that soft bed, and be lord of all here – he is the true and real Lord Glenthorn, and to the wide world I'll make it known. Ay, be pale and tremble, do; it's your turn now: I've touched you now: but it's too late. In the face of day I shall confess the wrong I've done; and I shall call upon you to give back to him all that by right is his own.'

Ellinor stopped short, for one of my servants at this instant came into the room.

'My lord, Mr M'Leod desires me to let you know the guard has brought up the prisoners, and he is going to commit them to gaol, and would be glad to know if you choose to see them first, my lord.'

Stupified by all I had just heard, I could only reply, that I would come presently. Ellinor rushed past the servant, – 'Are they come? cried she. 'Where will I get a sight of them?' I staid for a few minutes alone, to decide upon what I ought to say and do. A multitude of ideas, more than had ever come in my mind in a twelvemonth, passed through it in these few minutes.

As I was slowly descending the great staircase, Ellinor came running, as fast as she could run, to the foot of the stairs, exclaiming, 'It's a mistake! it's all a mistake, and I was a fool to believe them that brought me the word. Sure Ody's not there at all! nor ever was in it. I've seen them all, face to face; and my son's not one of them, nor ever was: and I was a fool from beginning to end – and I beg your pardon entirely,' whispered she, coming close to my ear: 'I was out of my reason at the thought of that boy's being to suffer, and I, his mother, the cause of it. Forgive all I said in my passion, my own best jewel: you was always good and tender to me, and be the same still, dear. I'll never say a word more about it to any one living: the secret shall die with me. Sure, when my conscience has borne it so long, it may strive and bear it a little longer for your sake: and it can't be long I have to live, so that will make all easy. Hark! they are asking for you. Do you go your ways into the great parlour, to Mr M'Leod, and think no more of any thing at all but joy. My son's not one of them! I must go to the forge, and tell Christy the good news.'

Ellinor departed, quite satisfied with herself, with me, and with all the world. She took it for granted that she left me in the same state of mind, and that I should obey her injunctions, and *think of nothing but joy*. Of what happened in the great parlour, and of the examinations of the prisoners, I have but a confused recollection. I remember that Mr M'Leod seemed rather surprised by my indifference to what concerned me so nearly; and that he was obliged to do all the business himself. The men were, I believe, all committed to gaol, and Joe Kelly turned king's evidence; but as to any further particulars, I know no more than if I had been in a dream. The discovery which Ellinor had just made to me engrossed all my powers of attention.

CHAPTER XVII

'Le vrai n'est pas toujours vraisemblable,'[79] says an acute observer of human affairs. The romance of real life certainly goes beyond all other romances; and there are facts which few writers would dare to put into a book, as there are skies which few painters would venture to put into a picture.

When I had leisure to reflect, I considered, that as yet I had no proof of the truth of Ellinor's strange story, except her own assertions. I sent for her again, to examine her more particularly. I was aware, that, if I alarmed her, I should so confuse her imagination, that I should never obtain the truth; therefore I composed myself, and assumed my usual external appearance of nonchalance. I received her lolling upon my sofa, as usual, and I questioned her merely as if to gratify an idle curiosity.

'Troth, dear,' said she, 'I'll tell you the whole story how it was, to make your mind asy, which, God knows, mine never was, from that minute it first came into my head, till this very time being. You mind the time you got the cut in your head – no, not you, jewel; but the little lord that was then, Christy there below that is. – Well, the cut was a terrible cut as ever you seen, got by a fall on the fender from the nurse's arms, that was drunk, three days after he was born.'

'I remember to have heard my father talk of some accident of this sort, which happened to me when I was an infant.'

'Ay, sure enough it did, and that was what first put him in the notion of taking the little lord out of the hands of the Dublin nurse-tenders, and them that were about my lady Glenthorn, and did not know how to manage her, which was the cause of her death: and he said he'd have his own way about his son and heir any way, and have him nursed by a wholesome woman in a cabin, and brought up hardy, as he, and the old lord, and all the family, were before him. So with that he sends for me, and he puts the young lord, God bless him, into my arms himself, and a *donny* thing he was that same time to look at, for he was but just out of the surgeon's hands, the head just healed and scarred over like; and my lord said there should be no more doctors never about him. So I took him, that is, Christy, and you, to a house at the sea, for the salt water, and showed him every justice; and my lord often came to see him whilst he was in the country; but then he was off, after a time, to Dublin, and I was in a lone place, where nobody came, and the child was very sick with me, and you was all the time as fine and thriving a child as ever you see; and I thought, to be sure, one night, that he would die wid me. He was very bad, very bad indeed; and I was sitting up in bed, rocking him backwards and forwards this ways: I thought with myself, what a pity it was the young lord should die, and he an only son and heir, and the estate to go out of the family the Lord knows where; and then the grief the father would be in: and then I thought how happy he would be if he had such a fine *babby* as you, dear; and you was a fine *babby* to be sure: and then I thought how happy it would be for you, if you was in the place of the little lord: and then it came into my head, just like a shot, where would be the harm to change you? for I thought the real lord would surely die; and then, what a gain it would be to all, if it was never known, and if the dead child was carried to the grave, since it must go, as only poor Ellinor O'Donoghoe's, and no more about it. Well, if it was a wicked thought, it was the devil himself put it in my head, to be sure; for, only for him, I should never have had the sense to think of such a thing, for I was always innocent like, and not worldly given. But so it was, the devil put it in my head, and made me do it, and showed me how, and all in a minute. So, I mind, your eyes and hair were both of the very same colour, dear; and as to the rest, there's no telling how those young things alter in a few months, and my lord would not be down from Dublin in a hurry, so I settled it all right; and as there was no likelihood at all the real lord would live, that quieted my conscience; for I argued, it was better the father should have any sort of child at all than none. So, when my lord came down, I carried him the child to see, that is you, jewel. He praised me, greatly for all the care I had taken of his boy; and said, how finely you was come on! and I never see a father in greater joy; and it would have been a sin, I thought, to tell him the truth, after he took the change that was put upon him so well, and it made him so happy like. Well, I was afeard of my life he'd pull off the cap to search for the scar, so I would not let your head be touched any way, dear, saying it was tinder and soft still with the fall, and you'd cry if the cap was stirred; and so I made it out, indeed, very well; for, God forgive me, I twitched the string under your chin, dear, and made you cry like mad, when they would come to touch you. So there was no more about it, and I had you home to myself, and, all in good time, the hair grew, and fine thick hair it was, God bless you; and so there was no more about it, and I got into no trouble at all, for it all fell out just as I had laid it out, except that the real little young lord did not die as I thought; and it was a wonder but he did, for you never saw none so near death, and backwards and forwards, what turns of sickness he took with me for months upon months, and year after year, so that none could think, no more than me, there was any likelihood at all of rearing him to man's estate. So that kept me easier in my mind concerning what I'd done; for as I kept saying to myself, better the family should have an heir to the estate, suppose not the right, than none at all; and if the father, nor nobody, never found it out, there was he and all the family made happy for life, and my child made a lord of, and none the wiser or the worse. Well, so I down-argued my conscience; and any way I took to little Christy, as he was now to be called – and I loved him, all as one as if he was my own – not that he was ever as well-looking as Ody, or any of the childer I had, but I never made any differ betwixt him and any of my own – he can't say as I did, any how, and he has no reason to complain of my being an unnat'ral mother to him, and being my foster-child I had a right to love him as I did, and I never wronged him in any way, except in the one article of changing him at nurse, which he being an infant, and never knowing, was never a bit the worse for, nor never will, now. So all's right, dear, and make your mind asy, jewel; there's the whole truth of the story, for you.'

'But it is a very strange story, Ellinor, after all, and – and I have only your word for it, and may be you are only taking advantage of my regard for you to make me believe you.'

'What is it, plase your honour?' said she, stepping forward, as if she did not hear or understand me.

'I say, Ellinor, that after all I have no proof of the truth of this story, except your word.'

'And is not that enough? and where's the use of having more? but if it will make you asy, sure I can give you proof – sure need you go farther than the scar on his head? If he was shaved to-morrow, I'd engage you'd see it fast enough. But sure, can't you put your hand up to your head this minute, and feel there never was no scar there, nor if all the hair you have, God save the mark, was shaved this minute, never a bit of a scar would be to be seen: but proof is it you want? – why, there's the surgeon that dressed the cut in the child's head, before he ever came to me; sure he's the man that can't forget it, and that will tell all: so to make your mind asy, see him, dear; but for your life don't let him see your head to feel it, for he'd miss the scar, and might suspect something by your going to question him.'

'Where does he live?' interrupted I.

'Not above twelve miles off.'

'Is he alive?'

'Ay, if he been't dead since Candlemas.'

At first I thought of writing to this man; but afterwards, being afraid of committing myself by writing, I went to him: he had long before this time left off business, and had retired to enjoy his fortune in the decline of life. He was a whimsical sort of character; he had some remains of his former taste for anatomy, and was a collector of curiosities. I found him just returned from a lake which he had been dragging for a moose-deer's horns, to complete the skeleton of a moose-deer, which he had mounted in his hall.[80] I introduced myself, desiring to see his museum, and mentioned to him the thigh-bone of a giant found in my neighbourhood; then by favour of this bone I introduced the able cure, that he had made of a cut in my head, when I was a child.

'A cut in your head, sir? Yes, my lord, I recollect perfectly well, it was a very ugly cut, especially in an infant's head; but I am glad to find you feel no bad effects from it. Have you any cicatrice on the place? – Eleven feet high, did you say? and is the giant's skeleton in your neighbourhood?'

I humoured his fancy, and by degrees he gave me all the information I wanted without in the least suspecting my secret motives. He described the length, breadth, and depth, of the wound to me; showed me just where it was on the head, and observed that it must have left an indelible mark, but that my fine hair covered it. When he seemed disposed to search for it, I defended myself with the giant's thigh-bone, and warded off his attacks most successfully. To satisfy myself upon this point, I affected to think that he had not been paid: he said he had been amply paid, and he showed me his books to prove it. I examined the dates, and found that they agreed with Ellinor's precisely. On my return home, the first thing I did was to make Christy a present of a new wig, which I was certain would induce him to shave his head; for the lower Irish agree with the beaux and belles of London and Paris, in preferring wigs to their own hair. Ellinor told me, that I might safely let his head be shaved, because to her certain knowledge, he had scars of so many cuts which he had received at fairs upon his skull, that there would appear nothing particular *in one more or less*. As soon as the head was shaved, and the wig was worn, I took an opportunity one day of stopping at the forge to have one of my horse's shoes changed; and whilst this was doing, I took notice of his new wig, and how well it fitted him. As I expected, he took it off to show it me better, and to pay his own compliments to it.

'Sure enough, you are a very fine wig,' said he; apostrophizing it as he held it up on the end of his hammer, 'and God bless him that give it me, and it fits me as if it was nailed to my head.'

'You seem to have had a good many nails in your head already, Christy,' said I, 'if one may judge by all these scars.'

'Oh yes, please your honour, my lord,' said he, 'there's no harm in them neither; they are scratches got when I was no wiser than I should be, at fairs, fighting with the boys of Shrawd-na-scoob.'

Whilst he fought his battles o'er again, I had leisure to study his head; and I traced precisely all the boundary lines. The situation, size, and figure of the cicatrice, which the surgeon and Ellinor had described to me, were so visible and exact, that no doubt could remain in my mind of Christy's being the real son of the late Lord and Lady Glenthorn. This conviction was still more impressed upon my mind a few days afterwards. I recollected having seen a file of family pictures in a lumber-room in the castle; and I rummaged them out to see if I could discover amongst them any likeness to Christy: I found one; the picture of my grandfather, – I should say, of *his* grandfather, – to which Christy bore a striking resemblance, when I saw him with his face washed, and in his Sunday clothes.

My mind being now perfectly satisfied of the truth of Ellinor's story, I was next to consider how I ought to act. To be or not to be Lord Glenthorn, or, in other words, to be or not to be a villain, was now the question. I could not dissemble to my conscience this plain state of the case, that I had no right to keep possession of that which I knew to be another's lawful property; yet, educated as I had been, and accustomed to the long enjoyment of those luxuries, which become necessaries to the wealthy; habituated to attendance as I had been; and, even amongst the dissipated and idle, notorious for extravagance the most unbounded and indolence the most inveterate; how was I at once to change my habits, to abdicate my rank and power, to encounter the evils of poverty? I was not compelled to make such sacrifices; for though Ellinor's transient passion had prompted her to threaten me with a public discovery, yet I knew that she would as soon cut off her own right hand as execute her threats. Her affection for me, and her pride in my consequence, were so strong, that I knew I might securely rely upon her secrecy. The horrid idea of being the cause of the death of one of her own children had for a moment sufficient power to balance her love for me; yet there was but little probability that any similar trial should occur, nor had I reason to apprehend that the reproaches of her conscience should induce her to make a voluntary discovery; for all her ideas of virtue depended on the principle of fidelity to the objects of her affection, and no scrupulous notions of justice disturbed her understanding or alarmed her self-complacency. Conscious that she would willingly sacrifice all she had in the world for any body she loved, and scarcely comprehending that any one could be selfish, she, in a confused way, applied the maxim of 'Do as you would be done by', and was as generous of the property of others as of her own. At the worst, if a law-suit commenced against me, I knew that possession was nine-tenths of the law. I also knew that Ellinor's health was declining, and that the secret would die with her. Unlawful possession of the wealth I enjoyed could not, however, satisfy my own mind; and, after a severe conflict between my love of ease and my sense of right – between my tastes and my principles – I determined to act honestly and honourably, and to relinquish what I could no longer maintain without committing injustice, and feeling remorse. I was, perhaps, the more ready to do rightly because I felt that I was not compelled to it. The moment when I made this virtuous decision was the happiest I had at that time ever felt: my mind seemed suddenly relieved from an oppressive weight; my whole frame glowed with new life; and the consciousness of courageous integrity elevated me so much in my own opinion, that titles, and rank, and fortune, appeared as nothing in my estimation. I rang my bell eagerly, and ordered that Christy O'Donoghoe should be immediately sent for. The servant went instantly; but it seemed to me an immoderately long time before Christy arrived. I walked up and down the room impatiently, and at last threw myself at full length upon the sofa: the servant returned.

'The smith is below in the hall, my lord.'

'Show him up.' – He was shown up into the ante-chamber.

'The smith is at the door, my lord.'

'Show him in, cannot you? What detains him?'

'My brogues, my lord! I'd be afraid to come in with 'em on the carpet.' Saying this, Christy came in, stepping fearfully, astonished to find himself in a splendid drawing-room.

'Were you never in this room before, Christy?' said I.

'Never, my lord, plase your honour, barring the day I mended the bolt.'

'It is a fine room, is not it, Christy?'

'Troth, it is the finest ever I see, sure enough.'

'How should you like to have such a room of your own, Christy?'

'Is it I, plase your honour?' replied he, laughing; 'what should I do with the like?'

'How should you feel if you were master of this great castle?'

'It's a poor figure I should make, to be sure,' said he, turning his head over his shoulder towards the door, and resting upon the lock: 'I'd rather be at the forge by a great *dale*.'

'Are you sure of that, Christy? Should not you like to be able to live without working any more, and to have horses and servants of your own?'

'What would I do with them, plase your honour, I that have never been used to them? sure they'd all laugh at me, and I'd not be the better o'that, no more than of having nothing to do; I that have been always used to the work, what should I do all the day without it? But sure, my lord,' continued he, changing his voice to a more serious tone, 'the horse that I shod yesterday for your honour did not go lame, did he?'

'The horse is very well shod, I believe; I have not ridden him since: I know nothing of the matter.'

'Because I was thinking, may be, it was that made your honour send for me up in the hurry – I was afeard I'd find your honour mad with me; and I'd be very sorry to disoblige you, my lord; and I'm glad to see your honour looking so well after all the trouble you've been put to by them *rubbles*, the villains, to be *consarting* against you under-ground. But, thanks be to God, you have 'em all in gaol now. I thought my mother would have died of the fright she took, when the report came that Ody was one of them. I told her there could not be no truth in it at all, but she would not mind me: it would be a strange unnatural thing, indeed, of any belonging to her to be plotting against your honour. I knew Ody could not be in it, and be a brother of mine; and that's what I kept saying all the time; but she never heeded me: for, your honour knows, when the women are frighted, and have taken a thing into their heads, you can't asy get it out again.'

'Very true: but, to return to what I was saying, should not you like to change places with me, if you could?'

'Your honour, my lord, is a very happy jantleman, and a very good jantleman, there's no doubt, and there's few but would be proud to be like you in any thing at all.'

'Thank you for that compliment. But now, in plain English, as to yourself, would you like to be in my place – to change places with me?'

'In your honour's place – I! I would *not*, my lord; and that's the truth, now,' said he, decidedly. 'I would not: no offence – your honour bid me to speak the truth; for I've all I want in the world, a good mother, and a good wife, and good *childer*, and a reasonable good little cabin, and my little *pratees*, and the grazing of the cow, and work enough always, and not called on to *slave*, and I get my health, thank God for all; and what more could I have if I should be made a lord to-morrow? Sure, my good woman would never make a lady; and what should I do with her? I'd be grieved to see her the laughing-stock of high and low, besides being the same myself, and my boy after me. That would never answer for me; so I am not like them that would overturn all to get uppermost; I never had any hand, art, or part, in a thing of the kind; I always thought and knew I was best as I am; not but what, if I was to change with any, it is with you, my lord, I would be proud to change; because if I was to be a jantleman at all, I'd wish to be of a *ra-al* good *ould* family born.'

'You are then what you wish to be,' said I.

'Och!' said he, laughing and scratching his head, 'your honour's jesting me about them kings of Ireland, that they say the O'Donoghoes was once: but that's what I never think *on*, that's all idle talk for the like of me, for sure that's a long time ago, and what use going back to it? One might as well be going back to Adam, that was the father of all, but which makes no differ now.'

'But you do not understand me,' interrupted I; 'I am not going back to the kings of Ireland: I mean to tell you, that you were born a gentleman – nay, I am perfectly serious; listen to me.'

'I do, plase your honour, though it is mocking me, I know you are; I would be sorry not to take a joke as well as another.'

'This is no joke; I repeat, that I am serious. You are not only a gentleman, but a nobleman: to you this castle and this great estate belongs, and to you they shall be surrendered.'

He stood astonished; and, his eyes opening wide, showed a great circle of white in his black face.

'Eh!' cried he, drawing that long breath, which astonishment had suppressed. 'But how can this be?'

'Your mother can explain better than I can: your mother, did I say? she is not your mother; Lady Glenthorn was your mother.'

'I can't understand it at all – I can't understand it [at] all. I'll *lave* it all to your honour,' said he, making a motion with his hands, as if to throw from him the trouble of comprehending it.

'Did you never hear of such a thing as a child's being changed at nurse?'

'I did, plase your honour; but *my* mother would never do the like, I'll answer for *her*, any way; and them that said any thing of the kind belied her; and don't be believing them, my lord.'

'But Ellinor was the person who told me this secret.'

'Was she so? Oh, she must have been *draaming*; she was always too good a mother to me to have sarved me so. But,' added he, struggling to clear his intellects, 'you say it's not my mother she is; but whose mother is she then? Can it be that she is yours? 'tis not possible to think such a great lord was the son of such as her, to look at you both: and was you the son of my father Johnny O'Donoghoe? How is that again?'

He rubbed his forehead; and I could scarcely forbear laughing at his odd perplexity, though the subject was of such serious importance. When he clearly understood the case, and thoroughly believed the truth, he did not seem elated by this sudden change of fortune; he really thought more of me than of himself.

'Well, I'll tell you what you will do then,' continued he, after a pause of deep reflection; 'say nothing to nobody, but just keep asy on, even as we are. Don't let there be any surrendering at all, and I'll speak to my mother, that is, Ellinor O'Donoghoe, and settle it so; and let it be so settled, in the name of God, and no more about it: and none need never be the wiser; 'tis so best for all. A good day to your honour, and I'll go shoe the mare.'

'Stay,' said I; 'you may hereafter repent of this sudden determination. I insist upon your taking four-and-twenty hours – no, that would be too little – take a month to consider of it coolly, and then let me know your final determination.'

'Oh! plase your honour, I will say the same then as now. It would be a poor thing indeed of me, after all you done for me and mine, to be putting you to more trouble. It would be a poor thing of me to forget how you liked to have lost your life all along with me at the time of the 'ruction.[81] No, I'll not take the fortin from you, any how.'

'Put gratitude to me out of the question,' said I. 'Far be it from me to take advantage of your affectionate temper. I do not consider you as under any obligations to me; nor will I be paid for doing justice.'

'Sure enough, your honour desarved to be born a gentleman,' said Christy.

'At least I have been bred a gentleman,' said I. 'Let me see you again this day month, and not till then.'

'You shall not – that is, you *shall*, plase your honour: but for fear any one would suspect any thing, I'd best go shoe the mare any way.'

CHAPTER XVIII

What riches give us, let us then inquire –
Meat, fire, and clothes – What more? – Meat, clothes, and fire.[82]

The philosophy we learn from books makes but a faint impression upon the mind, in comparison with that which we are taught by our own experience; and we sometimes feel surprised to find that what we have been taught as maxims of morality prove true in real life. After having had, for many years, the fullest opportunities of judging of the value of riches, when I reflected upon my past life, I perceived that their power of conferring happiness is limited, nearly as the philosophic poet describes; that all the changes and modifications of luxury must, in the sum of actual physical enjoyment, be reduced to a few elementary pleasures, of which the industrious poor can obtain their share: a small share, perhaps; but then it is enjoyed with a zest that makes it equal in value, perhaps, to the largest portion offered to the sated palate of ennui. These truths are as old as the world; but they appeared quite new to me, when I discovered them by my own experience.

During the month which I had allowed to my foster-brother for reflection, I had leisure to philosophize, and my understanding made a rapid progress. I foresaw the probability of Christy's deciding to become Earl of Glenthorn; notwithstanding that his good sense had so clearly demonstrated to him in theory, that, with his education and habits, he must be happier working in his forge than he could be as lord of Glenthorn Castle. I was not dismayed by the idea of losing my wealth and rank; I was pleased with myself for my honest conduct, and conscious of a degree of pleasure from my own approbation, superior to what my riches had ever procured.

The day appointed for Christy's final determination arrived. I knew by the first motion of his shoulder as he came into the room, what his decision would be.

'Well, Christy,' said I, 'you will be Earl of Glenthorn, I perceive. You are glad now that I did not take you at your word, and that I gave you a month's time for consideration.'

'Your honour was always considerate; but if I'd wish now to be changing my mind,' said he, hesitating, and shifting from leg to leg, 'it is not upon my own account, any way, but upon my son Johnny's.'

'My good friend,' said I, 'no apology is necessary. I should be very unjust if I were offended by your decision, and very mean if, after the declarations I have made, I could, for an instant, hesitate to restore to you that property which it is your right and your choice to reclaim.'

Christy made a low bow, and seemed much at a loss what he was to say next.

'I hope,' continued I, 'that you will be as happy when you are Earl of Glenthorn, as you have been as Christy O'Donoghoe.'

'May be not, plase your honour; but I trust my childer will be happy after me; and it's them and my wife I'm thinking of, as in duty bound. But it is hard your honour should be astray for want of the fortin you've been bred to; and this weighs with me greatly on the other side. If your honour could live on here, and share with us – But I see your honour's displeased at my naming *that*. It was my wife thought o'that; I knew it could not do. But then, what I think is, that your honour should name what you would be pleased to keep to live upon: for, to be sure, you have a right to live as a gentleman, that have always lived as one, as every body knows, and none better than I. Would your honour be so kind, then, as just to put down on a bit of paper what you'd wish to keep; and that same, whatever it is, none shall touch but yourself; and I would not own a child for mine that would begrudge it you. I'll step down and wait below while your honour writes what you plase.'

The generosity of this man touched me to the heart. I accepted from him three hundred a year; and requested that the annuity I allowed to the unfortunate Lady Glenthorn might be continued; that the house which I had built for Ellinor, and the land belonging to it, might be secured to her rent-free for life; and that all my debts should be paid. I recommended Mr M'Leod in the strongest manner, as an agent whose abilities and integrity would be to him an invaluable treasure.

Christy, when I gave him the paper on which I had stated these requests, took a pen instantly, and would have signed his name without reading it; but to this I absolutely objected.

'Well, then,' said he, 'I'll take it home, and read it over, and take time, as you desire, to consider. There's no danger of my changing my mind about this: I hope your honour can't think there is.'

The next day, on returning it to me, he observed, that it was making very little of him to put down only such a trifle; and he pressed me to make the hundreds thousands: – this I refused.

'But I hope your honour won't object to what I am going to propose. Is not there a house in London? and is not there another in England, in the country? and, sure, I and mine can't live there and here and every where at once: if you'd just condescend to occupy one of them, you'd do me a great pleasure, and a great sarvice too; for every thing would be right, instead of going wrong, as it might under an agent, and me at a distance, that does not know well how to manage such great estates. I hope you'll not refuse me that, if it's only to show me I don't lose your honour's good-will.'

The offer was made with so much earnestness, and even delicacy, that I could not abruptly refuse it at the moment, though one of these magnificent houses could be of no use to me with an income of £300 *per annum*.

'As to the annuity,' continued Christy, 'that shall be paid as punctual as the day: Mr M'Leod will pay it; and he shall have it all settled right, and put upon a stamp, by the lawyers, in case any thing should happen me. Then, as to Ellinor, sure, she is my mother, for I never can think of her any other way; and, except in that single article of changing me at nurse, was always the best of mothers to me. And even that same trick she played me, though very wicked, to be sure, was very nat'ral – ay, very nat'ral – to *prefar* her own flesh and blood if she could: and no one could be more sorry for the wrong she did me than she is now: there she is crying at home, ready to break her heart: but as I tell her, there's no use in repenting a thing when once it is done; and as I forgive her, none can ever bring it up against her: and as to the house and farm, she shall surely have that, and shall never want for any thing. So I hope your honour's mind will be asy on that matter; and whatever else you recollect to wish, *that* shall be done, if in my power.'

It is with pleasure that I recollect and record all these instances of goodness of heart in poor Christy, which, notwithstanding the odd mixture of absurdity and sense in his language and ideas, will, I make no doubt, please my readers, though they cannot affect them as much as they affected me.

I now prepared for my departure from Glenthorn Castle, never more to return. To spare me from unnecessary mortification, Christy had the wonderful self-command to keep the secret faithfully, so that none of the people in the neighbourhood, nor even my servants, had the slightest idea of the truth. Having long talked of returning to England, the preparations for my journey excited no surprise. Every thing went on as usual, except that Christy, instead of being at the forge, was almost every day at the whiskey-shop.

I thought it proper to speak openly of my affairs to Mr M'Leod: he was the only person who could make out a correct list of my debts. Besides, I wished to recommend him as agent to the future earl, to whom an honest and able agent would be peculiarly necessary, ignorant, as he was, both of the world and of business; and surrounded, as he must probably be, on his accession to his estate, by a herd of vulgar and designing flatterers.

Albeit not easily moved to surprise, Mr M'Leod really did, for an instant, look astonished, when I informed him that Christy O'Donoghoe was Earl of Glenthorn. But I must resolve not to stop to describe the astonishment that each individual showed upon this occasion, else I shall never have finished my story.

It was settled that Mr M'Leod should continue agent; and, for his credit, I must observe that, after he was made acquainted with my loss of rank and fortune, he treated me with infinitely more respect and regard than he had ever shown me whilst he considered me only as his employer. Our accounts were soon settled; and when this was done, and they were all regularly signed, Mr M'Leod came up to me, and, in a low voice of great emotion, said, 'I am not a man of professions; but when I say I am a man's friend, I hope I shall ever be found to be so, as far as can be in my power: and I cannot but esteem and admire the man who has acted so nobly as you have done.'

M'Leod wrung my hand as he spoke, and the tears stood in his eyes. I knew that the feeling must indeed be strong, which could extort from him even these few words of praise, and this simple profession of regard; but I did not know, till long afterwards, the full warmth of his affections and energy of his friendship. The very next day, unfortunately for me, he was obliged to go to Scotland, to his mother, who was dying: and at this time I saw no more of him.

In due legal form I now made a surrender of all claim upon the hereditary property of the Earl of Glenthorn, and every thing was in readiness for my journey. During this time poor Ellinor never appeared at the castle. I went to see her, to comfort her about my going away; but she was silent, and seemingly sullen, and would not be comforted.

'I've enough to grieve me,' said she: 'I know what will be the end of all; I see it as plain as if you'd told me. There's no hiding nothing from a mother: no, there's no use in striving to comfort me.' Every method which I tried to console her seemed to grieve her more.

The day before that which was fixed for my departure, I sent to desire to see her. This request I had repeatedly made; but she had, from day to day, excused herself, saying that she was unwell, and that she would be up on the morrow. At last she came; and though but a few days had elapsed since I had seen her, she was so changed in appearance, that I was shocked the moment I beheld her countenance.

'You don't look well, Ellinor,' said I: 'sit down.'

'No matter whether I sit or stand,' said she, calmly; 'I'm not long for this world: I won't live long after you are gone, that's one comfort.'

Her eyes were fixed and tearless; and there was a dead unnatural tranquillity in her manner.

'They are making a wonderful great noise nailing up the boxes, and I seen them cording the trunks as I came through the hall. I asked them, could I be of any use: but they said I could be of none, and that's true; for, when I put my hand to the cord, to pull it, I had no more strength than an infant. It was seven-and-twenty years last Midsummer-day since I first had you an infant in my arms. I was strong enough then, and you was a sweet babby. Had I seen that time all that would come to pass this day! But that's over now. I have done a wicked thing; but I'll send for Father Murphy, and get absolution before I die.'

She sighed deeply, then went on speaking more quickly.

'But I can do nothing until you go. What time will you go in the morning, dear? It's better go early. Is it in the coach you'll go? I see it in the yard. But I thought you must leave the coach, with all the rest, to the rightful heir. But my head's not clear about it all, I believe – and no matter.'

Her ideas rambled from one subject to another in an unconnected manner. I endeavoured in vain to recall her understanding by speaking of her own immediate interests; of the house that was secured to her for life; and of the promise that had been made me, that she should never *want for any thing*, and that she should be treated with all possible kindness. She seemed to listen to me; but showed that she did not comprehend what I said, by her answers; and, at every pause I made, she repeated the same question –

'What time will you go in the morning, dear?'

At last I touched her feelings, and she recovered her intellect, when I suddenly asked, if she would accompany me to England the next morning.

'Ay, that I will,' cried she, 'go with you through the wide world.'

She burst into tears, and wept bitterly for some time.

'Ah! now I feel right again,' said she; 'this is what I wanted; but could not cry this many a day – never since the word came to me that you was going, and all was lost.'

I assured her that I now expected to be happier than I had ever been.

'Oh!' cried she: 'and have you never been happy all this time? What a folly it was for me, then, to do so wicked a thing! and all my comfort was, the thinking you was happy, dear. And what will become of you now? And is it on foot you'll go?'

Her thoughts rambled again.

'Whatever way I go, you shall go with me,' said I. 'You are my mother; and now that your son has done what he knows to be honest and just, he will prosper in the world, and will be truly happy; and so may you be happy, now that you have nothing more to conceal.'

She shook her head.

'It's too late,' said she, 'quite too late. I often told Christy I would die before you left this place, dear; and so I will, you will see. God bless you! God bless you! and pray to him to forgive me! None that could know what I've gone through would ever do the like; no, not for their own child, was he even such as you, and that would be hard to find. God bless you, dear; I shall never see you more! The hand of death is upon me – God for ever bless you, dear!'

She died that night; and I lost in her the only human being who had ever shown me warm, disinterested affection. Her death delayed for a few days my departure from Glenthorn Castle. I staid to see her laid in the grave. Her funeral was followed by crowds of people: by many, from the general habit of attending funerals; by many, who wished to pay their court to me, in showing respect to the memory of my nurse.

When the prayers over the dead were ended, and the grave closed, just as the crowd were about to disperse, I stood up on a monument belonging to the Glenthorn family; and the moment it was observed that I wished to address the multitude, the moving waves were stilled, and there was a dead silence. Every eye was fixed upon me with eager expectation. It was the first time in my life that I had ever spoken before numbers; but as I was certain that I had something to say, and quite indifferent about the manner, words came without difficulty. Amazement appeared in every face when I declared myself to be the son of the poor woman whom we had just interred. And when I pointed to the real Earl of Glenthorn, and when I declared that I relinquished to him his hereditary title and lawful property, my auditors looked alternately at me and at my foster-brother, seeming to think it impossible that a man, with face and hands so black as Christy's usually were known to be, could become an earl.

When I concluded my narrative, and paused, the silence still continued; all seemed held in mute astonishment.

'And now, my good friends,' continued I, 'let me bid you farewell; probably you will never see or hear of me more; but, whether he be rich or poor, or high or low-born, every honest man must wish to leave behind him a fair character. Therefore, when I am gone, and, as it were, dead to you, speak of me, not as of an impostor, who long assumed a name and enjoyed a fortune that was not his own; but remember that I was bred to believe myself heir to a great estate, and that, after having lived till the age of seven-and-twenty, in every kind of luxury, I voluntarily gave up the fortune I enjoyed, the moment I discovered that it was not justly mine.'

'*That* you did, indeed,' interrupted Christy; 'and of that I am ready to bear witness for you in this world and in the next. God bless and prosper you wherever you go! and sure enough he will, for he cannot do other than prosper one that deserves it so well. I never should have known a sentence of the secret,' continued he, addressing his neighbours, 'if it had not been for *his* generosity to tell it me; and even had I found it out by any *maracle*, where would have been the gain of that to me? for you know he could, had he been so inclined, have kept me out of all by the law – ay, baffled me on till my heart was sick, and till my little substance was wasted, and my bones rotten in the ground; but, God's blessing be upon him! he's an honest man, and *done* that which many a lord in his place would not have done; but a good conscience is a kingdom in itself, and *that* he cannot but have, wherever he goes – and all which grieves me is that he is going away from us. If he'd be prevailed with by me, he'd stay where he is, and we'd share and share alike; but he's too proud for that – and no wonder – he has a right to be proud; for no matter who was his mother, he'll live and die a gentleman, every inch of him. Any man, you see, may be made a lord; but a gentleman, a man must make himself. And yourselves can witness, has not he reigned over us like a gentleman, and a *raal* gentleman; and shown mercy to the poor, and done justice to all, as well as to me? and did not he take me by the hand when I was persecuted, and none else in the wide world to *befrind* me; and did not he stand up for me against the tyrants that had the sway then; ay, and did not he put himself to trouble, day and night, go riding here and there, and *spaking* and writing for me? Well, as they say, he loves his ease, and that's the worst can be said of him; he took all this pains for a poor man, and had like to have lost his life by it. And now, wherever he is and whatever, can I help loving and praying for him? or could you? And since you will go,' added he, turning to me with tears in his eyes, 'take with you the blessings of the poor, which, they say, carry a man straight to heaven, if any thing can.'

The surrounding crowd joined with one voice in applauding this speech: 'It is he that has said what we all think,' cried they, following me with acclamations to the castle. When they saw the chaise at the door which was to carry me away, their acclamations suddenly ceased – 'But is he going? – But can't he stay? – And is he going this minute? troth it's a pity, and a great pity!'

Again and again these honest people insisted upon taking leave of me, and I could not force myself away without difficulty. They walked on beside my carriage, Christy at their head; and in this species of triumph, melancholy indeed, but grateful to my heart, I quitted Glenthorn Castle, passed through that park which was no longer mine, and at the verge of the county shook hands for the last time with these affectionate and generous people. I then bid my postilion drive on fast; and I never looked back, never once cast a lingering look at all I left behind. I felt proud of having executed my purpose, and conscious I had not the insignificant, inefficient character, that had formerly disgraced me. As to the future, I had not distinctly arranged my plans, nor was my mind during the remainder of the day sufficiently tranquil for reflection. I felt like one in a dream, and could scarcely persuade myself of the reality of the events, that had succeeded each other with such astonishing rapidity. At night I stopped at an inn where I was not known; and having no attendants or equipage to command respect from hostlers, waiters, and inn-keepers, I was made immediately sensible of the reality, at least, of the change in my fortune; but I was not mortified – I felt only as if I were travelling incognito. And I contrived to go to bed without a valet-de-chambre, and slept soundly, for I had earned a sound sleep by exertion both of body and mind.

CHAPTER XIX

In the morning I awoke with a confused notion that something extraordinary had happened; but it was a good while before I recollected myself sufficiently to be perfectly sensible of the absolute and irrevocable change in my circumstances. An inn may not appear the best possible place for meditation, especially if the moraliser's bedchamber be next the yard where carriages roll, and hostlers swear perpetually; yet, so situated, I, this morning as I lay awake in my bed, thought so abstractedly and attentively, that I heard neither wheels nor hostlers. I reviewed the whole of my past life; I regretted bitterly my extravagance, my dissipation, my waste of time; I considered how small a share of enjoyment my wealth had procured, either for myself or others; how little advantage I had derived from my education, and from all my opportunities of acquiring know-ledge. It had been in my power to associate with persons of the highest talents, and of the best information, in the British dominions; yet I had devoted my youth to loungers, and gamesters, and epicures, and knew that scarcely a trace of my existence remained in the minds of those selfish beings, who once called themselves my friends. I wished that I could live my life over again; and I felt that, were it in my power, I should live in a manner very different from that in which I had fooled away existence. In the midst of my self-reproaches, however, I had some consolation in the idea that I had never been guilty of any base or dishonourable action. I recollected, with satisfaction, my behaviour to Lady Glenthorn, when I discov-ered her misconduct; I recollected that I had always shown gratitude to poor Ellinor for her kindness; I recollected with pleasure, that when trusted with power I had not used it tyrannically. My exertions in favour of my foster-brother, when he was oppressed, I remembered with much satisfaction; and the steadiness with which I behaved, when a conspiracy was formed against my life, gave me confidence in my own courage; and, after having sacrificed my vast possessions to a sense of justice, no mortal could doubt my integrity: so that upon the whole, notwithstanding my past follies, I had a tolerably good opinion of myself, or rather good hopes for the future. I was certain, that there was more in me than the world had seen; and I was ambitious of proving that I had some personal merit, indepen-dent of the adventitious circumstances of rank and fortune. But how was I to distinguish myself?

Just as I came to this difficult question, the chambermaid inter-rupted my reverie, by warning me in a shrill voice, that it was very late, and that she had called me above two hours before.

'Where's my man? send up my man. O! I beg your pardon – nothing at all: only, my good girl, I should be obliged to you if you could let me have a little warm water, that I may shave myself.'

It was new and rather strange to me to be without attendants; but I found that, when I was forced to it, I could do things admirably well for myself, that I had never suspected I could perform without assistance. After I had travelled two days without servants, how I had travelled with them was the wonder. I once caught myself saying of myself, 'that careless blockhead has forgot my nightcap'. For some time I was liable to make odd blunders about my own identity; I was apt to mistake between my old and my new habits, so that when I spoke in the tone and imperative mode in which Lord Glenthorn had been habituated to speak, people stared at me as if I was mad, and I in my turn was frequently astonished by their astonishment, and perplexed by their ease of behaviour in my presence.

Upon my arrival in Dublin, I went to a small lodging which Mr M'Leod had recommended to me; it was such as suited my reduced finances; but, at first view, it was not much to my taste; however, I ate with a good appetite my very frugal supper, upon a little table, covered with a little table-cloth, on which I could not wipe my mouth without stooping low. The mistress of the house, a North-country woman,[83] was so condescending as to blow my fire, remarking, at the same time, that coals were a *very scarce article*; she begged to know whether I would choose a fire in my bed-room, and what quantity of coals she should lay in; she added many questions about boarding, and small-beer, and tea, and sugar, and butter, and blankets, and sheets, and washer-women, which almost overwhelmed my spirits.

'And must I think of all these things for myself?' said I, in a lamentable tone, and I suppose with a most deplorable length of face, for the woman could not refrain from laughing: as she left the room, I heard her exclaim, 'Lord help him! he looks as much astray as if he was just new from the Isle of Skye.'

The cares of life were coming fast upon me, and I was terrified by the idea of a host of petty evils; I sat ruminating, with my feet upon the bars of the grate, till past midnight, when my landlady, who seemed to think it incumbent upon her to supply me with common sense, came to inform me that there was a good fire burning to waste in the bed-room, and that I should find myself a deal better there than sitting over the cinders. I suffered myself to be removed to the bedchamber, and again established my feet upon the upper bar of the grate.

'Lack! sir, you'll burn your boots,' said my careful landlady; who, after bidding me good-night, put her head back into the room, to beg I would be sure to rake the fire, and throw up the ashes safe, before I went to bed. Left to my own meditations, I confess I did feel rather forlorn. I reflected upon my helplessness in all the common business of life; and the more I considered that I was totally unfit for any employment or profession, by which I could either earn money, or distinguish myself, the deeper became my despondency. I passed a sleepless night, vainly regretting the time that never could be recalled.

In the morning, my landlady gave me some letters, which had been forwarded to me from Glenthorn Castle: the direction to the Earl of Glenthorn scratched out, and in its place inserted my new address, '*C. O'Donoghoe, Esq., No. 6, Duke-street, Dublin.*' I remember, I held the letters in my hand, contemplating the direction for some minutes, and at length read it aloud repeatedly, to my landlady's infinite amusement: – she knew nothing of my history, and seemed in doubt whether to think me extremely silly or mad. One of my letters was from Lord Y—, an Irish nobleman, with whom I was not personally acquainted, but for whose amiable character and literary reputation I had always, even during my days of dissipation, peculiar respect. He wrote to me to make inquiries respecting the character of a Mr Lyddell, who had just proposed himself as tutor to the son of one of his friends. Mr Lyddell had formerly been my favourite tutor, the man who had encouraged me in every species of ignorance and idleness. In my present state of mind I was not disposed to speak favourably of this gentleman; and I resolved that I would not be instrumental in placing another young nobleman under his guidance. I wrote an explicit, indignant, and I will say eloquent letter, upon this occasion; but, when I came to the signature, I felt a repugnance to signing myself, C. O'Donoghoe, and I recollected, that as my history could not yet be public, Lord Y— would be puzzled by this strange name, and would be unable to comprehend this answer to his letter. I therefore determined to wait upon his lordship, and to make my explanations in person: besides my other reasons for determining on this visit, I had a strong desire to become personally acquainted with a nobleman of whom I had heard so much. His lordship's porter was not quite so insolent as some of his brethren; and though I did not come in a showy equipage, and though I had no laced footmen to enforce my rights, I gained admission. I passed through a gallery of fine statues, to a magnificent library, which I admired till the master of the house appeared, and from that moment he commanded, or rather captivated, my attention.

Lord Y— was at this time an elderly gentleman.[84] In his address, there was a becoming mixture of ease and dignity; he was not what the French call *manièré*; his politeness was not of any particular school, but founded on those general principles of good taste, good sense, and good nature, which must succeed in all times, places, and seasons. His desire to please evidently arose not from vanity but benevolence. In his conversation, there was neither the pedantry of a recluse, nor the coxcombry of a man of the world: his knowledge was select; his wit without effort, the play of a cultivated imagination: the happiness of his expressions did not seem the result of care: and his allusions were at once so apposite and elegant, as to charm both the learned and the unlearned: all he said was sufficiently clear and just to strike every person of plain sense and natural feeling, whilst to the man of literature it had often a further power to please, by its less obvious meaning. Lord Y—'s superiority never depressed those with whom he conversed; on the contrary, they felt themselves raised by the magic of politeness to his level; instead of being compelled to pay tribute, they seemed invited to share his intellectual dominion, and to enjoy with him the delightful pre-eminence of genius and virtue.

I shall be forgiven for pausing in my own insignificant story, to dwell on the noble character of a departed friend. That he permitted me to call him my friend, I think the greatest honour of my life. But let me, if I can, go on regularly with my narrative.

Lord Y— took it for granted, during our first half hour's conversation, that he was speaking to the Earl of Glenthorn: he thanked me with much warmth for putting him on his guard against the character of Mr Lyddell; and his lordship was also pleased to thank me for making him acquainted, as he said, with my own character; for convincing him how ill it had been appreciated by those, who imagined that wealth and title were the only distinctions which the Earl of Glenthorn might claim. This compliment went nearer to my heart than Lord Y— could guess.

'My character,' said I, 'since your lordship encourages me to speak of myself with freedom, – my character has, I hope, been much changed and improved by circumstances; and perhaps those, which might at present be deemed the most unfortunate, may ultimately prove of the greatest advantage, by urging me to exertion. – Your lordship is not aware of what I allude to; a late event in my singular history,' continued I, taking up the newspapers which lay on his library table – 'my singular history, has not yet, I fancy, got into the public newspapers. Perhaps you will hear it most favourably for myself.'

Lord Y— was politely, benevolently attentive, whilst I related to him the sudden and singular change in my fortune: when I gave an account of the manner in which I had conducted myself after the discovery of my birth, tears of generous feeling filled his eyes; he laid his hand upon mine when I paused –

'Whatever you have lost,' said he, 'you have gained a friend. Do not be surprised,' continued he, 'by this sudden declaration. Before I saw you this morning, your real character was better known to me than you imagine. I learnt it from a particular friend of mine, of whose judgement and abilities I have the highest opinion, Mr Cecil Devereux; I saw him just after his marriage; and the very evening before they sailed, I remember, when Lady Geraldine and he were talking of the regret they felt in leaving Ireland, among the friends whom they lamented that they should not see again, perhaps for years, you were mentioned with peculiar esteem and affection. They called you their generous benefactor, and fully explained to me the claim you had to this title – a title which never can be lost. But Mr Devereux was anxious to convince me that he was not influenced by the partiality of gratitude in his opinion of his benefactor's talents. He repeated an assertion, that was supported with much energy by the charming Lady Geraldine, that Lord Glenthorn had *abilities to be any thing he pleased*; and the high terms in which they spoke of his talents, and the strong proofs they adduced of the generosity of his character, excited in my mind a warm desire to cultivate his acquaintance; a desire which has been considerably increased within this last hour. May I hope that the Irish rapidity, with which I have passed from acquaintance to friendship may not shock English habits of reserve; and may not induce you to doubt the sincerity of the man, who has ventured with so little hesitation or ceremony, to declare himself your friend?'

I was so much moved by this unexpected kindness, that, though I felt how much more was requisite, I could answer only with a bow; and I was glad to make my retreat as soon as possible. The very next day, his lordship returned my visit, to my landlady's irrecoverable astonishment; and I had increasing reason to regard him with admiration and affection. He convinced me, that I had interested him in my concerns, and told me, I must forgive him if he spoke to me with the freedom of a friend: thus I was encouraged to consult him respecting my future plans. Plans, indeed, I had none regularly formed; but Lord Y—, by his judicious suggestions, settled and directed my ideas without overpowering me by the formality of advice. My ambition was excited to deserve his friendship, and to accomplish his predictions. The profession of the law was that to which he advised me to turn my thoughts: he predicted, that, if for five years I would persevere in application to the necessary preparatory studies, I should afterwards distinguish myself at the bar, more than I had ever been distinguished by the title of Earl of Glenthorn. Five years of hard labour! the idea alarmed, but did not utterly appal my imagination; and to prevent my dwelling upon it too long at the first, Lord Y— suddenly changed the conversation; and, in a playful tone, said, 'Before you immerse yourself in your studies, I must, however, claim some of your time. You must permit me to carry you home with me to-day, to introduce you to two ladies of my acquaintance: the one prudent and old – if a lady can ever be old; the other, young, and beautiful, and graceful, and witty, and wise, and reasonable. One of these ladies is much prepossessed in your favour, the other strongly prejudiced against you – for the best of all possible reasons, because she does not know you.'

I accepted Lord Y—'s invitation; not a little curious to know whether it was the old and prudent, or the young, beautiful, graceful, witty, wise, and reasonable lady, who was much prepossessed in my favour. Notwithstanding my usual indifference to the whole race of *very agreeable young ladies*, I remember trying to form a picture in my imagination of this all-accomplished female.

CHAPTER XX

Upon my arrival at Y— House, I found two ladies in the drawing-room, in earnest conversation with Lady Y—. In their external appearance they were nearly what my friend had described; except that the beauty of the youngest infinitely surpassed my expectations. The elegance of her form, and the charming expression of her counte-nance, struck me with a sort of delightful surprise, that was quickly succeeded by a most painful sensation.

'Lady Y—, give me leave to introduce to you Mr O'Donoghoe.'

Shocked by the sound of my own name, I was ready to recoil abashed. The elderly lady turned her eyes upon me for an instant, with that indifference with which we look at an uninteresting stranger. The young lady seemed to pity my confusion; for though so well and so long used to varieties of the highest company, when placed in a situation that was new to me, I was unaccountably disconcerted. Ah! thought I, how differently should I be received were I still Earl of Glenthorn!

I was rather angry with Lord Y—, for not introducing me, as he had promised, to this fair lady; and yet the repetition of my name would have increased my vexation. In short, I was unjust, and felt an impatience and irritability quite unusual to my temper. Lady Y— addressed some conversation to me, in an obliging manner, and I did my best to support my part till she left me: but my attention was soon distracted, by a conversation that commenced at another part of the room, between her and the elderly lady.

'My dear Lady Y—, have you heard the extraordinary news? the most incredible thing that ever was heard! For my part, I cannot believe it yet, though we have the intelligence from the best authority. Lord Glenthorn, that is to say, the person we always called Lord Glenthorn, turns out to be the son of the Lord knows who – they don't mention the name.'

At this speech I was ready to sink into the earth. Lord Y— took my arm, and led me into another room. 'I have some cameos,' said he, 'which are thought curious, would you like to look at them?'

'Can you conceive it?' continued the elderly lady, whose voice I still heard, as the folding-doors of the room were open: 'Changed at nurse! One hears of such things in novels, but, in real life, I absolutely cannot believe it. Yet here, in this letter from Lady Ormsby, are all the particulars: and a blacksmith is found to be Earl of Glenthorn, and takes possession of Glenthorn Castle, and all the estates. And the man is married, to some vulgarian of course: and he has a son, and may have half a hundred, you know; so there is an end of our hopes; and there is an end too of all my fine schemes for Cecilia.'

I felt myself change colour again. 'I believe,' said I to Lord Y—, 'I ought not to hear this. If your lordship will give me leave, I will shut the door.'

'No, no,' said he, smiling, and stopping me; 'you ought to hear it, for it will do you a great deal of good. You know I have undertaken to be your guide, philosopher, and friend; so you must let me have my own way: and if it should so happen, hear yourself abused patiently – Is not this a fine bust of Socrates?'

Some part of the conversation in the next room I missed, whilst his lordship spoke. The next words I heard were –

'But, my dear Lady Y—, look at Cecilia – Would not any other girl be cast down and miserable in Cecilia's place? yet see how provokingly happy and well she looks.'

'Yes,' replied Lady Y—, 'I never saw her appear better: but we are not to judge of her by what any other young lady would be in her place, for I know of none at all comparable to Miss Delamere.'

'Miss Delamere!' said I to Lord Y—. 'Is this the Miss Delamere who is heir at law to –'

'The Glenthorn estate. Yes – do not let the head of Socrates fall from your hands,' said his lordship, smiling.

I again lost something that was said in the next room; but I heard the old lady going on with –

'I only say, my dear, that if the man had been really what he was said to be, you could not have done better.'

'Dearest mother, you cannot be serious,' replied the sweetest voice I ever heard. 'I am sure that you never were in earnest upon this subject: you could not wish me to be united to such a man as Lord Glenthorn was said to be.'

'Why? what was he said to be, my dear? – a little dissipated, a little extravagant only: and if he had a fortune to support it, child, what matter?' pursued the mother: 'all young men are extravagant now-a-days – you must take the world as it goes.'

'The lady who married Lord Glenthorn, I suppose, acted upon that principle; and you see what was the consequence.'

'O, my dear, as to her ladyship, it ran in the blood: let her have married whom she would, she would have done the same: and I am told Lord Glenthorn made an incomparably good husband. A cousin of Lady Glenthorn's assured me that she was present one day, when her ladyship expressed a wish for a gold chain to wear round her neck, or braid her hair, I forget for what; but that very hour Lord Glenthorn bespoke for her a hundred yards of gold chain, at ten guineas a yard. Another time she longed for an Indian shawl, and his lordship presented her next day with three dozen real India shawls. There's a husband for you, Cecilia!'

'Not for me, mamma,' said Cecilia, laughing.

'Ah, you are a strange romantic girl, and never will be married after all, I fear.'

'Never to a fool, I hope,' said Cecilia.

'Miss Delamere will, however, allow,' said Lady Y—, 'that a man may have his follies, without being a fool, or wholly unworthy of her esteem; otherwise, what a large portion of mankind she would deprive of hope!'

'As to Lord Glenthorn, he was no fool, I promise you,' continued the mother: 'has not he been living prudently enough these three years? We have not heard of late of any of his *extraordinary landaus*.'

'But I have been told,' said Cecilia, 'that he is quite uninformed, without any taste for literature, and absolutely incapable of exertion – a victim to ennui. How miserable a woman must be with such a husband!'

'But,' said Lady Y—, 'what could be expected from a young nobleman bred up as Lord Glenthorn was?'

'Nothing,' said Cecilia; 'and that is the very reason I never wished to see him.'

'Perhaps Miss Delamere's opinion might be changed if she had known him,' said Lady Y—.

'Ay, for he is a very handsome man, I have heard,' said the mother. 'Lady Jocunda Lawler told me so, in one of her letters; and Lady Jocunda was very near being married to him herself, I can tell you, for he admired her prodigiously.'

'A certain proof that he never would have admired me,' said Cecilia; 'for two women, so opposite in every respect, no man could have loved.'

'Lord bless you, child! how little you know of the matter! After all, I dare say, if you had been acquainted with him, you might have been in love yourself with Lord Glenthorn.'

'Possibly,' said Cecilia, 'if I had found him the reverse of what he is reported to be.'

Company came in at this instant. Lord Y— was called to receive them, and I followed; glad, at this instant, that I was not Lord Glenthorn. At dinner the conversation turned upon general subjects; and Lord Y—, with polite and friendly attention, *drew me out*, without seeming to do so, in the kindest manner possible.

I had the pleasure to perceive that Cecilia Delamere did not find me a fool. I never, even in the presence of Lady Geraldine, exerted myself so much to avoid this disgrace.

After all the company, except Mrs and Miss Delamere, were gone, Lord Y— called me aside.

'Will you pardon,' said he, 'the means I have taken to convince you how much superior you are to the opinion that has been commonly formed of Lord Glenthorn? Will you forgive me for convincing you that when a man has sufficient strength of mind to rely upon himself, and sufficient energy to exert his abilities, he becomes independent of common report and vulgar opinion? He secures the suffrages of the best judges; and they, in time, lead all the rest of the world. Will you permit me now to introduce you to your prudent friend and your fair enemy? Mrs Delamere – Miss Delamere – give me leave to introduce to you the late Earl of Glenthorn.'

Of the astonishment in the opening eyes of Mrs Delamere I have some faint recollection. I can never forget the crimson blush that instantaneously spread over the celestial countenance of Cecilia. She was perfectly silent; but her mother went on talking with increased rapidity.

'Good Heavens! the late Lord Glenthorn! Why, I was talking – but he was not in the room.' The ladies exchanged looks, which seemed to say, 'I hope he did not hear all we said of him.'

'My dear Lord Y—, why did not you tell us this before? Suppose we had spoken of his lordship, you would have been answerable for all the consequences.'

'Certainly,' said Lord Y—.

'But, seriously,' said the old lady, 'have I the pleasure to speak to Lord Glenthorn, or have I not? I believe I began, unluckily, to talk of a strange story I had heard; but perhaps all this is a mistake, and my country correspondent may have been amusing herself at the expence of my credulity. I assure you I was not imposed upon; I never believed half the story.'

'You may believe the whole of it, madam,' said I; 'the story is perfectly true.'

'O! my good sir, how sorry I am to hear you say it is all true! And the blacksmith is really Earl of Glenthorn, and has taken possession of the castle, and is married, and has a son! Lord bless me, how unfortunate! Well, I can only say, sir, I wish, with all my heart, you were Earl of Glenthorn still.'

After hearing from Lord Y— the circumstances of what he was

pleased to call my generous conduct, Mrs Delamere observed, that I had acted very generously, to be sure, but that few in my place would have thought themselves bound to give up possession of an estate, which I had so long been taught to believe was my own. To have and to hold, she observed, always went together in law; and she could not help thinking I had done very injudiciously and imprudently not to let the law decide for me.

I was consoled for Mrs Delamere's reprehensions by her daughter's approving countenance. After this visit, Lord Y— gave me a general invitation to his house, where I frequently saw Miss Delamere, and frequently compared her with my recollection of Lady Geraldine —. Cecilia Delamere was not so entertaining, but she was more interesting than Lady Geraldine: the flashes of her ladyship's wit, though always striking, were sometimes dangerous; Cecilia's wit, though equally brilliant, shone with a more pleasing and inoffensive light. With as much generosity as Lady Geraldine could show in great affairs, she had more forbearance and delicacy of attention on every-day occasions. Lady Geraldine had much pride, and it often gave offence; Cecilia, perhaps, had more pride, but it never appeared, except upon the defensive: without having less candour, she had less occasion for it than Lady Geraldine seemed to have; and Cecilia's temper had more softness and equability. Perhaps Cecilia was not so fascinating, but she was more attractive. One had the envied art of appearing to advantage in public – the other, the more desirable power of being happy in private. I admired Lady Geraldine long before I loved her; I loved Cecilia long before I admired her.

Whilst I possibly could, I called what I felt for Miss Delamere only esteem; but when I found it impossible to conceal from myself that I loved, I resolved to avoid this charming woman. How happy, thought I, would the fortune I once possessed now make me! but in my present circumstances what have I to hope? Surely my friend Lord Y— has not shown his usual prudence in exposing me to such a temptation; but it is to be supposed, he thinks that the impossibility of my obtaining Miss Delamere will prevent my thinking of her, or perhaps he depends on the inertness and apathy of my temper. Unfortunately for me, my sensibility has increased since I have become poor; for many years, when I was rich, and could have married easily, I never wished to marry, and now that I have not enough to support a wife, I immediately fall desperately in love.

Again and again I pondered upon my circumstances: three hundred a-year was the amount of all my worldly possessions; and Miss Delamere was not rich, and she had been bred expensively; for it had never been absent from her mother's mind, that Cecilia would be heiress to the immense Glenthorn estate. The present possessor was, however, an excellent life, and he had a son stout and healthy, so all these hopes of Mrs Delamere's were at an end; and as there was little chance, as she said (laughing), of persuading her daughter to marry Johnny, the young lord and heir apparent, it was now necessary to turn her views elsewhere, and to form for Cecilia some suitable alliance. Rank and large fortune were, in Mrs Delamere's opinion, indispensable to happiness. Cecilia's ideas were far more moderate; but, though perfectly disinterested and generous, she was not so romantic, or so silly, as to think of marrying any man without the probability of his being able to support her in the society of her equals: nor, even if I could have thought it possible to prevail upon Miss Delamere to make an unbecoming and imprudent choice, would I have taken advantage of the confidence reposed in me by Lord Y—, to destroy the happiness of a young friend, for whom he evidently had a great regard. I resolved to see her no more – and for some weeks I kept my resolution; I refrained from going to Y— House. I deem this the most virtuous action of my life; it certainly was the most painful sacrifice I ever made to a sense of duty. At last, Lord Y— came to me one morning, and after reproaching me, in a friendly manner, for having so long absented myself from his house, declared that he would not be satisfied with any of those common excuses, which might content a mere acquaintance; that his sincere anxiety for my welfare gave him a right to expect from me the frankness of a friend. It was a relief to my mind to be encouraged in this manner. I confessed with entire openness my real motive: Lord Y— heard me without surprise.

'It is gratifying to me,' said his lordship, 'to be convinced that I was not mistaken in my judgement, either of your taste, or your integrity; permit me to assure you, that I foresaw exactly how you would feel, and precisely how you would act. There are certain moral omens, which old experience never fails to interpret rightly, and from which unerring predictions of the future conduct, and consequently of the future fate of individuals, may be formed. I hold that we are the artificers of our own fortune. If there be any whom the gods wish to destroy, these are first deprived of understanding; whom the gods wish to favour, they first endow with integrity, inspire with understanding, and animate with activity. Have I not seen integrity in you, and shall I not see activity? Yes; that supineness of temper or habit with which you reproach yourself has arisen, believe me, only from want of motive; but you have now the most powerful of motives, and in proportion to your exertions will be your success. In our country, you know, the highest offices of the state are open to talents and perseverance; a man of abilities and application cannot fail to secure independence, and obtain distinction. Time and industry are necessary to prepare you for the profession, to which you will hererafter be an honour, and you will courageously submit.

> – Time and industry, the mighty two,
> Which bring our wishes nearer to our view.[85]

As to the probability that your present wishes may be crowned with success, I can judge only from my general knowledge of the views and disposition of the lady whom you admire. I know that her views with respect to fortune are moderate; and that her disposition and excellent understanding will, in the choice of a husband, direct her preference to the essential good qualities, and not to the accidental advantages, of the candidates for her favour. As to the mother's influence, that will necessarily yield to the daughter's superior judgement. Cecilia possesses over her mother that witchcraft of gentle manners, which in the female sex is always irresistible, even over violent tempers. Prudential considerations have a just, though not exclusive, claim to Miss Delamere's attention. But her relations, I fancy, could find means of providing against any pecuniary embarrassments, if she should think proper to unite herself to a man who can be content, as she would be, with a competence, and who should *have proved himself able, by his own exertions, to maintain his wife in independence.* On this last condition I must dwell with emphasis, because it is indispensable; and I am convinced that without it Miss Delamere's consent, even after she is of age, and at liberty to judge for herself, could never be obtained. You perceive, then, how much depends upon your own exertions; and this is the best hope, and the best motive, that I can give to a strong and generous mind. Farewell – Persevere, and prosper.'

Such was the general purport of what Lord Y— said to me; indeed, I believe that I have repeated his very words, for they made a great and ineffaceable impression upon my mind. From this day I date the commencement of a new existence. Fired with ambition, – I hope generous ambition, – to distinguish myself among men, and to win the favour of the most amiable and the most lovely of women, all the faculties of my soul were awakened: I became active, permanently active. The enchantment of indolence was dissolved, and the demon of ennui was cast out for ever.

CHAPTER XXI

If, among those who may be tempted to peruse my history, there should be any mere novel readers, let me advise them to throw the book aside at the commencement of this chapter; for I have no more wonderful incidents to relate, no more changes at nurse, no more sudden turns of fortune. I am now become a plodding man of business, poring over law-books from morning till night, and leading a most monotonous life: yet occupation, and hope, and the constant sense of approaching nearer to my object, rendered this mode of existence, dull as it may seem, infinitely more agreeable than many of my apparently prosperous days, when I had more money, and more time, than I knew how to enjoy. I resolutely persevered in my studies.

About a month after I came to town, the doors of my lodgings were blockaded by half a dozen cars, loaded with huge packing cases, on which I saw, in the hand-writing which I remembered often to have seen in my blacksmith's bills, a direction to *Christopher O'Donoghoe, Esquire – this side upwards: to be kept dry.*

One of the carmen fumbled in what he called his pocket, and at last produced a very dirty note.

My dear and honourable foster-brother, larning from Mr M'Leod, that you are thinking of *studdeing*, I send you inclosed by the bearer, who is to get nothing for the *carrige*, all the bookes from the big booke-room at the castle, which I hope,

being of not as much use as I could wish to me, your honour
will not scorn to accept, with the true veneration of

Your ever-loving foster-brother,
and grateful humble servant,
to command.

PS. No name needful, for you will not be astray about the
hand.

This good-natured fellow's present was highly valuable and useful
to me.

Among my pleasures at this studious period of my life, when I
had few events to break the uniform tenor of my days, I must
mention letters which I frequently received from Mr Devereux and
Lady Geraldine, who still continued in India. Mr Devereux was
acquainted with almost all the men of eminence at the Irish bar;
men who are not mere lawyers, but persons of literature, of agreeable
manners, and gentlemanlike habits. Mr Devereux wrote to his friends
so warmly in my favour, that, instead of finding myself a stranger in
Dublin, my only difficulty was how to avoid the numerous invitations
which tempted me from my studies.

Those gentlemen of the bar who were intimate with Mr Devereux
honoured me with particular attention, and their society was peculiarly useful, as well as agreeable, to me: they directed my industry
to the best and shortest means of preparing myself for their profession; they put into my hands the best books; told me all that experience had taught them of the art of distinguishing, in the mass of
law-precedents, the useful from the useless: instructed me in the
methods of indexing and common-placing; and gave me all those
advantages, which solitary students so often want, and the want of
which so often makes the study of the law appear an endless maze
without a plan. When I found myself surrounded with books, and
reading assiduously day and night, I could scarcely believe in my
own identity; I could scarcely imagine that I was the same person,
who, but a few months before this time, lolled upon a sofa half the
day, and found it an intolerable labour to read or think for half an
hour together. Such is the power of motive! During the whole time I
pursued my studies, and kept my terms, in Ireland, the only relaxation I allowed myself was in the society at Lord Y—'s house in

Dublin, and, during my vacations, in excursions which I made with his lordship to different parts of the country. Lord Y— had two country seats in the most beautiful parts of Ireland. How differently the face of nature appeared to me now! with what different sensations I beheld the same objects!

> No brighter colours paint th' enamell'd fields,
> No sweeter fragrance now the garden yields;
> Whence this strange increase of joy?
> Is it to love these new delights I owe?[86]

It was not to love that I owed these new delights, for Cecilia was not there; but my powers of observation were awakened, and the confinement and labour to which I had lately submitted gave value to the pleasures of rest and liberty, and to the freshness of country air, and the beautiful scenes of nature. So true it is, that all our pleasures must be earned, before they can be enjoyed. When I saw on Lord Y—'s estates, and on those of several other gentlemen, which he occasionally took me to visit, the neat cottages, the well-cultivated farms, the air of comfort, industry, and prosperity, diffused through the lower classes of the people, I was convinced that much may be done by the judicious care and assistance of landlords for their tenantry. I saw this with mixed sensations of pleasure and of pain – of pain, for I reflected how little I had accomplished, and how ill I had done even that little, whilst the means of doing good to numbers had been in my power. For the very trifling services I did some of my poor tenants I am sure I had abundant gratitude; and I was astonished and touched by instances of this shown to me after I had lost my fortune, and when I scarcely had myself any remembrance of the people who came to thank me. Trivial as it is, I cannot forbear to record one of the many instances of gratitude I met with from a poor Irishman.

Whilst I was in Dublin, as I was paying a morning visit to Lord Y—, sitting with him in his library, we heard some disturbance in the inner court; and looking out of the window, we saw a countryman with a basket on his arm, struggling with the porter and two footmen.

'He is here; I know to a certainty he is here, and I *shall* see him, say what you plase now!'

'I tell you my lord is not at home,' said the porter.

'What's the matter?' said Lord Y—, opening the window.

'See, there's my lord himself at the window: are not you ashamed of yourself now?' said the footman.

'And why would I be ashamed that am telling no lies, and hindering no one?' said the countryman, looking up to us with so sudden a motion that his hat fell off. I knew his face, but could not recollect his name.

'Oh! there he is, his own honour; I've found him, and *axe* pardon for my boldness; but it's *becaase* I've been all day yesterday, and this day, running through Dublin after *yees*; and when certified by the lady of the lodgings you was in it here, I could not lave town without my errand, which is no more than a cheese from my wife of her own making, to be given to your honour's own hands, and she would not see me if I did not do it.'

'Let him come up,' said Lord Y—. 'This,' continued his lordship, turning to me, 'reminds me of Henry the Fourth, and the Gascon peasant with his *fromages de bœuf*.'[87]

'But our countryman brings his offering to an abdicated monarch,' said I.

The poor fellow presented his wife's cheese to me with as good a grace as any courtier could have made his offering. Unembarrassed, his manners and his words gave the natural and easy expression of a grateful heart. He assured me that he and his wife were the happiest couple in all Ireland; and he hoped I would one day be as happy myself in a wife as I *desarved*, who had made others so; and there were many on the estate remembered as well as he did the good I did to the poor during *my reign*.

Then stepping up closer to me, he said, in a lower voice, 'I'm Jimmy Riley, that married *ould* Noonan's daughter; and now that it is all over I may tell you a bit of a *secret*, which made me so eager to get to the speech of your honour, that I might tell it to your own ear alone – no offence to this gentleman, before whom I'd as soon say it as yourself, *becaase* I see he is all as one as another yourself. Then the thing is – does your honour remember the boy with the cord round his body, looking for the birds' eggs in the rock, and the nonymous bit of a letter that you got? 'Twas I wrote it, and the *gossoon* that threw it to your honour was a cousin of my own that I sent, that nobody, nor yourself even, might not know him: and the way I got the information I never can tell till I die, and then only to the priest, *becaase* I swore I would not never. But don't go for to think it was by being a *rubble* any way; no man can, I thank my God, charge me with indifference. So rejoiced to see you the same, I wish you a good morrow, and long life, and a happy death – when it comes.'

About this time I frequently used to receive presents to a considerable amount, and of things which were most useful to me, but always without any indication by which I could discover to whom I was indebted for them: at last, by means of my Scotch landlady, I traced them to Mr M'Leod. His kindness was so earnest and peremptory, that it would admit neither thanks nor refusals; and I submitted to be obliged to a man for whom I felt such high esteem. I looked upon it as not the least of his proofs of regard, that he gave me what I knew he valued more than any thing else – his time. Whenever he came to Dublin, though he was always hurried by business, so that he had scarcely leisure to eat or sleep, he used constantly to come to see me in my obscure lodgings; and when in the country, though he hated all letter-writing, except letters of business, yet he regularly informed me of every thing that could be interesting to me. Glenthorn Castle he described as a scene of riotous living, and of the most wasteful vulgar extravagance. My poor foster-brother, the best-natured and most generous fellow in the world, had not sufficient prudence or strength of mind to conduct his own family; his wife filled the castle with tribes of her vagabond relations; she chose to be descended from one of the kings of Ireland; and whoever would acknowledge her high descent, and whoever would claim relationship with her, were sure to have their claims allowed, and were welcome to live in all the barbaric magnificence of Glenthorn Castle. Every instance that she could hear of the former Lady Glenthorn's extravagance or of mine – and, alas! there were many upon record, she determined to exceed. Her diamonds and her pearls, and her finery, surpassed every thing but the extravagance of some of the Russian favourites of fortune. Decked out in the most absurd manner, this descendant of kings often, as Mr M'Leod assured me, indulged in the pleasures of the banquet, till, no longer able to support the regal diadem, she was carried by some of the meanest of her subjects to her bed. The thefts committed during these interregnums were amazing in their amount, and the jewels of the crown were to be replaced as fast as they were stolen. Poor Christy all this time was considered as a mean-spirited *cratur*, who had no notion of living like a prince; and whilst his wife and her relations were revelling in this unheard-of manner, he was scarcely considered as the master of the house: he lived by the fireside disregarded in winter, and in summer he spent his time chiefly in walking up and down his garden, and picking fruit. He once made an attempt to amuse himself by mending the lock of his own room door; but he was detected in the fact, and exposed to such loud ridicule by his lady's favourites, that he desisted, and sighing said to Mr M'Leod – 'And isn't it now a great hardship upon a man like me to have nothing to do, or not to be let do any thing? If it had not been for my son Johnny's sake, I never would have quit the forge; and now all will be spent in *coshering*,[88] and Johnny, at the last, will never be a penny the better, but the worse for my consinting to be lorded; and what grieves me more than all the rest, *she* is such *a negre*,* that I haven't a guinea I can call my own to send, as I'd always laid out to do at odd times, such little tokens of my love and duty, as would be becoming to my dear foster-brother there in Dublin. And now, you tell me, he is going away too, beyond sea to England, to finish making a lawyer of himself in London; and what friends will he find there, without money in his pocket? and I had been thinking this while past, ever since you gave me notice of his being to quit Ireland, that I would go up to Dublin myself to see him, and wish him a good journey kindly before he would go; and I had a little *compliment* here, in a private drawer, that I had collected *unknownst* to my wife; but here last night she *lit* upon it, and now that her hand has closed upon it, not a guinea of it shall I ever see more, nor a farthing the better of it will my dear foster-brother ever be, for it or for me; and this is what grieves me more than all, and goes to the quick of my heart.'

When Mr M'Leod repeated to me these lamentations of poor Christy, I immediately wrote to set his heart at ease, as much as I could, by the assurance that I was in no distress for money; and that my three hundred a year would support me in perfect comfort and independence, whilst 'I was making a lawyer of myself in London'. I farther assured my good foster-brother, that I was so well convinced of his affectionate and generous disposition towards me, that it would be quite unnecessary ever to send me tokens of his regard. I added a few words of advice about his wife and his affairs, which, like most

---

* An Irishman in using this word has some confused notion that it comes from *negro*; whereas it really means niggard.

words of advice, were, as I afterwards found, absolutely thrown away.

Though I had taken care to live with so much economy, that I was not in any danger of being in pecuniary embarrassments, yet I felt much distress of another kind in leaving Ireland. I left Miss Delamere surrounded with admirers; her mother using her utmost art and parental influence to induce Cecilia to decide in favour of one of these gentlemen, who was a person of rank and of considerable fortune. I had seen all this going on, and was bound in honour the whole time to remain passive, not to express my own ardent feelings, not to make the slightest attempt to win the affections of the woman who was the object of all my labours, of all my exertions. The last evening that I saw her at Lord Y—'s, just before I sailed for England, I suffered more than I thought it was in my nature to feel, especially at the moment when I went up to make my bow, and take leave of her with all the cold ceremony of a common acquaintance. At parting, however, in the presence of her mother and of Lord Y—, Cecilia, with her sweet smile, and, I think, with a slight blush, said a few words, upon which I lived for months afterwards.

'I sincerely wish you, sir, the success your perseverance so well deserves.'

The recollection of these words was often my solace in my lonely chambers at the Temple;[89] and often, after a day's hard study, the repeating them to myself operated as a charm that dissipated all fatigue, and revived at once my exhausted spirits. To be sure, there were moments when my fire was out, and my candle sinking in the socket, and my mind over-wearied saw things in the most gloomy point of view; and at these times I used to give an unfavourable interpretation to Cecilia's words, and I fancied that they were designed to prevent my entertaining fallacious hopes, and to warn me that she must yield to her mother's authority, or perhaps to her own inclinations, in favour of some of her richer lovers. This idea would have sunk me into utter despondency, and I should have lost, with my motive, all power of exertion, had I not opposed to this apprehension the remembrance of Lord Y—'s countenance, at the moment Cecilia was speaking to me. I then felt assured, that his lordship, at least, understood the words in a favourable sense, else he would have suffered for me, and would not certainly have allowed me to go away with false hopes. Re-animated by this consideration, I persevered – for it was by perseverance alone that I could have any chance of success.

It was fortunate for me, that, stimulated by a great motive, I thus devoted my whole time and thoughts to my studies, otherwise I must, on returning to London, have felt the total neglect and desertion of all my former associates in the fashionable world; of all the vast number of acquaintance, who used to lounge away their hours in my company, and partake of the luxuries of my table and the festivities of my house. Some whom I accidentally met in the street, just at my reappearance in town, thought proper, indeed, to know me again at first, that they might gratify their curiosity about the paragraphs which they had seen in the papers, and the reports which they had heard of my extraordinary change of fortune; but no sooner had they satisfied themselves that all they had heard was true, than their interest concerning me ceased. When they found, that, instead of being Earl of Glenthorn, and the possessor of a large estate, I was now reduced to three hundred a year, lodging in small chambers at the Temple, and studying the law, they never more thought me worthy of their notice. They affected, according to their different humours, either to pity me for my misfortunes, or to blame me for my folly in giving up my estate; but they unanimously expressed astonishment at the idea of my becoming a member of any active profession. They declared that it was impossible that I could ever endure the labour of the law, or succeed in such an arduous career. Their prophecies intimidated me not; I was conscious that these people did not in the least know me; and I hoped and believed that I had powers and a character which they were incapable of estimating: their contempt rather excited than depressed my mind, and their pity I returned with more sincerity than it was given. I had lived their life, knew thoroughly what were its pleasures and its pains; I could compare the ennui I felt when I was a Bond-street lounger with the self-complacency I enjoyed now that I was occupied in a laborious but interesting and honourable pursuit. I confess, I had sometimes, however, the weakness to think the worse of human nature, for what I called the desertion and ingratitude of these my former companions and flatterers; and I could not avoid comparing the neglect and solitude in which I lived in London, where I had lavished my fortune, with the kindness and hospitalities I had received in Dublin, where I lived only when I had no fortune to spend. After a little time, however, I became more reasonable and just; for I considered that it was my former dissipated mode of life, and imprudent choice of associates, which I should blame for the mortifications I now suffered from the desertion of companions, who were, in fact, incapable of being friends. In London I had lived with the most worthless, in Dublin with the best company; and in each place I had been treated as, in fact, I deserved. But, leaving the history of my feelings, I must proceed with my narrative.

One night, after I had dined with an Irish gentleman, a friend of Lord Y—'s, at the west end of the town, as I was returning late to my lodgings, I was stopped for some time by a crowd of carriages, in one of the fashionable streets. I found that there was a masquerade at the house of a lady, with whom I had been intimately acquainted. The clamours of the mob, eager to see the dresses of those who were alighting from their carriages, the gaudy and fantastic figures which I beheld by the light of the flambeaux, the noise and the bustle, put me in mind of various similar nights of my past life, and it seemed to me like a dream, or reminiscence of some former state of existence. I passed on as soon as the crowd would permit, and took my way down a narrow street, by which I hoped to get, by a shorter way than usual, to my quiet lodgings. The rattling of the carriages, the oaths of the footmen, and the shouts of the mob still sounded in my ears; and the masquerade figures had scarcely faded from my sight, when I saw, coming slowly out of a miserable entry, by the light of a few wretched candles and lanterns, a funeral. The contrast struck me: I stood still to make way for the coffin; and I heard one say to another, 'What matter how she's buried! I tell you, be at as little expence as possible, for he'll never pay a farthing.' I had a confused recollection of having heard the voice before: as one of the bearers lifted his lantern, I saw the face of the woman who spoke, and had a notion of having seen her before. I asked whose funeral it was; and I was answered, 'It is one Mrs Crawley's – Lady Glenthorn that was,' added the woman. I heard no more: I was so much shocked, that I believe I should have fallen in the street, if I had not been immediately supported by somebody near me. When I recovered my recollection, I saw the funeral had moved on some paces, and the person who supported me, I now found, was a clergyman. In a mild voice, he told me that his duty called him away from me at present, but he added, that if I would tell him where I could be found, he would see me in the morning, and give me any information in his power, as he supposed that I was interested for this unfortunate woman. I put a card with my address into his hands, thanked him, and got home as well as I could. In the morning, the clergyman called upon me – a most benevolent man, unknown to fame; but known to all the wretched within the reach of his consolatory religion. He gave me a melancholy account of the last days of the unhappy woman, whose funeral I had just seen. I told him who I was and what she had been to me. She had, almost in her last moments, as he assured me, expressed her sense of, what she called, my generosity to her, and had shown deep contrition for her infidelity. She died in extreme poverty and wretchedness, with no human being who was, or even seemed, interested for her, but a maid-servant (the woman whose voice I recollected), whose services were purchased to the last, by presents of whatever clothes or trinkets were left from the wreck of her mistress's fortune. Crawley, it seems, had behaved brutally to his victim. After having long delayed to perform his promise of marrying her, he declared that he could never think of a woman who had been divorced in any other way than a mistress: she, poor weak creature, consented to live with him on any terms; but, as his passions and his interest soon turned to new objects, he cast her off without scruple, refusing to pay any of the tradesmen, who had supplied her while she bore his name. He refused to pay the expences even of her funeral, though she had shared with him her annuity, and every thing she possessed. I paid the funeral expences, and some arrears of the maid's wages, together with such debts for necessaries as I had reason to believe were justly due: the strict economy with which I had lived for three years, and the parting with a watch and some other trinkets too fine for my circumstances, enabled me to pay this money without material inconvenience, and it was a satisfaction to my mind. The good clergyman who managed these little matters became interested for me, and our acquaintance with each other grew every day more intimate and agreeable. When he found that I was studying the law, he begged to introduce me to a brother of his, who had been one of the most eminent special pleaders[90] in London, and who now, on a high salary, undertook to prepare students for the bar. I was rather unwilling to accept of this introduction, because I was not rich enough to become a pupil of this gentleman's; but my clergyman guessed the cause of my reluctance, and told me that his brother had charged him to overrule all such objections. 'My brother and I,' continued he, 'though of different professions, have, in reality, but one mind between us; he has heard from me all the circumstances I know of you, and they have interested him so much, that he desires, in plain English, to be of any service he can to you.'

This offer was made in earnest; and if I had given him the largest salary that could have been offered by the most opulent of his pupils, I could not have met with more attention, or have been instructed with more zeal than I was, by my new friend the special pleader. He was also so kind as to put me at ease by the assurance that whenever I should begin to make money by my profession, he would accept of remuneration. He jestingly said, that he would make the same bargain with me that was made by the famous sophist Protagoras of old with his pupil, that he should have the profits of the first cause I should win – certain that I would not, like his treacherous pupil Evathlus, employ the rhetorician's arms against himself, to cheat him out of his promised reward.[91] My special pleader was not a mere man of forms and law *rigmaroles*; he knew the reason for the forms he used: he had not only a technical, but a rational knowledge of his business; and, what is still more uncommon, he knew how to teach what he had learnt. He did not merely set me down at a desk, and leave me skins after skins of parchment to pore over in bewildered and hopeless stupidity; he did not use me like a mere copying machine, to copy sheet after sheet for him, every morning from nine till four, and again every evening from five till ten. Mine was a law tutor of a superior sort. Wherever he could, he gave me a clue to guide me through the labyrinth; and when no reason could be devised for what the law directs, he never puzzled me by attempting to explain what could not be explained; he did not insist upon the total surrender of my rational faculties, but with wonderful liberality would allow me to call nonsense, nonsense; and would, after two or three hours' hard scrivening, as the case might require – for this I thank him more than all the rest – permit me to yawn, and stretch, and pity myself, and curse the useless repetitions of lawyers, sinking under the weight of *declarations*, and *replications*, and *double pleas*, and *dilatory pleas*;

> *Of horse pleas, traverses, demurrers,*
> *Jeofails, imparlances,* and *errors,*
> *Averments, bars,* and *protestandoes.*

O! Cecilia, what pains did I endure to win your applause! Yet, that I may state the whole truth, let me acknowledge, that even these, my dullest, hardest tasks, were light, compared with the burden I formerly bore of ennui. At length my period of probation in my pleader's office was over; I escaped from the dusky desk, and the smell of musty parchments, and the close smoky room; I finished *eating my terms* at the Temple, and returned, even, as the captain of the packet swore, 'in the face and teeth of the wind', to Dublin.

But, in my haste to return, I must not omit to notice, for the sake of poetical equity, that just when I was leaving England, I heard that slow, but sure-paced justice at last overtook that wretch Crawley. He was detected and convicted of embezzling considerable sums, the property of a gentleman in Cheshire, who had employed him as his agent. I saw him, as I passed through Chester, going to prison, amidst the execrations of the populace.

CHAPTER XXII

As I was not, as formerly, asleep in my carriage on deck, when we came within sight of the Irish shore, I saw, and hailed with delight, the beautiful Bay of Dublin. The moment we landed, instead of putting myself out of humour, as before, with every thing at the Marine Hotel, I went directly to my friend Lord Y—'s. I made my *sortie* from the hotel with so much extraordinary promptitude, that a slip-shod waiter was forced to pursue me, running or shuffling after me the whole length of the street, before he could overtake me with a letter, which had been 'waiting for my honour, at the hotel, since yesterday's Holyhead packet'. This was a mistake, as the letter had never come or gone by any Holyhead packet; it was only a letter from Mr M'Leod, to welcome me to Ireland again; and to tell me, that he had taken care to secure good well-aired lodgings for me: he added an account of what was going on at Glenthorn Castle. The extravagance of *my lady* had, by this time, reduced the family to great difficulties for ready money, as they could neither sell nor mortgage any part of the Glenthorn estate, which was settled on the son. My poor foster-brother had, it seems, in vain attempted to restrain the wasteful folly of his wife, and to persuade Johnny, the

young heir apparent, to *larn* to be a *jantleman*: in vain Christy tried
to prevail on his lordship to 'refrain drinking whisky *preferably* to
claret': the youth pleaded both his father's and mother's examples;
and said, that as he was an only son, and his father had but a life-
interest in the estate, he *expected* to be indulged; he repeated continually 'a short life and a merry one for me'. Mr M'Leod concluded
this letter by observing, 'that far from its being a merry life, he never
saw any thing more sad than the life this foolish boy led; and that
Glenthorn Castle was so melancholy and disgusting a scene of waste,
riot, and intemperance, that he could not bear to go there'. I was
grieved by this account, for the sake of my poor foster-brother; but it
would have made a deeper impression upon me at any other time. I
must own that I forgot the letter, and all that it contained, as I
knocked at Lord Y—'s door.

Lord Y— received me with open arms; and, with all the kindness
of friendship, anticipated the questions I longed, yet feared, to ask.

'Cecilia Delamere is still unmarried – Let these words be enough to
content you for the present; all the rest is, I hope, in your own power.'

In my power! – delightful thought! yet how distant that hope! For
I was now, after all my labours, but just called to the bar; not yet
likely, for years, to make a guinea, much less a fortune, by my
profession. Many of the greatest of our lawyers have gone circuit for
ten or twelve years, before they made a hundred a year; and I was
at this time four-and-thirty. I confessed to my Lord Y—, that these
reflections alarmed and depressed me exceedingly: but he encouraged me by this answer – 'Persevere – deserve success; and trust the
rest, not to fortune, but to your friends. It is not required of you to
make ten thousand or one thousand a year at the bar, in any given
time; but it is expected from you to give proofs that you are capable
of conquering the indolence of your disposition or of your former
habits. It is required from you to give proofs of intellectual energy
and ability. When you have convinced me that you have the knowledge and assiduity that ought to succeed at the bar, I shall be
certain that only time is wanting to your actual acquisition of a
fortune equal to what I ought to require for my fair friend and
relation. When it comes to that point, it will, my dear sir, be time
enough for me to say more. Till it comes to that point, I have
promised Mrs Delamere that you will not even attempt to see her
daughter. She blames me for having permitted Cecilia and you to

see so much of each other, as you did in this house when you were last in Ireland. Perhaps I was imprudent, but your conduct has saved me from my own reproaches, and I fear no other. I end where I began, with "Persevere – and may the success your perseverence deserves be your reward." If I recollect right, these were nearly Miss Delamere's own words at parting with you.'

In truth, I had not forgotten them; and I was so much excited by their repetition at this moment, and by my excellent friend's encouraging voice, that all difficulties, all dread of future labours or evils, vanished from my view. I went my first circuit, and made two guineas, and was content; for Lord Y— was not disappointed: he told me it would, it must be so. But though I made no money, I obtained gradually, amongst my associates at the bar, the reputation for judgement and knowledge. Of this they could judge by my conversation, and by the remarks on the trials brought on before us. The elder counsel had been prepared in my favour, first by Mr Devereux, and afterwards by my diligence in following their advice, during my studies in Dublin: they perceived that I had not lost my time in London, and that *my mind was in my possession*. They prophesied, that from the moment I began to be employed, I should rise rapidly. Opportunity, they told me, was now all that I wanted, and for that I must wait with patience. I waited with as much patience as I could. I had many friends; some among the judges, some among a more powerful class of men, the attorneys: some of these friends made for me by Mr Devereux and Lady Geraldine; some by Lord Y—; some, may I say it? by myself. Yet the utmost that even the highest patronage from the bench can do for a young barrister is, to give him an opportunity of distinguishing himself in preference to other competitors. This was all I hoped; and I was not deceived in this hope. It happened that a cause of considerable moment, which had come on in our circuit, and to the whole course of which I had attended with great care, was removed, by an appeal, to Dublin. I fortunately, I should say prudently, was in the habit of constant attendance at the courts: the counsel who was engaged to manage this cause was suddenly taken ill, and was disabled from proceeding. The judge called upon me: the attorneys, and the other counsel, were all agreed in wishing me to take up the business, for they knew I was prepared, and competent to the question. The next day the cause, which was then to be finally decided, came on. I sat up all night to look over my documents, and to make myself sure of my points. Ten years before this, if any one had prophesied this of me, how little could I have believed them!

The trial came on – I rose to speak. How fortunate it was for me, that I did not know my Lord Y— was in the court! I am persuaded that I could not have uttered three sentences, if he had caught my eye in the exordium of this my first harangue. Every man of sensibility – and no man without it can be an orator – every man of sensibility knows that it is more difficult to speak in the presence of one anxious friend, of whose judgement we have a high opinion, than before a thousand auditors who are indifferent, and are strangers to us. Not conscious who was listening to me, whose eyes were upon me, whose heart was beating for me, I spoke with confidence and fluency, for I spoke on a subject of which I had previously made myself completely master; and I was so full of the matter, that I thought not of the words. Perhaps this, and my having the right side of the question, were the causes of my success. I heard a buzz of thanks and applause round me. The decree was given in our favour. At this moment I recollected my bargain, and my debt to my good master the special pleader. But all bargains, all debts, all special pleaders, vanished the next instant from my mind; for the crowd opened, Lord Y— appeared before me, seized my hand, congratulated me actually with tears of joy, carried me away to his carriage, ordered the coachman to drive home – fast! fast!

'And now,' said he to me, 'I am satisfied. Your trial is over – successfully over, – you have convinced me of your powers and your perseverance. All the hopes of friendship are fulfilled: may all the hopes of love be accomplished! You have now my free and full approbation to address my ward and relation, Cecilia Delamere. You will have difficulties with her mother, perhaps; but none beyond what we good and great lawyers shall, I trust, be able to overrule. Mrs Delamere knows, that, as I have an unsettled estate, and but one son, I have it in my power to provide for her daughter as if she were my own. It has always been my intention to do so: but, if you marry Miss Delamere, you will still find it necessary to pursue your profession diligently, to maintain her in her own rank and style of life; and now that you have felt the pleasures of successful exertion, you will consider this necessity as an additional blessing. From what I have heard this day, there can be no doubt, that, by pursuing your profession, you can secure, in a few years, not only ease and competence, but affluence and honours – honours of your own earning. How far superior to any hereditary title!'

The carriage stopped at Lord Y—'s door. My friend presented me to Cecilia, whom I saw this day for the first time since my return to Ireland. From this hour I date the commencement of my life of real happiness. How unlike that life of *pleasure*, to which so many give erroneously the name of happiness! Lord Y—, with his powerful influence, supported my cause with Mrs Delamere, who was induced, though with an ill grace, to give up her opposition.

'Cecilia,' she said, 'was now three-and-twenty, an age to judge for herself; and Lord Y—'s judgement was a great point in favour of Mr O'Donoghoe, to be sure. And no doubt Mr O'Donoghoe might make a fortune, since he had made a figure already at the bar. In short, she could not oppose the wishes of Lord Y—, and the affections of her daughter, since they were so fixed. But, after all,' said Mrs Delamere, 'what a horrid thing it will be to hear my girl called Mrs O'Donoghoe! Only conceive the sound of – Mrs O'Donoghoe's carriage there! – Mrs O'Donoghoe's carriage stops the way!'

'Your objection, my dear madam,' replied Lord Y—, 'is fully as well founded as that of a young lady of my acquaintance, who could not prevail on her delicacy to become the wife of a merchant of the name of *Sheepshanks*. He very wisely, or very gallantly, paid five hundred pounds to change his name. I make no doubt that your future son-in-law will have no objection to take and bear the name and arms of Delamere; and I think I can answer for it, that a king's letter may be obtained, empowering him to do so. With this part of the business allow me to charge myself.'

I spare the reader the protracted journal of a lover's hopes and fears. Cecilia, convinced, by the exertions in which I had so long persevered, that my affection for her was not only sincere and ardent, but likely to be permanent, did not torture me by the vain delays of female coquetry. She believed, she said, that a man capable of conquering habitual indolence could not be of a feeble character; and she therefore consented, without hesitation, to intrust her happiness to my care.

I hope my readers have, by this time, too favourable an opinion of me to suspect, that, in my joy, I forgot him who had been my steady friend in adversity. I wrote to M'Leod, as soon as I knew my own happiness, and assured him that it would be incomplete without his sympathy. I do not think there was at our wedding a face of more sincere, though sober joy, than M'Leod's. Cecilia and I have been now married about a twelvemonth, and she permits me to say, that she has never, for a moment, repented her choice. That I have not relapsed into my former habits, the judicious and benevolent reader will hence infer: and yet I have been in a situation to be spoiled; for I scarcely know a wish of my heart that remains ungratified, except the wish that my friend Mr Devereux and Lady Geraldine should return from India, to see and partake of that happiness of which they first prepared the foundation. They first awakened my dormant intellects, made me know that I had a heart, and that I was capable of forming a character for myself. The loss of my estate continued the course of my education, forced me to exert my own powers, and to rely upon myself. My passion for the amiable and charming Cecilia was afterwards motive sufficient to urge me to persevering intellectual labour: fortunately my marriage has obliged me to continue my exertions, and the labours of my profession have made the pleasures of domestic life most delightful. The rich, says a philosophic moralist,[92] are obliged to labour, if they would be healthy or happy; and they call this labour exercise.

Whether, if I were again a rich man, I should have sufficient voluntary exertion to take a due portion of mental and bodily exercise, I dare not pretend to determine, nor do I wish to be put to the trial. Desiring nothing in life but the continuance of the blessings I possess, I may here conclude my memoirs, by assuring my readers, that after a full experience of most of what are called the pleasures of life, I would not accept of all the Glenthorn and Sherwood estates, to pass another year of such misery as I endured whilst I was 'stretched on the rack of a too easy chair'.[93]

The preceding memoirs were just ready for publication, when I received the following letter:

HONOURED FOSTER-BROTHER,

Since the day I parted yees, nothing in life but misfortins has happened me, owing to my being overruled by my wife, who would be a lady, all I could say again it. But that's over, and there's no help; for all and all that ever she can say will do no good. The castle's burnt down all to the ground, and my Johnny's dead, and I wish I was dead in his place. The occasion of his death was owing to drink, which he fell into from getting too much money, and nothing to do – and a snuff of a candle. When going to bed last night, a little in liquor, what does he do but takes the candle, and sticks it up against the head of his bed, as he used oftentimes to do, without detriment, in the cabin where he was reared, against the mud-wall. But this was close to an ould window curtain, and a deal of ould wood in the bed, which was all in a smother, and he lying asleep after drinking, when he was ever hard to wake, and before he waked at all, it appears the unfortunit *cratur* was smothered, and none heard a sentence of it, till the ceiling of my room, the blue bedchamber, with a piece of the big wood cornice, fell, and wakened me with terrible uproar, and all above and about me was flame and smoke, and I just took my wife on my back, and down the stairs with her, which did not give in till five minutes after, and she screeching, and all them relations she had screeching and running every one for themselves, and no thought in any to save any thing at all, but just what they could for themselves, and not a sarvant that was in his right rason. I got the ladder with a deal of difficulty, and up to Johnny's room, and there was a sight for me – he a corpse, and how even to get the corpse out of that, myself could not tell, for I was bewildered, and how they took me down, I don't well know. When I came to my sinses, I was lying on the ground in the court, and all confusion and screaming still, and the flames raging worse than ever. There's no use in describing all – the short of it is, there's nothing remaining of the castle but the stones; and it's little I'd think o'that, if I could have Johnny back – such as he used to be in my good days; since he's gone, I am no good. I write this to beg you, being married, of which I give you joy, to Miss Delamere, that is the *hare* at law, will take possession of all immediately, for I am as good as dead, and will give no hindrance. I will go back to my forge, and, by the help of God, forget at my work what has passed; and as to my wife, she may go to her own kith and kin, if she will not abide by me. I shall not trouble her long. Mr M'Leod is a good man, and will follow any directions you send; and may the blessing of God attind, and come to reign over us again, when you will find me, as heretofore,

Your loyal foster-brother,
CHRISTY DONOGHOE

Glenthorn Castle is now rebuilding; and when it is finished, and when I return thither, I will, if it should be desired by the public, give a faithful account of my feelings. I flatter myself that I shall not relapse into indolence; my understanding has been cultivated – I have acquired a taste for literature, and the example of Lord Y— convinces me, that a man may at once be rich and noble, and active and happy.

Written in 1804.
Printed in 1809.

APPENDIX

Review-article (anonymous) by R. L. and Maria Edgeworth of John Carr's
The Stranger in Ireland *(London: 1806)*, Edinburgh Review *10 (April 1807), 40–60.*

This little-known review-article by the Edgeworths begins and ends decorously, doing what a knowledgeable comprehensive review ought to do. It opens with a historical survey of the best accounts of Ireland by English strangers – Spenser, Davies and Young. A longer section at the end returns to the journalistic manner 'mainland' British readers are used to, that of an assumed impartiality, but its account of current social problems leaves no doubt that it is the work of an Irish resident with warm opinions. As one of relatively few sustained non-fictional treatments of contemporary Ireland by either of the Edgeworths outside the Tales, it has some interest in itself, and even more when read in conjunction with the fiction. It clarifies and reinforces the didactic side of the Tales, by itemizing the planks of the liberal Whig political platform for Ireland – mass education, better administration of justice, Catholic emancipation, religious equal rights, and an end to English commercial protectionism. It also throws into relief how policy is played down in the Tales or conveyed in another language, that of allegory. (See Introduction, pp. 33ff.)

The middle part directs itself to Carr's book, which the Edgeworths decry as under-researched, over-written and over-priced. Here, much less conventionally, they develop at length the conceit that Carr found a lot of his material in an earlier publication. The source they pretend he plagiarized is Robert Jephson's once-celebrated Dublin squib of 1771, the verse *Epistle to Gorges Edmond Howard*, which was accompanied by richly comic annotations spuriously attributed to a man described by Swift as the 'prince of Dublin printers', George Faulkner (1699–1775). The fake panegyric to Howard, a Dublin lawyer and alderman, is in the familiar Augustan tradition of the satire on literary dullness. But Jephson (1736–1803), the friend in 1760s London of Garrick, Johnson, Burke and Goldsmith, and subsequently a moderately successful playwright in both capitals, does more than merely repeat the Pope circle's imaginary pedant Martin Scriblerus. Jephson's footnotes transform the real-life publisher into a rich comic creation. A naive, prolix, self-advertising Faulkner appears to speak in his own voice, and at the same time to conjure up the packed, heterogeneous pages of his best-known product, the paper he owned, edited and largely wrote, the *Dublin Journal*.

To observe that Carr's pompous prose style and frequent blundering are reminiscent of the portrait of Faulkner is already offensive. To allege that the Englishman Carr steals from the Irishman Jephson, having misread his wit, is a much more complicated insult, and above all it is an Irish joke on the English. This section of the review is in effect coded for Irish readers, who to begin with would be more likely to remember and appreciate the squib's range of reference to Dublin life and personalities, and the memorable impression it gives of the chaotic columns of the *Dublin Journal*. The Edgeworths 'lift' the squib by giving it a co-author, Walter Hussey Burgh (1741–1783), Irish lawyer, parliamentary orator and a leading architect of the eighteen-year independence of the Dublin parliament. They also quote enough of the *Epistle to Howard* to show how intertwined London and Dublin print cultures were in the previous century – especially in those periods when literary wits intervened in the public sphere, such as the peak years of English literary opposition to Walpole, from 1736, when Faulkner briefly found himself in Newgate for publishing a political libel. Just as there is a learned strand in *Castle Rackrent*, to be picked up by readers who can identify Thady's quotation from the 2nd Duke of Ormond, so the review calls up the historical memory of the vitality and British significance of eighteenth-century Dublin culture between Swift's day and the coming of the Ascendancy.

As a lampoon, this part of the review anticipates two chapters of *Ennui*. When the tourist Lord Craiglethorpe visits Ormsby Villa (Ch.IX), Lady Geraldine adopts him as the butt of one of her practical jokes, feeding him with 'the stale jests and misinformation... the old stories of bulls and blunders' of which the review complains; she is his supplier, the part Jephson allegedly plays in the review. In Ch.XIII Glenthorn himself goes to the Giant's Causeway and Killarney, the high points of Ireland's tourist circuit. By the time he reaches Killarney his fatigue is such that he can only 'quote' his guidebook. The footnote in question (pp. 251–2) parodies Carr's overblown description of Killarney's celebrated stag-hunt, complete with its allusion to Jaques's weeping deer in *As You Like It* (II. i). The idea of the tourist overwhelmed by previous descriptions comes from a subjoined 'letter' sent from Killarney in the *Epistle to Howard* (p. 15, note t): to attempt to describe it would require the ablest pen of the ancient poets, or of modern poets, the famous painter of said lake, wherefore, I shall never attempt it.'

The Edgeworth review in 1807 and *Ennui* in 1809 both contribute to a literary *cause célèbre* with Carr's book at its centre. In 1807 Edward Dubois (1774–1850), English wit, editor and minor satirical novelist, published a pamphlet called *My Pocket-book, or Hints for 'A Right Merrie and Conceited Tour, in quarto; to be called, "The Stranger in Ireland", in 1805. By a Knight Errant'*. Carr retaliated with an action for libel against the publishers Vernor, Hood and Sharpe. The case was tried before Lord Ellenborough and a special jury at London's Guildhall (1 August 1808). Carr lost it, on grounds given by Ellenborough and upheld by the jury, that literary burlesque was fair comment. The defendants issued their shorthand version of the trial separately in 8vo and 12vo, respectively called *Libel!* and *Liberty of the Press!* (both 1808). But, though topical and interesting enough as a legal dispute touching on the freedom to comment, this English court-case ignored the aspect of Carr's book exercising Edgeworth throughout, its slur on the cultural standing of Ireland and Dublin. In *Ennui* Edgeworth uses Lady Geraldine, her Irish wit, to satirize Carr, who becomes the butt of the people he tries to patronize.

The Stranger in Ireland; or, a Tour in the Southern and Western Parts of that Country in the Year 1805. By John Carr, Esq. of the Honourable Society of the Middle Temple; Author of a Northern Summer, or Travels round the Baltic; the Stranger in France, &c. &c.

We were glad to see a tour through Ireland by Mr Carr; for though a hasty traveller, and an incorrect writer, we judged, from his former publications, that he had talents for observation, and for lively description. We expected that he would throw new lights upon the state of Ireland; that country, for which, as Lord Chesterfield said, 'God has done so much and man so little'. The union has certainly created a demand for a statistical, economical, moral and political view of Ireland, with a clear explanation of the causes which have, for nearly three centuries, impeded its progress in civilization; and a statement of such remedies as sound policy and practical humanity suggest for its improvement.

Spenser, who was secretary to one of the lord lieutenants in the reign of Elizabeth, and Sir John Davies, who was attorney-general and speaker of the House of Commons in Ireland in the reign of James the I, have left full and able accounts of the state of that country in their times. The Irish were then a nation of wandering shepherds, and feudal freebooters. The English *pale* extended but to a few counties immediately round Dublin; all without were excluded from the benefit of the English laws and protection. On the confines of the pale, and in the English *marches*, a continual warfare was carried on between the natives and the settlers; but in these petty contests there was little of that chivalrous spirit which distinguished our Scottish borderers. Neither in prose or verse could the history of these marauders be told with grace or dignity. Spenser, however, gives an entertaining account of their septs and clans, their Brehon laws, their *Boolies*, their *Cosheerings*, their *Stucas*, their long mantles, and their saffron-coloured linen. The methods which he proposed for the civilization of the Irish, were the abrogation of the Brehon, and the adoption of the English laws; the dispersing English soldiers and settlers over the country to overawe the rebellious, and to induce the well-disposed to imitate examples of better modes of life. He recommended also the establishing of garrisons and magazines for corn, and the building of villages, and country schools near every parish church for the instruction of the common people.

Sir John Davies, who wrote but a few years after Spenser died, gives a similar account of the country, but adds, in his '*Progress through the Wastes and wildest Parts of the Kingdom*', and in his History of the Settlement in Ulster, an interesting view of the efforts made to accelerate the progress of civilization, and the success with which these judicious attempts were attended. The right claimed by the soldiers, to take at will, from the peasantry, man's meat, and horse's meat, and even money; the *damnable* custom (as Sir John justly styles it) of coin and livery, a custom 'which, established in hell, as it was in Ireland, would have overturned the kingdom of Beelzebub', was abolished. The pernicious customs of tanistry and gavel-kind, by which the descent of property was rendered uncertain, and its sub-division an encouragement of idleness, were now broken through. The lands were set, and their descent established according to the actual English law. The Brehon laws were altogether abrogated, and something like a rational and equal administration of justice commenced. The number of judges of assize were increased, and they went regular circuits through the kingdom; 'whereas the cir-cuits, in former times, went but round about the pale, like the circle of the cynosura about the pole'. Trials by jury were instituted; but Sir John observes, that 'many of the poor people were very unwilling to be sworn of the juries, lest, if they condemned any man, his friends, in revenge, should rob, or burn, or kill them for it; the like mischief having happened to divers jurors since the last session holden there'.

Sir John Davies, who shows himself a true friend to Ireland, made efforts, in this *Progress*, to inquire into the state of the church lands and benefices; 'but my lords the bishops were not well pleased that laymen should intermeddle with these things, and did ever answer, Let us alone with that business. Take you no care of that.' The churches were miserably out of repair: such as were got up for presentation only thatched; and, says Sir John, 'the poor vicars that came to our camp were most ragged, ignorant creatures, not worthy the meanest of their livings, though those were many of them but of 40s. per annum'. The non-residence of the protestant bishops was much complained of; and a proverb is quoted, which was frequently in the mouth of one of the greatest of these prelates, 'That an Irish priest is no better than a milch cow.'

Davies, as well as the great Bacon, had sagacity enough to predict, that unless measures of liberal policy were adopted for the govern-ment of the country, 'Ireland *civil* would become more dangerous than Ireland *savage*'. What Davies could, he did; and what he could not effect, he suggested. He obtained amnesties for the offences of the rebels who returned to their allegiance; remission of old debts and quit-rents due to the crown: he obliterated, as far as possible, the remembrance of antient feuds and party distinctions; restrained the excesses of the soldiery; and, besides establishing a regular administration of justice, did his utmost to obtain some education for the poor of the country.

Of the progress of civilization in Ireland after this time, and of the steps by which it was retarded or advanced, we have no distinct view. There have, indeed, appeared voluminous pamphlets, professing to treat of the state of the country; but these relate chiefly to party questions. Arthur Young's Tour has been much and deservedly applauded as a faithful and lively picture of that kingdom when he saw it; but that was nearly thirty years ago. Much remains to be learned; and we therefore opened with eagerness a new tour through Ireland, which we hoped would represent to us Ireland as it was, and as it is. But, alas! we were miserably disappointed. We found Mr Carr's quarto, a book of stale jests, and fulsome compliments. All the old stories of bulls and blunders, which, as we are informed, have for years past been regularly brought forward for the recreation of every new lord-lieutenant and his secretary, are here collected for the edification of the public. The Stranger in Ireland was, it seems, upon his arrival, bountifully supplied, by the hospitable Hibernians, with all the *good things* in which that convivial nation abounds. With a little more taste and judgement, he might have arranged these so as to afford agreeable entertainment to his readers; but, to save himself the trouble of thought or arrangement, he has emptied and overwhelmed us with his common-place book. For one beauty this work is indeed eminently distinguished, – for the beauty of contrast; that species of contrast, which results from want of order, where grave and gay, just and absurd, fine and vulgar, sublime and ludicrous, succeed each other, so as to create in the highest degree the pleasure of *unexpectedness*. This pleasure, indeed, gradually abates as we proceed; for we are at length taught to expect the recurrence of these strange figures, which come round and round again like the pictures in a Savoyard's magic-lantern; whilst the same tone of a show-man, kept up incessantly, must at last weary the most enduring ear. Let no impatient reader of this volume resort to the index in hopes of skipping with celerity and advantage. The table of contents will rather mislead than direct; it will entice him on, and leave him disappointed and provoked. The knack of giving *good* heads to chapters has been carried to a high and treacherous state of perfection.

We are often cheated into reading a stupid chapter, as we are entrapped in the newspapers by the beginning of some paragraph, apparently about Newton or Buffon, – about some new discovery in optics, or natural history, which proves in the end nothing more than a lottery advertisement. Our Author's table of contents may be most inviting to the large tribe of anecdote-mongers and desultory readers; but surely, numerous as they are, their taste should not have been exclusively consulted, to the utter neglect of the interests of purchasers, who set some little value upon their money or their time.

Besides being disappointed in the solid contents, we were disgusted with the manner of this book. It is worse written than any of Mr Carr's former tours. The style is both careless and affected, trivial and inflated; his fine sentences are sometimes without meaning, and often without grammar; and his high-flown descriptions, which are neither prose nor poetry, frequently terminate in striking instances of the bathos. For example, take the following account of his arrival at Killarney.

'The evening, shrouded in black clouds charged with rain, rapidly set in; the wind roared; and only the light-blue smoke of the cabin relieved the universally deep embrowned sterility of the scene. *In these and most other districts the milk of sheep is used.*'

His description of Mucross-Abbey is not inferior.

'The graceful ruins of Mucross-Abbey on our right, half embosomed in a group of luxuriant and stately trees, *influenced, as soon as seen, the bridles of our horses.*'

It is a pity that our tourist, before he began to describe Killarney, had not attended to the monition of a celebrated author, who thus writeth:

'I have at length seen what I have long wished to see, – this wondrous lake! To attempt to describe it, would require the ablest of the antient poets, or of modern poets; wherefore I shall never attempt it.'*

Though we regret, that Mr Carr did not attend to this dissuasive paragraph, yet we do not accuse him of being ignorant of the merits

* The Epistle to Gorges Edmond Howard, Esq., with notes by George Falkener, Esq., was the production of Hussey Burgh Jephson, and some other wits, during the administration of Lord Townsend in Ireland.

of the performance in which it is contained; for his style frequently reminds us of the manner of the author to whom it is attributed, – the celebrated George Falkener. In his peculiar use of pronouns, in his heterogeneous anecdotes, and in his mode of dragging into a sentence a multitude of words and ideas foreign to the principal purpose, Mr Carr is not inferior to this great original; the resemblance of style is indeed so striking, that we should almost suspect him of studied imitation. We shall select a few parallel passages.

Mr Carr says,

'I cannot help gratifying my readers in this stage of our tour with the result of an active and anxious inquiry, which I made of the existence of a custom in some parts of Ireland, equally cruel and impolitic, &c. It is with real pleasure that I have it in my power, upon the authority of several gentlemen of great respectability residing in various parts of Ireland, to state, that at this day *the custom of ploughing and harrowing by the horse's tail* does not exist. Long since, it shocked the humanity and excited the interference of the legislature; for I find that, in the year 1634, when Lord Strafford was lord-deputy, an act was passed against this cruel usage.'

Mr Falkener said before him,

'The Irish formerly *ploughed by the tail with bullocks*. But upon Dr Swift's voyage to the Houynhams being published, and his saying so much in praise of horses, this barbarous, horrid, atrocious, shocking, detestable, cruel, nefarious custom, was abolished by act of Parliament. See an abridgment of the Irish *Statues*, sold by me in Parliament Street.'

Carr

informs us, 'that *Ceres* bears a strong affinity to the Irish word *Cuirim*, or *Cairim*, to sow or plant; and that *Treabtalamb*, a plougher of the earth, is not unlike *Triptolemus*.'

Falkener,

more modest than Carr in his pretensions, claims only the improvement of the plough for the Irish.

'Ploughs are an instrument for turning up the earth, first invented by Triptolemus, a near relation of the goddess *Ceres*, and afterwards much improved by Mr John Wynne, baker, of the Dublin Society.'

Again, our authors have a coincidence of thought and expression on the happy subject of bulls.

CARR

'An Irishman and a bull form a twin thought in an Englishman's mind; long and inveterate prejudices have made them as inseparable in reflection as a bull and his horns. I went to France in the full persuasion of seeing a race of lean men, and found them of the ordinary size and stature; and many of them of a bulk and vigour that an untravelled Englishman would reluctantly give credit to. I went to Ireland, expecting a bull to fly out of every Irishman's mouth every third time he spoke. That the lower classes make bulls, I believe, because I have been well informed that they do, and because the lower classes of other countries make them also.'

George Falkener, who was as tender upon the subject of blundering, and as zealous for the honour of the Irish as Mr Carr seems to be, volunteered in their defence; and, as Mr Carr jumbles together the French and Irish in his vindication, Mr Falkener, with equal propriety, drags the Germans and Irish into the same exculpatory paragraph.

'The Germans are, in general, supposed to be a proud people. Julius Caesar and Mr Nugent give them this character; but the Irish are very unjustly charged with a talent of blundering; but it is well known that the people express themselves in their native tongue, the English, with more perspicuity and precision. The Dean of St Patrick was of this opinion, who, though born and bred in England, always declared himself, when sober, to be an Irishman.'

At Cork we expected some good jokes; because Mr Falkener, to whose authority we may refer with implicit confidence, informs us, that Attica was called the Cork of Greece. Accordingly, we find that our traveller's taste for wit improved as he approached Cork. As he was going up a hill, having humanely helped a carrier to reload his car, the witty native thanked him in the following attic manner.

'Ah, may your Honour live long, very long!'

The brilliancy of this repartee is to be equalled only by the Kerry postilion's wit, thus recorded page 175.

'Your Honour' – said our driver, upon our observing that one of his horses plunged – 'that mare is always very *unasy* in going down hill.'

From these bon-mots, and from the various anecdotes of King Donahue – Lord Castlereagh and his young friend Sturrock – the immaculate St Bridget – Carrolan and Miss Bridget Cruise – that celebrated antiquarian Mr Grose and the butcher – Lord Avonmore and the calf – from these and a thousand more,

'Ah, dread the thousand still unnamed behind!'

we are convinced that Mr Carr has the same indefatigable taste for collecting anecdotes of celebrated characters, for which Mr Falkener was distinguished. [. . .]

Mr Carr is not merely the eulogist of wits and poets: every man he meets is well-bred, witty, eloquent, generous, admired, or at least well-known; every lady, of course, is fair and elegant, accomplished, amiable, graceful, enchanting, perfectly well informed or distinguished for talents. He is the most courteous, and the most fortunate of travellers; he wins his easy way from house to house, and leaves, at every hospitable mansion, according to the custom of ancient Irish bards, a *planxty*, celebrating the virtues, charms, or high descent of the hostess. Far be it from us to censure the generous overflowings of gratitude: but we must own, that our author has, on some occasions, startled our Scottish notions of economy, by the profuseness of his remuneration for trifling civilities .[. . .]

It is but justice to Mr Carr to display some of his best anecdotes, which we shall do, without prejudicing the reader against them by exaggerated epithets of praise.

Page 41 – 'The dress of the beggars in Dublin is deplorably filthy, and induced a wit to say, that he never knew what the beggars in London did with their cast clothes, till he found that they were sold to the Dublin beggars.'

Page 84 – 'It was upon the steps of this place (the General Post Office in Dublin) that Curran and Lord — were standing, when the latter, who had voted for the Union, as he looked towards the late Parliament-House, which was then in a forlorn state of mutilation, observed – "How shocking our old Parliament-House looks, Curran!" To which the witty barrister finely replied – "True, my Lord, it is usual for murderers to be afraid of ghosts."' [. . .]

We extract the following passages, not only as favourable specimens of the author's manner, but as just representations of the Irish, and as slight circumstances from which the politician and philosopher may draw some important conclusions.

'The next morning I attended the quarter-sessions (at Killarney) at which a barrister presided. At this meeting, the character of the people was strikingly developed. The greatest good humour prevailed in the court, which was a large, naked room, with a quantity of turf piled up in one corner of it. Every face looked animated; scarcely any decorum was kept; but justice was expeditiously, and I believe substantially, administered by the barrister, who is addressed by that name, and who appeared to be perfectly competent to the discharge of his judicial duties. He was elevated above the rest. A fellow, like every one of his countrymen in or out of court, loving law in his soul, projected himself too forward to hear a cause which was proceeding: the officer of the court, who, like the bell in Peeping Tom of Coventry, made a horrible noise by endeavouring to keep silence, struck this anxious unlucky wight a blow on the head with a long pole, almost sufficiently forcible to have felled an ox: the fellow rubbed his head: all the assembly broke out in a loud laugh, in which the object of their mirth could not resist joining. Instead of counsel, solicitors pleaded: one of them was examining a rustic, a witness on behalf of his client when I entered: the poor fellow suffered answers, unfavourable to the party for whom he appeared, to escape him; upon which, after half a dozen imprecations, the solicitor threw the testament on which he had been sworn at his head; a second laugh followed: another fellow swore backwards and forwards ten times in as many minutes; and whenever he was detected in the most abominable perjury, the auditory was thrown into convulsions of merriment.' [. . .]

We perfectly agree with our author in the opinion, that some reform is much wanted in this mode of administering justice in Ireland. He was fortunate in seeing assistant barristers, who did honour to the choice of government, by maintaining *some* decorum in their courts. But the integrity or abilities of those individuals to whom power is delegated, cannot, in the judgement of a good legislator, be any excuse for the imprudence, or any compensation for the hazard, of entrusting it to them without proper restrictions .[. . .]

[. . .] we have been assured that assistant barristers in Ireland are permitted to plead as counsel at assizes, in the very counties where they preside at sessions. Does it never happen, that he who has been judge at the sessions, becomes an advocate at the assizes in the same cause? Have opulent or powerful clients no influence in such delicate situations? Do party prejudices and electioneering politics produce no bias? It would be easy to obviate all suspicion, by making it a rule, that assistant barristers should never be appointed to act in the counties where their own property lies, and that they should never plead as lawyers in the counties where they act as judges at sessions. Any increase of salary which may be necessary to remunerate these gentlemen for these privations, will be money well bestowed, as it will materially improve the administration of this branch of justice in Ireland.

Mr Carr rises above himself, when inspired with eloquence by virtuous indignation at the sight of the horrible state of the House of Industry in Limerick. He speaks of it as an eye-witness; we cannot therefore doubt the facts. They are a disgrace to that city. The manner in which they are now described by a popular writer will probably promote the correction of these abuses. If this prophecy should prove true, we shall rejoice that Mr Carr has written this quarto: and, from the benevolence apparent in all this gentleman's writings, we are convinced, that the consciousness of having obtained a material benefit for his fellow-creatures would amply repay him for all the pains and penalties of authorship.

The account of the Dublin House of Industry confirms us in an opinion, which we have long entertained, and which cannot be more concisely expressed than in the words of our judicious countryman Dr Gray,* 'Fields of industry are better than houses of industry.' What avail houses of industry, and orphan houses, and parish schools, to mend the morals of the people of Dublin, when in one street alone there are fifty-two houses licensed to sell spirits! 'That a revenue derived from such a source should be an object worthy of encouragement, it is impossible to believe,' says Mr Carr. 'It might as well impose a tax upon coffins, and inoculate all its subjects with the plague.'

The chief part of the information in Mr Carr's book, is comprised in the last chapter, entitled, 'General Remarks'. Amongst other serious topics, he there adverts to the state of education in Ireland. Upon this subject he speaks liberally, though in rather too high-flown language.

* Essential Principles of the Wealth of Nations illustrated, &c.

'Education,' says he, 'has never beamed on the poor Irish man; sentiments of honour have never been instilled into him; and a spirit of just and social pride, improvement and enterprise, have never opened upon him. The poor Irishman looks around him, and sees a frightful void between him and those who, in well-regulated communities, ought to be separated from each other only by those gentle shades of colouring that unite the brown russet to the imperial purple. He has no more power of raising himself, than an eagle whose wings have been half shorn of their plumage. The legislature has rarely noticed him but in anger, – when that ignorance, which it has never stooped to remove, has precipitated him into acts incompatible with social tranquillity, and repugnant to his nature.'

We learn with great satisfaction, that since the above was written, a Board of Education has been appointed in Ireland, composed of men of character, talents, rank, fortune and popularity. From their united efforts, their country has much to expect. They are to inquire into the state of the schools in Ireland; and we hope that they will endeavour to establish a good system of instruction for the lower classes of the people. By instruction, we do not mean merely reading, writing, and arithmetic; in these, if we have not been misinformed, the lower Irish are sufficiently well taught, even in their *hedge-schools* (which, by the by, might with more propriety be called *ditch*-schools). In arithmetic, especially, the boys are said to be wonderfully expert. We are told that, in a great public charity in Dublin; and in parts of Armagh, writing and arithmetic have been long since taught by Mr Lancaster's method. The Irish learn, whatever they wish to learn, quickly, and with the greatest facility. But it is in moral instruction that they are deficient, and to raise a demand for this, and to administer it properly, are the great difficulties. It will be no easy task to breed up children to have totally different habits and principles from their parents, without destroying that filial and parental affection, which is the great bond of society, and without which no national education can be fundamentally good or permanent. It will be no easy task to change the associations of pleasure, pride and mirth, which the Irish children early form with the ideas of cheating, stealing, prevaricating and lying. To convince their understandings that honesty is the best policy, and that their duty to God and their neighbour is likewise their duty to themselves, might be easily accomplished; but the moral demonstration would have no more effect on their conduct, than any of the demonstrations of the missionaries at Otaheite, unless their associations and habits were changed by some strong or constant motives.

To substitute the sturdy pride of plain-dealing, for the delight of successful cunning, must be a work of time, especially where the people are, from their poverty and *subordinate* situation, continually tempted to deceive; and where party-politics and religious prejudices incline a vast proportion of the population to consider the remainder as fair game for flattery and deception. We agree with Mr Carr in the manly opinion which he has well expressed, that

'Nothing but a frank and liberal system of education, which shall be wholly free from the *suspicion* of aiming at religious conversion directly or indirectly, can promote the great object of enlightening the poorer classes of society in Ireland.'

All our author says about *proselytism* is excellent; we consider it as by far the most valuable part of the book; and from 'a stranger in Ireland', we hope that it will not shock any individuals but that it may produce its just effect upon the good sense of all parties. Mr Carr pays a tribute, and, as we are assured, a well-merited tribute of approbation to the ladies of Ireland, for their benevolent indefatigable exertions to improve the education of the poor children in their country. He mentions several well-conducted schools under the patronage, and, what is much better than the patronage, under the daily superintendance, of ladies in every respect qualified for the task. From these schools we may reasonably hope salutary and immediate effects. From a board of education we can expect only well-digested plans, which, if steadily pursued, may in time produce a general change in the habits of the people. We hope that it will not be thought to arise from national partiality, if we advert to the state of education in our own country, and if we say that Ireland may look with advantage to North Britain, for an example of the success which rewards the labour and expense bestowed on national instruction.

Our author writes judiciously against *eleemosynary* education. He justly observes, that it would be better to accept of sixpence per annum as payment, than to offer instruction gratis: in all countries, and particularly in Ireland, the pride of parents and children would revolt from the idea of suing for education *in forma pauperis*. This is an honest pride, for which nothing half so good can be substituted by charity or ostentation. We hope, as Mr Carr does, that the poor laws and poor rates of England may never be introduced into Ireland.

Page 519 – Mr Carr has fallen into one of those common prejudices, which usually ensnare the hunter after popular discontents. He inveighs bitterly against a race of farmers, who have obtained the name of Middlemen, from their holding an interest in lands between the proprietor and the terre-tenant. Every tyro in political economy, who has read Smith's Wealth of Nations, should know the utility of factors in all mercantile transactions. And in what does a middleman differ from a factor? He collects the value of the produce, and pays it to a land merchant at home, or exports it to a land merchant abroad. A nobleman or gentleman, who lets land for one, or for several years, does nothing more than sell raw materials to a manufacturer; and the middleman is a merchant or factor, who buys the raw material wholesale, and retails it to the workman. When this process is omitted, the landlord is obliged to employ deputies or agents, who are not connected with the under tenant by any common tie of interest .[. . .] the agent is a greater oppressor than the middleman. Where middlemen are interposed, the profit made by the agent falls to their share. It is true, that they let the lands at the highest price; but they must bear the loss, if the tenant fails; and knowing this, they are interested in every loss or gain that happens to their subtenant. The middleman is, like the doctor, desirous of gain; but it is never his interest to destroy the patient. Wherever large capital is deficient, the system of middlemen *must* prevail. In the time of Jack Cade's rebellion, the same complaint against monopolizers of lands was the watch-word of his adherents; and so late as the reign of Elizabeth, there was a similar cry in England against engrossing farms. But till capital has been collected by numbers, numbers cannot enter into competition for farms: the large capitalists alone can stock them; and the under tenants must be dependent upon such farmers for the small portions of land, which, in Ireland, supply them with the means of existence. Our author despatches, in two sentences, that great question in political economy, what is the best food for the poor? We shall here only put in our caveat against the peremptory manner in which it is decided. Whoever has seriously considered the subject, and has read what has been written by Malthus on population, and by Selkirk on emigration, will not lightly hazard a decision. The Irishman's reply to Mr Carr's inquiry into the cause of the great population of Ireland, deserves a serious investigation. 'By Jasus, Sir, it's all the potato.'

Either we are misinformed, or Mr Carr is strangely mistaken with regard to the average price of labour in Ireland, which he states at 18d. per day. This appeared such an extraordinary assertion, that we were at the trouble of looking over the whole book to verify our reference, which at last we found (page 505). In our search, we discovered the cause of his mistake. He had learned (page 419), that the price of labour, *near Cork*, is 16d. or 18d., which is certainly not a high rate in the neighbourhood of the second city in Ireland: but to call this the average price of labour through the kingdom is a gross error. Such careless assertions we deem most unpardonable blunders; because they mislead all who attempt to reason upon such false *data*. For instance, how could Malthus himself reconcile the wretchedness of superabundant population with such high wages of labour, and such low price of provisions, as Mr Carr has stated? We are well assured, that the average wages of labour in Ireland do not amount to half the sum which he has mentioned. Those who make a tour through a country, see objects in a new, and often in a more entertaining point of view, than persons whose long residence in the country have rendered most objects familiar; but, on certain points, we can hope to obtain accurate information from those only who have lived in the country, and who, in their political and economical observations, have taken time into the account.

Mr Carr has, with much address, evaded the discussion of many questions on which parties run high in Ireland; by this policy he probably hopes to be favourably judged by both sides. But it should not be the prime object of a man of talents to steal into popularity: his pride should be, to stand forward in the cause of truth, to do his utmost to serve his fellow-creatures, disdaining the clamours of ignorance and prejudice, secure of his reward from the good and wise; or, if disappointed of this honest fame, able to rest satisfied with his own approbation. There is a fashion amongst many well-meaning timid persons, of avoiding to speak upon what are called *dangerous* subjects; as if the danger were created by inquiring into the means of defence; or as if it could be dissipated by pretending that it does not exist. Talk of danger, and it will appear, – seems to be the maxim of this childish superstition.

Every body knows, that there have been insurrections and rebellions in Ireland: that, in 1796, nothing but the dispersion of the French fleet by a storm saved that kingdom from conquest: that, in 1798, the plot by which the city of Dublin was to have been *revolutionized*, was not discovered or counteracted, till a few hours before the moment appointed for its execution: that, in the same year, an inconsiderable French force effected an invasion of Ireland, were joined by numbers of the natives, and penetrated to the centre of the island: that, in 1803, a nobleman, high in office, and of most respectable character, was assassinated in the metropolis; and that, by this premature murder, in which the rabble indulged themselves contrary to the wishes and orders of their leaders, the plan of another insurrection was disconcerted.

But these are things of which the timid will not speak, and of which the foolhardy will not think. The rash do yet more mischief in politics than the timorous; they will not suffer you to believe that danger ever exists, notwithstanding the most alarming symptoms; and they consider it as a proof of want of courage, or want of loyalty, to suspect, that things which have been so lately, may recur.

'Ireland' say they, 'is now perfectly quiet; and it is ridiculous and wicked to suppose, that it will ever again be in a state of disturbance. There have been Thrashers, to be sure, within these few months in that kingdom; but these were honest, poor, ignorant fellows, who had no bad designs: they collected in large bodies, to be sure, went about at night armed, to administer unlawful oaths; but the Thrashers' oath was merely not to pay tithes to proctors, and to obey Captain Thrasher; but nobody knew who this captain was, so that the oath was of no consequence. And those who refused to take it, were only dragged out of their beds and ducked; or delivered over to Captain Carder, to have their backs *carded* (that is, flayed with a steel instrument used in dressing flax).

> 'But all this was done with jollity,
> Midnight shouts and revelry.'

'And these political maskers were all in fancy dresses; white caps on their heads, and white shirts over their clothes; some over uniforms, it is said; – but no harm was done. Besides, their cause was so popular, that most of the middling farmers favoured them, and many of the thinking men approved of the end, and objected only to the means. Now, however, the whole affair is settled by special commission; the poor wretches, who have been tried and condemned, have suffered, and are a sufficient warning to the rest; *though* they have been generally pitied, because it was obvious that they were merely tools in the hands of others, and actually did not know what they were about. At all events, the country is now perfectly quiet; and we may all sleep in peace.'

Yes! – sleep in peace, like the rash fools who sleep at the foot of Mount Vesuvius – secure, because, say they, there has been lately an eruption of the mountain, and, may be, there will not be another in our times.

It is in vain to palter and palliate. Ireland never will be perfectly safe, till the causes of discontent among the great body of the people are removed. Complete *Catholic emancipation*, as it is called, should be granted to them; nothing less will do. As to the right, the arguments in favour of the abolition of the slave-trade are not more clear, than those in favour of the Catholic emancipation. But as to the expediency, – it is alleged, if we grant the Catholics this, they will ask more. *Then* it will be time to refuse; but the surmise that people will encroach, is no argument against granting them their rights. Expediency can never permanently stand against justice. And after all this, expediency exists merely in imagination. Popery is a mere bugbear. The fear of a Catholic interest in a British parliament is absurd. The Catholic gentry in Ireland, of property sufficient to become members of the senate, are few, compared with the Protestants; and, what is of more consequence, their interests are the same as those of the Protestants. Their property is subject to the same danger from invasion or insurrection. The old claims to forfeited Irish estates could never be substantiated, without despoiling the present opulent Catholics. Property against numbers, is a contest decidedly in favour of property, as long as the possessors of property manage their advantages with prudence: but oppression makes the danger which it fears.

The Irish Catholics, *upon their taking the oaths of allegiance and Supremacy*, should, in their political right, be put exactly on a footing with all the other subjects of the empire; and should be relieved from the burthen of tithes paid to ministers from whom they receive no instruction. Might not their priests, too, be paid by government? They would then be properly dependent. The late grant to the

College of Maynooth, for the education of Catholics, is liberal and prudent. It is to be hoped, however, that that college is subject to frequent visitations. We should know what books are put into the hands of the students; not with a view of interfering in the least with religious tenets, but to secure some pledge that the youth are properly educated. In all other colleges the *course* is universally known. With these precautions, and with this just toleration, all the lower classes of the Catholic religion in Ireland would be safe, and good subjects; not only when English troops are in the country, but in all circumstances. In case of an invasion, it would not be their interest to join the enemy. It is a common Irish proverb, that 'those who are upon the ground can go no lower'. Raise them, and their fear of falling begins to operate. In most countries, the lowest class of the people is in the situation of the ass in the fable, caring not who is master, since he must always carry his paniers; but the ass ceases to be in this, his usual state of neutrality, if his paniers be too heavily laden, and if he have hopes that his new master will lighten his burthen.

Independently of all that can be done by the Legislature, much may be effected towards making the different classes of people in Ireland coalesce, by the good sense of individuals, in their daily conversation and intercourse with each other. All signs of party hatred should be suppressed; all party words forborn. The appellations of orangemen and *croppies* should never be heard: *Protestant ascendancy* should never be talked of; nor should the term *an honest man* be used exclusively to designate a Protestant. If this liberal policy were universally adopted, Ireland would indeed be perfectly quiet and secure. And it would become, not only a secure, but a flourishing part of the British empire, if commercial as well as religious jealousies could cease. This is another subject, which a writer, publishing a quarto on Ireland, should have discussed. The discussion would lead us far beyond our limits, which we have already transgressed: but we cannot avoid observing, in general, that it is a farce to talk of an incorporating union having taken place between two countries, whilst the frontiers of each are guarded by a host of customhouse officers; whilst the inhabitants cannot pass or repass from either country, without undergoing a search as rigorous as if they were in an enemy's territory; whilst the duties and drawbacks of excise operate as checks upon the transfer of property, and even upon locomotion.

NOTES

Introduction

1. Marilyn Butler, *Maria Edgeworth: A Literary Biography* (Oxford: Clarendon Press, 1972), p. 359. (Henceforward, Butler.)
2. Étienne Dumont to M.E., 1 November 1813; University College London, MS. Bentham 174/24.
3. [F. Jeffrey], *Edinburgh Review* XIV (July 1809), 383.
4. Sydney Smith to Lady Holland, 20 January 1814 (*Letters of Sydney Smith*, ed. N. C. Smith (Oxford: O.U.P., 1953), I, p. 244).
5. Walter Scott, 'Postscript, which should have been a Preface' to *Waverley* (Edinburgh: Adam & Charles Black, 1877), II, p. 420.
6. J. G. Lockhart, *Life of Scott*, Ch. 82; quoted from the 'family journal' of Mrs John Davy, recording her drive with Scott in Malta in December 1831.
7. Edgeworth to Mrs Stark, 6 September 1834; quoted in Butler, pp. 240–41.
8. For the tendency to equate *Castle Rackrent* with John Langan's voice, innocently reported, see Emily Lawless, *Maria Edgeworth* (1904), p. 92; Butler, especially pp. 357–60; and Roger McHugh and Maurice Harmon, *A Short History of Anglo-Irish Literature* (Dublin, 1982), p. 87: 'The spontaneity of the narrative and the authenticity of Thady and of all the family anecdotes on which his history is based are thus explicable.' For a critique of the practice, see Iain Topliss, 'The Novels of Maria Edgeworth: Enlightenment and Tutelage', Ph.D. thesis, University of Cambridge (1985), pp. 182 ff.
9. Francis Beaufort, in conversation with Joseph Farington, March 1817 (*Farington Diary*, ed. J. Greig (1928), viii, p. 217). See Butler, pp. 353ff., and George Watson's Introduction to his edition of *Castle Rackrent*, Oxford English Novels (Oxford: O.U.P., 1964), for details concerning the evolution of *Castle Rackrent*.
10. J. F. Marmontel, 'Éléments de Littérature', *Œuvres Complètes*, 18 vols. (Paris, 1818), XII, pp. 524–5. See Topliss's good discussion (note 8 above), pp. 182–6.
11. Ibid., pp. 522–3.
12. Ibid., p. 523.
13. Nancy Armstrong, *Desire and Domestic Fiction* (Oxford: O.U.P., 1987), p. 65.
14. '*Castle Rackrent* can be read as an analysis of the peasant threat, transposed from the level of overt violence from outside, to that of the covert erosion from within of a moribund and corrupt landlordism.' Tom Dunne, 'Maria Edgeworth and the Colonial Mind', O'Donnell Lecture (Dublin: National University of Ireland, 1985), p. 7.
15. P. F. Sheeran, 'Some Aspects of Anglo-Irish Literature from Swift to Joyce', *Yearbook of English Studies* 13 (1983), 102.

16. Dunne, op. cit., p. 8.
17. *Ormond*, (1817) Ch. 3; II. 66 *Castle Rackrent*, p. 73n.
18. See *Castle Rackrent*, p. 110, and Topliss, op. cit., pp. 194–5.
19. Marianne Elliott, *Partners in Revolution: the United Irishmen and France* (New Haven: Yale U.P., 1982), pp. 6–7.
20. See Note on the Text, n.3.
21. Francis Edgeworth (1657–1709), nicknamed Protestant Frank, raised a regiment in 1689 in support of King William, and the following year briefly served in the Horse Guards in Flanders under the Duke of Ormond. Thereafter Ormond remained his patron and became godfather to his youngest son. Frank, his disreputable brothers and his father Sir John, who was a gambler and a spendthrift, are the Edgeworth ancestors closest in character and experience to the Rackrent dynasty, according to a family memoir composed in the mid eighteenth century by Edgeworth's grandfather, Richard Edgeworth. See H. E. and H. J. Butler, *The Black Book of Edgeworthstown and Other Edgeworth Memories, 1585–1817* (London: Faber & Gwyer, 1927), pp. 17–52.
22. Denis Donoghue, 'Being Irish Together', *Sewanee Review* 84 (Winter 1976), 133, and W. J. McCormack, *Ascendancy and Tradition in Irish Literary History, 1793–1939* (Oxford: Clarendon Press, 1985), p. 5.
23. P. F. Sheeran, op. cit., p. 100, developing the arguments of A. Memmi, *The Coloniser and the Colonised* (London, 1974), p. ix.
24. P. B. Shelley, *Laon and Cythna*, Canto II, xliii; and Grattan, quoted in Steven Watson, *The Reign of George III* (Oxford: Clarendon Press, 1960), p. 392.
25. For modern commentary on the figuring of gossip in the domestic novel, see Patricia Meyer Spacks, *Gossip* (Chicago: Chicago U.P., 1985), and M. Butler, Introduction to *Emma* by Jane Austen (London: Everyman Library, 1991).
26. See John Horne Tooke, *Diversions of Purley*, 2 vols. (1786, 1805); Hans Aarsleff, *The Study of Language in England, 1780–1860* (Princeton, 1967); John Barrell, 'The Language Properly So Called', in *English Literature in History, 1730–80* (London: Hutchinson, 1983); Olivia Smith, *The Politics of Language* (Oxford: O.U.P., 1984). Cf. *Castle Rackrent*, Glossary-note, p. 123 and n. 46.
27. W. Wordsworth to John Wilson, 7 June 1802, *Letters of William and Dorothy Wordsworth* I, ed. Shaver (Oxford: O.U.P., 1967), pp. 354–5.
28. M.E. to Fanny Robinson, n.d., 1782; quoted Butler, p. 91.
29. Edgeworth uses the Conclusion to *Irish Bulls* to challenge the 'nativist' precepts that genuine Irishness is to be sought in the history of the Dark Ages, or that ethnicity is the key to Irish identity. Like most Protestant interpreters, Edgeworth begins Irish history from the time of the arrival of the English: 'it is a matter of indifference to us whether the Irish derive their origin from the Spaniards, or the Milesians, or the Welsh' (I, pp. 278–9). The nationalist historian assailed in this passage is Sylvester O'Halloran, author of *An Introduction to the Study of the History and Antiquities of Ireland* (1772) and *A General History of Ireland from the Earliest Accounts to the Close of the Twelfth Century* (1778). O'Halloran's work underwent a revival as the Union gave a sharper, more nationalist significance to its concentration on early Irish history, which is no doubt why in 1802 the Edgeworths reacted

brusquely. Afterwards Edgeworth incorporates the Celtic past into her hybrid Ireland, e.g. by introducing the real-life O'Halloran, unnamed, as the eccentric surgeon in *Ennui* (see *Ennui*, pp. 276–7 and n. 80), and by bringing him on by name as an idealized antiquarian in *The Absentee*. For a discussion of Count O'Halloran, see W. J. McCormack, *Ascendancy and Tradition in Irish Literary History, 1793–1939* (Oxford: Clarendon Press, 1985), pp. 135–62. R. B. McDowell gives an account of the scholarly Celtic Renaissance, *Ireland in the Age of Imperialism and Revolution, 1760–1801* (Oxford, 1979), pp. 150–55.

30. R. L. and Maria Edgeworth, *Essays on Irish Bulls*; *Tales and Novels by Maria Edgeworth*, 18 vols. (London: Baldwin & Cradock, 1832), I, pp. 190–91.

31. For example, from Scotland she acquired as correspondents Elizabeth Hamilton (1758–1804), author of the satirical novel *Memoirs of Modern Philosophers* (1798) and the provincial novel *The Cottagers of Glenburnie* (1808), and Dugald Stewart (1753–1828) and his wife Helen. The latter also corresponded widely with Stewart's former pupils, an influential network.

32. See Butler, p. 291.

33. M.E. to Sophy Ruxton, 26 February 1805; quoted in Butler, pp. 209–10.

34. Louis MacNeice, *Varieties of Parable* (Cambridge, 1965). The Clark Lectures, delivered at Cambridge in 1963.

35. In 1810, while the fifth edition of *Castle Rackrent* was being planned, R. L. Edgeworth pressed Edgeworth to provide a new episode to follow Condy's death, which would bring the story into post-Union times. She refused, on the grounds that she was already writing a story about a family of Irish absentees, the Tipperarys, as a sub-plot in a new novel set in England (afterwards *Patronage*, 1814). It was, she thought, a tale in which she could say what she still had to say about modern Ireland (see Butler, pp. 277–8). So *Castle Rackrent* went to press without substantive additions. When two years later Edgeworth needed another tale, preferably Irish, for the second series of *Tales of Fashionable Life*, she did extract this family, renamed the Clonbronys, as the central characters of their own tale, *The Absentee*.

36. Adam Smith, *The Wealth of Nations*, I, v; *Glasgow Edition*, ed. R. H. Campbell and A. S. Skinner (Oxford: Clarendon Press, 1976), I, 54.

37. Ibid., II, iii, 1–2; *Glasgow Edition*, I, 330–31.

38. Ibid.

39. Ibid., II, iii, 7; I, 333.

40. Ibid., IV, ix, 13; II, 668.

41. Ibid., IV, ix, 7; II, 665–6. This passage may be the source of the name 'Rackrent' for M.E.'s fictional family. Her original choice of name, 'Stopgap', derived from the Irish rural practice of using a cart as an improvised gate. See *Castle Rackrent*, p. 66 and n. 10.

42. Young stressed the economic importance of agriculture to Ireland, but he also criticized the inefficiency of many Irish practices ('five centuries behind England in the management of arable crops' (II, 20)). In the steep social hierarchy he saw everywhere, and in the oppressive treatment of the poor,

he recognized a 'domineering aristocracy'. He concluded that Ireland would benefit from economic union with England, since even if the loss of their local importance drove out some of the wealthier gentry, 'the kingdom would lose ... an idle race of country gentlemen, and, in exchange, their ports would fill with ships and commerce.' Arthur Young, *Tour in Ireland* (1780), ed. A. W. Hutton, 2 vols. (London: George Bell, 1892), II, 22; ibid., I, 59, 69.

43. Emma Rothschild, 'Adam Smith and Conservative Economics', forthcoming, *Economic History Review* (1992).

44. T. Flanagan, *Irish Novelists, 1800–1850* (New York, 1959), p. 23.

45. For W. Cullen, *First Lines of the Practice of Physic*, see *Ennui*, n. 72. John Mullan surveys eighteenth-century medical opinion of hypochondria and some of its literary implications in his *Sentiment and Sociability* (Oxford: O.U.P., 1988), pp. 201–40.

46. Adam Smith, *Theory of Moral Sentiments*, IV, i, 10; IV, ii, 8. *Glasgow Edition of the Works and Correspondence of Adam Smith*, I, ed. D. D. Raphael and A. L. MacFie (Oxford: Clarendon Press, 1976), pp. 183, 189–90.

47. See Bibliography, pp. 57–8.

48. Stephen Gwynn, *Irish Literature and Drama* (London: Nelson, 1936), p. 54. For an invaluable account of the ideological pressures on twentieth-century criticism, see Terence Brown, *A Cultural History of Ireland, 1922–85* (London: Fontana, 1981).

49. For the place of early Unionist debate within the civic humanist tradition, I am indebted to a paper by Istvan Hont, 'Civic Humanism and Reason of State: Unionist Ideas in Ireland, *c.* 1689–1707', delivered at Pembroke College, Cambridge, January 1991.

50. R. L. and M. Edgeworth, *Memoirs of R. L. Edgeworth, Esq.*, 2 vols. (London, 1820), II, 252. Cf. the Preface to *Castle Rackrent*, p. 63 and the concluding passage of *Irish Bulls*.

51. S. Deane, in *Ireland's Field Day* (London: Hutchinson, 1985), p. 50.

52. *Quarterly Review* vii (1812), 330, 336. W. J. McCormack suggests (*Ascendancy and Tradition*, p. 130) that Croker's own anonymous satirical pamphlet, *An Intercepted Letter from J— F— Esq., Writer at Canton, to his Friend in Dublin Ireland* (1804) may be a reference and a minor source in *The Absentee*.

53. Adam Smith, *Essays on Philosophical Subjects: with Dugald Stewart's Account of Adam Smith, Glasgow Edition*, III, ed. W. P. D. Wightman, J. C. Bryce and I. S. Ross (Oxford: Clarendon Press, 1980), pp. 39–40.

54. J. W. Croker, *Quarterly Review*, vii, 329.

55. For example, the stories of Mrs Clarke, Juvenal and the *Lives* of some of the emperors. See *Ennui*, the first two chapters and notes.

56. Lady Pamela Fitzgerald (1776?–1831) was widely believed to be the daughter of the educationalist Mme de Genlis and of Philippe, Duke of Orléans. She was certainly an adopted daughter of the former, and Orléans made a handsome settlement on her before her marriage. Fitzgerald married her in France in December 1792, and she accompanied him to Dublin. Part of the Edgeworths' interest in Pamela arose from admiration for her (supposed)

mother. They visited Genlis in Paris in 1803, when R. L. Edgeworth informed her he had defended Pamela in the Irish parliament. Maria Edgeworth's first work intended for publication was a translation (1782) of Genlis: see Introduction, p. 6.

57. In *The Absentee* (1832), vi, p. 128; in *Irish Bulls*, i, pp. 243–4; in A. J. C. Hare, *Life and Letters of Maria Edgeworth* (1894), ii, pp. 202–3.

58. Richard Wellesley, 1st Marquis Wellesley, was Governor-General from 1797 to 1805, and one of the most hawkish and expansionist architects of British India. His younger brother Arthur Wellesley, future Duke of Wellington and husband of the Earl of Longford's daughter Kitty Pakenham, was a field officer responsible for some victories in these wars.

59. See Eric Stokes, *English Utilitarians and India* (Oxford: Clarendon Press, 1959), Ch. 1, 'The doctrine and its setting', pp. 1–80.

60. Cf. especially Darnton's *The Literary Underground of the Old Regime* (Cambridge, Mass.: Harvard U.P., 1982).

61. See n. 29, above.

62. Most of this material will be found in the memoir made by Edgeworth's grandfather, Richard Edgeworth, eventually published as *The Black Book of Edgeworthstown*; see Butler, pp. 14–15.

63. Butler, pp. 112–24.

64. See McCormack for the real and fictional O'Hallorans and Grace Nugent: cited n. 29.

65. See S. Gilbert and S. Gubar, *The Madwoman in the Attic* (New Haven: Yale U.P., 1979), pp. 149–51.

Note on the Text

1. M.E. to Mrs Ruxton, 29 January 1800; quoted in Butler, p. 290.

2. See *Castle Rackrent*, n. 10, for signs that while in the process of writing M.E. changed the name of the family whose annals she is relating.

3. Of the thirteen proposed corrigenda, only the four 'literals' were implemented. Most of the others were suggestions for new notes. Another corrigendum, on the back endpaper of the same copy, was added to the Glossary in 1810. See n. 33, below; and Watson, Appendix A, pp. 116–17, for the Butler copy notes.

4. See Introduction, n. 35.

5. See *Ennui*, p. 175 and n. 30.

Castle Rackrent

1. (p. 61) The Preface was probably written by R. L. Edgeworth, Maria Edgeworth's father, though perhaps with her assistance. It was immediately followed in the first edition by 'Advertisement to the English Reader' and the Glossary, which the advertisement announces. These follow the text in

the second edition of 1800, and all subsequent editions.

2. (p. 62) *a man of genius and virtue*. Samuel Johnson's *Life of Savage* (1744) was reissued as one of his *Lives of the Poets* (1779–81). It takes a sympathetic view of the life and character of the poet, murderer and alleged blackmailer Richard Savage (d. 1747), who claimed to be the illegitimate son of Richard Savage, 4th Earl Rivers (?1660–1712) by Anne, Countess of Macclesfield. Margaret Cavendish, Duchess of Newcastle (?1624–1674), published her husband's *Life* (1667), but could not literally have written a life of the poet, who was born after her death. The point is that the Duchess and Johnson each wrote a biography which conspicuously whitewashed its subject.

3. (p. 63) *Squire Western or Parson Trulliber*. Squire Western is the coarse country squire and father of the heroine in Fielding's *Tom Jones* (1749), and Parson Trulliber the country clergyman and pig farmer in Fielding's *Joseph Andrews* (1742).

4. (p. 63) *When Ireland loses her identity by an union with Great Britain*. The Irish Parliament of 1782–1800 had achieved constitutional autonomy, in that it was no longer subject to Parliament at Westminster. The bill proposing the abolition of the Dublin parliament, in favour of seats for Irish M.P.s in the Westminster parliament, began its progress through the Dublin parliament in 1799 but was not completed until July 1800. For R. L. Edgeworth's involvement, see Introduction, pp. 34–5.

5. (p. 65) *Holantide*. Hallowe'en, 31 October.

6. (p. 66) *almost his household stuff*. Spenser, *Prose Works*, ed. R. Gottfried (Baltimore: Johns Hopkins Press, 1949), 11 (1561–1608), pp. 99–101. From *A Vewe of the Present State of Ireland* (1596), regarded by Edgeworth as the first of the classic English writings on Ireland; see Appendix, p. 327. For Spenser's use of the dialogue format, see Introduction, p. 17. M.E.'s original footnotes were sent to the publisher with the text in time to be printed routinely at the foot of the page.

7. (p. 66) *true and loyal to the family*. A phrase with Jacobite connotations, since it alludes to James Butler, 2nd Duke of Ormond (1665–1745), who served the last Stuart monarchs but lived in exile under the first Hanoverians. See Introduction, pp. 13–14.

8. (p. 66) *bear the surname . . . of Rackrent*. Thady or his 'editor' does not say so, but Sir Patrick's change of surname may have been accompanied by or represent a change of religion. By the harsh penal laws enacted against Irish Catholics in 1690, a Catholic could not inherit land from a Protestant unless he conformed to the Church of Ireland. Nor could he practise law, or stand for Parliament – both of which Condy subsequently does. All four Rackrents would have had to be Protestants. Thady is plainly a Catholic, but his son Jason would have had to become a Protestant in order to practise law and to purchase land from a Protestant. Catholics regained rights in respect of land by the Relief Act of 1782; as lawyers, for most purposes, in 1793.

9. (p. 66) *Moneygawls*. Moneygawl's (1832), Castle-Moneygawls (1800) (inconsistent with Moneygawls, p. 87).

10. (p. 67) *Castle Rackrent*. Castle Stopgap (1800). Edgeworth seems to have

intended at an early stage of writing to use Stopgap as the name of the family and the estate, a reference presumably to Sir Tallyhoo's custom of using a car instead of a regular gate (see p. 66). For a possible source in Adam Smith for the name Rackrent, meaning extortionate rent, see Introduction, p. 31 and n. 41.

11. (p. 67) *He that goes to bed* . . . Watson notes two versions of this traditional song, one in *Rollo: or the Bloody Brother* (1639), II, ii, a play by John Fletcher and others, a second in Thomas Fuller, *Gnomologa: Adages and Proverbs* (1732), no. 6219.

12. (p. 69) *Linen Board to distribute gratis*. Linen was a leading Irish manufacture, based on locally-grown flax. The Dublin-based Linen Board encouraged its development throughout Ireland, but it really flourished only in a triangle in eastern Ulster in the counties of Antrim, Down and Armagh.

13. (p. 69) *replevying*. Recovering [cattle or goods] distrained or taken from him, upon his giving security to have the case tried in a court of justice (*O.E.D.*).

14. (p. 70) *heriots*. Herriots (1800). A feudal service, of the best live beast 'or dead chattel', paid to the lord (landlord) on the death of the tenant (*O.E.D.*).

15. (p. 70) *learning is better than house or land*. Traditional, though Watson finds two versions in plays: Samuel Foote's *Taste* (1752), I. i, and David Garrick's prologue to Goldsmith's *She Stoops to Conquer*, l. 28.

16. (p. 70) *fee-simple of the . . . appurtenances*. Fee in feudal law relates to the word fief: a heritable estate in land, held on condition of homage and service to a superior lord (*O.E.D.*). 'Appurtenances', of Anglo-French derivation, is a minor property-right or privilege (*O.E.D.*).

17. (p. 71, n.) *loy*. A narrow spade.

18. (p. 71) *abatements*. A legal term, of Anglo-French derivation, for a reduction in value or the end of an action (*O.E.D.*).

19. (p. 73) *£500*. 500*l*. (1832 and previous editions). Here and subsequently emended to the modern form.

20. (p. 73) *Rackrent*. Stopgap (1800). See n. 10, above.

21. (p. 77) *nabob*. Originally a high government official in Moslem India, from the same word as Urdu *nawab*. Thence (*O.E.D.* 1764) a (British) person who has returned from India with a large fortune.

22. (p. 79, n.) *The editor was acquainted . . . imprisonment*. The pretence of a male editor, taking down the illiterate Thady's reminiscences, is maintained throughout the text and in subsequent editions, after the acknowledgement of M.E.'s authorship in 1801. Elizabeth Malyn (?1692–1789) retained the name of her third husband, Baron Cathcart (d. 1740) when she married her fourth husband, the Irish fortune-hunter Colonel Hugh Macguire, in 1745. When she refused to give up her property and jewels he abducted her from England to his estate in Co. Fermanagh, and kept her locked up there until his death in 1764. MS. evidence suggests M.E. or another member of the family had met the bailiff who escorted Lady Cathcart back to England: see Watson, p. 125, n. 28; Edward Ford, *Tewin-Water: or the story of Lady Cathcart* (Enfield, 1876), and *Gentleman's Magazine* 70 (1789), 766–7.

23. (p. 80) *my lady Rackrent*. My lady Stopgap (1800–1815).

24. (p. 80) *my pretty Jessica. The Merchant of Venice*, V. i. 21.

25. (p. 81) *ames-ace*. aims-ace (1800–1815). A double ace, the lowest throw at dice.

26. (p. 83) *vails*. Tips.

27. (p. 85) *Continuation of the Memoirs of the Rackrent Family*. For the circumstances of composition, see Introduction, pp. 4–5.

28. (p. 85) *the college of Dublin*. Trinity College, Dublin, the only Irish university at this time. See above, n. 8, and below, n. 51.

29. (p. 85) *white-headed boy*. Editions of 1800–1815 have the following footnote: '*White-headed boy* is used by the Irish as an expression of fondness. – It is upon a par with the English term *crony*. – We are at a loss for the derivation of this term.' *O.E.D.*, giving the meaning 'favourite', describes the expression as an Irish colloquialism, and dates its first example 1820.

30. (p. 86) *friends*. A standard eighteenth-century usage, now archaic, meaning those interested in Condy's well-being, including members of Condy's family.

31. (p. 90) *carried off . . . to Scotland*. Owing to the differences between Scottish and English law relating to marriages, under-age English and Irish couples seeking to marry without parental consent went to Scotland. M.E.'s parents, Richard Lovell Edgeworth and Anna Maria Elers, apparently eloped to Scotland in 1763 from her home in Oxfordshire, because he was nineteen and lacked his father's consent.

32. (p. 95) *had little thought of a contest*. These circumstances resemble R. L. Edgeworth's candidature for the Co. Longford seat in February 1796, though he lost the election. Details of Condy's campaign could also have been suggested by two English election campaigns M.E. knew about at second hand, one in Oxfordshire in 1754 in which her maternal grandfather Paul Elers was involved, and another at Andover in which her father's friend Sir Francis Delaval stood as a candidate. See Butler, pp. 118–20 and p. 21 n. 3, and R. L. and M. Edgeworth, *Memoirs of R. L. Edgeworth*, 2 vols. (1820), I, pp. 85–6, 128–33.

33. (p. 96, n.) This footnote, and the related Glossary-note about the turf, were both added to the fifth edition (1810).

34. (p. 98) *custodiam*. A term in Irish law for a three-year grant of Crown lands made by the Exchequer to the lessee.

35. (p. 102) Goethe's *Sorrows of Young Werther* (1774) was first translated into English in 1779, and remained a popular sentimental classic for the remainder of the century.

36. (p. 106) *gripers*. Extortioners.

37. (p. 108) *Sarrah*. For Sorrow, euphemism for the Devil: an imprecation.

38. (p. 110) *the childer*. A footnote in the 1800–1825 editions reads: 'This is the invariable pronunciation of the lower Irish.'

39. (p. 112) *wake*. The accompanying Glossary-note was written by R. L. Edgeworth. See unpublished letters from M.E. to Letty Ruxton, 29 January 1800; to Sophy Ruxton, 7 May 1800; to Charlotte Sneyd, August or September 1806 (National Library of Ireland, MS. 10, 166–7).

40. (p. 113, n.) *taplash*. Washings of casks or glasses; dregs.
41. (p. 118) *gauger*. Exciseman.
42. (p. 121) *Mr Young's picture of Ireland*. Arthur Young, *Tour in Ireland* (1780). The paragraph after the reference to Young, beginning 'It is a problem . . .' and dealing with the Union, closely reflects Young's view of the question. See Introduction, n. 42.
43. (p. 122) *The Warwickshire militia . . . drink whiskey*. The Warwickshire militia were part of the large extra detachment of troops (some 80,000) diverted from the war with France to police Ireland in the 1790s. The Irish produced both beer and whiskey, but during the 1790s brewers successfully pleaded that beer was nutritious while the effects of whiskey were almost all negative. In 1795 the Irish parliament abolished the tax on beer, which may have assisted its sales; R. B. McDowell points out that there is no evidence that distilling suffered (*Ireland in the Age of Imperialism and Revolution* (Oxford: O.U.P., 1979), p. 13).
44. (p. 123) GLOSSARY. The device of an accompanying commentary is very unusual in the eighteenth-century novel, though not unprecedented: Beckford's oriental tale *Vathek* (1787) has one. For later works of fiction M.E. supplied no more than footnotes, but she provided a 75-page Glossary for Mary Leadbeater's *Cottage Dialogues among the Irish Poor* (1811; see Introduction). In this respect Walter Scott's *Waverley Novels*, beginning 1814, which are copiously supplied with learned prefaces, appendices, commentaries and footnotes, seem indebted to *Castle Rackrent*.
45. (p. 123) *Some friends . . . following Glossary*. In 1800–1815 editions this was printed as 'Advertisement to the English Reader', on a separate page; in 1800A, among preliminaries, immediately following the Preface; in 1800B–1815, following the tale.
46. (p. 123) Glossary-note to p. 66. John Horne Tooke, *Diversions of Purley* (vol. I, 1786; vol. II, 1805), I, 102 ('if') and 202 ('but'). Tooke proposed a drastic simplification of the theory of language, by reducing the parts of speech necessary to meaning to two (nouns and verbs); conjunctions, particles and interjections were supposed to have evolved from abbreviations of the essential elements. Tooke's propositions made modern English rational and above all autonomous: he encouraged study of 'the parent language' rather than the so-called learned languages, Latin and Greek (pp. 99–100). For the political radicalism of such language theories, see Introduction, pp. 19–20.
47. (p. 124) Glossary-note to p. 68. The passage quoted is from William Beauford's 'Caoinan: or some account of the antient Irish lamentations', *Transactions of the Royal Irish Academy* IV, 41, 42, 43, 43–4.
48. (p. 127) Glossary-note to p. 69. *thirty turkies*. In the Edgeworth–Butler family copy, this is emended in ink, in M.E.'s hand, to 'sixty turkies', but the change was never implemented.
49. (p. 129) Glossary-note to p. 70. Though interest in Northern European early or folk literatures was pioneered in the mid eighteenth century by Gray, Percy, Elstob and others in Britain, Herder in Germany and Mallet

in Switzerland, references to Slavonic and certainly Estonian literature remained much rarer. Edgeworth's source unidentified.

50. (p. 130) Glossary-note to p. 71. Thomas Parnell (1679–1718), poet and friend of Swift and Pope, was born and educated in Dublin, and from 1716 was vicar of Finglas, Co. Dublin. 'In Britain's isle, and Arthur's days' is line 1 of his narrative poem 'The Fairy Tale', which is written in an archaic style based on Spenser's. Pope afterwards revised it. The poem tells how the hunchback Edmund happens to see the fairies dancing, he pleases them, and they remove his hump; afterwards his rival in love, Sir Topaz, seeks out the fairies in the hope of a reward, and they punish him by wishing the hump on him. It is odd that M.E. thinks a 'British' story belongs to 'ancient English' history. Even more than the Irish, Scottish eighteenth-century writers were fond of using early British history and legend, and the words Britain and British, as counters to English chauvinism.

51. (p. 132) Glossary-note to p. 74. *St Omer's . . . Maynooth*. Minnouth (1800–1815). Corrected in ink in the Butler copy. St Omer's, near Calais, was the nearest seminary in which English-speaking Catholic boys could be trained for the priesthood during the eighteenth century. After the relaxation of some of the penal laws against Catholics in 1793, St Patrick's College, Maynooth, Co. Kildare, was opened in 1795.

52. (p. 132) Glossary-note to p. 82. *the Curragh*. As the best-known Irish racecourse, the Curragh, in Co. Kildare, was (and is) the centre for the breeding, training and sale of horses, for which Ireland is famous.

53. (p. 134) Glossary-note to p. 86. *naggin*. Presumably noggin, meaning a small cup and hence a small measure of drink.

54. (p. 135) Glossary-note to p. 95. *Bona Dea*. The good goddess, object of ancient mystery cults special to women.

55. (p. 136) Glossary-note to p. 95. *There is no woman where there's no reserve*. Untraced.

56. (p. 136) Glossary-note to p. 95. David Garrick's *High Life below Stairs* (1759), attributed on first publication to J. Townley, was one of the most popular late eighteenth-century stage comedies.

57. (p. 136) Glossary-note to p. 96. Added 1810; sketched on an endpaper of the Butler copy, in M.E.'s hand: 'at a dispute between Mr McConchy & Mr E about boundaries – an old man a tenant of Mr M's cut a sod from Mr E's land & cutting out a square from Mr M's land on the opposite side inserted the McConchy sod and standing upon it when the *viewers* came gave evidence that the ground he stood upon was Mr McConchy's'. The incident described took place in the course of a lawsuit between M.E.'s grandfather Richard Edgeworth and the great-grandfather of a McConchy who was still currently a neighbour. (R. L. Edgeworth to Mr Frederick, 25 June 1812, unpublished letter, National Library of Ireland.)

58. (p. 137) Glossary-note to p. 112. *Wake*. See n. 39 above for the MS. evidence that this entry is R. L. Edgeworth's.

59. (p. 138) Glossary-note to p. 112. *Deal on, deal on . . .* Traditional song.

Ennui

1. Epigraph to *Tales of Fashionable Life*, '*Tutta la gente . . .*'. First appearance in the second edition, 1809. 'Everyone listened smilingly to the pretty little tales, in which they all saw the faults of other people rather than their own; or if they suspected their own, they believed that no one else would do so.' Verse in the manner of Gian Carlo Passeroni's *Cicerone* (4 vols., Venice, 1764), a work to Sterne, which in the guise of a long digressive biography of the Roman orator satirizes modern foibles and vices.

2. (p. 143) 'What do you do at Potsdam?' I asked Prince William [Wilhelm] one day. 'Sir,' he replied, 'we pass our lives conjugating the same verb: "I am bored, you are bored . . . I was bored, I will be bored, etc.".' (Dieudonné Thiebault, *Mes Souvenirs de vingt ans de séjour à Berlin; ou Frederic le Grand, sa famille, sa cour*, 5 vols. (Paris, 1804).)

3. (p. 144) *Anglois*. M.E. and her publishers use the standard older form of French spelling, gradually replaced under Voltaire's influence from the third quarter of the eighteenth century, though not abandoned by the Académie Française until 1835.

4. (p. 147) *very extraordinary landaus*. From January to June 1809 the British public was regaled with the scandal of the Duke of York, third in line to the throne and Commander-in-Chief of the army, and his clever mistress, Mrs Mary Anne Clarke, who had compensated for the Duke's slowness in paying her allowance by selling promotions, especially in the army. Among the prodigious expenses of her household (estimated annual running costs, £10,000), were two carriages and eight to ten horses. In Mrs Clarke's trial for conspiracy (1809), the Court of King's Bench heard that another leading actor in the scandal, Colonel Wardle, M.P., sent his wife in a barouche (or landau) to a Brook Street hotel with a letter to one Major Hogan, in which the major found a £500 banknote. (M. A. Clarke, *The Rival Princes* (London, 1810); Elizabeth Taylor, *Authentic Memoirs of Mrs Mary Ann Clarke*, second edition (London, 1809).)

5. (p. 147) *repeaters*. Fob watches which strike hours, quarters, etc.

6. (p. 148) *O! ressource assurée . . . .* 'O, certain remedy! come, stir these idlers from their apathy! their vacant minds are at least amused by avarice disguised as pleasure!' Unidentified.

7. (p. 148) *St James's-street*. Among the gentlemen's clubs in St James's Street, S.W., then and now, are Brooks's, Boodle's and White's. The first had a particular notoriety about 1800 as the club where Charles James Fox gambled all night. Edgeworth requested help from friends for stories of high life for *Ennui*, listing many in a notebook (see p. 24). At Christmas 1804 she wrote to her cousin Sophy Ruxton that her neighbour Lord Longford had given her 'a great many ex. anecdotes of gaming – eating & drinking – which will all *tell* in *Ennui*' (Butler, p. 247).

8. (p. 149) *fee-simple*. See *Castle Rackrent*, n. 16.

9. (p. 152) *Eliogabalus*. Verse in the manner of Samuel Butler's satire on Presbyte-

rian enthusiasm, *Hudibras* (1663–8), a much-used mode for a further century. For Elagabalus, see n. 13 below.

10. (p. 153) *quatre assiettes . . . des confitures.* 'four plates of different soups; a whole pheasant; a partridge; a large plateful of salad; mutton sliced in its own gravy, with garlic; two good servings of ham; a plateful of cakes; fruit and preserves!'. The literary notebook containing five pages of notes for *Ennui* includes more notes for *Professional Education*, for example: 'To get behind the scenes in the education of princes, see the mems of Mme de Bavière, mother of the Regent.' [i.e., the Princess Palatine, whose son became regent of France on the death of Louis XIV in 1715.] 'Notes from Dictionnaire des portraits historiques. Anecdotes et traits remarquables des hommes illustrés.' (Many entries in French follow the latter.)

11. (p. 153) *. . . 400 oysters.* The 'Roman historian' to whom this story is attributed is Cordus; Edgeworth seems to be using a collection of *Lives* of Roman emperors, in print since the sixteenth century, and supposedly compiled in the fourth century, the authorship of which remains disputed. The 'imperial glutton' in question is Clodius Albinus, who attempted to become emperor on the death of Commodus in A.D. 192, but was challenged and killed by Severus. These stories about Clodius have the hallmark of disinformation by a successful rival. The list quoted occurs in the entry on Clodius, 11.3, *Scriptores Historiae Augustae*, 3 vols. (Loeb Classical Library), I, 483.

12. (p. 153) turbot consultation *immortalized by the Roman satirist.* See Juvenal, *Satire* IV, in which a fisherman from Ancona presents the Emperor Domitian with a gigantic turbot (*Lat.* rhombus, a highly prized fish). Finding there is no dish big enough, Domitian summons his Privy Council to discuss the problem. As soon as they have dealt with it he dismisses them – to their relief, since Domitian has a record of executing senators. Partly a tilt at Roman luxuriousness, *Satire* IV also portrays a despotic court and an enfeebled political elite.

13. (p. 153) *Heliogabalus . . . any confession he could make.* See entry on Elagabalus, 29.6, *Scriptores Historiae Augustae* (Loeb Classical Library), II, 165. Elagabalus, Roman emperor A.D. 218–222, was formerly the fourteen-year-old priest of the sun-god of Emesa, in Asia Minor. A preoccupation of his short reign was to establish his eastern religion at Rome. This goal helped generate a hostile mythology about his folly and degeneracy; the 'records' of his reign must have been favourite schoolboy reading in the eighteenth century.

14. (p. 154) *Egyptian* salon. A craze for Egyptian décor and artefacts was stimulated by Napoleon Bonaparte's invasion of Egypt in 1798.

15. (p. 154) *Montaigne and his sausage.* Michel de Montaigne (1533–92), essayist and traveller: anecdote unidentified.

16. (p. 154) *a'weary of the sun. Macbeth*, V. v. 49.

17. (p. 159, n.) Sir John Davies, *A Discoverie of the True Causes why Ireland was never entirely subdued . . . until . . . James I* (Dublin, 1761), *printed exactly from the* [*first*] *edition in 1612*, pp. 124–5.

18. (p. 159, n.) For quotation see Lodge, *Peerage of Ireland* (1754), II, 107: the nurse, Joan Harman, journeyed to Milan about 1550. Lord Thomas Fitzmau-

rice (1502–90), 16th Lord of Kerry by a (Norman) Irish title created 1181, was an ancestor of the Petty-Fitzmaurice family who from the mid eighteenth century also acquired titles in the English peerage – Earl of Shelburne, followed by Marquis of Lansdowne. Thomas Fitzmaurice was a romantic figure, according to Lodge 'the most beautiful man of his age, and of such great Strength, that within a few months before his death . . . not three men in Kerry could bend his bow'. At times he appeared at the court of Elizabeth I, but in old age (1581–5) took up arms against the English and his own neighbours who supported them, such as the Earl of Ormond. This footnote establishes a connection between Ellinor and Irish rebellion against English rule (see n. 19, below).

19. (p. 160) *O'Neill, the Irish black-beard.* Hugh O'Neill, 2nd Earl of Tyrone (1540?–1616), Elizabeth I's most formidable Irish opponent. After being brought up in England he returned to Ireland and at first co-operated with Elizabeth's commanders there. Later he quarrelled with one of them, Sir Henry Bagenal, and in 1591 eloped with Bagenal's sister Mabel, making her his third wife. After he flaunted his mistresses before her, she returned to her brother's house. O'Neill became the spearhead of Irish resistance for the rest of Elizabeth's reign, but under James I left the country and died in exile in Rome.

20. (p. 165) *'Twas doing nothing was his curse* . . . . Untraced verse, in the manner of La Fontaine's fables.

21. (p. 167) *the poor king of Spain and* le brasier. Story untraced.

22. (p. 167) *High Life below Stairs.* See *Castle Rackrent*, n. 56.

23. (p. 168) *parliamentary panegyrists of boxing and bull-baiting.* Two parliamentary efforts to abolish the vulgar sport of bull-baiting, on 18 April 1800 and 26 May 1802, were successfully opposed by the Tory M.P. for Norfolk, William Windham, supported in 1800 by George Canning and in 1802 by General Gascoyne and others. In the first debate Windham also defended cudgels and boxing, arguing that 'the amusements of our people were always composed of athletic, manly and hardy exercises, affording trials of their courage, conducive to their health, and to their objects of ambition and of glory'. (*Speeches in Parliament of William Windham*, 3 vols. (London, 1812), pp. 334–5.) The wartime surge of patriot enthusiasm for popular pastimes was also served by, for example, Joseph Strutt, *Sports and Pastimes of the English People* (1801).

24. (p. 169) *Es-tu contente à la fleur de tes ans* . . . . '"Are you happy in the prime of your life? Have you got your own tastes and amusements? You must lead quite an agreeable life." The other answered in two words, "I'm bored." "That's unfortunate," said the fairy. "I think the great thing is to be at home."' In the manner of La Fontaine.

25. (p. 169) *Holyhead.* then and now, a leading port of embarkation from England to Ireland.

26. (p. 169) *hotels in London.* Noblemen's Dublin houses converted into hotels at this time included the Shelburne and the Gresham.

27. (p. 171) Sorrow *better chaise in the county.* See *Castle Rackrent*, n. 37.

28. (p. 171) *no better . . . than this same*; n., *Verbatim*. The chemist Humphry Davy afterwards told Byron that he supplied materials for this episode when he visited Edgeworthstown in July 1806. Byron commented in his journal, 'So *much* the better – being *life*.' ('Detached Thoughts', 15 October 1821 – 18 May 1822, *Letters and Journals* 9, ed. L. Marchand (London: John Murray, 1979), p. 34.) But in an undated letter (?May 1805) M.E. alludes to a suggestion by her cousin Sophy Ruxton that the amusing coaching scene should be made the subject of a frontispiece. See Butler, p. 237. The episode may well all be from life, but is not apparently all from Davy.

29. (p. 175) *tester or a hog . . . English shilling*. Tester, a sixpence; a hog, an English shilling, worth a penny more than an Irish shilling. See Introduction, p. 22, for other metaphorical Irish terms for coins.

30. (p. 175) Footnote first added to the fourth edition, 1813.

31. (p. 182) Probably the most sustained version of a classic scene in Edgeworth's writing about Ireland – the landlord's (or magistrate's) confrontation with lower-class petitioners. See also *Castle Rackrent*, Glossary-note to p. 86, on docking the entail; *Irish Bulls*; and Edgeworth's Glossary to Mary Leadbeater's *Cottage Dialogues among the Irish poor* (1811). Such scenes implicitly connect the fictional landlord with R. L. Edgeworth: cf. his experiences on returning to Ireland as a young man after some years in England. (R. L. and M. Edgeworth, *Memoirs of Richard Lovell Edgeworth* (1820), I, pp. 198, 234–5.)

32. (p. 184) *King of Prussia . . . mouse-traps in his dominions*. See Mirabeau, *Secret Memoirs of the King of Prussia*, English trans. (1798) of *Histoire secrète de la cour de Berlin, ou Correspondance d'un voyageur français* (Paris, 1789).

33. (p. 195) *Qu'est-ce que la raison . . . une gueule comme celle-là*. 'What's the use of low-voiced reason against a talker who bawls like that?' Not in the Concordance to Molière's *Works*.

34. (p. 198) *half a dozen penal statutes*. '. . . in parliament in the 44th year of the reign of Elizabeth . . . [a member] said a J.P. was a living creature that for half a dozen of chickens would dispense with a whole dozen of penal statutes' (Edmund Bohun, *The Justice of the Peace, his Calling and Qualifications* (1693), pp. 118–19).

35. (p. 199) *There was a lady lov'd a swine . . . .* Traditional. Listed in M.E.'s notebook, p. 70 ('There was a lady loved a hog . . .') as 'song for nurse'.

36. (p. 200, n.) Sir George Shuckburgh, 'Observations made in Savoy, in order to ascertain the height of mountains by means of the Barometer', *Philosophical Transactions* [of the Royal Society] 67 (1777), pt. 2, pp. 513–97, especially p. 535.

37. (p. 201) *glass windows . . . in England*. William Harrison, 'Description of England', Ch. 12: 'Of the Maner of building and Furniture of our Houses', in Raphael Holinshed, *The Chronicles of England, Scotland and Ireland* (1577), new edition, 6 vols. (London: J. Johnson, 1807), I, 314–16.

38. (p. 203) *her voice was agreeable*. In the 1809–25 editions, continues 'though rather loud', M.E. dropped the latter three words in 1832 for reasons of decorum. See Butler, p. 297.

39. (p. 203) *lord lieutenant's levées.* Dublin Castle was the vice-regal residence and the seat of Irish government.

40. (p. 203) *prôneuse.* 'Puffer', or advertiser.

41. (p. 204) *cognomens.* Cognomen, 3rd or family name of a Roman citizen; agnomen, 2nd cognomen or 4th name; hence, nickname (1811) (*O.E.D.*).

42. (p. 210) *Il faut avouer ... talent pour le silence.* 'It must be said that this gentleman has a great talent for silence.' Quip attributed by the Edgeworths to Talleyrand during their visit to Paris in 1802–3.

43. (p. 210) *we live but to oblige him.* Perhaps a squib by one of the Edgeworth family aimed at John Carr during his visit to Edgeworthstown in 1805.

44. (p. 211) See Appendix (pp. 324–42) for John Carr's *The Stranger in Ireland*, which is ridiculed in Craiglethorpe's methods of research and Lord Glenthorn's travels in Ireland

45. (p. 219) *Full little knowest thou that hast not tried ....* Spenser, *Mother Hubbard's Tale*, 895 ff.

46. (pp. 220) *a full equivalent for the jest.* Shakabac, a poor man, is invited by the rich Barmecide to a feast in Baghdad. But the dishes the Barmecide calls up are imaginary. Shakabac humours his host by pretending to eat until 'wine' is served. Then he pretends to get drunk and cuffs the Barmecide, thus winning the contest of wits and his host's approval. (*Arabian Nights*, 180th and 181st nights.)

47. (p. 220) *Not to know him, argues yourself unknown. Paradise Lost*, IV, 830.

48. (p. 224) Proud *as I am, I'll put myself to school.* Adapted from Pope, *Imitations of Horace*, Epistle I, i, 47: 'Late as it is, I put myself to school.'

49. (p. 224) We *never mention Hell to ears polite.* Pope, *Epistle* V, *To Burlington*, 1, 149.

50. (p. 224) *to touch the brink of all we hate.* Pope, *Moral Essays*, II, 52.

51. (p. 224) *Humane-society.* Royal Humane Society, founded in 1774 by William Hawes.

52. (p. 226) *En petit compris vous pouvez voir ....* 'In a small compass here you see one who was greatly renowned. The lover of the loved one vanquished pen, tongue, toil and respectfulness. O gentle soul, so highly honoured: who can praise you, except by silence? When the subject is greater than the speaker, his words fail him.' M.E. copied the epitaph to Petrarch's Laura, written by Francis I, king of France (1515–1547), into her notebook for *Ennui* (p. 68), giving no source.

53. (p. 227) *statue of snow.* The anecdote about Michelangelo and his patron Pietro de Medici is told by Giorgio Vasari in his *Lives of the most eminent painters, sculptors and architects* (Florence, 1550). (English translation, London: Everyman Library, 1963), IV, pp. 112–13. It appears in M.E.'s notebook (p. 63) incorrectly associated with Leonardo da Vinci.

54. (p. 228) *Allons, mademoiselle, parlez ... ensuite autre chose.* 'Come, mademoiselle, talk – you'll see, madame, how well she talks – She saw that I hesitated, and thought she should help me out, as you hum a tune to tell a singer which song you want – Talk a bit about religion, mademoiselle, and

then you can speak of something else.' (*Mémoires de madame la baronne de Staal, écrits par elle-même*, 3 vols. (London, 1787), I, pp. 124–5; English translation (London, 1759), p. 64.) The scene occurs in Paris in 1710, when the young Mlle de Launay, fresh from her convent education, is shown off by the Duchesse de la Ferté to the Duchesse de Noailles.

55. (p. 228) *a poet to do all that there work*. The London firm of Packwood's, manufacturers of razors, was celebrated for its brilliant marketing: its advertisements anticipated the modern jingle. See N. McKendrick, 'George Packwood and the Commercialization of Shaving', in McKendrick, Brewer and Plumb, *The Birth of a Consumer Society* (Bloomington: Indiana U.P., 1982), pp. 146–94. The heroine of Edgeworth's *Belinda* (1801) overhears herself described among a group of young men as 'as well advertized as Packwood's razor strops'. *Belinda*, Ch. 2.

56. (p. 228) *starling in the Sentimental Journey*. Sterne, *A Sentimental Journey Through France and Italy*, ed. Gardner D. Stout, Jr. (Berkeley: University of California Press, 1967); pp. 197–205.

57. (p. 229) *Persian language*. Persian, the language of the Moghul court at Delhi, continued in the eighteenth and early nineteenth centuries to be the main Asian language of government in the British territories in India.

58. (p. 230) *with another lover*. Gottfried August Bürger, celebrated in England for his eerie ballad *Lenore* (1770, English translation 1796), was for many years married to Dorette Leonhart, while he loved and wrote poems to her sister Auguste. The marriage Edgeworth describes is his third. Features of Bürger's first and third marriages apparently reappear in two Edgeworth tales, *Vivian* (1812) and 'Angelina', *Moral Tales* (1801).

59. (p. 231) *sing mournful ditties to a mistress's eyebrow*. As *You Like It*, II. vii. 149, but Shakespeare has 'ballads'. Cupid loved the mortal girl Psyche, whose name means 'a butterfly'. 'Love occupies a vast space' anticipates Byron's 'Love in man's life's a thing apart,/Tis woman's whole existence' (*Don Juan*, I, 194, 1–2).

60. (p. 231) . . . *the vinegar of marriage*. Untraced.

61. (p. 231) *No more for Amynta fresh garlands I wove*. Entry in M.E.'s notebook, following notes on Scott's *Lay of the Last Minstrel*; 'song by Sir Gibert [sic] Elliott'. 'Amynta', a song beginning 'My sheep I neglected, I broke my sheep hook', the best-known poem of Sir Gilbert Elliott, 3rd baronet of Minto (1722–77), first appeared in Yair's *Charmer* (1749), vol. I.

62. (p. 232) *philosophers . . . inimical to states*. The view adopted by Burke in his *Reflections on the Revolution in France* (1790), *Letter to a Noble Lord* (1796), etc. Conservative anti-intellectualism was rife in 1797–8, the date of the main action of *Ennui*: cf. the counter-revolutionary French 'exposé' by the Abbé Barruel, *Mémoires pour servir à l'histoire du Jacobinisme* (1797), the satirical journal, *The Anti-jacobin* (1797–8), and the many novels lampooning Godwin, Priestley, Price and other revolutionary sympathizers.

63. (p. 232) *bévue*. Blunder, mistake – or 'bull'.

64. (p. 232) *the savage's classification of animals*. ?Buffon, *Histoire Naturelle*, 44 vols. (1749–), trans. W. Kenrick *et al.* (London, 1775).

65. (p. 234) *poems of Sir William Jones.* Many of the poems of the orientalist Sir William Jones (1746–94) appeared only posthumously, in A. M. Jones's *The Works of Sir William Jones*, 6 vols. (1799–1801). As imitations of Hindu, Persian, Arab and classical originals, they enjoyed a considerable vogue for the next twenty years, especially after the appearance of a one-volume *Poetical Works of Sir William Jones* in Bell's *Poets of Great Britain*, vol. 61 (1807).

66. (p. 238) *sure of her consent.* John Gregory, *A Father's Legacy to his Daughters* (new edition, 1789), pp. 104–6.

67. (p. 240) *the Surfaces.* A reference to the character of the hypocrite Joseph Surface in Sheridan's *The School for Scandal* (1777).

68. (p. 244) *rebellion broke out in Ireland.* After some years of agrarian unrest in the Catholic south and more purposeful planning of armed resistance stemming largely from Ulster, the United Irishmen headed a force of 15,000 men which captured the town of Wexford in late May 1798. In June their main force lost a pitched battle at Vinegar Hill; the Wexford rising was then bloodily suppressed. A French force of 900 professional soldiers under General Humbert landed in Co. Mayo on 22 August 1798 and, accompanied by peasant volunteers, advanced to within a score of miles of Edgeworthstown before being defeated in September near Granard. These historical events 'date' the action of Chs. XII–XVIII.

69. (p. 248) *And, for the book of knowledge fair . . . .* Milton, *Paradise Lost*, III, 47–9.

70. (p. 250) *hypochondriacism.* William Cullen, *First lines of the practice of physic*, new edition (Edinburgh, 1796), III, p. 299. Hints for Glenthorn's neurotic symptoms and suggestions for activities that might relieve them – gambling, exercise, a journey, excitement – clearly derive from this standard medical treatise. See Introduction, p. 32 and n. 45.

71. (p. 250) *forming all together . . . cannot be rivalled.* William Hamilton, *Letters concerning the North Coast of the County of Antrim* (1790), pt. II, p. 33.

72. (p. 251) *Guide to the Lakes.* Apparently a parody of Carr's overwritten description of the Killarney stag-hunt: see Appendix. F. S. Bourke, *A Handlist of Books relating to Killarney*, The Bibliographical Society of Ireland VI, no. 2 (Dublin, 1953) lists eight titles of books and pamphlets before 1809, none with precisely this title.

73. (p. 252) *Now my weary lips I close . . . .* Gray, 'Descent of Odin', refrain, beginning at l. 50 (*Poems of Gray, Collins and Goldsmith*, ed. R. Lonsdale, pp. 223–8).

74. (p. 254) *give us places.* Anecdote possibly heard from M. A. Pictet, Genevese traveller, visitor to Edgeworthstown (1801) and author of *Voyage de trois mois en Angleterre, en Écosse et en Irlande* (Geneva, 1802). But for a critique of French Enlightenment thinkers' admiration for the English parliamentary system and an indictment of its pervasive corruption, see Joseph Fievée's *Lettres sur l'Angleterre* (London, 1802).

75. (p. 255) *like to have their fools.* See Smith, *The Wealth of Nations* (1776), and Introduction, p. 29.

76. (p. 258) *. . . his master's meat.* In La Fontaine's fable, 'The Dog and His

Master's Dinner', a dog bringing home some meat is attacked by a mastiff
and a pack of curs. In Edward Marsh's translation,

> Against such numbers, what could Trusty do?
> The meat was doomed, so much was manifest,
> And 'twas but reason he should profit too.
> 'Gently, pray gently, Sirs!' he made request,
> 'I'll take my chunk, and you can share the rest . . .'

La Fontaine's Fables (London: Heinemann, 1933), Bk VIII, 7, p. 241.

77. (p. 261) united-man. United Irishmen, association of Catholics and Protestants seeking the overthrow of British administration in Ireland. See n. 68 above.

78. (p. 266) *yeomen in coloured clothes*, i.e. un-uniformed militia, or volunteer constabulary. The Yeomanry were largely raised by Protestant landlords.

79. (p. 273) *Le vrai n'est pas toujours vraisemblable*. 'Life is not always lifelike'. Boileau, *Art poetique*, chant III, l. 48: '*Le vrai peut quelquefois n'être pas vraisemblable.*'

80. (p. 277) . . . *mounted in his hall*. The surgeon of the skull with antiquarian tastes is Sylvester O'Halloran, whom R. L. Edgeworth knew of as a fellow founder-member of the Royal Irish Academy. Though best known for scholarly books on early Irish history (see Introduction, p. 20 and n. 29), O'Halloran practised as a surgeon specializing in head injuries, and wrote a scholarly article on this topic (on trepanning) in a journal to which Edgeworth had access; the same volume is cited in the Glossary to *Castle Rackrent* (see Glossary-note on 'Whillaluh'). Details from O'Halloran's article are used for the blacksmith-earl's head injury and for the supposed earl's fall from his horse in Ch. III. (*Transactions of the Royal Irish Academy* IV (1790), 151–70.)

81. (p. 282) '*ruction*. Insurrection, or rebellion.

82. (p. 283) What riches give us, let us then inquire . . . . Pope, *Moral Essays*, III, 79–80.

83. (p. 293) *a North-country woman*. Not a woman from the north of England, as the wording suggests in modern English, but from Scotland.

84. (p. 294) Lord Y— . . . *an elderly gentleman*. An idealized portrait of James Caulfield, 4th Viscount and 1st Earl Charlemont (1728–99), Irish peer, member of the Johnson circle, and a moderate leader of the Anglo-Irish campaigners who in 1782–3 brought the Ascendancy Parliament into being. For R. L. Edgeworth's dealings with him at this time, see Butler, p. 95. The complimentary portrait of Charlemont relates more to his role as first President of the Royal Irish Academy, an organization founded in 1787 which was dedicated to the advancement of progress in Ireland through the pursuit of all branches of knowledge, though especially science.

85. (p. 304) *Time and industry, the mighty two* . . . . Matthew Prior, *Henry and Emma*. (1708), ll. 149–50.

86. (p. 307) *No brighter colours paint th'enamell'd fields* . . . . Untraced.

87 (p. 308) *his* fromages de boeuf. Henry IV of France (reigned 1589–1610) came from Gascony and was said to have retained 'all the habits of a country

gentleman of his native Béarn', as exemplified in this popular story of his fondness for home cooking.

88. (p. 310) *coshering*. Feasting, especially entertainment given by Irish chiefs for their followers, or exacted from followers by chiefs. See Sir John Davies, *True Causes* (n. 17), cit., p. 124.

89. (p. 311) *the Temple*. In order to qualify as a lawyer a would-be Irish barrister had to study, reside and eat a regulation number of meals (see p. 316) in one of the City of London's medieval Inns of Court, for example, the Temple or Gray's Inn. R. L. Edgeworth put in terms at the Temple in 1765–8.

90. (p. 314) *special pleaders*. Members of Inns of Court specializing in the drawing up of pleadings, a category formalized in 1804 (*O.E.D.*).

91. (p. 315) *Protagoras ... Evathlus ... promised reward*. Protagoras (480–411 B.C.) was a celebrated sophist and teacher, who allegedly invented the dialectical method of argument known as Socratic. He was also the first teacher to demand payment from pupils, but Evathlus refused to pay on the grounds that he had never been successful in argument. Protagoras replied, 'But if I gain my case, I naturally receive the fruits of my victory, and so would you obtain the fruits of yours.' Diogenes Laertius, *Lives and Opinions of the Philosophers*, trans. C. D. Yonge (Bohn, 1880).

92. (p. 321) *a philosophic moralist*. Probably William Cullen, whom Edgeworth has already described as a philosopher. See n. 70, above.

93. (p. 321) *stretched on the rack of a too easy chair*. Pope, *Dunciad* (1743), IV, 342.